SABOTEUR

A Novel of Love and War

SABOTEUR

A Novel of Love and War

DEAN HUGHES

DESERET
BOOK
SALT LAKE CITY, UTAH

Library of Congress Cataloging-in-Publication Data

Hughes, Dean, 1943-
  Saboteur : a novel of love and war / Dean Hughes.
     p.   cm.
  ISBN-10 1-59038-619-1 (hardbound : alk. paper)
  ISBN-13 978-1-59038-619-4 (hardbound : alk. paper)
  1. Mormons—Fiction. 2. Japanese Americans—Evacuation and relocation,
1942-1945—Fiction. [1. World War, 1939-1945—Fiction.] I. Title.
  PS3558.U36S23 2006
  813'.54—dc22   2006013668

Printed in the United States of America
R. R. Donnelley and Sons, Crawfordsville, IN

10   9   8   7   6   5   4   3   2   1

To my grandson
Steven Hughes

CHAPTER 1

ANDY GLEDHILL STOOD under the columned portico at the front of the Hay-Adams Hotel. He had turned his back to the wind and folded his arms across his chest, but he was still shivering. He had always wanted to visit Washington, and now he was just across Lafayette Park from the White House, but he had no overcoat, and a cold, wind-driven rain had been falling since he had arrived the day before. He had wanted to look around a little, but not in this weather, and he was too nervous anyway. *What am I doing here?* he kept asking himself.

When he had arrived at the hotel, he'd taken a look at the White House, dim in the gray light of the December afternoon. He'd always thought it was bigger, grander. *I've seen nicer houses than that in Salt Lake,* he'd found himself thinking. But his brain had felt as dull as the light outside. He had spent the previous night sitting up on a train from Georgia to North Carolina, only to learn that he had to board a bus and ride all day to Washington. He had gone to bed immediately and stayed there for twelve hours, but he had slept fitfully and then awakened suddenly, alarmed until he remembered where he was. He felt out of place in a room with such ornate draperies and plaster moldings on the ceiling. As a boy, in the desert of central Utah, he had liked to sleep under the stars in a sleeping bag, wriggling until the sand fit his back. He wished he were there now.

A groggy buzz still filled Andy's head as he waited in front of the hotel. He'd gone outside to be sure he didn't miss the car that was coming for him, but the doorman had been too attentive, so he had stepped farther away. Now, however, the cold had penetrated even the heavy wool of his army dress uniform. His kneecaps were jerking, his hands shaking. He liked to be in control of his life; since his first day of boot camp at Fort Ord, California, the previous winter, he had hated the sense that someone was always making up his mind for him—scheduling his days, deciding what he would do and when and even why.

A gray Chevrolet arrived on time—at 0900 hours—but with nothing to identify it as a government car. Andy waited as the driver leaned across the seat, took a cigarette from his lips, and said, "Are you Lieutenant"—he glanced at a sheet of paper lying on the seat—"Ander Gledhill?"

"It's André."

"Yeah . . . well."

Andy pulled off his hat, then reached for the front door handle, but the driver motioned with his thumb to the backseat. The car was filled with smoke as gray as the seat covers. On the train, and then again on the bus, almost everyone around him had smoked continually. He had had enough of it.

"Can you tell me where we're going?"

"Headquarters." The driver was a man in his late forties or maybe older. He had a bald spot in back, and his scalp was pink and rough, the same as his face. Andy rolled down his window a crack and tried to breathe some better air. He had been in the army a year, and he figured by now he should be used to cigarette smoke, but his eyes always swelled in a smoky room and his throat constricted, the same as when sagebrush put out its pollen.

"What headquarters?" Andy asked.

"OSS."

"What is that exactly? I never heard of it until yesterday."

The man looked in the rearview mirror, his eyes squinted as though he wanted to get a good look at the idiot in the backseat. "You mean you don't even know what it means?"

"I know it's the Office of Strategic Services, but that could be almost anything."

"I guess."

Andy hated how condescending the man sounded, but it was a tone he had almost come to expect—even from a working stiff like this guy.

The driver shifted the car into gear and drove out from under the portico, then glanced over his shoulder to check for traffic. In a friendlier voice, he added, "Some guys say that OSS means 'Oh, So Social.' You know, because all those jerks down at the E Street Complex keep their noses stuck so high in the air."

Andy had no idea what the E Street Complex was, but he didn't ask. He wasn't going to sound stupid again. It was just like the army to tell a guy to go somewhere and not tell him why.

The driver turned right onto H Street and then glanced over his shoulder again. "OSS is brand-new, from what I hear—but no one tells me much of anything. The word going around is, they train people to be spies."

That was what Andy had figured. He had also made some other assumptions—and they all bothered him. *I don't have to volunteer for anything,* he told himself, and then he rolled his window down a little more.

"This smoke bothering you?" the man asked.

"Yeah, actually, it is." Andy had rarely said anything like that, but he was feeling this morning that he needed to speak up for himself a little more.

The driver stubbed out his cigarette and opened his own window a crack, but he didn't say another word, which was fine with Andy. On the car radio, playing softly, he could hear a man—Dick Haymes, he

3

thought—singing "It Had to Be You." Whisper Harris liked that song; he remembered dancing to it at Van's Dance Hall in Delta. He wished he could breathe a little more of *that* air—the sweet scent of her shampooed hair. He thought of the big mirror ball, the colored lights reflecting off it and off all the other mirrors in the room, everything turning into a shimmering glow.

The driver made a couple of turns, and then Andy saw E Street on a corner sign. They continued west a couple of blocks and turned into a driveway with a gate that read "National Health Institute" across the top. The car stopped in front of a small but stately two-story building with marble columns at the entrance. The driver said, "This is it, no matter what the sign says. Tell the receptionist—the girl just inside the front door—what you're here for. She'll get you to the right office."

"Okay, thanks." Andy walked fast up the steps as the rain blew against the side of his face. He pushed his way through the front door, tucked his officer's hat under his arm, and stepped in front of a gray metal desk.

The receptionist—a dark-haired girl close to his own age—paid no attention for a time, but when she looked up, her eyelashes fluttered. Andy didn't mind lipstick, but girls in the East smeared it on like grease on an axle, bloodred. Whisper wore a little lipstick when she dressed up, but what Andy liked better was the smoothness of her bare lips, and he loved her creamy skin, even her freckles. He had known her all his life, but he had kissed her for the first time only a few weeks before he had left home.

The girl leaned her head to one side and said, smiling, "What, pray tell, may I do for *you?*"

Eastern girls. They did know how to flirt. "I'm Lieutenant André Gledhill. I was told to report here this morning. I have a letter." He reached into the inside pocket of his jacket, tried one side, but ended up finding the letter in the other.

But by then she was holding up both her hands, palms facing out. "Don't show it to me. I know where you're supposed to go. Just sit down over there for a minute." She stood. "I'm just an office girl. Don't tell me *anything.*"

"I'm sorry, I thought . . ." But he didn't know what he thought. He shoved one hand into a pants pocket, decided he shouldn't do that, and pulled it back out.

"That's all right. You'll catch on." She really was pretty, with olive skin and long eyelashes, and clearly she knew that he was noticing. "My name's Mary Deluca, by the way. And while I have the chance, just let me mention one thing." She leaned forward with her hands on the desk, winked, then whispered, "If you need someone to show you around while you're in town, I'd be *more* than happy to help you out. And I do know this town." She made a little twirl with her finger.

Andy smiled back, but he didn't know what to say.

"Not interested?"

"Just a little preoccupied right now," he said. But he liked the way she was looking at him. In college, at the University of Utah, he had enjoyed turning the heads of the coeds on campus. He found himself smiling again, in spite of himself, so he added, "My dad told me about girls like you."

"How did *he* know?" She winked again, and then she walked down a hall, her hips rotating under a tight blue skirt, her high heels clicking, echoing. She came back with a tall man, at least fifty, in a charcoal-colored suit—double-breasted, with pinstripes. He looked more like a big-city lawyer than a spy. His hair was thinning, but his face and head were tanned. Andy thought he looked like a tennis player, and he seemed the type. "Lieutenant Gledhill, hello," he said, reaching out his hand. Andy wondered whether he should salute, but he couldn't very well do that when the man was offering to shake hands. "My name is Edmund

Chambers. I work with General Donovan. Would you step into my office with me, please?"

Andy had met a guy in Officer Candidate School who had gone to Yale. He had sounded like this Chambers—almost British. Andy followed the man down the hall, which was lined with gray marble. The air smelled like a pool hall—smoky again, with the hint of a men's room nearby. Andy's letter had come from a General William Donovan. He had heard of a "Wild Bill" Donovan, who had been a hero in the Great War. He figured this Donovan must be the same guy.

Inside, Chambers stepped behind his big desk. He motioned for Andy to take a chair across from him. It was a plain office—four beige walls—but the desk was quality work, walnut, and on it was a picture of a younger Chambers with three well-scrubbed boys and a nicely dressed wife. She also looked like a tennis player, trim and tan. "Lieutenant, I know you're wondering what this is all about," Chambers said. He leaned back in his chair as though he had lots of time. "But for now, this is just a chance to get to know you. Depending on what comes of our conversation, you may be on your way back to Fort Bragg tomorrow. On the other hand, we may want to talk to you about . . . other possibilities."

Chambers reached into his shirt pocket, inside his suit coat, and Andy knew what was coming. Chambers pulled out a pack of Chesterfields, knocked them on the side of his hand until a few of the cigarettes slipped out, then reached to offer one to Andy. When Andy declined, he pulled one out for himself, tapped the end against the package, put it in his mouth, then used a silver cigarette lighter to light up.

"I see from your report that you're from a place called Delta, Utah. That's a very small town, I take it."

"Yes, it is."

"Tell me about your family."

"I have three sisters and a brother. We're just regular people."

"Isn't your dad a prominent man?"

6

"Well . . . I guess you could call him that. He has some businesses—a bank and a truck and tractor dealership—and he's the mayor."

"I thought he was a Mormon bishop?"

"He is. But that's not like a Catholic bishop. He doesn't wear robes and all that stuff. He'll serve for a while, and then he'll get released, and someone else will get called. That's how it is in our church."

"What about you? Were you the fair-haired boy in town—the son of the mayor and bishop and business leader?" Andy saw in the lift of Chambers's eyebrows that he found something comical in that description.

"No, not really."

"Oh, please. Be honest. There can't be many young men like you in a little Utah town."

"Look, you can make fun of us, but—"

"Fun? Who's making fun? You're quite the fellow." Chambers slapped his hand on a manila folder in front of him. "I've read your report."

Andy didn't respond. He knew what he had been in Delta. He'd been the center of a lot of things at the high school—sports, mainly—but he'd been resented, too. He'd spent his childhood, especially his teen years, trying to prove himself to boys who cared more than anything about how tough a guy was on the football field or whether he could handle himself in a fistfight.

"I understand you speak French like a native," Chambers said. "Can you tell me how that came about?"

"My mother is French. My dad was in Europe during the first war and he met my mom over there. They got married in France, and then he brought her home to Utah."

"So you spoke French in your home?"

Don't give me this. You know all about me. Let's get down to business. What bothered Andy was that he had spent the better part of a year, most of 1942, being trained. He had finished a "90-day wonder" officer

7

training course as well as jump school—all to become a paratrooper. And that was what he wanted. He had reported at Fort Bragg, eager to take on his assignment with the 82ⁿᵈ Airborne, and the first thing his new CO had done was hand him a letter instructing him to report here. It was the last line of the letter that had struck Andy hard: "Do not, under any circumstances, report to anyone, including your family, the content of this message." He had taken a guess that his language background had something to do with his being summoned here, and now that was exactly where Chambers was going. One possibility was that the OSS needed translators, but that wasn't what he saw in the steady way Chambers was watching him.

"Well, yeah, we spoke the language quite a bit at home. But I spent time in France, too. Mom had a hard time adjusting to the desert heat, so she liked to go home when she could. She took us kids along, and I was the oldest, so I spent a lot of summers in France. I grew up speaking French about the same as English."

"Where in France?"

"In the south. Not too far from Arles—a little town called Tarascon."

"How wonderful."

"It was. But it's not near the beaches. It's in the Rhone Valley, away from the Mediterranean."

"Yes. Between Arles and Avignon. That's a beautiful region."

Andy was surprised. Chambers clearly knew the area, and his French pronunciation was correct. "It is beautiful," Andy agreed. "But it was hard for me as a kid to leave my friends every summer." He didn't mention that the boys in town had called him "Frenchy" and made fun of the clothes his mom bought for him in Europe.

Chambers nodded. He held his cigarette not far from his lips, the smoke winding past his face in a little plume, his eyes never leaving Andy. "Could you pass for a Frenchman?"

"I don't know. Not many French have hair as light as mine."

8

"But if natives heard you speak, would they know you were an American?"

So this was definitely not about translating. Andy felt the tightness in his throat again. "I met a Frenchman on the train the other day. He picked up that I spoke with a dialect—the one they speak in the south of France—but he seemed to think I was French."

"My report says that you were getting ready to be a missionary when the war broke out." Chambers tapped some ashes into an ashtray on his desk. His motions were graceful, as though he were relaxing at his country club, and the way he intoned "missionary" hinted his disdain. But what bothered Andy most was that the man knew about his personal plans. That sort of thing was not in his military records. Someone had been doing a background check on him.

"Well, yeah. I was going to finish out the school year and graduate from college, and then I was planning to go. But I don't know how you'd know that."

Chambers didn't bother to say.

Andy glanced again at the bare walls. It was as though Chambers wanted the office to feel like an interrogation room.

"So is that what you plan, after the war, to spend your life as a missionary?"

"No, it's not like that. A lot of people in our church serve missions for a couple of years."

"And what do you do during that time?"

"We go door to door, mostly, and we teach about our church. If people want to join, we baptize them."

"Where? In Africa, or—"

"No. In the U.S. or Europe, or—you know—anywhere."

"So there are Mormons outside of Utah?"

"Yes, sir."

"I had no idea."

"I'm sure you didn't," Andy said, and he let a little resentment flow back to the man.

Chambers looked surprised. His eyes tightened, as if to say, "What's this? Have I struck a sore spot?" He sat for a time, then suddenly leaned forward and rested his elbows on his desk. "So how do you feel about killing people?"

Andy hesitated. "The same as anybody, I guess," he finally said.

"What's that supposed to mean?"

"Right after the Japs attacked Pearl Harbor, I quit college and signed up. I'm ready to do what I have to do."

"But I guess you'd rather be off recruiting people into your church."

Andy didn't know where to start. He wasn't some *zealot,* the way Chambers was implying. "I don't think anyone *wants* to go to war," Andy said. "But I'm well trained now, and I'll—"

"I know the army's given you some training. But you've been taught all your life, 'Thou shalt not kill.' What if you had to kill a man face-to-face? Stick a knife through his ribs? Or reach around from behind him and cut his throat?"

This was exactly what bothered Andy. He'd figured the OSS might be that sort of outfit. He was trained to fight, not to slither around like a snake. He had thought everything over on the bus, and he'd decided to say that he would prefer to stay with his Airborne unit, but he wasn't going to let Chambers think he was afraid to do his duty. "Look, I'll put our Mormon boys up against anybody. I don't want some Nazi kicking down my front door. As far as I'm concerned, I'm defending my mom and my sisters and my hometown. And I'm defending *freedom.* I'm ready to *die* for those things, if that's what it takes."

Chambers had begun to laugh in the middle of all that, and now he was shaking his head. "That's a very pretty little speech, son. Freedom and motherhood and the good old red, white, and blue. Brings tears to my eyes."

Andy had no idea how to respond to that, but he knew he wanted to get back to his unit as soon as possible.

"Mormons believe in the Bible, don't they?"

"Yes, sir."

"Well, let me tell you something, and notice, there's no 'Star-Spangled Banner' playing in the background." He hesitated and stared at Andy. "You can't love your enemy when you're about to cut his heart out. I don't care what the *good book* says."

Andy had thought about that. But some of the best men in the Book of Mormon had fought and killed when they had to. It wasn't like he was going out looking for someone to knock off.

Chambers took his time, as though he liked giving Andy time to squirm. "I'll tell you what, Gledhill," he finally said. "I think maybe I'm going to send you back to Fort Bragg. I had my doubts when I looked through your paperwork, and now that I talk to you, I'm pretty sure my instincts were right. Sometimes you can just *feel* that a guy is all talk—and won't be able to cut it when the pressure is on. I don't like it when a man says, 'I'll do what I have to do.'"

"I'm not a coward, sir."

Chambers stood. He put out his cigarette, and then he walked around to the front of his desk, sat on it, crossed his arms, and looked down at Andy. "We're looking for people who know how to jump out of airplanes and who speak good French. But we need *men*. We're not looking for Sunday school teachers. I'd be more impressed if you told me you'd been in a barroom fight and chewed some guy's jugular vein in half. I want to believe you can break a man's neck with your bare hands and then go back and drink a few beers to celebrate."

"I disagree," Andy said. "In fact, I'd say just the opposite. Guys who believe something have more to fight for."

"Not if it's meekness and love they believe in. That's not going to cut it with us."

Andy wasn't going to listen to this stuff any longer. He stood up, looked Chambers straight on, and said, "That's fine. I'll go back to my unit—that's where I want to be anyway. But when this war is over I'm going to find you, look you in the eye, and tell you what I did. I guess you want some guy who brags that he's a steely-eyed killer. I don't do that. But I'll *show* what I can do when the time comes."

Chambers stepped forward. Andy didn't move back, but he hated the closeness: the smell of Chambers's wool suit, the large pores in the skin of his nose. "You don't know that, Gledhill. It's what you tell yourself, but I don't believe it. I think you're a mama's boy. I think you're going to *fail* as a soldier."

"No, I'm not. And you have no right to say that to me."

"I'm just telling you the truth." He breathed into Andy's face, the heavy smell of tobacco on his breath. "You might as well face it now before you lead a bunch of men into trouble."

"Listen, I've never failed at *anything,* and I'm not going to start now. You talk like you're tough, but you'll be sitting at a desk while us Airborne guys are dropping behind enemy lines."

Now it was Chambers who didn't answer.

"*Isn't that right?*"

"The truth is, I don't know where I'll be."

Andy had heard Chambers's hesitation, and he felt the triumph. "Well, I know what I'm going to do. I'm going to fight like a man—and I hope I never see you again." He took a step toward the door.

"Sit down."

Andy turned back. "Why should I? You're a civilian. I don't have to follow your orders."

"Actually, I have military rank," Chambers said. "I'm a lieutenant colonel. But I'm not going to pull rank on you. If you want to leave, go ahead. But before you walk out, I'd like to explain a few things to you."

Andy knew that he really ought to leave. He had won his little victory and he should make his exit, but he remained standing for a few seconds, and then he did sit down. He couldn't resist finding out what this was all about.

Chambers walked back around his desk and took his seat again. "Someday we're going to invade Europe," he said. "But certain things have to be ready behind the lines. We can find plenty of people who've studied languages in college, but we need operatives who can pass themselves off as natives. We'll need intelligence so we know what we're doing, but the men who go in might also have to fight, and they might have to kill. They might have to eliminate obstructions, and that could mean killing stealthily, viciously—and doing it without regret. I'm just telling you honestly that I have my doubts you can do that. I don't question your loyalty; I question your capability."

Andy wanted to say, *Fine. I'm heading back to Fort Bragg,* but the guy was calling him out and Andy knew it. He didn't want to admit how disgusting the whole thing sounded to him.

"So that's it?" Chambers asked. "You have nothing to say?"

"What do you want me to say?"

"Okay, that's enough. Get out of here. And don't say a word to anyone about this meeting." Chambers stood and nodded toward the door.

Andy didn't move.

"Go on. Leave. I don't want to look at you. You claim you're a fighter, but you get awfully silent when you find out that we're looking for *killers.*"

Andy stood up. He knew he would hate himself the rest of his life if he walked away with his tail between his legs. "I can handle it," he said.

"Handle what?"

"I can kill. I'll stand up for what's right. That's what you need—not just a guy who's able to kill, but someone willing to die, if that's what it takes."

But Chambers was laughing again. "How old are you, Lieutenant?" he asked.

"Twenty-two."

"Oh, I'm glad to hear that. I would have sworn you were sixteen. You sound like some high school kid. 'Put me in the game, Coach. I'll give my all for the team.'"

"All right, fine. I'm going back to North Carolina. You find yourself some guy who tells you how *evil* he is." Andy turned to leave, but his breath was coming hard. He spun back and said, "Or maybe I'll stab *you* in the ribs. I hate phonies like you. You'll never pull a trigger. You'll sit here in this office and think you're a war hero. So don't try to tell me that I'm going to fail. Go out and put your own life on the line. That's what I'm doing."

Chambers nodded, and Andy thought he saw a hint of a smile. "You finally sound like you mean what you say, Gledhill. I was wondering whether you ever would." He motioned toward the chair. "Why don't we talk a little more?"

Andy had known what was coming. He had seen it in Chambers's eyes, the way they had relaxed at the very moment Andy had threatened to stab him. What Andy knew just as clearly was that the guy had manipulated him to get that very reaction.

Andy sat down, but he felt his breath coming even harder. This wasn't the first time in his life he had taken the bait this way. Back when he'd been a kid and had come back from France at the end of summer, he'd had to prove himself every time. Once he had jumped into an irrigation canal even though he hadn't learned to swim—had done it because the boys said that he didn't dare. He had gone down into all that dark water until his feet found mud, and then he had pushed up and fought his way, more than swum, back to the bank. He hadn't known it back then, but he'd recognized later that he'd jumped in the water because he was the "bishop's boy" and "Frenchy."

"I suppose you just passed your first interview—or at least the initial screening," Chambers said, and now his smile was not so subtle. He was also lighting up again. He took a long tug on his cigarette and let the smoke seep from his nose. "You want a cigarette now?" he asked, smiling a little. "I think you need one."

Lay off, Chambers. You're not funny.

"There's still a question you have to ask yourself. You're prepared to drop behind enemy lines to fight. But are you prepared, if caught, to be tortured? Perhaps tortured to death?" Chambers hesitated only a second, and before Andy could answer, added, "I'll let you think about that for a few minutes."

But the question was stunning. Andy hardly knew how to think about it.

"Here's the thing, Lieutenant. As we try to get a foothold in Europe, we'll take *thousands* of casualties, and if we don't do everything just right, we'll get thrown back into the sea. We're going to need men on the ground long before that landing takes place. We'll need to know the German order of battle, troop strength, fuel supplies, everything. It's going to take reconnaissance men—spies. I'm thinking now that *maybe* you could be one of them."

Andy raised his head. This didn't sound like killing.

"You *might* get the job, but that's only if you get through the rest of this process—some tests and more interviews—and if you get past that, then you'll have to survive our training school, and I'll tell you right now, it's tough."

Andy nodded.

"We need to put a million soldiers in Europe to win this war, maybe more. But for a time the whole operation will depend on a few hundred men, and maybe some women. The actions of a small group of people could change the history of the world. We need to get to know you a lot better before we determine that you're good enough to be one of that group."

Andy had always known that his chances for survival with the Airborne might not be great. This actually didn't sound any worse. And the idea of changing history—Chambers should have said that a long time ago. Andy had said all along that he wanted to do his part, and this sounded important.

"But there really might be more involved than reconnaissance. We need to know, and not just from your saying so, that you can kill—swiftly and mercilessly, when the time comes. So we'll look at you closely during training, which will start right after the first of the year."

There was something strange about all this—this civilized man, clearly well educated, talking about killing "mercilessly." Andy couldn't help wondering what God must think of the nations of the world, all training their young people to kill, taking such a dim view of mercy, seeking out men who could perform hideous acts without normal pangs of conscience.

"Do you have a girl back home?"

Andy was taken by surprise. "Actually, yes, sir, I do."

"What's her name?"

"Her real name is Wilma, but I've never called her that in my whole life. She's always been known as Whisper."

"Is she sweet and soft-spoken?"

Andy laughed. "She's sort of that way now, I guess, but when she was a kid, she could outrun most of the boys in town, and she wasn't afraid of snakes or anything else."

"It sounds as though you grew up together."

"We did. She was a little younger, but I can't remember a time when I didn't know her."

Chambers nodded, watching Andy as though he were still trying to get a read on him. "So how do you feel about all this, Gledhill? Are you still in? Or do you want to leave now?"

"Send me in, Coach," Andy heard himself say, but he didn't laugh. And then he added, "Someone has to do it, and I can. So I think I should."

Chambers grinned, his big, smoke-stained teeth showing fully for the first time. "All right. Depending on how things go with your other interviews, I may be talking to you again."

Chambers got up and walked with Andy back to Mary, who escorted him to an almost empty room. She had him sit down at a desk and then she set a stack of papers in front of him. She didn't flirt now. Andy had the feeling she felt sorry for him.

*   *   *   *   *

At the end of Andy's second day of interviews, Mary delivered Andy back to Chambers's office, and by then he understood that Chambers was the big gun, the one who would make the final decision. He was wearing a light gray suit this time, tailored as carefully as the one he had worn the day before, and a dark blue tie—silk, from before the war. And he was smoking another cigarette. "All right, Lieutenant Gledhill," he said, "we're going to give you a try. My men weren't overly impressed with you, if you want to know the truth, but we're going to see how you do in training. Don't feel bad if we flunk you out." He smiled. "That might tell you that you're normal. We don't use normal people in our operation."

Andy didn't smile.

"One thing may be obvious, but I don't know how to stress it enough. You cannot talk to *anyone* about what's happened here. You can tell your parents you're going to be in the Washington area for some training, but you can't even hint what you're actually going to be doing. After you finish here, you'll probably be shipped to England for further training, and it's the same thing over there. Not a word about what you're doing. This job will definitely involve a lot of lying. Are you ready for that?"

"Sure," said Andy. "I understand why I'll have to do it." But he hated the idea.

"Okay. We're going to give you a thirty-day leave. Return here on the sixth of January. Come to my office again, and by then I'll have your training schedule worked out. You'll be in the Washington area for several months. That much I can tell you for sure, but after that, it depends on what's happening with the war. Do you have any questions?"

"No, I . . . oh, should I wear a uniform when I come back, or—"

"Wear it while you travel, but once you get back here, you won't need it most of the time. Bring some civilian clothes—but once again, don't let your mother start asking any questions about that. You may want to buy some things back here."

"All right."

"Mary can help you make arrangements for your travel." He grinned. "In fact, if I know her, she'll be happy to put you up for the night—at her place." But then Chambers looked serious. "Or actually, I guess you don't . . . do that sort of thing."

"No, sir."

Chambers smiled. "Well, men with vices are vulnerable. But I've never much trusted a man without *any*. You don't even drink wine, do you?"

"No."

"You might have to do that a time or two—just to keep your cover, posing as a Frenchman. Try not to choke."

Chambers laughed, but the idea bothered Andy more than he dared admit. It hadn't occurred to him that lying to his family—and drinking—might be part of his job.

CHAPTER 2

ANDY HAD TO TAKE another long train ride—this time, all the way across America. By the time he reached Ogden, Utah, his brain was full of fog as thick as the smoke that was once again filling the troop car. Now he faced a bus ride that would last several more hours, stopping at every little town along the way. But on the bus he had a double seat to himself and he managed to wad himself up and sleep a little, and as he neared Fillmore, where his parents had agreed to pick him up, he actually began to come alive.

He had left the previous February and now it was winter again; he felt the loss of the seasons he'd missed. As he watched from the bus window, he saw big stretches of snow-covered sagebrush, rabbit brush, and the dark round junipers that, he had learned in college, were not really cedars, even though Utahns called them that. It struck him that this land would not be beautiful to just anyone riding through on a bus—certainly not to people who had lived among the hardwood forests in the East. But the space was vast, the texture gritty, and at the edge of it all, white-capped mountains stood like blue-gray phantoms on the horizon. He knew these stretches of land. He'd chased horned toads out there, caught garter snakes with his hands, and found arrowheads and chunks of amber-colored topaz lying on top of the ground amidst the sagebrush.

He'd grown up sunburned and snow burned, always outside, always running.

He had also played at war out there, hiding in the brush.

Bang, bang. I gotcha.

No you din't. You missed.

He and his friends had often died, but they always stood up and played again. Now they were all gone to this real war.

Long before he needed to, Andy pulled his jacket down from the shelf above his seat. He was still wearing his Class A uniform—what soldiers called "pinks and greens," although he failed to see anything pink in the shirt. When the bus finally stopped in Fillmore, he twisted in his seat to scan the road, but it wasn't until he climbed down the steps that he saw Belle, his mother, walking toward him. She had apparently been staying out of the wind in the old Pontiac, which Andy could see parked down the street. He hurried toward her and took her in his arms. She had always been the prettiest and the best-dressed woman in Delta—if a little flamboyant in her choices. "Oh, Andy," she said, "it's so good to have you home."

He heard the hint of her French accent—which he only noticed when he hadn't seen her for a time—but to him she sounded elegant more than foreign. He stepped back and looked at her. "Hey, you didn't have to get dressed up," he said. She was wearing a black wool coat, a red scarf, and a feathery red hat with a net that hung to her dark eyebrows. And black gloves. Mom loved to wear gloves when she dressed nicely—white ones in summer, even in the heat.

"Of course I had to dress up. This is the best day for me in a long, long time." She touched his cheek with those soft, cloth gloves. "You look so handsome, Andy." Mom had called him André most of his life. It was only in recent years that she had given in and called him what everyone else did.

"Where's Dad?"

"Oh, you know your father. He was going to come with me, but someone came into the bank at the last minute and needed him for something—probably church or town business, not banking. Nothing's changed with him." Dad always promised Mom that he wouldn't run for mayor again, but no one else wanted the job, or at least no one wanted to replace Dad, so he had stayed on, now for more than twelve years. He spent as much time as he could at the bank, but he rarely stopped by at his truck and tractor dealership. He depended on old Raymond Healey, who had worked for him for over twenty years. There were no new vehicles coming out now, anyway. The big car makers in Detroit had shut down their regular operations for the duration of the war and were making jeeps and tanks instead. Raymond sold a few used trucks, when he could get any, but mostly he spent his time keeping old wrecks on the road.

People in town thought that Bishop Gledhill was rich, and he did have some money wrapped up in real estate and his businesses, but surely not as much as folks thought he did. The families in town who had real money were those who produced and sold alfalfa seed. Delta had become a center for that. Of course, wealth was relative in central Utah. The war was finally breaking the back of the Depression, but better times were slow in coming out here. Dad tried to help everyone, sometimes through the Church and sometimes out of his own pocket. If he was "rich," that only meant that Mom had a nice coat; it didn't mean she had bought a new one this winter.

Andy stepped back toward the bus and met the bus driver coming toward him with his duffel bag. "Hey, I could have gotten that," Andy said.

"I didn't want to put it down in the snow," the driver told him.

There wasn't much snow left. Most of a recent storm had melted away. But Andy knew what the man meant: *You're one of our soldiers. It's the least I can do.* Andy had seen that attitude all across the country.

Andy thanked him, shook his hand. "Best of luck to you, young man," the driver said. The words reminded Andy of his new assignment—and to not drop any hints to his mother.

But once they were in the car, she didn't ask questions at first. She talked about home. "Your sisters are excited to see you, and Flip wanted to leave school early and ride over with me. I told him no, but he'll be waiting at the house when we get there."

Andy had three sisters: Adele, who was twenty and currently in Salt Lake attending the University of Utah; Marie, a senior in high school; and Christiane, sixteen, known as Chrissy. Andy's little brother was four-teen. His name was actually Phillip—a compromise on Phillippe—but he had always been Flip, even to his schoolteachers.

"Has he grown much yet?"

"No. I'm afraid not. He's going to be like your father, I think. Your dad grew four inches after he graduated from high school."

"It's hard for a boy when he's always the smallest. I know. I was that way for quite a while myself."

"But you didn't let it bother you as much."

Andy thought of how Flip had been when he was little, with his front teeth missing and his hair in his eyes. Andy would wrestle with him on the floor and rough him up, but the kid would come back for more, grinning. "He's a nice boy," Andy said. "More than I ever was."

"I wouldn't say that. He's got a soft heart, but you do too. You're like most boys—*and men*—scared to death that someone might find out about it."

A storm was blowing in from the northwest. In the distance, Andy could see dark, knobby clouds. He didn't like snow once it lay in dirty piles on Main Street, but there was nothing he loved more than watching a storm. Some of his favorite memories were of blizzard days when school was closed, sitting with his mother in the kitchen while his sisters played in their bedroom. He remembered the dizzying smell of baking cinnamon rolls, and Mom telling stories. Dad mostly just said what needed to be said, but Mom could meander through stories for hours, connecting one to the next with no real thread of logic. Andy had been almost grown before he realized that her true stories—at least the details—were as imagined as her fictions.

Most people in town liked Mom well enough, but Andy had heard them joke about her fancy hats and her polished fingernails. He once heard a local man say, "Bishop and Belle, they don't seem much alike, but I guess the bishop don't mind the way she is. He treats her good." That was all true, in a way, but Mom wasn't snooty, the way some people thought. Andy was old enough to remember when she was still trying to accept this gray and brown land as a place she could think of as home. She had made her accommodations as best she could.

Mom had told Andy once, when he was maybe nine or ten, "I grew up with so much beauty around me. I didn't recognize what I'd had until I came here. That's why I make things as pretty as I can." She had been arranging cut roses at the time, with her back to Andy. He'd understood for the first time why she worked so hard to keep her roses thriving—pruning them and feeding them deep once a week, carrying water to them one bucket at a time. He remembered how she had set the vase in the center of the table and then turned around and rested her hand on Andy's hair. He had seen her sadness, and he'd believed since that moment that there was some suffering connected with growing up.

Belle drove out of Fillmore and onto the narrow road that lay straight across the land. The world looked like a black-and-white movie under the darkening sky. Every detail was familiar to Andy: the blacktop road with no line down the middle; the hum of the tires; the smell of dust in the drafty car; the scraped snow rolled up on the sides of the road; the fence posts capped with leaning white towers, so hardened by the cold that they didn't blow off in the wind.

This was the way home. It was who he was, every inch of it.

"Adele still worries me," Mom said.

"What's she doing now? Has she found her a beau up at the U?"

"Oh, yes. Lots of them. She's in love every time I talk to her—with someone new. What she doesn't do is put any effort into her studies."

"She needs to find herself a husband."

"No. She needs to grow up. And she's not showing any sign of it. I'm glad she *hasn't* found anyone just yet."

Andy knew what Mom meant, but sometimes he envied Adele. "She won't grow up," he said. "She'll be a kid forever."

Andy watched his mother, who didn't like to take her eyes off the road when she was driving. She didn't smile, didn't respond for a time, and she was serious when she said, "I fear you might be right, Andy. I worry more about her than any of you kids."

"You always have."

Andy watched the clouds. They were hanging back for now, but they were swelling, and they would hit the valley before another hour was gone. By then, Mom and Andy would be home, and then the storm could do as it pleased.

"Andy, what about you? What's the army going to do with you?"

He saw the connection in his mother's thoughts. Maybe Adele was her biggest worry, but surely Andy's situation represented her greatest fear. "I wanted to talk to you about that, Mom. I might not end up a paratrooper after all. After Christmas, I'm going to Washington to get some more training. Maybe my French is going to come in handy. I could actually end up with a desk job."

Andy had prepared these words and had practiced them on the train. He was telling the truth, sort of. Not everyone who took OSS training would end up behind enemy lines. One of the interviewers had told him that some agents would have to process the information gleaned by the in-country spies. Andy had told the man that he didn't want to sit out the war shuffling papers, but that could still happen. For now, Mom didn't have anything to worry about; Andy would be in Washington for weeks or months, and then probably in England for a time.

"What do you mean, Andy? What would you be doing?"

"Translating, maybe. I'm not sure."

"But I don't understand. What kind of training are you talking about?"

"I don't know myself. It's all new to me. I'll know more about it later."

"Is it at a school or an army camp or . . ."

"A school, I guess you'd say. I just got my orders. I don't know what they call it."

But now she glanced his way, and he saw what he had discovered many times in his life—she knew when he was lying. "Is it something you can't tell me, Andy?"

"No. Not at all. Once I find out what it's all about I'll write to you and explain it."

"I've thought about things they might want you to do with your French. Some of the possibilities worry me."

Andy wanted to put her mind at rest, but there was nothing he could say.

"Andy, what about Whisper?"

"What do you mean?"

"What are you going to tell her? She needs to know what your intentions are. She's waiting for you to propose. I'm sure you know that."

"Do you think it's fair for me to do that now?"

The wind was picking up, gusting, whistling in one of the back windows. "It's unfair *not* to ask her, Andy. You've done everything but say the words."

Andy knew what Mom meant, but he wasn't sure she was right. The war could last a long time, and Andy didn't know what his chances were of getting home.

*   *   *   *   *

Whisper Harris had put in a long day at Bishop Gledhill's bank, where she worked as a teller and secretary and, half the time, as manager. She wanted to be excited about Andy's arrival, but she was scared. She had an idea that before the day ended she would finally know how she stood with him. He had left for college when she was sixteen, and she had known then that she wanted to wait for him however long she needed to, even if he went on a mission after college. But he had never asked her to do that, and she had never told him how she felt about him. Each time he returned—for Christmas or summers—she had waited to see what she would discover in his eyes. It was only this last year, just before he joined the army, that she had finally found what she had been looking for. But she didn't know what to expect today. Andy always said he liked Delta, but how long could that last when he was seeing so much of the world? She had loved him at ten and thirteen as much as now, but he hadn't even noticed her most of his life, and he had never made any promises.

So the day was tedious, and she knew that, as always, she would measure the time from his arrival in town until he showed up to see her. He would be tired today after such a long trip, so maybe she wouldn't hear from him until tomorrow. Or maybe he wouldn't appear at all this time. He had probably met sophisticated girls back East, and he might have recognized Whisper for what she really was—the country kid back home.

Bishop Gledhill stepped out of his office at about 3:30. He pulled his watch from his vest pocket. "Well," he said, "Belle should have picked up Andy by now if the bus is on time."

"The bus is never on time," Whisper said, and she laughed. She didn't want the bishop to pick up any hint that she was worried.

But Bishop Gledhill smiled back at her as if to say, *I know what's on your mind, dear.*

It was what she always sensed from him—that he knew her better than anyone did, and knew everyone in Delta the same way. He was tall, but other than that, he looked nothing like Andy. He was nearing fifty now. Whisper knew that because Sister Gledhill sometimes teased him. Belle was four years younger than he, and she liked to remind him of that. But Belle said everything that came into her head, and the bishop chose his words carefully. He wasn't a handsome man, with his red, round face and his swelling middle. Whisper doubted that he ever had been good-looking, but Belle, the pretty young French girl, had fallen for him long ago, and Whisper understood why. Lots of people tried to be good; Bishop Gledhill just was.

It was true that the bishop could get down in the mouth, even a little cranky at times. He could also use those careful words of his to cut people down to size—when they had it coming. She had heard him in his office one day with the door closed, talking—shouting, really—at a man who had hit his wife. Whisper had actually been shocked by the things the bishop had said. He had used the word *damn* a time or two; she hadn't imagined he would ever do that. But Whisper had pounded her desk with her fist each time he did, and she had said out loud, "You tell him, Bishop. It's just what he deserves."

Bishop Gledhill was the center of everything in Delta. He set the tone at every First Ward sacrament meeting, every ward party, every town event. No one cared whether he was acting as mayor or bishop; it was all the same. He listened to people's personal problems. He showed up when a family tragedy occurred. He got calls in the middle of the night when someone was sick, and he, like Doctor Noorda, would get out of bed and make house calls, the two often arriving at the same time. Doc would heal the body, when he could, and Bishop Gledhill, the spirit. More often than not, though, Doc Noorda would join the bishop and lay his hands on a patient's head before prescribing medicine or setting a broken bone.

What Whisper knew about Andy was that he was a mix of his parents: more talkative than his father; more introspective than his mother; but gentle, even though not many ever knew that side of him. He had played hard, knocked around with the other boys in town, and later had been an intense high school football player and a wrestler, but he had always seemed to feel things more deeply than most of the boys in town. Once a boy had killed a robin with a rock, and Andy had shown his indignation. Every kid knew it was all right to kill sparrows or barn swallows, but a robin was untouchable. Andy had called the boy a few names that the bishop wouldn't have liked, but afterward, he and Whisper and Adele had buried the bird, and Whisper had seen how carefully he had placed it in the hole and then patted the soil around it.

Whisper had liked to play with the boys, even after elementary school. She was as entranced by Andy as every other kid in town was. By then, he wasn't going off to France so often, and he had somehow taken over as the boy everyone followed. Once, running in a dress, Whisper had fallen and skinned her knee. Andy had walked her home, with all the other kids trailing along. "I'm not crying," Whisper had told him, and Andy had only said, "I know," even though they both knew that she was.

Whisper had seen Andy through his rebellious years, when the title "bishop's son" had become almost too much of a burden. He had taken up swearing for a while, and had done it pretty proficiently. He had also saved up rotten eggs and, along with a couple of his friends, had attacked the girls walking home from church on Easter Sunday. Whisper thought it was funny, how much the girls howled, but it was a scandal in town. "Maybe the bishop needs to spend a little more time at home, teaching his own children how to behave," one of the "injured" girls' mothers had told Whisper's mom. But Sister Harris had said, "Andy's a good boy at heart. He'll be just like his father someday. I'd bet a dozen *good* eggs on that."

"Andy's going to be too tired to hold his head up when he gets here," Whisper told the bishop.

He patted her shoulder as if to say, *Don't worry; he'll want to see you soon,* but he didn't say it. He only smiled and walked back into his office.

*   *   *   *   *

As Belle drove into Delta, Andy loved seeing everything. The whole "downtown" was only three blocks long, but Main Street was even wider than the streets of Salt Lake City. In the middle of the street, as always, was a huge, decorated Christmas tree. There were a couple of filling stations; two drugstores; Dad's bank and dealership; Hatch's City Café on one side, the Gem Café on the other; D. Steven's department store; an auto parts place; Quality Market, a grocery store; the Crest movie house; Moody Brothers Feed and Seed; a barber shop; Nona's Beauty Shop; Hilton Brothers Motor Company; a bakery; a cleaners; and the sugar factory that processed sugar beets at the end of the street by the railroad line. And of course, the crown jewel of the town was Van's Dance Hall, above the auto parts store. Every inch was fancy, with glass mosaics, a thousand mirrors, and the great mirror ball with a replica of the Salt Lake Temple on top.

Delta, Andy knew, would look funny if transplanted to the East, but it was wonderful to him. He knew every crack in the sidewalks and every owner of every store—and all the owners' kids. He remembered the time he and Oscar Evertson had raced their horses down a side street and crossed Main just as a little truck was driving through. Oscar's horse had hit the truck, and Oscar had been thrown all the way over the top. For a couple of days there had been a question as to whether Oscar would live, and Andy had sat the whole time outside his house, waiting to know. Dad had been there too, at least half the time, and he had finally come out and said, "He's awake and talking. Doc says he'll be all right." And now Oscar was in the Pacific somewhere, serving in the navy.

Belle turned at 200 West—the street everyone in Delta called "Silk Stocking Way." But to Andy that seemed something of a joke as he thought of it now. There wasn't a house in all of Delta that was truly fancy. Belle drove south a couple of blocks and then pulled into the driveway at home. Andy saw Flip running across the lawn to the car. The kid wasn't worried about the patches of snow that still remained in the shade of the old willow tree out front. But as Andy stepped out of the car, Flip stopped short. For a moment he looked up at Andy as though he wasn't sure what he was supposed to do. But Andy reached out and grabbed him, then hugged him against his chest. Mom was right, he hadn't grown—but he did seem a little older. After all, he hadn't jumped into Andy's arms. "Hey, kid, how you doing?" Andy asked.

Flip was still clinging to him. "I'm good. Same as always. How long are you going to be home?"

Andy was pretty sure Flip knew the answer. Maybe he was just trying to think of something to say. "'Til New Year's. I gotta leave on the second of January."

"Will we have time to go over to the church and play some basketball?"

Andy finally let go of Flip and looked down at him. "Let's do it every day. I gotta stay in shape while I'm home. I can't let myself get flabby. What about you? How's your game?"

"Terrible. The guys don't want me to play Junior M-Men ball for the ward because I'm too short. I gotta work on my set shot so I can make some long ones."

"Okay. We'll work on that." Andy looked toward the house. Chrissy was standing on the porch. She was wearing a skirt and blouse, no coat, and she was folding her arms against her middle, obviously cold. She was pretty, like Mom, with the same dark hair and eyes. Andy and Flip and

Adele were the ones who had gotten lighter hair from Dad—at least the color Dad's hair had been before it had grayed so much the last few years. But Flip didn't have Dad's round cheeks. He was not just short; he was skinny. His face was all bones. He really wasn't much to look at. Still, he had that great whole-face smile, and he never had been able to hide his emotions, no matter what he was feeling. He was beaming now, and Chrissy was walking down the steps, not willing to tromp through the snow, but clearly eager to receive her own hug. So Andy left his duffel bag and strode across the lawn to her. He wrapped her in his arms. She did look older, more filled out.

Andy started up the stairs with Chrissy and then heard Flip grunting as he tried to catch up, carrying the big duffel bag. Andy reached back to take it, but Flip said, "It's okay. I've got it." And he did. The kid was strong as fencing wire, always had been.

As Andy reached the porch, the screen door swung open and Marie stepped out. She had changed more than anyone. She was a woman. "Marie," Andy said, "you're beautiful." She had always been shy, and she blushed terribly now, but she reached for Andy, and he grabbed her and pulled her into his arms.

Andy had almost forgotten how happy he could be. He had left so many times that he rarely got homesick, but the joy of being here, seeing everyone, hit him harder than he had expected. He had teased his sisters all their lives, and they had sometimes lost patience with him, but he liked what he felt from them now.

Inside, everyone sat down in the living room—which, as always, was much too warm. Mom was always cold in winter, and she kept the old furnace full of coal, stoked up and burning strong. Everyone asked the usual questions—about the train ride, about his training. Andy knew there actually was a lot to talk about, but his weariness was hitting him hard again. He wanted to take a nap before dinner, but he also wanted to see Whisper. And he knew how she was—if he was in town a few hours before he stopped over, she would take it the wrong way. He was about to ask Mom if he could borrow the car when the front door opened and Dad came in. He had obviously walked to work that day, as he usually did. He stepped inside and yelled, "Hello!" but then he bent down to release the buckles on his galoshes.

"Hey, Mister, what are you doing home in the middle of the day?" Andy called. "You must have banker's hours." Dad was leaning against the wall, balancing himself as he pulled off one of the galoshes and then the other. By then, Andy had reached him. When Dad finally righted himself, he grabbed Andy by the shoulders, kissed his cheek, and then pulled him into his arms. Dad had kissed Andy for as long as he could remember. Maybe it was something he had learned in France, but it surely wasn't something most fathers in Delta would ever do. Still, it never embarrassed Andy.

"How long have you been here?" Bishop Gledhill asked.

"I just got in. My bus was a little late. But I was about to make a quick run over to the bank—to say hello to you. And, you know, to Whisper."

Dad walked into the living room, keeping an arm around Andy's shoulders. "Yes, I think I'd do that. But talk to me a minute first." Dad stepped over to Mom and gave her a peck on the cheek.

"Ron," Belle said, "let him go now. You can talk to him when he gets back."

So Andy borrowed the car and made a quick run to the bank, but that turned out to be awkward. There were customers at the teller's window, and talking to Whisper in front of them was embarrassing. So Andy merely said, "I just wanted to say hello. Will you be home after dinner?"

He got some knowing smiles from LuRane and Elbert Jenkins, so he figured he'd better say something to them. He shook each of their hands. "How's Marlin doing, Brother Jenkins?" he asked. "Is he man enough for the marines?"

"He thinks he is, I guess. But you know Marlin. He writes us a letter about four lines long and he don't tell us much of anything."

"Is he someplace where he can go to church?"

"He has to go to the Protestant services," Sister Jenkins said. "I guess they lump Mormons in that way. But he doesn't like it. I told him, 'You never did like to sit through church meetings, so don't blame it on something like that.'"

"I'll tell you, though," Andy said, "most guys get a lot more religious once they know they're shipping out to the war."

"That's right," Brother Jenkins said. "We've seen some of that already. Last letter, he said to send him his Book of Mormon."

"Marlin's all right. He'd give you the shirt right off his back. He told me once that he'd thought about serving a mission but he was just a little too scared."

"I know," said Brother Jenkins. "He's about like me. Your dad asked me to talk in sacrament meeting one time and I did it, but the best I remember, I had to change my underwear right after the meeting."

Andy laughed and glanced at Whisper. He had no idea what he could say to her. But the Jenkinses seemed to know what he was thinking. "Hey, we better take care of our business and get along so you can give your girl a kiss," Sister Jenkins said.

Whisper looked away and pretended not to hear, but her face was red. Andy knew he was in over his head. "Oh, no. I've got to run. You finish up here, and I'll see Whisper later."

She glanced up long enough to nod to him, and then Andy left. He wished by then that he hadn't stopped by, but it had been nice to get a look at her. She seemed prettier every time he saw her. She had reddish hair, sort of half blonde, and lots of freckles that had been kind of ugly when she was fourteen but looked perfect now with her pale green eyes.

When Andy got home, his dad was in his office and Mom was getting started on dinner. Andy stepped into Dad's office, just off the living room. It was a little room that had once been a nursery in the old house, but Dad used it to talk to all the people who came to see him on church or town or business matters. There had always been a steady parade of people through the Gledhill home.

"Come in, Andy. Sit down," Dad said. "Your mother was just telling me that you've been reassigned to Washington, D.C. What is it you're going to be doing there?"

Andy sat in one of the two chairs Dad always kept in front of his desk. He went through his routine again, answering without answering, promising to let his dad know more later. Dad finally said, "Your mother thinks maybe you're getting a dangerous assignment—because of your language background. She's awfully worried."

Andy clasped his hands together and looked down at them. He tried to think what he should say. "Dad, I'm trained to be a paratrooper. Mom knows that as well as you do. There probably isn't any job in the army more dangerous than that. I still might end up with the 82nd Airborne, and if I do, I'll probably drop behind the lines whenever the big invasion takes place. Any assignment I might get in Washington couldn't be more dangerous than that."

Bishop Gledhill nodded. "That's true, I guess, but not exactly comforting. Do you worry much about all that?"

"A little, I guess. But it doesn't do much good to dwell on it. I'll just do what I have to—when the time comes."

Dad smiled a little. He had had some dental work done since Andy had been home last, and a gold inlay on one of his front teeth called too much attention to itself. Andy didn't like the look of it, but he knew what that smile meant. He had seen it all his life. When Andy started blowing smoke, Dad didn't go for it. "You think about it plenty, Andy. I know you do. When I shipped out to Europe in 1917, I couldn't gather enough saliva to spit with. And the worst part was, everything turned out just as bad as I feared."

Andy grinned. "Is that supposed to make me feel better?"

"All I'm saying is, I know you're scared—and for good reason. What I doubt, though, is that you understand what war is all about. I don't think you can know that until you get there."

"I guess not."

"In our war, I saw good men—men who'd gone to church every Sunday before they shipped over there—lose every bit of their faith."

"I've been in the army almost a year, Dad. I've handled things all right."

"I know. But I wish you'd had a chance to serve your mission. I think that would have done a lot for you. You've always gone after life hard and done pretty much what you're supposed to do. But I've never heard you say much of anything about having a testimony."

"I guess I'd rather *do* what's right—not talk about it."

Dad took a good look at Andy, and they both knew the truth. Religion had never really gotten top priority in Andy's life. "Andy, you may get in a situation where you can't go to church for a long time. But I hope you'll always pray. You'll need the Lord with you."

"I've done just fine with that so far, Dad. I don't get down on my knees when other men are around, but I pray. Every day."

"That's good." Dad nodded. "But I suspect you're going to face some new things this time around. Some people can kill and not let it bother them. Or at least they claim they can. But for me, it was the lowest I ever felt in my life."

"The thing is, Dad, this is a war that's got to be fought. That's what keeps me going, knowing I'll be fighting on the same side God's on."

"I know. And I'm proud of you that you signed up right off when the war broke out."

Andy smiled. "But if I had my druthers, I'd just stay right here in Delta, never leave again."

"That's exactly what I felt while I was gone. And it's why I'm still

35

here. Your mother always wished we could move to Salt Lake or some-place a little bigger, but I feel better here with these people than I could in any other place in the world."

Andy nodded, and he looked at the floor for a time. It was hard to imagine what he would face these next few years, and there were so many ways that it could end badly. "Will you give me a father's blessing before I leave, Dad?" he asked.

"You know I will. I was hoping you'd ask."

CHAPTER 3

ANDY WAS BEYOND TIRED by the time he finished dinner. He wished that he could wait until morning and then spend all day with Whisper, but she would be working at the bank in the morning, and he did want to have some time with her. So after he ate, he put on a pair of civilian trousers and a sport shirt, neither of which fit because he was bigger in the chest and smaller in the waist than he had been a year ago, and then he found his old galoshes in the back of the hallway closet. The storm had hit by then, and snow was coming down hard. According to the weather report on KSL radio, this was not supposed to be a huge storm, but weathermen were often wrong, and the announcers on the Salt Lake City stations talked mostly about northern Utah and had little to say about the central part of the state.

Most people had little tread on their tires these days, with new tires rationed so carefully, so drivers had to put chains on, and that was more trouble than Andy wanted. So he found his old overcoat in the closet and borrowed one of Dad's felt hats. He tugged on his galoshes and called to his mother that he wouldn't be late, then set out for Whisper's house, just one street west and one block to the south. He felt foolish dressed in such ill-fitting clothes, but he didn't want to tromp around in the snow in his uniform.

What he did like was the stillness outside. People were staying home in this weather, so there were few sounds. The wind had died down, and the snow was settling over the town like feathers. He did hear a voice, probably a mother calling for her kids to come inside, but the sound was distant, vibrating like a note from a violin string. All this was as different from Washington, D.C., as anything he could imagine. At the corner just down from his house he stopped and looked at a streetlight. He focused his eyes on the light and on the snow fluttering past it until the moment came when the snow seemed to halt, as though stuck in space, and the lamp took off, rising upward. It was an illusion, like a train moving on a parallel track, but Andy remembered when he had first noticed that little trick here under this very lamp in another snowstorm long ago. A whole childhood came back to him—that immense time when he had thought he would be a kid forever. He looked away, then stared at the light again, let the reversal of motions happen in his brain once more, and suddenly he wanted to cry. This place was enough for him, these memories, the snow biting at his face. He didn't want to leave again, and he didn't want any of what lay ahead for him.

But he ducked his head and crossed the street, his galoshes crunching in the dry snow. When he reached Whisper's house his face was still stinging but he was warm inside his coat. He found himself hoping she would want to come out with him so they could walk and she could feel what he was feeling. Sometimes, back when they had been kids together, they had built snow forts with the other kids in the neighborhood. Andy remembered kneeling in the snow, pressing together snowballs, the snow sticking to his woolen mittens, and he remembered the wars, the attacks and counterattacks, Andy yelling out commands, leading his troops, then directing the repair of the fort after the battle. He remembered the tense excitement as he and his soldiers made more snowballs, whispered about the next onslaught, and laughed in spite of themselves—and the disappointment when parents finally called them inside. The memory was powerfully appealing to him tonight: that kind of war, that kind of peace.

When Whisper opened the door, Andy could see that she had dressed up a little more since that afternoon. He didn't dare ask her to come outside. She was wearing a pretty green dress—a church dress. Whisper had told him once that she liked green because it brought out the color in her eyes. He noticed now that it was true. But the vibrations running through him seemed to have more to do with her slim waist, the long lines of her, the fall of her reddish hair along her neck, the quiet way she was smiling.

"Come in," she said, but she didn't turn away to give him much room to come inside without stepping close to her. Andy wasn't sure what to do. Where were her parents? Should he go ahead and kiss her now or maybe wait until he was leaving? But she still didn't step away, and he thought he knew what she was telling him. So he bent toward her, kissed her lightly for a moment, and then found himself pulling her into a full embrace. He felt her slimness through her soft dress, felt those vibrations again, felt all the air leave his chest. Bishop Gledhill had been warning Andy for years that kissing seemed innocent enough, but it could get a young couple excited, and then mistakes could happen. Andy hadn't always listened to his dad, but he sensed now how difficult things could get if he kissed Whisper too much while he was home.

Whisper stepped back, but she didn't pull away entirely. She touched his cheek. "You're cold," she said.

"Only my face," Andy told her, smiling. He wanted to say that he was burning inside or something like that—some line that an actor might use in a movie. But he wasn't good at that kind of thing, so he let it go.

"It's so good to have you home."

The words that came to Andy were, *I love you, Whisper,* but he didn't say them. He didn't say anything. Instead, he took her back into his arms and held her, and once again he wished that he could cry.

When Whisper pulled away from him, Andy was certain that her parents must be sitting in the living room, just around the corner. He could hear the radio: Lowell Thomas, in his deep voice, announcing the evening news. Whisper took Andy's coat and hat and hung them on the hall tree, then walked him into the living room. Just as he had thought, Brother and Sister Harris were sitting by their big walnut console radio, one on each side. Sister Harris reached and turned the volume down. Brother Harris set his newspaper aside and stood up. "Hello, Andy," he said. "Wilma told us you were in town. Looks like you brought a snowstorm with you."

"Naw, someone else must've brought that. It was raining where I came from."

Brother Harris smiled and nodded. He was a thin man with no fleshiness at all in his face. He wore wire-rimmed glasses with thick lenses that magnified his eyes. Life had been hard on him. He operated a little insurance company in town, but during the Depression lots of people had had to drop their coverage—or they had lost their possessions worth insuring. Brother Harris had eked out a living, and Bishop Gledhill had worked out some arrangements so that he hadn't lost his house—tiny place that it was—but Whisper and her brothers had never had much. Andy could remember a time when Adele had gotten a new coat and had given her old one to Whisper. It was well worn by then and too short the first day Whisper put it on, but she had said she was happy with it. Years later she had told Andy how ashamed she had been for all her friends to know that she had to wear Adele's hand-me-downs.

The Harrises chatted with Andy for a few minutes, and then, as though by previous agreement, they excused themselves, walked to the kitchen, and left Andy and Whisper alone. Music was playing on the radio by then—big band music from one of the dance halls in New York

City. A woman was singing: "Dream, when you're feeling lonely, dream, when you're feeling blue." Whisper turned the volume back up a little, but the two paid little attention to the music. They talked about people they knew, about all their friends who were away at war and what Whisper had heard about them, and then they talked about Andy's transfer to Washington, D.C. Once again Andy said as little about that as possible. When Whisper suggested that he might be able to avoid going into battle, he let her think that was true.

"You're tired, aren't you?" Whisper asked after a time. "I can see it in your eyes."

"I didn't sleep much on the train. I never have been able to sleep sitting up."

"I doubt I could either. I'd want to see everything, even at night. It must be exciting to cross the country like that. I've still never been outside of Utah."

"Out in the middle of the country the land isn't very interesting—mostly just flat, with lots of big farms."

"I know. But I'd like to see that. I'd like to see *anything.* Everyone talks about California and the ocean and the palm trees, and about picking oranges and lemons. I've always wanted to go down there and pick some."

"I don't know. Little ol' Delta looks awfully good to me right now. I'd come home and stay if I could."

She smiled, seemed to think about that, and then she asked, "With me, Andy?"

It was the most forward thing she had ever said to him—probably the most forward thing she had said in her life. He knew how he had been looking at her, and what his eyes must be saying to her, but still, he didn't answer. He had told himself on the train that he had to be careful. If he and Whisper made too many promises, that might be a mistake.

Whisper certainly saw his confusion, and she flushed, the skin across her cheekbones brightening under her freckles. But she surprised him again. "Andy, I need to know," she said. "I'm almost twenty-one. You've been coming and going all these years and you've never said what you expect of me."

Andy knew that, of course, and he had even thought, before he'd been called to Washington, of buying her an engagement ring for Christmas. But this new business with the OSS changed things in Andy's mind. Maybe he was in no more danger than he had been with his Airborne unit, but it felt worse to him, seemed more inevitable that something would go wrong. He had asked himself over and over during the long train ride whether he had much chance of surviving behind enemy lines and what it would do to Whisper if they got engaged and then he got himself killed. If he avoided commitments, maybe that would be best for her. But if that were what he intended, he shouldn't have held her in his arms the way he had; he should have acted more aloof. It was too late for that, so he said more than he should have: "Whisper, it's hard to say the right thing right now. Everything's so up in the air. If I was going to be here, you know what I would ask."

"It doesn't matter. Ask me. I know you have to go again. But if I know that much—that I'm the one you want—then I can wait forever."

She was sitting too far away to touch, with the big radio between them, but he wanted to hold her again and didn't dare. It wasn't just that her parents were in the next room; he needed to think more about their situation and not just let his emotions run away. But she was blinking back tears, trying hard not to come undone. He knew what it had cost her to be so direct with him. "This whole thing is not fair to you, Whisper. What if something happens to me?"

"You mean, what if you die?"

"Well, sure."

"I thought you were going to be in Washington."

"I am. For a while. After that, I don't know."

"Then let's get married now. We could go up to the Salt Lake Temple before you leave again. Then I'd know that I'm going to have you in the next life even if you don't make it home from the war."

"But Whisper, what would that do to you? You have to live *this* life before you start the next one."

"I'd manage all right. But if you died, and I never knew what I meant to you—or whether I could still have you on the other side—that would be the worst of all."

Andy had thought about all that, considered it both ways, and he knew how much it would hurt him if she found someone else while he was gone. But if she did find someone else, she could have a home and children—the things she always said she wanted. If she put all her hope in Andy, and he was killed, she might miss her chance. She was already past the age when most girls got married. Maybe the most selfish thing he could do was to make promises.

But Andy wasn't saying anything, and he could see that his silence was destroying Whisper. It was so unlike her to take this risk, and she was clearly regretting that she had done it, so he said what he knew she needed to hear. "I love you, Whisper. I'll always love you." He got up from his chair, took her hands and pulled her up, then held her in his arms again. He felt her mold to him, felt the ache in himself.

"You've never said that, Andy. I've wanted you to tell me that since I was a little girl."

He pulled his head back, looked at her, and smiled. "I was more interested in catching horny toads at the time."

"I know you were. And in high school you were more interested in cars and football and all your buddies."

Andy had known all this—how much Whisper had cared for him— but he hadn't thought of it then the way he did now. He had been hurting this girl forever. She had stuck with him when he had hardly bothered with her, and the truth was, back in his teenage years he had never thought much at all about marrying her. She was just a skinny girl with freckles. He had only liked her because she wasn't as scared of snakes as most girls, wasn't afraid to swim in the irrigation canal. He had dated her as much as anything because he could relax around her and think of things to say. It was only when he had been getting ready to leave for the army that he first recognized how much she mattered to him.

But there was no question in Andy's mind now. All his resolve about avoiding promises was slipping away. "I do want to marry you, Whisper. I do want you to wait for me. But how can I ask you to do that when—"

"I'm going to wait for you, Andy. I can't help it. Now that you've told me you love me, it's what I'll do whether you ask me or not."

"Whisper, listen. There's something I have to tell you." He tried to look more solemn. She needed to understand. "I think my odds of coming home are not good. I can't tell you why that's the case. I'm already saying more than I'm supposed to say. But you need to be ready for the worst. I don't like putting that worry on you, but you have to understand what you're getting into."

"Andy, I can't help it. I don't have any choice. I didn't decide to love you. I just do."

"I love you, too, Whisper. And I want you to wait for me. But it's the most selfish thing I've ever done in my life, to ask you to do it."

"It's all right. It's all I've ever wanted."

And now it seemed the same to Andy—all he wanted and maybe all he ever had.

*   *   *   *   *

Flip got up early the next morning. He shoveled snow from the front steps and made a pathway out to the street and one to the gravel driveway. The fact was, no one in the family was likely to drive that day. The snow had fallen much of the night and piled up maybe six or seven inches. It wasn't a giant storm, but Dad would walk to work, and Mom wasn't likely to take the car out. What Flip wished was that he could stay home from school for the day. It would be cold after the storm, and he could sit in the kitchen with Andy and Mom and listen to them talk. Maybe he could ask Andy about some of the places he'd been, and about jumping from an airplane. Then maybe they could get Dad's key to the church and go over and play basketball in the recreation hall. By the time Flip got home from school that afternoon, his sisters would be coming in and they would chatter with Andy all about the boys they liked and about school, and Flip would hardly get the chance to ask his questions.

When Flip finished his work, he left the shovel and his galoshes on the front porch and stepped in through the front door. He heard his mother call, "Flip, don't track a lot of snow inside."

"I didn't," he called back. "I took my boots off outside."

"That's good. Hang your coat up."

Flip had been ready to drop his coat on the floor, since he would be using it again before long, but he hung it in the hall closet and then walked into the kitchen. "What's gotten into you this morning?" she asked. "Up so early, out shoveling already?"

"It's one of my chores."

"Yes. But your father usually has to get you out of bed to do it."

"I woke up, so I got up."

"And you're excited to have your brother home, aren't you?"

Flip didn't want to admit that. "What's for breakfast?" he asked instead.

"Waffles."

"And bacon. I can smell it."

Dad loved a big breakfast, and Mom got up every day to make one for him, but she didn't always start the day sounding quite so lively. Flip knew she was just as excited as he was to have Andy around. "I doubt you'll see your brother before you go to school. He was dead tired when he went to bed last night."

"He probably stayed up too late, over there necking with Whisper Harris." Flip had not been pleased that Andy, on his first night home, had spent his time with Whisper—although he hadn't told anyone he felt that way.

"Oh, is that what you think he was doing? He might have been reading the scriptures with her, for all you know."

"Oh, sure. Whisper's the prettiest girl in Delta. I think he's got more than the Bible on his mind when he goes to see her." Flip sat down at the little pine table in the kitchen. In the dining room was a heavy maple one, big enough for the whole family, and Dad expected everyone to gather around it for supper at night, but breakfast was hit-and-miss anymore, with everyone leaving at different times.

Mom was stirring up the batter for the waffles, but she turned enough to look toward Flip. "I didn't know you thought Whisper was so pretty."

Flip felt the heat come into his face. He sometimes went by the bank after school to sweep the floors and empty the wastepaper baskets, and when he did, he took a look at Whisper every time he got a chance. She was slender as a willow, and she had the nicest smile he had ever seen. She liked him, too. She would chat with him sometimes, and she didn't tease. She was almost the only person he had ever known who didn't find some reason to make fun of him. She just talked about things—maybe about the sunny weather or about someone who had come into the bank that afternoon. It was like the way grownups talked to each other. Flip thought she was probably the nicest person he had ever met, not just the prettiest. "I didn't say I thought she was pretty," Flip finally said. "It's just what everyone calls her—the prettiest girl in town."

"Well, she probably is, and to me, the best one, too. I hope she and

Andy did do a little kissing last night. I don't want him to leave town this time without putting a ring on her finger."

Flip hoped that too. He had thought for a long time that Whisper was almost part of the family, working at the bank and everything, and Andy's girlfriend.

In a few minutes Dad came down the hallway, smelling of Old Spice and dressed in his white shirt and tie, his leather braces strapped over his shoulders and bending around his stomach. "Smells good, Belle," he said, walking over and giving her a peck on the cheek. "Do you think I could get a fried egg, over easy, with that waffle?"

"What do you think this is, a café?" Mom walked to the "icebox"— as Dad still called the refrigerator he had bought not long before the war broke out—and she got out a bowl of eggs.

Flip liked to see Dad so happy in the morning, joking with Mom. He was never harsh or angry the way Calvin Archer's father was, but sometimes he was silent in the morning, as though he had way too much on his mind.

Flip ate with his dad, and then, after Mom called to them, Marie and Chrissy showed up. They ate in a second shift. Flip waited and listened to them gab. They were also cheerier than usual and wondering what had happened at Whisper's house the night before. But Andy didn't show up to answer that question, and it was only as Flip was pulling his coat out of the closet, having waited until the last possible moment to leave, that Andy strolled down the hall, still in his brown flannel pajamas. "Hey, Flip, let's play some ball when you get home this afternoon," he said, and nothing could have pleased Flip more.

He was happy all day at school, and happier that afternoon when Andy helped him with his dribbling and with his set shot. "It doesn't matter if you're a little shorter than some of the boys," he told Flip. "You're quick. And that's just as important as being tall. Get set for that long shot, and if your guy comes out to cover you, give him a fake and dribble past him. You can do it. All you gotta do is practice real hard until you have the confidence. That's what it takes."

Flip believed it. He had never been good at sports, but he hadn't known he was quick. From now on, he was going to practice a whole lot more. Then, when Cal tried to guard him, he would dribble right on by. He probably never would be good enough to play for Delta High, but if he worked hard enough, he could play for the ward team and not just sit on the bench all the time.

Andy wanted to end their practice much sooner than Flip would have liked. Flip hoped they would still have some time to talk about the army. Maybe Whisper would come over to their house that evening and Andy wouldn't leave. Flip grabbed his coat off a chair on the side of the court and was about to pull it on when Andy said, "We better cool off a little, so we're not sweating when we go outside."

"Yeah. Okay," Flip said.

"Besides, I want to talk to you about something before we leave."

Flip could hardly believe this could happen. No one in the family was there; he and Andy could just talk by themselves. Andy sounded serious, too.

Andy sat down on one of the wooden folding chairs along the wall and Flip sat next to him. There wasn't much heat in the old hall, and some of the big windows were loose. Andy's hair was matted with sweat, steam coming off it. "I guess you know I went to see Whisper last night," Andy said.

Flip thought of joking about that, telling Andy that he'd probably been kissing her, but Andy was looking way too solemn. Flip didn't want to act like a kid. "I know. You said you were going over there."

"Well, she and I did a lot of talking. We're trying to figure out about the future, you know. I guess it's not much of a secret that I'd like to marry her someday."

Andy finally smiled, but Flip tried not to. "Mom always told me that you probably would," Flip said. "Did you get engaged last night?"

"No. Not exactly. But we made some promises, and that kind of worries me. I keep trying to think what she's going to do for fun with me gone so long. Who's going to take her to a church dance or to a show or something like that?"

Flip didn't see the point exactly. He shrugged and said, "I don't know."

"I don't know either, but I'm afraid she'll just stay home all the time. And that isn't fair to her."

"She doesn't get down in the mouth or anything like that," Flip said. "She's not like Adele, all happy one day and in a bad mood the next."

"I know. But she does *feel* unhappy sometimes. She just doesn't let on. She told me that herself."

Flip nodded. He could hardly believe that Andy would reveal something like that to him. He knew he would think of Whisper a little differently from then on.

"Anyway, I need your help, Flip. You'll be fifteen this summer, and pretty soon you'll be getting interested in things you don't care so much about right now. What I was thinking was that you could just sort of look out for Whisper. You could go with her to a picture show, or you could even walk with her to a dance. You wouldn't have to dance with her all the time, but you could watch out for her. There are guys around who'll bother a girl if she walks home from a dance by herself, but you could walk with her and make her feel safe."

Flip couldn't have been more astounded if Andy had asked him to go off with him to the war. He was almost sure he couldn't take Whisper—a grown woman—to a dance, but Andy seemed to mean what he was saying. Flip was not about to tell him that he wouldn't do it. "I guess we do have to watch out for these Japs around here now," he said. "They could cause some trouble."

"What Japs?"

"The ones they brought in from California. You know about that camp, don't you?"

"I heard about it. But they don't come into town, do they?"

"Not much. But I've heard people say we have to watch out. They might try to bust out, and then we could have some big problems over here. There's lots more Japs out there than white people here in town. I heard Vern Danielson talking, down at the bank, and he said we all ought to keep our rifles loaded, just in case."

"I don't know, Flip. I doubt that's anything to worry about. I met some Japs when I was in California and they were nice folks. Farmers mostly."

"They aren't so nice when they're dropping bombs on Pearl Harbor or torturing all the prisoners they take."

"Those are the ones from Japan. These people at the camp have all been living in America."

"Vern said a Jap's a Jap, no matter how long they live over here. They don't ever start thinking like us. They read newspapers from Japan and all that kind of stuff."

Andy shrugged. "Vern talks a lot, Flip. I doubt he's ever met a Jap in his whole life."

"He said he had. And he said—"

"Well, anyway, they've got barbed wire around those people out there, and armed guards. I don't think they'll be bothering anyone. I'm just talking about some guy who gets liquored up, or something like that, and tries to give a girl a hard time. It's just not a good idea for a girl to walk home alone these days."

"Sure. I know what you're talking about."

"Whisper is really nice, and she's easy to talk to. Walking her home will actually be a good way for you to learn how to go out on dates, so you'll be ready when you start wanting to do that. In fact, even more than a show or a dance, the best thing might be just to go over and sit on the porch with her sometimes on summer nights. She gets really lonely."

"But wouldn't she want to talk to a grown-up?"

"She can do that too. But she needs a friend. Most of her girlfriends are married now and busy with their babies, and all the guys are in the service somewhere. But she told me how much she likes you, and how you talk to her at the bank sometimes. I just thought, maybe ol' Flip could be a good friend to her. I might not get back here for *years,* Flip, and she's going to get more lonesome all the time. You'll be almost grown yourself by then." Suddenly Andy laughed. "In fact, I better be careful. You might try to steal her away from me."

"Oh, sure. Big chance of that."

Andy threw his arm around Flip's neck and got him in a headlock. "If you try, I'll have to fight you for her when I get back."

Flip fought back just a little, to make a show of it, but he was still feeling strange about the things Andy had asked him. It made his stomach a little bit sick just to think of walking to a dance with Whisper holding his arm, like he was her boyfriend.

"So what do you say? Will you do it?" Flip didn't answer, so Andy let go of his neck, turned him, and looked in his face. "Will you?" he asked again.

"I guess I could try."

"Look at me, Flip. I've gotta tell you what I'm really talking about." Flip did look in his eyes. "I've got no business asking her to wait. But she does want to, so I'm just trying to think how she can manage it. I guess, in a way, I want you to watch out for some of the guys who might come home ahead of me and start chasing her. I'm selfish, Flip. I love her. So I want you to keep her safe for me. Will you promise me you'll try to do that?"

"You mean, try to scare other guys away from her?"

"No. I don't expect you to fight anyone off, exactly. But time is going to go by, and she'll probably start to wonder after a while if she did the right thing to make promises to me. You can be there when she needs to talk about that, and you can maybe remind her a little, if she starts to change her mind." Andy shook his head. "I don't know, Flip. Maybe I'm trying to ask too much of you, but I need someone around here trying to hang on to her for me if a bunch of guys are after her. Can you do that?"

"I'm not sure. I'd do my best, I guess."

"Here's the thing. There might be some times—long times—when I can't write to her, and she might think I'm losing interest in her. But if I can't write, the trouble is, I won't even be able to tell her why. I can't even tell you why that could happen. But if I don't write to her, keep telling her I haven't changed my mind about her. She'll just need to hear that sometimes."

Flip nodded.

"It's not bad duty, Flip. I've been around this country some, and I don't think I've ever seen anyone prettier than she is. I've seen showier girls, but when you talk about real beauty, she beats all comers in my book."

Flip believed Andy, but he wasn't about to start talking about something like that.

"There's something else I'm worried about." Andy folded his arms in front of him and looked down at the floor. "Soldiers die. That's just how it is. If I get shot up and don't make it back, Whisper's going to need a good friend—someone who's been her friend all along. Maybe there will be a girlfriend, or something like that. I don't know. But she'll need all the support she can get. Will you promise me you'll do your best to help her out, if something like that happens? Mom and Dad would do all they could, but she might want someone to talk to, and they don't always have the time."

Flip thought his heart had stopped. Andy couldn't die. And what in the world could he say to Whisper if he did?

"I know how hard that sounds. But can you try?"

"Yeah. I'd try."

"Hey, that's my little brother—the best one I've got." He grabbed Flip in another headlock. This time Flip was too weak to put up any fight at all. "Don't worry, though. I plan to get back. I feel like I have to now."

*   *   *   *   *

Four weeks later Andy was on another bus. He had spent part of every day with Whisper, and they had talked all about their future: what they wanted out of life and where they would live. Whisper had always liked the idea of living in a bigger town, but Andy watched her give way to his vision. "Dad said I can take over the bank," Andy had told her. "Maybe Flip and I could do that together. Or maybe Flip would want the farm. But Delta is *home,* and I need to know I can come back to it, once the war is over."

"That'd be fine," Whisper had told him. "I want a pack of kids, I know that, and they're probably better off in a small town."

So a lot had been said, but the two hadn't gotten engaged. That was Andy's decision. "I don't want it so you can't go to a dance and have a good time. I need to feel like I didn't rope you to a chair in your mother's kitchen. And I want to feel like you were here when I got back because you wanted to be." Then he told her about Flip's promise, that he would take her to the movie house sometimes, or to a dance, if she wanted to go.

Andy kept staring out the window, watching everything slip away from him. He studied the snow-covered desert so he could remember it, and he watched the highway, a black slice right up the middle of all that white, and he wanted to think that he really would return down that same road someday.

He tried to think realistically about what his odds of getting home might be. No matter how he pictured things, the numbers didn't look good. Chambers had said that the success of the invasion of Europe would change the history of the world, and Andy knew he couldn't turn his back on what had to be done there. But he wondered whether he should have made promises to the world and then made promises to Whisper besides.

CHAPTER 4

ANDY COULD SEE the man he had to kill. The dark figure was standing with his back turned, a clear silhouette in the moonlight. Andy took careful steps, held his double-edged stiletto low by his side, hardly breathed as he edged closer. Then he rushed the man. He grasped the sentry around the neck in a choke hold, bent him back, and drove the knife into his back. Raul, Andy's partner, hurried around the sentry to grab his rifle before it dropped to the ground, but by then Andy knew something was wrong. The knife had struck something pillowy. He jerked the knife back and thrust it again, this time lower, but Major Fairbairn was already screaming at him.

"Armand, think what I've tried to teach you! What did you do wrong?"

But Andy wasn't certain yet what had happened. He released his hold on the dummy and felt its back, checking to see what his knife had actually struck. "I didn't notice it in the dark, sir. He's got a backpack on."

"Yes, he's wearing a knapsack, and you paid no mind. What is it I try to drive into you people? Tell me that, Armand." No one used his real name here. Andy's code name was simply Armand, with no last name.

"Observe *everything*," Andy said. It was Fairbairn's constantly repeated admonition.

"Yes, that's right. I brought you out here on a moonlit night to make it easy for you, but remember, you won't always have that luxury. By the time you stab a man a second time, he'll shout so loud everyone in the guardhouse—anyone within a mile—will know what's going on. Put short, Armand, you're a dead man, and so's poor Raul there, who didn't have the good sense to be a second pair of eyes for you."

Andy had been concentrating on the procedure he had learned: how to snatch the man and where to drive the knife. He had practiced the move in the daylight several times. It hadn't occurred to him that the major would cross him up with something new. Part of the problem was, Andy had been only half awake when the major had called on him to make his attack. All the members of Andy's training unit—fourteen men from the barracks and four women from a nearby cabin—had been rousted out of their bunks at three o'clock in the morning, then forced to dress quickly and fall in outside.

"It's always something different. Do you understand that, Armand? You have to be ready for anything. Sentries don't stand and wait to be stabbed in the back. And they don't always do things the way they did the night before, even if you've studied their patterns several times. What you did there was not bad—if you don't mind trading your life for the life of that sentry. But if you want to survive, you have to look lively every second of every day, even if you've just been pulled away from a comfortable bed."

"Not that comfortable," one of the men said, and everyone laughed.

Andy could see the other trainees gathered in a tight group, with only their faces visible under the glow of the moon. They were his friends now, but he knew very little about any of them. What they shared was what they had survived together: all the running, the early morning workouts in the cold, the long days of drill and classes. The training camp, on the Canadian-side shores of Lake Ontario, might be a pretty spot in the summer—a wilderness of woods and meadows—but it was cold in April and had been worse in March when the school had started, and the rough barracks the men lived in did little to hold out the cold wind.

Andy hadn't found the physical work any harder than the training he had been through in boot camp, OCS, and jump school, but some of the trainees seemed much less prepared, and he had found himself pulling for them, helping them, feeling the shared burden of Fairbairn's demands. These people were not destined to fight together, other than in pairs, and after the weeks here they might never see one another again. In truth, he was not sure that he would have chosen any of them as friends. There were eccentrics among them, even fanatics, and some seemed entirely too titillated by the clandestine nature of their work, but the group was surviving a tough challenge together and six of the original trainees had already dropped out. Those who remained felt a bond.

"Aw right," Fairbairn barked, with his Scottish intonation. Andy could see the steam burst from his mouth in puffs, then drift into the moonlight. "Them cots of yours are like a cloud in heaven compared to the cold ground you're gonna sleep on some nights out in the woods, or rolled up under a hedgerow. You Yanks are used to a soft life."

His remarks were greeted by a mumbled response and a couple of sarcastic comments. A lot of the trainees were not Yanks at all, or if they were, hadn't been in the United States all that long. More than half of them were immigrants who spoke English as their second language—or in some cases, their fourth or fifth language.

Fairbairn was as hard-nosed as they came. He did everything by the book—but it was his own book. He was an officer in the British military, but he had gained his fame as the Assistant Commissioner of the Municipal Police in Shanghai. He had developed methods of silent killing that were being taught all around the world now. All the OSS trainees knew his nickname—"Fearless Dan"—and they called him that behind his back, but it was "Major Fairbairn" to his face.

"Aw right, Armand and Raul, let's try this again, only this time, let's make it interesting. Kill *me,* not the dummy. And I won't be wearing no bloody knapsack." He walked a few paces away and turned his back. "Come on, now. Come after me, and stab me through."

This was nothing new. Fairbairn liked to set up these situations. And the trainee usually ended up flat on his back, the breath knocked out of him. Rumor had it that Fairbairn was the first westerner ever to earn a black belt in jujitsu, and he knew other martial arts too, but he had developed his own technique, which he called "gutter fighting." Fighting him was like taking on a crazed dog, and Andy wanted nothing to do with trying to stab the man.

Still, he had no choice but to try. Andy and Raul lined up again, and Andy started his approach, taking slow steps. He was ten or twelve feet away when he heard a little crunch under his foot, nothing more than a leaf smashing, but Fairbairn swung around. "Who's there?" he whispered, sounding almost desperate.

Andy held his ground, unsure what he should do.

"No, no, Armand. I've shot you by now. The instant I turned, you had to react."

Andy wasn't sure whether they would start again, so he waited.

"Well, what is it? What are you going to do? Come after me."

Andy rushed forward, slashing backhanded with his knife, as Fairbairn had taught him to do, but the major slipped to the side, grabbed Andy's arm, and pulled him on by, at the same time chopping viciously at Andy's forearm. Pain shot through his arm. The knife dropped from his hand, and he knew he was beaten, but Fairbairn wasn't finished. He reached across Andy, grabbed hold of his fatigues at the shoulder, and jerked him around. In the same motion he slammed his knee hard between Andy's legs. The pain burst through his groin and Andy dropped to the ground. He hunched himself into a lump and rolled onto his side on the grass. He couldn't breathe, couldn't think.

Fairbairn was yelling at him, but he had no idea what the man was saying.

By then, Raul had dropped down next to Andy. "Take long breaths," he was saying. "You'll be all right in a minute or two."

But Andy didn't think so. Pain like this wouldn't pass away quickly. Andy wished he had that knife now. He wouldn't hold back if he had another chance at the guy.

Fairbairn was saying, in a calm voice, not to Andy but to the others, "You may think, if you've broken a man's arm, you've done enough. But you have to debilitate him, and then you have to kill him. I didn't finish the job here, for obvious reasons, but once I have a man broken down the way Armand is, snapping his neck would be a simple matter. And a knife is even quicker, if it's used correctly."

Fairbairn paused, and then he called in Andy's direction, "Come now, Armand, that's about enough whining and moaning. You're all right. Get up now, and let's find out what we've learned."

Andy didn't think he could get up, but Raul helped him, and the major stepped closer, got a hand under Andy's arm, and, with Raul, pulled him up. Andy made it to his feet, but he stayed bent over. The ache in his groin had spread through his abdomen and into his thighs.

"Stand up straight, Armand. I don't mind that you made a mistake, but be a man about it now."

Andy straightened up, but he felt a wave of nausea.

Fairbairn stepped up to him, close, breathed into his face. "What would you like to do to me right now?" he asked. The stench of his breath was disgusting.

Andy didn't answer.

"What would you do to me this time if I handed that knife back to you? Answer me."

"Cut you in half."

"You had your chance. Why didn't you do it before?"

59

Andy had liked Fairbairn at times and found him annoying at others, but at this moment, he couldn't stand the man. He wasn't going to play his game. He refused to answer.

"I'll tell you what you told yourself. 'The poor bloke don't even have a weapon, and I've got a bloody knife. It's not right. I can't go after him for real.' Isn't that what you were thinking?"

Again, Andy didn't answer.

"Wasn't it? Tell me, Armand."

"You're my trainer. I'm not going to kill you."

"No, you certainly aren't. You're not good enough." Fairbairn turned back to the others. "You Yanks. You're like bloody Englishmen. Everything's got to be on the up-and-up. Fair play and all of that. But you've got to get all that out of your heads. It's kill or be killed, and that means that the bloke with the dirtiest tricks will win every time. You women, you saw where I kicked him, and you saw what that did to him. That's the best weapon you have, so use it. Or bite a man as hard as you can, rip some of his flesh in your teeth. Go for his eyes. Poke your finger all the way to his brains. Rip his mouth; the lips tear like paper. You're always better off with a weapon, but if you don't have one, use whatever you do have. Butt with your head, scratch with your fingernails, swing your elbows—whatever is free to strike with. And it's the same for the men, no matter what you learned about 'fighting fair' when you were growing up."

He turned back to Andy. "Do you think I acted in a sporting way, Armand? You were careful not to slice my arm with your knife, and then I done you like that, kneed you where it hurts the most. What do you think of a man who would do something like that?"

"I think he better not try it again."

"Oh, I like that spirit. We'll have another go at it—once your health is on the mend. But note this. I came out alive, and yet, *you* had a knife. A fight is a fight, and the only goal is to win. You learned *rules* growing up, didn't you? No biting, no scratching, no hitting below the belt. Isn't that how it was?"

"Yes, sir."

"And what if some big men—several of them—were trying to harm your mother? How would you fight them? You'd do whatever you had to, wouldn't you?"

"Yes, sir."

"Well, that's what this is all about, Armand. The Gestapo will hold nothing back if they get their hands on you, so you better be prepared to fight the same way."

Andy certainly understood, but the man hadn't had to kick him like that just to make his point. Andy tried to see what the others were feeling, whether any of them detested Fairbairn as much as he did at the moment, but they seemed quite entertained by the man's little lecture. A big fellow known as Dimitri was actually grinning. But then, Dimitri talked every day about his eagerness to get his first kill. Andy knew the man wasn't really French, although he spoke French well. But somewhere, he had clearly dealt with Nazis. He had said many times that he wanted more than anything to kill a Gestapo agent with his bare hands.

"I'll tell you the truth, Armand," Fairbairn continued. "I hurt you a little, but I held back. If I had used all my force, you wouldn't be on your feet yet—not for a long time. I saved you so you wouldn't miss our training in the morning, which starts in a couple of hours." He looked at the other trainees. "So everyone back to bed."

Fairbairn walked away, still grinning. This had clearly been fun for him.

Raul still had a hand on Andy's shoulder. "Are you all right now?" he asked. French was Raul's first language, and that was always more obvious when he was tired, as he clearly was now.

"No. I'm not," Andy said, but the pain actually was calming down. As it did, though, his anger only increased. "He didn't have to do that.

We're fighting on the same side. He just likes to show us that he's tougher than we are."

"No question. But that's why he wants you—because he thinks you're the toughest man in our group. It's his way of showing us we're not ready yet."

Andy thought that was true. He had felt almost from the beginning that Fairbairn wanted to bring Andy down and show everyone who the real man was. Andy had had more military training than most of the trainees, but that was misleading. Andy sometimes felt that he had the least commitment to what he was being trained to do. He wanted to do his part, as he had always said, but he didn't feel the hatred these people had apparently learned from experience. Andy suspected that Fairbairn sensed some of that and was singling him out for that reason.

At the moment, however, Andy was feeling the bite of the cold breeze again. He told Raul, "Let's just get back to bed." The truth was, though, he doubted that he could sleep. The ache in his groin hadn't diminished nearly enough. As he walked back toward the barracks, the men didn't tease him, as he thought they might, but Madeleine, a trainee who always had something to say, whispered, "Poor Armand. He's still bent over. Something terrible must have happened to him."

Some of the men did laugh at that, but Andy had no comment to make. When he got to his bunk, he sat down, then leaned forward and rested his elbows on his knees. He still wasn't ready to stretch out.

Raul sat on his own bunk, next to Andy's. Most of the men were hurrying to pull off their fatigues and get back into bed. The barracks were supposedly heated by an old coal stove in the corner, but it was never really warm at night, and by this time of the morning, the fire had always died down. Andy saw that Karl, an American with an accent that sounded western, was stoking the fire and adding some lumps of coal, but it was too late for that to do much good. "Dan said he held back," Raul told Andy. "But he brought his knee up pretty hard."

Andy's thinking had moved a step ahead. "I don't know if I want to do this, Raul."

"Do what?"

"When I joined up, I told the recruiter I wanted to get into the paratroopers. It sounded dangerous, but it was still the way I pictured war. I'd have a rifle in my hands, and if I faced the enemy, I'd try to shoot him before he shot me. I didn't ever think about knives and sneaking up behind people."

"We may never have to do that. We'll be gathering information and radioing it back to our people. We'll be saving lives, more than anything. We probably won't be killing anyone at all."

"You don't know that. Look at all the time we spend on sabotage and hand-to-hand fighting. We may be gathering information when we first go in, but before the invasion comes, we'll be blowing things up—or maybe even assassinating people we're told to take out."

This use of stilettos was only one of the fighting techniques the training unit had learned. Fairbairn had taught them to use the "tiger's claw," a clenched hand with the knuckles pressed forward. Those knuckles could be thrust into a man's eyes or used to break the bones in his face. The major had taught them to go limp when grabbed from behind, and then to grasp at any body part that could be damaged. Over and over he had stressed that the most vulnerable place on a man was his groin, and that they should rip at it in any way possible. It was true that the trainees had also spent a lot of time learning the use of Allied weapons as well as those of the enemy, and they had worked with plastic explosives that could bring down bridges or railway trestles, debilitate train engines, sink ships, even blow up buildings. They had been taught intelligence-gathering techniques, along with radio operation, and how to recruit and organize resistance circuits—called *Réseaux*—not only for gathering information but for setting up acts of sabotage. They had learned defensive techniques, too: how to behave when stopped by police or German interrogators; how to avoid little habits that were clearly American. All that made sense, but Fairbairn always came back to his fighting techniques.

"There's a difference between you and me," Raul said.

Andy raised his head to look at him.

"Sure, you wanted to go to war," said Raul. "Maybe you wanted the excitement. And you—"

"No. I'm not one of those guys. I'd rather stay home any day. But I knew we had to fight this war, and I wasn't going to sit home while other guys put their lives on the line."

"But when you say that, I know that you only *believe* that the Nazis are bad guys. I *know.* They took my country away from me."

"Be careful what you say, Raul." The trainees weren't supposed to know about one another's backgrounds. If Andy and "Raul" stayed together, as they were supposed to do, they would drop into France together. But if they were ever captured, it was better that neither knew anything he could reveal about the other. If Raul was from France, he might still have family there. It was just the sort of thing the Gestapo would want to know.

"I won't say anything. But you know I'm French. You know I'm going back to fight for *my* country. If you had Germans walking down the streets of your little town—wherever it is—you would feel different about this war."

Andy had told Raul that he was from a small town, and he had slipped and said something about Utah, which Raul had pretended to ignore, but Andy was pretty sure that was all he knew about him. "Sure," Andy said. "I understand that."

"I don't think you do. My grandmother lives in a nice little village, but it's full of Germans now. She's alone, and she can hardly get enough food to eat. The Germans are shipping all our food back to their own country. They're taking our coal, so people can't even stay warm. And worse than any of that is the fear. My grandmother is scared to go out, just to walk to the market. The Germans strut down the streets like they own the whole village."

Andy knew that until the previous fall, 1942, the southeast part of France had been called the "free zone." It had been run by the so-called Vichy government, which was really only a puppet regime for the Germans. But the Germans occupied all of France now. Andy had heard plenty of stories about the way Gestapo agents roamed the streets in French cities, checking papers and enforcing curfews. They were always trying to locate resistance groups, and once they thought they had a member of any of the underground organizations, they would beat and torture him to get other names. The trainers here at Camp X, as this remote place was called, told shocking stories of German brutality, obviously to build hatred for the Germans. The trainees were taught that they needed to be as brutal as the Gestapo.

But Raul was right about Andy's attitude. Germans weren't real to him. He could hate the idea of the Nazis, but he suspected that Germans were just people. He knew plenty of German Americans, and they weren't any different from anyone else. It was hard to believe that a philosophy could make monsters of people who had produced such great music and art and science. But Germans weren't marching through the streets of Delta, and it was hard to imagine that ever happening.

Andy's pain was finally letting up. He unbuttoned his fatigue shirt and pulled it off. Raul was doing the same thing. "How long have you been in America, Raul?" Andy asked. There seemed nothing wrong in his knowing that.

"Not long after France fell in 1940, my father decided to get us out. We went south and managed to . . . but maybe that's more than I should say."

Raul was a thin fellow, with dark hair and eyes. His black eyebrows against his soft, white skin seemed almost effeminate, and Andy had taken him as less than manly at first. Raul also smoked constantly, and Andy hadn't liked bunking next to him in the barracks, but Andy was learning that Raul possessed his own kind of toughness. He could run as long and hard as Andy could. He had also excelled at shooting Fairbairn's pop-up targets—all made to look like German soldiers—and at working his way through complicated obstacle courses. He didn't really have Andy's athletic skills, but he made up for that with sheer intensity. He wanted to get to this war, and he wanted to win it.

"My father had a brother in this country," Raul said. "We moved to the same town. This uncle had had a good business importing wines. But that's been dead since the war started. My father and uncle work hard just to put food on the table now. At least there are jobs. That's one thing the war has done."

"Will your family go back to France once we kick the Germans out?"

"I doubt it. But I'll go back, whether my parents do or not."

"Why? You speak good English. Won't you have more opportunities in the U.S.?"

"I'm French. I've never felt truly at home since I left my village. I've always planned to go back."

"But not like this."

"No. Not as a spy. But when I joined the army, I started asking questions about doing this kind of work. Someone told me about the OSS, and I started trying to get in."

"Do you want to stab a man in the back, the way we were doing tonight?"

The light went out, and someone called, "Armand, Raul, let's cut the chatter. We've gotta be up before long."

"All right," Andy called out.

"How're you feeling, Andy?" another voice asked. Andy recognized that it was Luis.

"I'll be all right."

"Not for a while, you won't."

Andy pulled off his fatigue trousers and allowed himself to do the unthinkable: drop them by his cot. But he figured no one would be back for an inspection now. He twisted himself onto his bunk, with his legs still pulled up. For the first time, he felt for damage. The swelling had begun, and the tenderness was even worse than he had expected. Once again, a thought came to mind that had plagued him daily since he had arrived at Camp X. When he had returned to Washington after Christmas, he had attended a school near the city, held on the grounds of a country club. After that he had been sent by train to Detroit, then picked up there and driven to this camp. No one outside the OSS even seemed to know that the camp existed, and it was apparently placed in this remote area of Canada so that no one would discover what was happening there. His letters were routed through Washington, and he was never allowed to say a word about where he was or what he was doing.

But on the train, and especially since his first day of training, he had asked himself over and over whether he wanted to stay with the OSS. Why not go back to his Airborne unit? He had stayed so far only because he hated the idea of being a quitter—and maybe to prove to Chambers that he could stick it out. But that seemed a stupid reason, finally, and he knew he soon had to make a real choice.

Andy heard Raul whisper, "Yes. I can stab a man in the back—if he's a Gestapo agent. I'll be disappointed if I never get the chance. I want to kill at least one for my grandmother. Those people have stolen her life from her—taken everything she loved, and did it in her old age. I want some revenge for that."

Andy understood that. He even tried to borrow Raul's motivation. But when he tried out the hatred in his own head, he still thought of a knife passing into a human body, and it felt like something wrong to do. What he preferred to think about was Whisper. He knew that his letters to her had been not only empty of content but empty of emotion. What he sensed every day was that she lived in a world that was already escaping him—hard to remember, even hard to imagine. But it was still the one thing he clung to. Someday he would go home, and Whisper would be waiting. He told himself over and over to believe in that, and he prayed for it every day.

CHAPTER 5

THE WINTER HAD passed slowly for Flip. He was relieved that Whisper seemed content to work at the bank, wait each day for Andy's letters, and stay at home on weekends. Now and then Flip would ask her, rather halfheartedly, if she wanted to go somewhere with him, but she usually declined. Once in the spring, however, she had taken him up on his offer to go to a show, and poor Flip had thought he would die of nervousness. It was a singing and dancing movie—*For Me and My Gal*—not the kind Flip liked very much.

Coming out of the Crest Theater, a few people had said to Whisper, "Hey, your date looks a little young for you," and stuff like that, but everyone knew what it was all about—that Whisper was taken, and Flip was more or less her little brother already. What bothered him was that he was almost fifteen, not exactly a little kid, but he looked more like twelve or thirteen and he knew it. Everyone in town seemed to forget that he was in ninth grade.

But Whisper didn't tease him about anything like that. When they had walked home that night, she had asked him whether he liked the movie, and Flip had only said, "It was okay, I guess. I like westerns better."

"I think I do too." Whisper laughed, and then she asked him about basketball. Flip had played on the ward Junior M-Men team, and he had practiced hard, almost every day after school. He could dribble better now, and when he got in a game, he played defense like a wild man, harassing the guy he guarded with so much energy that some of the players on his own team laughed at him. His shooting was also improving some—at least at practice—but out on the floor, in a game, he tried never to shoot, and the few times he had let one fly, he had been lucky to hit the rim. He had scored only one basket all season, but then, he had spent most of his time sitting on the bench. It didn't seem to matter whether he improved; he was still shorter by four or five inches than anyone else on the team.

"I'm not any good," he told Whisper. "I try about as hard as anybody, but I'm never going to be as good as Andy was."

"We all have different talents, Flip. Not everybody has to be good at sports. In high school, in gym class, I was the worst player at every sport."

But Flip didn't want to be compared to a girl. Instead of making up his mind that he didn't have to be good at sports, he decided to practice all the harder. The day would come, he told himself, when he would ask Whisper to come to one of his games and he'd be in the starting lineup and score a bunch of points. Maybe he would grow this year, and next season, if he practiced all summer, everyone would be surprised how good he was.

Flip saw Whisper at least a couple of times a week when he stopped by the bank to sweep the floors and clean the bathroom. He always talked to her for a while, but after the night he had taken her to the show, he didn't ask her to another one. Most of the pictures were about like that last one, and a couple were about the war. He didn't think she would want to see those. One day in early June, though, Flip was doing his cleaning in the bank when Whisper called him over to the teller window. "There's a dance at the church tomorrow night," she said.

"Everybody tells me I ought to get out of the house a little. Do you think you could walk with me over to the ward house?"

Flip had hoped for a long time that this would never happen. He knew what he had promised Andy, but he had never gone to Whisper's house just to talk, the way Andy had said, and above all he had never mentioned the ward dances. "I guess I could, but . . ."

"But you'd rather not?"

"No. I'm not saying that. I told Andy I would."

"You don't have to dance with me if you don't want to."

"It's not anything about *wanting*. I just plain don't know how. Chrissy tried to teach me, but I walked on her feet so many times, she finally gave up."

"Why don't you let me give you some lessons?"

Flip stared at her through the bars of the teller window. He couldn't believe she would come up with something like that. "No," he said. "I couldn't do that."

"Why not? You need to learn."

"Not really."

"Flip, your whole life you'll be expected to go to dances. I doubt a girl will ever want to marry you if you can't dance."

"I guess I'll have to be a bachelor," Flip said, grinning.

"Now, don't say that. You're getting so handsome, every girl in town is going to want to go out on dates with you. So you'll have to dance a lot."

Flip couldn't speak. He was still trying to get the words to register. Had she actually said he was handsome? Mom had said something like that too—said he was filling out and getting muscles, and how nice he was starting to look. But that was his mother. And he was still the shortest kid his age, even shorter than most of the girls.

"Why don't you come to my house a little early, before the dance, and we'll practice a few times. Then, when you get to the dance, you can ask a couple of the cute girls in the ward to dance with you."

"No. I don't want to do that." He looked at her shoulder, the little embroidered design that was sewn into her dress, but he hardly knew what he was seeing. He just knew he couldn't look into her pretty green eyes. "I don't want to bust your feet before you even get to the dance."

"I'm not worried about that. I'm a very good teacher. I'll have you dancing like Gene Kelly in that movie we saw."

"Oh, sure."

Flip put in one of the longest nights and days of his life after that. He asked Chrissy to teach him again, and stumbled around until she told him he was hopeless. That destroyed the bit of courage he had mustered, so he decided not to keep his promise, and he didn't show up at Whisper's house until it was time for the dance. But she didn't let that stop her. She asked him to come inside and dance in her living room. She explained the steps better than Chrissy had, put on a phonograph record, and then demonstrated, with him following behind her. That went fairly well. But then she took hold of his hand, facing him, smiling, and placed his other hand at her waist. His legs seemed to lock when he touched her. He could think only of his right hand, touching the cloth of her pretty rose-colored dress—and of her skin underneath. She started counting again, taking the steps she had showed him, and he gradually moved with her, actually doing fairly well. They danced one more, with Bing Crosby singing, "Moonlight becomes you; it goes with your hair," and he thought he found the rhythm in the song, something he had only guessed at before.

But in the recreation hall at the church, when Whisper asked him for a dance, he told her no, and then stood with Cal and some of the other boys. Whisper had said she probably wouldn't dance much and would just talk to some of the women in the ward, but she danced almost every time, and Flip watched her, thinking that he had held her the same way, just not quite so close. But he didn't tell his friends. He just watched.

When Lamont Archibald, the president of the YMMIA, announced in a loud voice that the next dance was girls' choice, Jane Moffet, the smallest girl in the ninth grade, walked up and asked, "Flip, may I have this dance?" It was like she figured they belonged together because they were both so short. He didn't like that, and he didn't think much of Jane with her curly, curly hair, but he knew it would be mean to tell her no. Cal and the other guys laughed when he walked out on the floor, but he saw their amazed looks when he danced all right. Flip actually felt pretty good about that, but he didn't ask any other girls to dance. He only danced one more time when they announced another girls' choice, and then it was with Sue Ann Lester, who was four or fives inches taller than he was. She muscled him around the floor to her own timing, and he got thrown off, so he didn't look as good that time. He was glad to hide away after that. At least Cal and the guys laughed mostly at Sue Ann, not him, and Cal said, "Sue Ann dances like a work horse. You couldn'ta got her under control with a bit in her mouth."

But Charlie Nash said, "Ol' Flip, he thinks he's Fred Astaire out there prancing around."

"No, I don't. I don't like dancing."

"You oughta dance with Whisper," Cal said. "And pull her right up next to you, like some of them guys do. You could even smooch her a quick one."

"Shut up," Flip told him. He didn't like the teasing, but even more, he didn't think anyone ought to talk about Whisper that way.

After a while, Whisper found Flip. "Would you mind if we went home now?" she asked. He heard Martin Jenson let out some sort of little laugh or gasp, like he couldn't believe what he'd just heard. But Flip didn't look over at the guy.

"No. That's fine. The sooner the better."

"Would you dance with me once before we go?"

"Naw. I'd rather not."

"Go ahead, Flip. Do it," Cal said, laughing, but Flip knew that Cal was still thinking about dancing close and all that. He wanted to punch the guy.

"You and little Jane looked *so cute* out there," Whisper said. "You're a good dancer already." Cal and Martin and Charlie all laughed, but Whisper said, "If you boys want to be as popular as Flip, you better start working on your dancing."

That was the last thing in the world Flip wanted Whisper to say. He knew what his buddies would say next time he saw them, when she wasn't around. But still, he kind of liked walking away with Whisper, with her holding his arm. He knew they envied him, no matter what they said.

Flip made it to the door and didn't look back, but then Jeff Jones came up behind them and said, "Hey, Whisper, are you leaving already?" Jeff was out of high school, but he was a year or so younger than Whisper.

Whisper turned around and said, "Yes, we are." Flip liked that she had said "we."

Some guy was with Jeff—a towheaded boy who wasn't from the ward and looked a little older than Jeff. Most guys like that were gone now, in the military. Jeff said, "You danced with my cousin, but he said he didn't tell you his name. It's Lamar Jones."

Whisper nodded at the boy with the light hair.

"I didn't think to say anything," Lamar said. He was blushing like a girl. He was wearing a tie with a deer painted on it, like he thought he was really fancy.

"Lamar lives over in Fillmore, but he drove over here for the weekend. If you want, me and him could give you a ride home, and then you wouldn't have to walk."

"That's all right. Flip takes good care of me, and it's a nice night to walk."

Lamar said, "I'd be more than happy to do it. We could run the boy home, too."

Flip didn't like this Lamar. He looked like a rabbit with all that white hair and a nose that was flattened out. Flip thought he'd like to punch him one and spread it out a little more, just for calling him "the boy."

"Lamar's going to be here the whole weekend," Jeff went on, "and a bunch of us are going to go swimming over at the volcano. If you want, you could go along with the rest of us."

The "volcano" was a hot spring close to Fillmore. People from all over the county swam there year-round, building bonfires in the winter so they didn't freeze when they got out of the warm water.

"I'd be happy to take you," Lamar said. He sounded a little anxious, as though he were afraid Jeff wasn't making it clear that it was Lamar who wanted her to go, not Jeff. Jeff had 4-F status with the army because he had broken both his legs when a tractor had turned over on him a few years back. He walked with a little limp, if you knew to watch for it.

"No, thanks," Whisper said. "But it was nice to meet you, Lamar." She took hold of Flip's arm and they walked out.

Flip felt as though she were actually leading him, not the other way around, but once they were outside, Flip let go of her and just walked by her side. "I think that Lamar is sweet on you," he said.

"I know," was all Whisper said, but she didn't have to say the rest, and that made Flip feel good. She wasn't going to let a guy like that take her mind away from Andy.

Whisper was quiet most of the way home. Flip thought of a couple of things to say to her, mostly about the weather, but Whisper seemed to be thinking about something else. It was a warm night, the last of the light still a hint in the sky, even though it was after ten o'clock. They walked under the trees along the street, the air smelling like warm sap, and Flip felt the ease of summer. It was strange to think, here in all this quiet, that a war could be going on.

"Flip, what are you going to do this summer?" Whisper finally asked when they were almost back to her house.

"Work on our farm, mostly. Cut hay and everything." But she already knew that. She had asked him at the bank. She even knew that his dad wouldn't have time to help much and was looking around for a farmhand to work with Flip. Workers were almost impossible to find.

Of course, Whisper was trying to be nice, Flip figured, just thinking up something to say. She was probably thinking, *I haven't even talked much with Flip.*

"Well, it was awfully nice of you to walk with me," she said, and she walked up the steps to her porch. She stopped and looked down, making Flip feel shorter than ever. But then Whisper said, "Come sit on the porch with me for just a few minutes, Flip. It's too nice a night to go in just yet."

Flip didn't want to do that, but he told her he would. He sat on the love seat in front of the front window, as far away from Whisper as he could get. "I hate this war," she said. "It feels like it's never going to end."

"Dad says our boys will be landing in Europe pretty soon, and then after that, we can start to think about when it might be over."

"It's going to be *years,* Flip. Andy told me that, but I don't think I believed it. Or at least I didn't think how long it would feel."

"Maybe it won't seem so slow after a while." Flip doubted that would be true, but he wanted to say the right thing if he could.

"I talked to Lorene Bickers tonight. Her brother is a pilot and he was shot down in the Pacific. He's still missing. She didn't say it, but she knows he's probably dead."

"My dad told us about that last night at supper." Flip knew exactly what Whisper was thinking. If it could happen to Ronnie Bickers, it could happen to Andy. It was just what Flip had thought when his dad had talked about it.

The two sat for a time, and Flip wanted to say something that would help—now that he knew what Whisper had been thinking about—but he couldn't think of a thing. There were lilacs by the porch, and he could smell their sweetness. It wasn't a smell Flip liked. It reminded him of his Grandma Gledhill's house when Grandpa had died and the whole house was filled with flowers. He didn't want to think of that and Andy at the same time.

"I hoped Andy would stay in an office in Washington," Whisper said. "He said he might. But now, since they sent him to England, I keep wondering, maybe he'll be back with the paratroopers, and he'll have to jump when the invasion finally starts. I ask him, every time I write, what exactly he's doing over there, and he never answers me about that. I think he would if he could, and that makes me worry about what he might be doing."

Mom was worried about that too, but Flip didn't want to scare Whisper any more than he had to. "He might be translating things from French. And it's secret, so he can't say anything. That's what my dad says."

"I know. Your dad's told me that too. I hope he's right."

Flip sat, quiet, and noticed for the first time that the crickets were making a racket.

"I promised myself I'd stay busy," Whisper said. "I thought it would be a good time to improve myself—read books and practice on the piano and all those things. And I wasn't going to be sad, ever. But it's going to be so long before I see him again."

"It doesn't matter how long it is. Just remember, everything is going to be great someday. Andy'll come back. And then you two can get married and have a family and everything. He'll keep all his promises. If Andy says he'll do something, he does it."

"I think you're the same way, Flip. You're going to be like Andy, and like your dad. Good as gold."

Flip shrugged, but he couldn't think what to say. He only knew that now that he was sitting there, he wanted to stay awhile yet. He liked the sound of the crickets and the warm night; he didn't even mind the smell of the lilacs as much as he usually did.

"What do you want to do when you grow up, Flip?"

"I don't know. Dad said I could take over the dealership, if we ever start getting cars again, or maybe the bank, depending on what Andy wants to do. But I don't think I'd like any of that very much. I'll be going in the army in three years. That's the one thing I know for sure. Maybe after the war, I'll just stay in. That way I could see a lot of places I'd never see otherwise. That's what I've been thinking lately, anyway."

"Oh, Flip, don't say that. I'm hoping this war won't last so long that it will take away all you younger boys. I was thinking about that tonight, how many of our high school boys will be gone before long."

"That's what they want, too. And so do I. We want to do our part, the same as any other man."

Whisper put her hand on Flip's arm and said, "Don't get too anxious to grow up. Enjoy these years. They're some of the best of your life."

But Flip didn't like that. If he got his chance to serve, he was going to apply for the paratroopers, the same as his brother, and he was going to show a lot of people that he wasn't a midget. He'd get his growth one of these days, and he'd be as much a man as anyone around, maybe more than most.

Whisper talked for a while after that, not saying much that was important, only going on about the nice summer night, and some about missing all the things that were rationed now, especially sugar for baking. But finally she said, "Well, maybe you better go home now, Flip. It's getting almost time for the dance to end, and your parents will be watching for you."

"It's okay. They know I was looking out for you tonight."

"Well, then, don't get me blamed for keeping you out late." She stood up, so Flip did too, and then she gave him a little pat on the shoulder and said, "Thanks so much, Flip. It was nice of you to sit and talk for a while. It's what I needed."

Flip didn't know quite what to say, so he just nodded and then told her goodnight. When he got home, he saw that the light was on in his dad's office, so he walked to the door and said, "I'm home, Dad."

The light was dim, with only a little table light on, and Dad didn't have a book or any paperwork in front of him. It seemed as though he had only been sitting there, maybe thinking. "So how was it, dancing with Whisper?" Bishop Gledhill asked, smiling.

"I didn't dance with her."

"Did you dance at all?"

Flip didn't want to get into all that, but he said, "Just on girls' choice dances."

That seemed to strike Dad as funny. He chuckled and shook his head. "Who asked you to dance?"

"Just a couple of the girls in the ward."

Bishop Gledhill leaned back in his chair. He was wearing an old short-sleeved sport shirt that he liked to put on in the evening after he had taken off his white shirt and tie. It was red and blue plaid and always looked a little wrong for Dad, even though he wore it so often. "I dropped by for a few minutes, but I only saw you over in the corner with your pals."

"Why didn't you bring Mom over and dance?"

"Actually, I was planning to do just that, but old Sister Glissmeyer died this afternoon. I had to go out there and help her daughter plan the funeral."

"Don't you get tired of all that? It seems like there's something like that to do just about every day."

"Well, sure, that's just the way it is. But I've known the Glissmeyers since I was a little boy. It's nice to sit down with the family on a day like this. Death is a nice thing, the way it makes us reflect a little. Their son Farrell, the one that moved to California and left the Church, he was there, and he told me he has some regrets about the way he's done some things, so I talked to him about that. He's softened a whole lot, and I felt like maybe I did a little good—at least to salve over some angry feelings in the family. I don't know if he'll come back to the Church, but maybe he's making a step in that direction."

That was Dad. He always thought something good was coming from anything that happened. He spent his whole life talking to people, trying to help them out of trouble, or settling family matters. Flip didn't think he would ever want to be like that—all wrapped up in other people's lives. And he thought maybe his mother would be a little happier if Dad would stay home more often. It seemed like almost every night Dad was off to a meeting or gone to visit someone, never home with Mom. Mom used to talk of getting away for a little trip or something, but now, with the war, she had even stopped talking about that. There was no gasoline to go any farther than Salt Lake once in a great while. Even that was only to visit Dad's brother and sister-in-law, and Mom always said, when she got back, that they made her tired with all their complaining about everything.

Flip felt the heat in the house. He didn't really want to go to bed. Besides, it still seemed early, the sun having lingered so long. "Dad, how long do you think the war will last?"

"It's hard to know, son." Dad had a way of making a simple question sound like a great, weighty one. "I hear people saying we'll have it done in a year, but I don't think so. I think we're looking at a pretty long go of it."

"Could it last until I'm eighteen?"

"Yes, it could. But I pray every day of my life that it won't. I hope you won't have to go."

"Some guys get their father to sign for them, and they join up at seventeen. That's less than two years off now."

"Well, don't start talking about that, because I won't sign."

"Don't you think I ought to do my part?"

Dad folded his arms across his chest. His arms were white and plump, with lots of blondish hair. Flip didn't like to look at them. "I'm not saying you shouldn't do your duty if the time comes, Flip. But it's nothing to hope for. I served, and now Andy's serving. Maybe that's enough for one family. I hope the war ends and we never fight another one."

"I don't feel like that, Dad. After the war, everyone's going to be talking about what they did, and I'll have to say that I went to school and farmed in the summer."

"War is not like it seems, son. It's not exciting. There's not one thing about war that a young man needs to experience."

"I'm not saying that it's exciting. But a man's got to defend his country. I talked to Alan Burke. He's joined the marines, and he's leaving next week. He picked the marines so he could fight the Japs. He says he can't wait to get some kills and pay them back for what they did at Pearl Harbor."

"Sit down a minute, Flip."

Flip could just about guess what was coming, and he really didn't want to hear it, but he sat in one of the two wooden chairs in front of Dad's desk. He looked at the picture of Jesus on the wall behind his dad, hung up in the middle of a bunch of roses on the wallpaper. He heard the big grandfather clock in the living room, but he didn't bother to think what time it was ringing out.

"The good Lord didn't bless any of those Burke boys with a whole lot of brains, but Alan came up short even by his family's standards. He's been going over to Oak City or Deseret since he was not much older than you, just to see if he could get into a fistfight with somebody. I guess he thinks that makes a man out of him when he finds some kid a little smaller and beats him up—but it *doesn't*. Now he thinks he'll be a bigger man if he can kill Japs. But I'm telling you, Flip, there's nothing that God abhors more than bloodthirst. If we have to kill to protect this country, then we'll do it. But it's not something we should ever hope for."

"Tell that to the Japs. They started it."

But Bishop Gledhill didn't say anything about that. He leaned forward with his elbows on his desk, the lamp making the side of his head glow yellow. "Flip, I know you're small for your age. But you won't always be. Growth is just a natural thing. It comes sooner or later, and we're not small people in our family, so you'll be good sized one day. You don't have to prove anything. And you don't have to get into a hurry."

"I didn't say anything about being small."

"I know. But you can't help but think about it. I know some of the boys give you a hard time about being a little shorter than they are."

"I don't care one thing about that, Dad. I was just talking about going to war. And all I'm saying is, I'll be ready when the time comes. I'm not scared off by Germans or Japs, either one."

"Flip, you don't want to kill a man, do you? Why would anyone want to do that?"

That wasn't the way Flip thought of it. And it wasn't the way he wanted to think about it. Dad had a way of making everything religious. He could quote a scripture about almost anything, and then make you feel guilty for doing what everyone else did without a second thought. So Flip got up. "I'm not talking about murdering anyone," he said. "I don't know why you want to make it sound like that." He loosened his necktie and unbuttoned his collar. He didn't know why his mother starched his white shirts so stiff. "I'm tired. I guess I'll go to bed."

"Flip, I'm just telling you that it's not like you imagine it. Every boy gets the wrong idea about war."

"Sure," Flip said, and he walked from the room, only saying "goodnight" when he was well down the hall. His bedroom was hot, so he opened his window, pulled his clothes off, and lay on his bed in his underwear. He didn't even pull back the bedding. He just lay on top of his cotton bedspread with his hands behind his head, and he thought about things he should have told Dad instead of what he'd said. He'd read a whole book about men who had won the Medal of Honor, and he didn't know whether he would do something like that, but he wouldn't back away the way his dad wanted him to do. He would fight like a man, and he'd face whatever he had to.

* * * * *

Whisper got up on Saturday morning, glad she didn't have to go to the bank, but not sure what she wanted to do with her day. She sometimes helped around the house, but her mother liked the house neat and spent every day of her life keeping it that way, so there wasn't much for Whisper to do. She did go outside for a while and help her dad in the garden. He didn't really love all the hoeing and weeding, but he had kept a big garden through all their bad years, and sometimes it had kept them eating—that and the rabbits they raised in a coop beyond the garden. As people across the nation had begun to put in "victory gardens" at President Roosevelt's request, most people in Delta just laughed. It's what they had always done. Whisper hoed, and even got down on her knees and pulled weeds around the squash and potato vines, but as the heat came on, her dad told her they had done enough.

Whisper went inside and took a bath, and then she told her mother she was going to walk over to visit Adele, who had recently come home from the University of Utah for the summer. Adele had been hired at D. Steven's department store, selling women's wear. She wasn't the most reliable employee, and everyone in town knew it, but she knew how to wear clothes. She could make a plain dress look snappy just by the way she walked around in it.

Whisper had seen Adele at the dance, and the two had chatted for a few minutes. Adele had said, "I'm not working tomorrow. Come on over and we'll think of something to do. Just not early." The girl did love her sleep.

When Whisper knocked on the door, Sister Gledhill opened it and said, "I'm glad you're here. Now I'll have an excuse to get Adele out of bed. It makes her dad upset when she sleeps all day."

"I could come back later, and—"

"No, I'm serious. It's almost eleven. I need to get her up." Then she smiled. "How did Flip do last night? Did he make a good escort?"

Whisper stepped into the house. It felt cooler inside than her own house did. She loved the elegant furniture in the living room, and she loved Sister Gledhill's easy way of talking, of thinking. Her own mother always seemed so stern about everything. "He danced with me at my house and did all right, but I asked him to dance at the church and he wouldn't do it."

"But he *did* dance with you before you went over?"

"Yes."

"My goodness. This is news. Flip told his dad that he danced some girls' choice dances, but I wondered whether he had done them any bodily harm."

"No. He did just fine. He looked really cute with that little Moffet girl."

"Is that who he danced with? He wouldn't tell me. Well, well. Andy, at that age, didn't like to dance either. But he got so he did all right. Maybe Flip will too." Sister Gledhill was wearing a white apron over a flowered housedress, and her hair was tied up in a loose roll at the back of her head, but somehow she looked dressed up. Maybe it was the gleaming white of her apron, or maybe it was her bright nails, but, as always, she looked wonderful to Whisper. Still, it was Sister Gledhill who said, "Oh, Whisper, you look so pretty on a Saturday morning. How do you do it? I was pretty once, you know, but I had to work at it more than you ever do. I'll get Adele."

All of that had come in a rush, as her communications usually did. She went striding off down the hall, calling back, "Just sit down in the living room—or in the kitchen."

Whisper walked into the living room and stood at the fireplace where the Gledhills kept a picture of Andy in his uniform. Whisper had some pictures of her own, but this was the one she especially liked. Andy looked handsome, his eyes so gentle, but he also looked playful, as though he were trying to be a serious military officer but was holding back a laugh. He had such a boy's face, his dimples showing a little, and a short lock of hair falling loose on his forehead. She remembered him when his hair had always been in his eyes, burnt white by the sun, and his face red from running.

Whisper liked to think of herself as part of this house, this family— the daughter-in-law. Sometimes she still wished that she and Andy had married before he had left; then she wouldn't have to imagine that she belonged here. When she had been younger, the Gledhills had seemed so rich, so secure. She knew now that they watched their expenses more than she had ever imagined, but still, they didn't worry constantly about money the way her parents did; she always felt the difference when she was here. Part of Andy's appeal, she had to admit to herself, was that he could give her comfort, an end to so much worry.

When Belle returned, she said, "I actually saw Adele in an upright position. Why don't you walk down to her bedroom and make sure she stays that way. I'll fix her a little breakfast, and you a lunch. How would that be?"

"Oh, no. Not for me. I'm fine."

"My dear. I'm French. When you come here, you get food. Accept that. You're going to be coming here all your life, and I'm always going to feed you. But I won't ruin that gorgeous figure of yours. I'll fix something light."

So Whisper walked down the hall and tapped at Adele's door. "Adele, it's Whisper."

"Come in."

Whisper stepped in and found Adele sitting on her bed, looking as though she were still asleep. "Why do my parents care how long I sleep?" she asked. "What possible difference can it make to them?"

"Early to bed, early to rise."

"They believe that, Whisper. They actually believe that. Or at least my father does, and Mom tries to please him. I'm twenty-one years old, and every time I come home, my parents make me feel like I'm thirteen all over again."

Whisper walked to a little chair that Adele kept in front of a dressing table. She turned the chair around and sat down. "They're such mean people. I'm well aware of that. Remember, I work for that ogre of a father of yours."

But Adele didn't laugh. She did laugh her way through most of life, but she never started early. She was almost boyish looking, sitting in her cotton nightgown, her short hair messed up. She could look spectacular when she worked at it, but she wasn't the natural beauty her mother was. Her face was like her father's, too round, even though she was skinny, and her skin was almost colorless without makeup, her eyes gray. "He's not mean. I didn't say that. He's just so sure he's right about everything, and he thinks I have to be exactly like him."

Whisper didn't think that was true at all. What the Gledhills had always wanted was for Adele to show a sign or two that she was going to be a responsible adult, and she rarely did. But Whisper loved something about that—the way Adele clung to her freedom. She had always been the girl in the neighborhood who thought up the best things to do, and dared to do more than Whisper would have done on her own. Whisper had been a tomboy and didn't scare off when it came to running a footrace with a boy or picking up a lizard, whereas Adele avoided everything of that sort. But it was Adele who had kissed a boy first, who had smoked a cigarette one time while all the other girls waited to see what might happen to her. And it was Adele who, during high school, could always wangle a ride and get herself and Whisper over to Hinckley or some of the other little towns to meet boys at ward dances. Whisper hadn't been boy crazy in the same way—except for her unexpressed feelings about Andy—but she loved the daringness she felt with Adele and never found in herself.

"So how was your big date with Flip?"

"He was cute. He tried to act as grown up as he could, but you saw what he did at the dance. He hid out most of the time. But what I want to know is, who was that fellow you were dancing with?"

"Who knows?" Adele said airily. "He mumbled his name, and I didn't care to know what it was. He kept clinging to me until I waved at Brig Simmons to cut in."

"What about back at the university? Are you in love with anyone up there?"

"No." Some of that Adele impishness appeared. "I have about ten boys chasing me, but I don't let them catch up. I've kissed some of them, just enough to get them all fired up, and then I play with their hearts. But they know I'm not the type to make a wonderful wife and mother, and they chase me anyway—so they deserve what they get. Boys don't really like nice girls, no matter what they tell you in your Gleaner class at MIA."

"Come on, Adele. You are nice."

"I plan to be someday. But not quite yet. What I really want to do is get away from the U and go off to California or somewhere like that. I want one of those jobs in the airplane factories. I want to be Rosie the Riveter for a while—make some money, buy some clothes, meet a bunch of service boys who are shipping out."

"You know better than that, Adele. Those guys only have one thing on their minds."

"Well, it's on my mind too—whether Daddy thinks it should be or not."

"Adele!"

"I didn't say I'd do it. But I'd sure like to flirt with some of those fellows, and then send them off to war still hot under the collar."

Whisper tried not to laugh, but she did. Then she caught herself. "Nothing like that interests me—except for seeing California. I've only kissed one boy in my life, and that's how I want it to stay. When Andy comes home, I want him to know I've been true to him every second he was gone."

"Oh, Whisper. I'm glad you're true to my brother. I want you to be my sister-in-law. But I've got to tell you, sweetheart: You really are boring."

CHAPTER 6

ANDY STOPPED ABRUPTLY and turned to look in a store window. He had to wait only a few seconds before a chubby man in a raincoat rounded the corner. His eyes met Andy's for a moment and he hesitated, but then he continued to walk in Andy's direction. Andy looked back at the shoes and suits in the window, let the man pass him by, waited several more seconds, and then reversed himself and headed back in the direction the man had come from. But just as Andy turned the corner, he glanced up the street and saw that light-colored raincoat. The man had also turned around and was on Andy's tail again. Andy laughed. The guy really wasn't very good at this.

Andy walked fast, turned left into an alley, and then saw that the store with the suits in the window had a back door. That entrance certainly wasn't intended for customers, but Andy tried the door and found it was unlocked, so he quickly stepped inside. He had actually entered a stockroom, full of shelves and boxes. Above him, a woman in a short skirt was standing on a ladder, reaching for a shoe box. Once she had the box in hand, she looked down at Andy. "May I help you?" she asked. She was a pretty girl, about twenty, but her legs—which he could see plenty of—were a little too thick.

"No, thanks. I just wondered if I could enter your shop this way."

"Well, aren't you cheeky?" She smiled. "This isn't a proper entrance for shoppers, I suppose you know." She climbed down the ladder.

"I can't tell you how sorry I am," he said with a smile of his own—his attempt to be charming.

She was flirting with him, holding her head at an angle, teasing with her eyes.

"You can't tell me you're sorry because you're not. You Yanks. You think you own our country."

"Don't we?"

"Not yet. But you're taking us over, a little at a time."

"Actually, I am sorry. Would it hurt anything if I just passed on through this way?"

"Mr. Stoneham won't mind—not if you buy a suit."

"Oh. Well, then, maybe I'll just go back out the way I came in." But he hesitated. The man in the raincoat might still be searching the alley.

"Do one or the other. Just don't stay here with me. That's something Mr. Stoneham *won't* understand." She finally seemed serious.

So Andy opened the back door a crack and looked out. He spotted his man at the far end of the alley, coming back his way. He shut the door. "I think I'll have a look at a suit," he said, stepping to another door.

"Not in that closet, you won't. Try the door over there."

Andy laughed and headed in the direction she had pointed. "Thanks," he said, glancing back.

She was smiling again. "Pass my way again—any time."

In the shop Andy spotted an older man hunched over a counter, studying some sort of paperwork. "I like that suit in the window," Andy said. "I want to take another look at it."

"Pardon me?"

But Andy was already hurrying on through. He opened the front door, walked out, did take a quick look in the window, and then hurried across the street. He saw a pharmacy and walked inside, then watched through the front window. In a few minutes he saw what he expected. The man in the raincoat waddled around the corner and down the street, casting his eyes in all directions. Andy stepped back from the window, only to hear, "Is there something I can help you with?"

Andy had told enough lies to last him for a bit, so he said, "No, thanks. I was actually hiding out for just a minute. Do you mind?"

A little man in a white coat and wire-rimmed glasses was staring at Andy. "By all means. Feel free. What else are we here for?"

"I'm sorry. We're a bother, we Americans, aren't we?"

"You're here to save us. That's what they tell us. But it wouldn't hurt if you bought a tin of tooth powder from time to time—and left our daughters alone."

Andy nodded and smiled, and the man smiled a little too. Andy said, "Tell your daughter I'm very sorry, but I'm busy this weekend. Perhaps some other time." And out he went. Behind him, he heard the man mumbling something about not actually having a daughter.

Andy pressed on to the bus stop, where he had been heading, and sat on a bench next to a tall man with a bowler hat. The man was reading a newspaper, but after a minute or so, he set the paper next to him on the bench and walked away. Andy picked up the paper and began to read, or at least pretended to. Inside one of the pages he found the envelope he was looking for. He tucked it into his coat pocket and then looked down the street for the bus. If he could make it back from Bournemouth to Beaulieu without his tail picking him up again, he would pass his test.

It was August, 1943, and Andy was receiving his final training at a "finishing school" near the village of Beaulieu—called "Bew-lee" by the English. The OSS planned to have all its own training schools in place soon, but for now some of the early recruits, initially trained in the United States, were receiving specialized training in England. Camp X had focused on physical conditioning and fighting skills. Camp B, in a wooded area of Maryland, where Andy and Raul had taken an additional course, had emphasized demolition, wireless operation, and surveillance. Trainees had been pushed to their physical and emotional limits, and those who couldn't take the pressure had been weeded out. But Beaulieu was different. Men were still pushed hard enough to keep fit, but most of the training was directed at the subtle skills of survival in a foreign country.

Andy and Raul lived in one of the charming, if cold, country houses on the grounds of the Beaulieu estate in the New Forest region, not far from the south coast of England. They were being trained by the British SOE—Special Operations Executive—an organization much like the American OSS. In fact, it was the organization General Donovan had modeled the OSS upon. The Brits had a good deal of experience in the spy business, but Americans, until now, had never felt a need for such activity and had even disliked the idea of it. Now, however, with the kinds of enemies the free world was facing, Americans were trying to catch up fast.

Andy, along with the other trainees in his group, had now completed five more parachute jumps. He had learned to jump through a hole in the belly of an airplane, to jump at low altitude, and to jump at night. And he had learned to dig a hole and bury his parachute as soon as he was on the ground.

Now that the Beaulieu training was nearing its end, the students were being put to some final tests. They had learned techniques for escaping when being tailed, but also how to follow someone else—more effectively than the man who had tried to follow Andy today. More important, they had practiced methods of posing as ordinary French citizens. Andy had noticed when he was growing up that his mother didn't turn the point of a piece of pie or cake toward herself, as Americans did, but now he learned that his mother's way was the normal way in France, and turning a pastry the American way could get him caught—and killed. He also had to be aware of what was happening in France because of the war. Bistros in most sections of France were only allowed to serve alcohol every other day. Most foods were rationed, and petrol was almost impossible to obtain. Every Frenchman would know these things, and agents were in danger of being caught unaware. One trainer told the story of an undercover agent blowing his cover by asking for "black coffee." Milk was very difficult to find in France these days, so coffee was always drunk black—when drunk at all—and little real coffee was available. People drank *ersatz* coffees, the most common one brewed from barley.

If an Englishman or American were to parachute into France in his own clothes, he wouldn't last long. Most people in France were wearing well-worn clothing these days. But more than that, if anyone was suspected of spying, Gestapo agents would check every inch of his clothing to be certain that French sewing methods had been used. The French sewed buttons in parallel stitches, not crossed, for example, and if the tailors who prepared the agents slipped up on such a detail, a cover could be blown. Andy had already spent more painful hours than he liked having his dental work redone. American and British dentists used a different technique than the French, and Gestapo agents had learned to look into the mouths of suspected agents.

Andy had learned "advanced skills" as well. He had a fair chance of cracking a safe now, or opening a locked door. He had been taught by a professional break-in man who had been released early from prison in order to instruct at Beaulieu. There were also techniques for steaming open a letter without leaving any sign of tampering. Coding, decoding, and advanced radio skills were another part of the program.

Perhaps most useful, a Frenchman for the Free French army who had slipped out of France taught methods of secretly recruiting *Réseaux*—resistance networks or pods. All through France small resistance groups had formed. They were often called the *Maquis,* a name derived from a tenacious brush that grew on the island of Corsica, but the designation implied unity, and there was actually little of that. The Free French groups were loyal to Charles de Gaulle, who had fled France after the Germans had overrun the country. He was operating out of London and used radio broadcasts to call the French to perform acts of sabotage and to undermine German control. But some groups were made up of Communists who tended to avoid unification with the Free French.

All through France healthy young men were being rounded up by the Gestapo and transported to Germany to work in factories. But many of these young men were avoiding that odious duty by hiding out in the mountains of southern France, and they were forming renegade resistance groups, doing reconnaissance and sabotage. Young women had joined them and, among other duties, had set up mobile hospitals to treat the wounded. These groups especially liked the title *Maquis*. Undercover agents like Andy and Raul would be expected to bring organization to any and all such groups, unify them, train them, and enlarge their numbers. The members would not only attempt to undermine German control, they would feed information to American and British teams, and that intelligence would then be signaled to London, where an OSS center had been established. At some point, as the time for the invasion of Europe neared, sabotage would escalate.

Andy caught his bus and enjoyed his ride back to Beaulieu. The morning had been misty and overcast, but the sky was clearing now and the green countryside was comforting. Stonehenge was not far away, and Andy held out a hope that he would see it before he left the area, though he doubted he would have the chance. Everything was focused now. The trainees found plenty of reason to laugh, and many of them drank a good deal when they were allowed the time, but everyone surely felt that things were getting serious now. Andy didn't know when he would make his jump into France, but he was sure the time wasn't too far off.

The bus ride made Andy think of the bus he had taken the winter before on his departure from Delta. But only the old seat covers and the dusty smell were similar. The appearance of the lush green farmland out-side couldn't have been more different from the Utah desert. Maybe that was part of why Andy found himself wondering, as he often did these days, whether he was still the same person. He knew he had acquired some physical hardness, some stamina, but more than that, a certain cyn-icism lay behind much of the talk among teachers and trainees, especially here in England, and Andy found himself thinking more like the people he spent his time with. He longed to get away on a Sunday and attend a Mormon church, or talk to someone who believed what he had been raised to believe, but his life at home seemed a distant memory now, and somehow outside of reality. Still, he vowed to not let himself change fun-damentally, to cling to things he had always trusted. He prayed every day, many times, and he kept in his pocket a little copy of the New Testament, which he read when he could find the time. The problem was, his prayers seemed more a matter of routine than of devotion, and he rarely felt anything he could identify as spiritual.

Andy wrote to Whisper often, twice a week or more when he could get the time, but increasingly, she seemed hard to conjure up in his mind. He remembered her pretty hair, her voice, the smell of her, but the way he and Whisper had thought and talked before he left felt foreign to him now. He wasn't sure he was still that kid who had been raised in the desert.

What all the trainees knew but never said was that they were being prepared to die. Trainers always talked to the men about improving their odds of coming back, but that didn't change the feeling that they would be dropped into the lion's den by parachute, and any mistake, at any time, would get them killed. Andy had worried about killing at one time, but he knew now that his ability to kill ruthlessly might be his salvation. Still, it was cynical to think that way, and it felt wrong, so mostly Andy tried not to think at all about the months ahead and what they would bring. A kind of fatalism had taken over his thought process, and it seemed to blank out thoughts of his future, thoughts of things sacred, even thoughts of life's meaning.

Andy found that he was saying less and less in his letters, revealing nothing partly because he wasn't allowed to but also because he didn't want to. It was better that Whisper never knew what was happening to him, better that his family didn't either. Flip was such a good kid. Andy hoped he would never have to go to war, or if he did, that he could learn to shoot, not to sabotage and assassinate. What Andy tried to believe was that he was going into a necessary state, like an animal disappearing into a den to hibernate, and that he could awaken later and return to himself. But for now, he couldn't try to be Andy. He was being remade into a creature of sorts, one that could live and attack by instinct.

When Andy arrived at the Beaulieu bus stop, he wasn't surprised to see two men waiting. He knew them—both trainers—but he also knew they would take on the role of Gestapo or police and check his papers. Andy had heard stories from other trainees about the harassment that followed each of these tests.

Andy stepped off the bus, made eye contact with one of the men, and greeted him in French. His trainers had taught him never to seem fearful of authorities. In France, if he were to spot someone checking him out, he should walk up to the man and ask the time or request directions. It was the best way to relieve suspicions.

"Please. Come with us," the man said, in French. "We're the police."

In the former free zone, collaborationist police known as the Milice had been created in the image of the Gestapo and were said to be just as vicious. Many other French policemen were less committed to the Germans but cooperated for their own safety. Most of the French knew that to survive they at least had to seem to accept German rule. Andy knew he must assume that any French policeman might use all the methods of the Nazis to break his cover.

Andy followed the men to a squat little building nearby—an administration building—and then into an interrogation room, with only a small table and three chairs inside. The spokesman, a man whose actual name was Henri Boulicaud, faced Andy, standing too close, and said, "May I see your papers, please." His words were polite but his tone hostile. The other man, Arthur Lindsay, stood next to Andy, also crowding him. Andy was carrying a set of counterfeit papers that included everything required of the French by the Germans. They were not the actual papers he would carry into France, but similar. When he dropped into France he would take with him perfect forgeries of identity cards, ration cards, food stamps, work permits, travel permits, paybooks, and any special papers he might need. He had been instructed to study his temporary papers carefully, but he had also been given a cover story to establish a false identity, and he had been grilled on the story several times.

Andy pulled out his billfold from his coat pocket and began to open it, but the "agent" took it from him. "*Monsieur* Chalon," he said, "what is the nature of your travel today?" Henri was a sallow-faced man with a drooping mustache and drooping bags under his eyes. His face never revealed much emotion.

"I was visiting my mother, who is very ill," Andy said. "She lives in Tarascon." He had been taught to use information that was familiar to him. He knew Tarascon—the town where he had lived in the summers when he was a boy—and could answer questions about it if he was pressed to do so.

"And you have a pass for this travel?"

"Yes, you see it there."

"And were you away from work, making this visit?"

"I work in the military bakery here in Dijon, but it was bombed last week. We are not back to work yet."

Henri stared into Andy's face, his eyes steady, intense. "But you were expected to help with repairs, no?"

"No. It's not my line of work. My supervisor told me this would be a good time to make my visit. My mother is not expected to live much longer."

Henri looked again at the papers and, in a friendlier voice, said, "Sit down. Make yourself comfortable." Andy sat at the table, and the trainers moved to the other side and sat across from him. Andy was surprisingly nervous. He didn't want to make a mistake and fail his test, but more than that, he knew that a situation like this, before long, may well determine whether he lived or died. He wanted to believe that he could manage all right. "So what do you bake in this military bakery, *boule de pain?*"

"Yes. Of course. But I'm only learning. I haven't worked there very long."

"I understand." Henri handed the papers back to Andy, but he continued to study his face. Andy tried to meet his gaze, not look away. "Will you have a cigarette, my friend?"

"No, thank you. I've quit smoking. It's too hard to get cigarettes these days."

"But you won't have one now?" Henri had taken a pack of cigarettes from his pocket, and he offered one to Arthur, who accepted. Again, he extended the pack toward Andy. "You won't have one?"

"I don't want to start again. It was difficult enough to quit."

"Yes, I know what you're saying. But tell me this. Where did you get such a nice haircut? You must have a fine barber."

"It was something special from my mother. She has a friend in Tarascon who cuts hair. I looked so shabby when I arrived at home, my mother sent me out to get it cut—she paid the barber herself."

Henri took a draw on his cigarette, then blew the smoke directly at Andy with just a hint of aggression, but with no change in his face. Andy held his breath for a time, but he tried not to show that he was bothered. "Is she a rich woman, your mother?"

"Oh, no. Of course not. But she has nothing to spend her money on now. She has a small pension."

"But I thought you said she was dying."

Andy was startled by his own inconsistency. He tried to think whether he had made a crucial mistake. "She's managing to get around a little right now," he said. "But she's been very weak. Her heart isn't good."

"She can't be elderly. How old is she?"

Andy thought of using his own mother's age, but then decided to add a few years. "She's just over fifty." And then, rather awkwardly, he added, "She's not elderly, but her heart has never been good." Andy could feel the sweat beading up on his upper lip.

"And what about your father?"

"He was killed long ago, in the first war."

Henri slowly leaned forward, holding the cigarette so its smoke curled in Andy's direction. "But that's not what your papers say."

Andy was stunned. He tried to think. But he knew better than to backtrack. Confidence was more important than accuracy. That concept had been driven into his head. "My papers say nothing of that, as I recall. It's certainly so, however. He fought with the great Marshall Petain and died at Verdun."

"A hero?"

"No. A simple soldier."

"So you bakers, what time do you have to get up every morning? Very early, I would guess." Henri leaned back now, almost smiled.

Arthur was watching Andy closely. He was a Londoner, refined in appearance, in a well-pressed suit and regimental striped tie, but his speech hinted at his Cockney origins.

"Middle of the night, I wager," he said in English, even though he had followed the conversation in French.

Was this to tempt Andy to slip into English? Andy ignored Arthur and answered Henri in French. "We start at three in the morning. It's not so bad once a man is accustomed to it." He laughed. "But I'm left with very few evenings for seeing girls."

"You have a girlfriend?"

"Not really. There are girls I sometimes—"

"Tell me their names," Henri said.

"Why? Are you looking for company?" Andy laughed again, but he was thinking frantically for names of girls.

"Tell me their names."

"I see a girl named Yvette sometimes."

"What's her family name?"

"Delamere." It was the name of a girl he had known in Tarascon, growing up.

"How often do you sleep with her?"

"Oh, no. It's not like that. She's someone I dance with."

"Where is it that you dance?"

Andy had definitely made a mistake this time. He knew no names of clubs or dance halls in Dijon. "Here and there. Wherever we—"

"Where did you dance with her recently?"

Henri was speaking faster now, sounding impatient. Andy tried not to change his own pace. "At a little dance hall. Paradise, it's called." Another name from Tarascon.

Henri glanced toward Arthur, who suddenly stood, placed his hand on the table, and leaned toward Andy. "There's no truth in this," he barked, this time in his school French. "You're lying. We have no such dance hall here."

"You must not go out much," Andy said, and he laughed. "Of course there is. It's not far from the bakery where I work."

"Then take us there," Henri said. "And while we're there, we want to meet this supervisor who sends you off on a journey just when he needs workers more than usual."

"Of course. I can take you to him. He doesn't work now, this time of day, but he will be there again in the morning."

But Andy had lost his confidence and he felt it.

"I don't think you're French. You don't look French to me. And there's something in your voice. It doesn't sound right. We know there are foreign agents causing trouble here. I think you're one of them."

"The only trouble I cause is when I bake the bread too long. I don't understand why you would say such a thing." But Andy was knotting up inside. He felt as though he had just gotten himself killed.

Henri finally motioned for Arthur to sit down. Then he said, "You did well at times, Armand, but you made mistakes. After such an interview, you would be taken in for further questioning, and you would be beaten and tortured. You might last a day or two before you turned on your partner and the members of your network—that is at least what we would hope, so others will have a chance to escape—but chances are you would tell them everything they wanted to know within a few hours."

Andy felt as though the interrogation hadn't ended. He still had to pass. "I won't break," he said. "I'll die first."

"It isn't dying that's difficult," Arthur said. "If they would let you die, anyone would choose that. It's the agony they put you through before you finally succumb. There comes a time when you beg for death."

Andy had thought about all this. The trainers had talked about inter-rogation techniques the Gestapo used, but always in general terms, as though they didn't want to give the trainees too much to think about. He knew that he would carry a cyanide pill with him, and that could be his escape from the torture, but he had always been taught at home that suicide was wrong, and he wondered what his family, what Whisper, would think of him if he took that way out.

"Tell us your mistakes," Henri said.

"I told you things I didn't have to, and then you forced me into details."

"That's right," Arthur said. "Don't start down a path you can't follow to the end. It's not surprising that you know little about Dijon. The materials we give you here are brief. But when you arrive in the town where you'll actually operate, you must learn all about it."

"Why Tarascon?" Henri asked.

"I lived there as a boy."

"That's good. You know things about it. It's a wise choice, but remember, many things have changed since you were there. It's wartime there, too, so you take a chance in being that specific."

"Still, you were reasonably cool under fire," Arthur said, in English. "When Henri told you that you were lying about your father, you stayed with your story. That's just the thing to do."

"But Armand, you still haven't mentioned your worst mistake," Henri said.

"I'm not sure what it was."

"Be careful when someone gives you information and asks you to agree. Dijon is known for its white bread—*boule de pain*—but it's not baked there now. Everyone eats black bread, the same as the *boches*. It's disgusting, and no one likes it, but it's what people have."

"What should I have said?"

"It's best to avoid things you don't know about. Don't say you're a baker if you can't provide the right details."

"You're going into France as a farmer," Arthur said. "That's something you know. But you'll need to learn everything you can about local techniques, equipment—all of that."

Andy nodded, but he still felt a little sick. He had made a mess of this, worse even than he had realized.

"Most situations are not this bad," Arthur said. "Usually, it's a simple check at a train station, and you'll have perfect forgeries to work with. They won't push you as hard as we did—unless you give them some reason to suspect you."

"And if they suspect you," Henri said, "they'll penetrate your cover. You have little chance if they continue to question you long enough. It's getting past the first few seconds—maybe a minute—that really matters."

Andy tried to find some hope in that, but a fear that had started the first day he had been recruited to the OSS was steadily deepening. He would probably die, he kept telling himself, and he tried to live with that, but it was living that scared him: facing danger every minute of every day.

"One other thing. Rarely would a Frenchman turn down a cigarette. If you're offered one, smoke it."

"I'd cough, I'm afraid. I really don't smoke."

"Yes, then, you must practice. Have one now."

"No, thanks."

Henri shrugged. "It's your life," he said. "Tell them you don't smoke, if that's what you prefer. But never admit that you haven't slept with your girlfriend. A Frenchman would rather lie than admit to such a thing."

Arthur and Henri both laughed, and Andy tried. He was also still trying to get his breath back. He would soon receive the final details of his cover story, and he vowed to prepare for every possibility.

That night he wrote to Whisper and made a better attempt to bring some feeling to what he said to her. He was afraid the boy he had once been existed only in her memory now. Maybe he could get back to himself if he fought to reject all the attitudes he was experiencing here and let her rethink him once he was home. After he wrote the letter, he prayed, did it sitting on his bed, since Raul was in the room. He asked the Lord to help him remember everything at home—all he'd learned, all he'd been—not to let it slip away. But even as he prayed, he felt the emptiness that never left him these days.

CHAPTER 7

FLIP WAS SITTING at the dinner table with his mother and sisters on an August evening. Dad finally hurried in, grabbed his chair, and pulled it out. "I'm sorry," he said as he was sitting down. "I was trying to think what I'm going to say at my meeting tonight." He tucked his napkin into his collar. It was what he always did—ate dressed up most nights and tried to keep his food off his tie. And he was usually in a hurry. It wasn't as though he was rattled and nervous all the time. He would stop and chat with almost anyone whether he had the time or not, but he had lots of things going on, and he was often running from one to another.

"What meeting is it tonight?" Mom asked. "Church, or—"

"No. It's town council. And Millie put so many items on our list, I don't know how we'll ever get to them all." Bishop Gledhill forked a pork chop onto his plate and scooped up some mashed potatoes. "I've got to be on my way in about five minutes."

"Slow down a little," Mom said. "They always start late anyway." But that was Mom's motto: Calm down, enjoy life. She kept busy herself, working in the house and yard, but she seemed to do everything with ease. What bothered Flip, though, was that she had been so quiet lately. He knew that she worried about Andy. Dad probably worried too, but he never said that he did.

Dad cut his pork chop in lots of bite-sized pieces, buttered up a thick slice of homemade bread, then began gobbling it all, chewing like a chipmunk, his cheeks swelling into knobs. Mom had taught Flip not to cut his meat that way, but to cut one piece at a time as he ate. Mom also ate without switching her knife and fork back and forth. That was the French way, she said. Maybe being calm was the French way, too. But it was hard for Flip not to eat fast himself. The kitchen was full of the smell of rhubarb pie tonight, and that was something Mom rarely baked anymore. Her ration of sugar didn't allow for it very often.

"Flip," Dad said, "I'm not going to have time to help you with this next cutting of hay. I talked to Mr. Schneider, from out at Topaz. I've arranged to have a young fellow from out there come in and work for us."

Flip was staring at his dad. He couldn't believe this. "I can cut it by myself, Dad. And Cal could—"

"No. I thought about that. You two aren't old enough. Cal's good-sized for his age, but you still need someone older. And the boys out there at Topaz are good workers. This young man will catch the camp bus into town day after tomorrow, and then he's going to sleep out at the little house on the farm for a while." Bishop Gledhill looked across the table at his wife. "Do you suppose, when you pack a lunch for Flip each day, you could make one up for the Japanese boy too?"

Belle nodded—once at her husband, and then again, more resolutely, at Flip.

Flip couldn't believe this was happening.

"I suppose we could just have him walk over here each night for dinner," Dad said. "That might be as easy as anything. It's either that or buy him some groceries and let him cook for himself out there. If he had some eggs and bacon, or something like that, maybe he could take care of his own breakfast."

Flip looked around at his sisters. They had all stopped eating. They were staring at Dad, who was still shoveling food in as though he had no idea he had said anything shocking. "Dad, I don't want to work with a Jap," Flip said. "I will, if you say I have to, but inviting him to sit down at our dinner table with us—that's another thing."

Bishop Gledhill was chewing. He didn't look at Flip for a time, but when he did, he said, "The last I heard, God made the Japanese, just the same as he did us. And I can't think of a single reason why any of God's children can't sit down together and partake of a meal."

Flip looked to his sisters again for support. They were still staring at Dad as though he had just announced that he wanted them to commit a murder. "Wait just a minute, Dad," Flip said. "It's the Japs who are killing our boys in the Pacific while we're sitting here eating our pork chops."

"Flip, this boy is from California. He's just as American as you are. Or as far as that goes, maybe you're not an American. After all, you have a French mother. Maybe we ought to send you back where you came from."

"We're not fighting the French, Dad."

"Flip, that's enough."

"Well, I'm not eating dinner with him," Adele said. She must have been going out somewhere that night because her hair was up in pin curls and she looked about half scary. When she was mad, her voice screeched like a bad clarinet, and that was what it was doing now.

"I'm not either," Marie said, and she was not usually one to take a stand about much of anything. Maybe she thought she was grown up now; she was heading off to college at the BYU in just a few weeks.

"That's fine, girls. After two or three nights without dinner, though, you might get a little hungry." Dad pulled the napkin from his collar. "Save a little of that pie for me, Belle. I'll eat it when I get home. I'd give half a dollar for a scoop of ice cream with it, but I guess there's no chance of that."

Belle was smiling. She watched her husband walk from the room, and then she looked around at her children. "I've known a few Japanese people," she said. "They've all been very nice."

"I don't care," Adele said, her voice pinching again. "I *won't* eat with a Jap. It isn't right. We've all got to stick together on this."

But Marie was losing confidence already. She wouldn't look at Adele. And Chrissy tended to side with Mom on almost any issue. All Flip could think was that Adele was going to cause a big family fight, as she usually did. He decided he would do what he had to do. He would work with the guy out at the farm. And then maybe he could pull Dad aside and tell him how bad it would look to people if they saw a Jap coming into their home—especially with three single daughters in the family. Of course, Dad probably wouldn't listen to something like that. He'd say that right was right, no matter what other people thought about it.

*   *   *   *   *

Two days later Flip was sitting under a gnarly cottonwood tree next to an irrigation canal with Tomitaro Tanaka. The two were eating lunch together. Flip hadn't said much to the boy—"Tom," he liked to be called—partly because they had been working hard, and partly because Flip had made up his mind not to be friendly. But Flip had to admit to himself, the guy wasn't at all what he had expected. He didn't seem to know he was a Jap. He talked like a regular American, not like the ones in the movies—saying "ah so" all the time—and he didn't have buck teeth and thick glasses like the ones in all the cartoon drawings in the newspapers. He actually seemed pretty much like most of the guys at Delta High School, and he dressed like them, too, with his jeans rolled up at the ankles and his short sleeves rolled up high. He wasn't much bigger than Flip, but he was strong. Flip had to say that for him. And he didn't waste any time. It was a hot day—the temperature on its way over a hundred—but Tom hadn't taken a break all morning.

Flip had talked to his friend Cal, and Cal had told him, "I wouldn't worry too much about working with the guy. No one's going to say nothing about that. Let the Japs cut our hay for us if they're willing to do it. It doesn't mean you have to be buddies with him."

"What makes you think I would?" Flip had asked. "I'll work with him, and that's all." He didn't tell the part about Dad wanting the guy to come to dinner. If he actually did come to the house, that would surely get around town sooner or later, but Flip wasn't going to spread the news himself.

"Just keep an eye on him," Cal said. "My dad thinks the Japs out at Topaz might try to break out, and if they do, the first thing they'll do is head for Delta. They'll slit people's throats, or whatever they have to do, then steal our cars and head back to California. They want to help the Jap pilots when they bomb San Diego, the same as they did over at Pearl Harbor."

Flip had heard the same stuff from other people. "I'll watch him all right. They're sneaky. They'll wait 'til you're not looking and then steal anything that isn't nailed down. Brother Buttars at the barber shop told me that. The drugstores in town have to watch them real close every time a bunch of them come in."

But now Flip and this Tom guy were leaning their backs against the same tree, both of them wet with sweat and caked with dirt. And they were eating the same kind of lunch. Maybe Tom had been raised on noodles and all that other stuff, but he seemed to know what fried chicken was all about, and he was putting it away fast, with lots of potato salad. He knew how to use a fork, too.

"What grade are you in, Phillip?" Tom asked. He had a way of saying things like he was forty instead of seventeen, or like he was your teacher and figured he knew just about everything.

"I'm starting ninth this fall."

"Is that at the high school?"

"No. Junior high."

"Do you play on any of the teams?" Tom stretched his legs out in front of him. He didn't have boots—just some worn-out oxfords, like the kind Flip wore to church. Flip wondered how he kept them from getting filled with dirt when he was out in the fields. Tom licked some of the grease off his fingers and unwrapped the waxed paper from a slice of rhubarb pie. Flip had tried to talk his mother out of sending any of that out here to the farm. He'd told her he was pretty sure Japs didn't eat anything like that, but ol' Tom took it down in about three bites.

"No. Probably not." Flip thought about saying that he played on a church team, but he didn't want to talk any more than he had to.

"I play baseball. We have a good team out at the camp. Even better than my high school team back in Berkeley, where I lived before."

"What position do you play?" Flip asked, mostly because he figured he had to say something.

"Second base. Or shortstop. And I bat first because I get on base most of the time."

"What? Lots of walks?"

Tom laughed. "Not me," he said. "I don't take pitches. I swing away." He pressed his fists together and made a swinging motion. "And once I'm on first, you might as well give me second because I'm going to steal it anyway."

"Sounds like you're pretty sneaky."

Flip was ready for a reaction. He wanted the guy to know he'd been insulted, but Tom said, "I'm fast. That's what I am. Do you want to race me?" He started to get up, like he really meant it.

"Naw. Not with our stomachs all full." The guy was a bragger, and Flip hadn't expected that—a Jap from a camp like Topaz, acting like he was a big shot.

"Anytime you want, we'll race. I'll give you a head start, five yards, and we'll race fifty. That's about down to that fence."

Flip knew how far fifty yards was. He didn't need to be told. But he looked down the road—really just two ruts along a barbed-wire fence—and tried to picture himself running all out, beating this little Jap by about twenty yards. The trouble was, he probably couldn't do it. Everyone always teased him about how slow he was—"slow as tar," "slow as a snail," or whatever else they came up with. Andy had tried to convince Flip he was quick, but Flip had decided that was just to make him feel good.

"My brother Andy—he's in the army now—he's the fast guy in our family. He was the star of just about every sport when he was in high school."

"Where is he?"

Flip couldn't believe he was letting himself get into this much of a conversation, but it was easy to forget that Tom was a Jap. He had black hair, and his eyes looked Japanese, but he talked like a regular guy. Everyone said Japs were yellow, but Tom was a little browner than Flip, and red from the sun. Flip couldn't see any sign of yellow. He wondered if the guy was different from most Japs. Flip had never really looked at one close up like this.

"Andy's in England," Flip said. "He's been trained as a paratrooper. He'll be fighting in Europe before long, killing Krauts." Flip hoped that Tom could fill in the blanks—know that Andy *and* Flip would do the same to Japs if they had the chance.

"That's what I want to get in on," Tom said.

"Get in on? What are you talking about?"

"The war. Over in Europe."

"You mean, fight for America?"

"Sure. Haven't you heard about the four-four-two?"

"The what?"

"The 442nd Regimental Combat Team. Everybody in it is Japanese American. The whole unit just shipped out for North Africa a couple of weeks ago. When I turn eighteen, I'm going to try to get in, but it's not easy. They only take the best."

Flip was almost sure that none of that was true. Tom wasn't just a bragger, he was a liar. The United States Army wasn't going to let in a bunch of Japs. Flip finished his pie and then put everything back in the basket his mother had sent. He decided he'd talked way too much to this guy.

Tom pulled out a red handkerchief from his pocket and wiped the sweat off his face. The heat was working its way into the shade, seeming to come right out of the dirt. The leaves on the cottonwood tree looked limp, and there weren't even any birds singing. It was good weather to dry hay, but not much good for anything else.

Tom was leaning back with his eyes shut when he said, without so much cockiness in his voice, "It's hard to know what to do, Phillip. Some of my friends at the camp say I shouldn't sign up. They figure our government stuck us away in the middle of nowhere when they had no right to do it, so they don't want to fight. But me, I look at it the opposite way. The best way to prove we're loyal is to go out and help win the war."

Flip still wasn't sure he was buying this story, even though Tom sounded like he knew what he was talking about. It just seemed kind of funny that no one around Delta had ever said anything about Japs fighting for America.

But Flip didn't say that. "I want to go myself, if the war lasts that long," he said.

Tom laughed. "I'll tell you what. Once me and my Japanese buddies get there, we'll put an end to the war *fast,* and then you won't have to worry about it."

"But I *want* to go. And don't let my size fool you. My brother was small when he was my age, and he's six foot tall now. I'm going to get my growth one of these days, the same as him."

"Hey, it's not how tall you are; it's what you got inside." Tom opened his eyes and sat up a little more. "I'm small, but I'm tip-top at just about everything. You know what I mean? Baseball. Track. I was president of my sophomore class, too. People like me, once they get to know me. That's what I got going. Who cares if I'm big or not?"

Flip was pretty sure he was hearing another story. "Were you class president out at the camp, or—"

"No. I'll be a senior this fall. That was back in California at a regular high school, and no one cared whether I was Japanese or anything else. I was the hottest dancer in the school, and I have a good personality. Can't you tell?" Tom laughed hard and long, his voice sort of chirpy. The surprising thing was, Flip thought maybe people did like him. He was cocky, no question, but he seemed like he might be kind of a good guy. Maybe he really had been president of his class.

"You ought to run for a class office when you get to high school," Tom said.

"Naw. I'd never do that. I'm not the type."

Something akin to a breeze actually moved the air a little, and a few tufts of late-clinging cotton glided down from the tree and drifted toward the barn. The poor old barn had never been painted, and the roof and walls were sagging now, like an old face.

"Hey, come on, Phillip, don't talk that way or you won't amount to anything. That's how I look at it. You gotta be positive, and you gotta set some goals for yourself. I want to have my own business someday and make some good bucks. You know what I'm talking about?"

"Sure. I might run my dad's bank someday. Maybe me and my brother."

"Your dad owns a bank?"

"Yup."

"Hey, you got it *made in the shade.* My dad had a nursery business back in California—raising trees and shrubs and everything—but we don't know what we'll have when we get back. When we got relocated, we rented our house and our business to a family, but they've never sent us any money."

Now that *had* to be a lie. If people weren't paying the rent, they couldn't just get away with it. It's what Flip had heard, that the Japs at Topaz wanted to put blame on the government and not admit they were getting what they deserved. The truth was, they actually had a good deal going for them. They didn't have to do much of anything but sit around and listen to the radio, and they got three square meals and a place to sleep. Brother Buttars had told Flip, "They're better off than a lot of people. If you ask me, they oughta be working for what they get."

Tom took a long swig of lemonade from a Mason jar Mom had sent with the lunches. Flip took another look at him. Tom was lean and hardened down, even sort of handsome, and after one morning out working with him, Flip knew the guy wasn't lazy. That didn't sound much like what Brother Buttars had been saying. But Tom did lie; Flip was almost sure of that. So maybe he really was sneaky, like everyone said.

"Do you like music, Phillip?"

"No one calls me Phillip. I'm mostly called Flip."

"Flip. I like that. It's a cool name. What kind of music do you like?"

"I don't know. Just songs, I guess. My sisters all like Frank Sinatra and my mom likes Bing Crosby, but I don't pay too much attention to any of that."

"I like dance music. Benny Goodman, Artie Shaw, Duke Ellington. Hot bands—you know what I mean? I can jump, man. Cut a rug. You know what I'm talkin' about?"

"What are you, like a zoot suiter?"

"Not me. I dress great. Back home, I had some good duds."

"So is that what you do out at the camp? Dance, and listen to the radio all day?"

"No. I don't get time. I've got another job out there. I work in the dining hall, serving up the food and washing the dishes. I put in forty-four hours a week and I only get eleven dollars a month for it. The highest pay at the camp is only about twenty bucks."

"That's more than Dad pays me."

Tom's head jerked around. "You better go on strike," he said. "You're worse off than a Jap." Tom laughed with his high-pitched squeal again, and he slapped Flip on the shoulder.

Flip couldn't help it; he laughed too. This guy wasn't anything like Flip had expected.

* * * * *

On Friday that week there was another dance at the ward. Whisper hadn't thought much about going, but when Flip called her Friday afternoon and asked her if she wanted to go, she decided she would. Earlier in the week she had received a letter from Andy that she wasn't happy about, and she had been feeling down ever since. She didn't think she would enjoy the dance much, but the thought of spending the whole weekend at home was worse.

So Whisper and Flip walked to the dance. On the way, Flip talked about cutting and baling hay all week, and Whisper tried to pretend she was listening. Flip was a great kid, but he was painfully self-conscious when he was around her. He always struggled to think of things to say, and when he did find something, he would go on and on, as if to fill up the quiet and escape some of his embarrassment. Tonight he kept talking about a Japanese boy he was working with, from Topaz. "He's not like you'd think," he told her. "He can do just about anything. He works hard, and he's a great baseball player. He wants to join the army, too. The American army."

Whisper heard in Flip's voice some of the enthusiasm he usually kept for his brother, and that was surprising. Flip had always been down on Japs. When Whisper had told him once how nice the people from Topaz were—the ones she had met in the bank—he had told her a bunch of things he had heard about Japanese people, mostly things he had been told at the barber shop.

At the corner, by Service Drug, Whisper and Flip met up with old Brother Wheatley and his wife. They were dressed up, him in the same old suit he had worn for as long as Whisper had known him, and his wife in a purple dress that had been around just as long. They never missed a dance. "Nice night, huh?" Brother Wheatley said. A pickup truck rolled past them on Main Street, the back full of young people, probably on their way to the dance too. "Look at that," Brother Wheatley said. "Those boys are wearing jeans. I don't think they ought to let them in, if that's how they're going to dress."

But Sister Wheatley said, "Maybe that's all they have, Harvey. You don't know."

"I do know. They can wear their Sunday best. That's what we always did when I was a boy, and we had less than these kids do."

Whisper smiled and glanced at Flip, and they walked on across the street. Flip was wearing a tie and his church pants, but when they got a little farther ahead of the Wheatleys he said, "I'd wear jeans too, if my mom would let me."

It was mostly the young people in the ward who had come to the dance, although there were a number of older ones, like the Wheatleys, who came to every dance. Lots of folks in town danced at Van's Dance Hall on Saturday nights, but there was a good deal of drinking and smoking there, and some preferred to avoid all that. Whisper felt rather ancient herself with so many teenagers at the dance. She did manage to talk Flip into dancing with her once, right after they arrived, but then he slipped off to his friends.

Whisper spotted some girls a little younger than herself talking in a group. She was walking toward them when someone touched her shoulder. "Hi. Do you remember me?"

"Sure I do. Hi." But she couldn't think of his name.

"Lamar Jones. I'm Jeff Jones's cousin, from over in Fillmore."

"Yes. I remember." Lamar had on a wool sport coat, in spite of the heat, and it was so tight for him that it bunched up under his arms. He appeared nervous, too, his face flushed.

"Would you like to dance?"

"All right."

Lamar was actually a pretty good dancer. Still, she planned to slip away after one dance, but when the music stopped, he kept hold of her hand and walked her over to say hello to Jeff and to introduce her to Jeff's date, Janeal, also from Fillmore. The way Jeff had his arm wrapped around Janeal, Whisper assumed that the two must have been going together for a while. Lamar's plan was obviously to keep dancing with Whisper and to tie in with Jeff and Janeal on some sort of double date. Whisper was nice to everyone, but she knew she couldn't let that happen, so she danced one more dance with Lamar, and then she said, "Thank you, Lamar," firmly, and walked away. She looked for that group of girls she had seen earlier, but they were apparently dancing, so she headed toward Flip, who was standing with his friend Cal and some of the other younger boys. "Flip," she whispered, "I don't think I want to stay. But you don't need to walk me home. I'm fine by myself."

She could see how embarrassed Flip was, and she knew why. His friends were all listening in and grinning. "Hey, I don't want to stay," Flip said. "I'll walk you home."

"No, really. It's still light out. I'll enjoy the walk."

But Flip paid no attention. He didn't look at the other boys, and he walked out with Whisper, not offering his arm or his hand, but staying next to her. Whisper was careful not to glance around. She didn't want to make eye contact with Lamar if he happened to be watching. What she really wished was that Flip would let her go on her own. She could stroll along the streets at her own pace, or maybe go for a longer walk somewhere. Flip tromped ahead as though he had to get where he was going as quickly as possible, and Whisper was in no hurry to get home.

"I noticed that white-haired cousin of Jeff Jones's is after you again," Flip said.

Whisper didn't answer. Flip was a nice boy, but he was young, even for his age. There were only so many things she could think to say to him, and she didn't want to make fun of Lamar. He was nice, and actually not all that bad-looking. If she weren't waiting for Andy, she might have considered him worth getting to know. Her problem was that she measured everyone against Andy.

Flip was soon talking about cutting hay again, and about the Japanese boy. Whisper merely walked alongside him and said little—and truthfully, listened even less. They were back to her house much too quickly, and Whisper was thinking she might say good-bye to Flip and then take that walk. The house was hot, and she hated to go inside.

"Are you okay?" Flip asked her just as she reached her front steps.

"Sure."

"You seem sort of sad."

"Well, I guess I am a little blue tonight."

"That's what Andy told me—that you would probably get that way sometimes, and maybe I could talk to you and help you out. But I don't think I know how to do that."

Whisper smiled. There was nothing complicated about Flip. He said whatever he thought. "When did Andy tell you that?"

"Just before he left—when he asked me if I'd look after you while he was gone."

"What else did he tell you?"

"I don't know. I can't remember exactly." Flip pushed his hands into his pants pockets. He'd gotten his hair cut shorter than usual—because of the heat, she supposed—but his little wave in front had come loose and was drooping on his forehead. "I know he did say that if it ever seemed like he wasn't coming back, always to tell you that he would, and for you not to lose hope."

Whisper wanted to believe that. But she had watched Andy's letters change. She didn't know what was going on with him now. The evening light was fading fast. Whisper looked at Flip, standing in the golden light, his face sunburned, his hair bleached out so it was almost as pale as his brother's. He looked sweet and serious. She felt bad that she hadn't been nicer to him. "Come and sit down for a minute," she said. All week she had said nothing to anyone, not even to Bishop Gledhill, about the letter Andy had sent her, but her feelings had been hard to keep inside.

Flip walked up the steps onto the porch and sat on the love seat. She smiled when she noticed how tightly he hugged the other end of the seat, staying as far from her as he could get. "I'm a little upset by something," she said. "I got a letter from Andy on Tuesday, and it seemed like he was taking back everything he promised me when he was home last winter."

"What do you mean?" Flip asked, sounding worried.

"He said it was probably awful to sit around and wait for him, and it wasn't fair to me. Then he went on about how long it might be before he'll ever get back. He even said, '*if* I get back.'"

"He said some things like that to me too, Whisper. But he said, 'If I can't write for a while, tell Whisper not to give up on me.'"

Whisper felt the words like cool air. She wanted so much to remember all the things Andy had said to her just before he had left. He hadn't promised that he would make it back, but he had promised to try, and he had promised her that he would always love her. "Flip, I'm glad he told you that, because he told me in this new letter that he wouldn't be able to write to me for a long time. Then he said I ought to start dating other fellows, and to reconsider whether I really should plan on waiting for him."

"He said that?"

Flip sounded angry, and Whisper liked that. She stretched her arm along the back of the love seat and touched Flip's shoulder. "The way he said it wasn't mean. He was trying to be nice about it. I think he just worries about me and doesn't want me to sit around for years and years while he's gone."

"But he shouldn't say something like that. He told Mom and Dad that he wouldn't be able to write for a while, but he didn't mention anything about giving up on you. If you ask me, Andy's turning nuts."

"Nuts?"

"You know what I'm saying."

"No, I don't."

"Any guy who would take a chance on losing you can't be thinking right. Most guys would give just about anything to be in Andy's shoes. Look at that rabbit-looking guy from Fillmore. He gets calf eyes every time he looks at you."

Whisper laughed. "Which is he? A rabbit or a calf?"

"He's a mix. Rabbit nose, rabbit hair, calf eyes. And he's ugly as a mud fence, all at the same time."

"Hey, he's not *that* bad."

"He is too. And if you want to dance more and don't want to dance with him, I'll practice really hard so I get better, and then I'll dance every single dance with you."

"Wow. That's quite a sacrifice." She laughed, but she could tell that Flip meant was he was saying. It touched her to see that, and part of her reaction was that there was just enough of Andy in his face and voice to bring back memories.

"It's not that bad," Flip said, seeming to take her words seriously. "I don't like to dance, and my friends think they're funny telling me a bunch of stuff when I do, but really, if that would help any, I'd do it." Then he grinned at himself and said, "Of course, I might ruin your shoes."

"You danced very well tonight. You didn't step on me once." But she caught herself smiling and admitted, "Well, maybe once."

"Maybe two or three times."

"But you're doing a lot better."

Flip looked pleased for a moment, but she saw the frustration return to his face. "I don't know what Andy's talking about. That time we talked over in the ward house, he said it wasn't exactly fair to ask you to wait, but he wanted you to do it anyway. Maybe he's just thinking more and more that it isn't fair."

"Or maybe he's met a pretty English girl."

"No."

"How do you know?"

"I know there's not a girl in all of England—or anywhere else— as . . ." But he stopped. And now she could see how red he was turning, even under his sunburn.

"As what?"

"Nothing."

"As pretty?"

"Sure, you're pretty. But you're a lot more than that. And Andy's going to make it back to you, no matter what he has to face."

Whisper leaned back and tried to think what Andy really did have on his mind these days. "Here's what I've been wondering," she finally said. "He keeps talking about taking more training, but he never says what kind of training. Maybe he's going into battle now. And maybe he's worried he won't come back. It's his way of preparing me, in case he doesn't make it."

Flip nodded. "That's what I think too. But don't worry, he's going to come home. You shouldn't ever doubt that."

Whisper had cried when she had first received the letter, but she hadn't cried since, and she had told herself she wasn't going to. But she felt tears drip onto her cheeks again now. "Oh, Flip, you're good for me. I do have to have more faith. It's good I've got you around."

Flip only shrugged, and he wouldn't look at her.

Whisper thought, as she often did, how much she hated this war—the way it pulled people apart, the way it changed people. She read in the Millard County newspaper every week about casualties—the wounds and deaths of local boys. But the paper couldn't account for all the other losses.

The crickets had started to chirp, and a little air had started to move, causing the leaves in the lilac bushes to rustle just a bit. She had sat here so many summers, always waiting. She wanted her life to start, had wanted it to start for as long as she could remember—but it was on hold again, as usual, and there was no change in sight.

CHAPTER 8

ANDY SAT IN the flight shack with Raul. An OSS officer from the London headquarters, a man named Hepworth, was with them, had been all day. It was almost ten o'clock—2200 hours—on a balmy September night, but Andy and Raul had started their preparations early that morning. They had been outfitted at the Grosvenor Square offices by people who made a science of disguising agents to look like natives in the countries they penetrated. Every article of clothing, from underwear and stockings on out, was either French or a carefully created duplicate. The plan was for Andy and Raul to pass themselves off as peasant farmers, so they wore shabby, patched denim overalls and jackets, and once on the ground they would don well-worn berets. But for the jump they would use helmets and camouflage coveralls. They also wore leather-topped wooden clogs, called *sabots*. Andy remembered from his childhood seeing French farmers wear that type of shoe, so he knew they were authentic; he just didn't like the feel of the things.

Raul and Hepworth sipped coffee and chatted about nothing very important. Andy had chosen to sit a little away from them on a bunk in the corner. He wanted some time to think and, actually, to pray. But he was surprisingly calm. It was good to face the danger he had been hearing about for the better part of a year instead of only thinking about it. Still, he was well aware that if he were going to die in this war, one of the most likely times for that to happen would come in the next seventy-two hours. Making a night jump was dangerous enough, but getting down and being located by local resistance forces without being discovered by Germans first, and then getting to a safe house and blending into a community—all that was chancy, with as much luck as skill involved.

Those things—the details of their initial actions in France—had been rehearsed hundreds of times with Andy and Raul, so much so that Andy didn't really have to go over them in his mind now. Images kept flashing into his head: the leap into darkness, the first contact with supporters. What hung in his mind more heavily, though, were thoughts of home. He had written to his parents, and to Whisper, to tell them that he wouldn't be writing again for some time; he didn't know how long. He had tried to offer Whisper a release from their promises without implying that he didn't care about her anymore, but he knew his letter had been a jumble of confused messages.

He kept imagining his parents getting a telegram that he had been killed or lost in action, and Dad and Mom going to visit Whisper to break the news to her. He knew how much that would hurt the three of them, and that actually pained him more than the thought of his own death. He hated to think of the decisions Whisper would have to make, and he worried what would happen to her if she kept the idea in her head that Andy was the only man for her. He knew now for certain that he had handled his departure all wrong. He had wanted her too much to let her go, and she had seemed not to believe in the possibility of his dying. Tonight, however, he was about to do something as dangerous as any soldier ever had to do—drop into the middle of enemy territory. The Gestapo was known for its brutality, and if he were caught, he would be treated not as a soldier but as a spy.

The door to the Nissen hut finally opened and a gust of cool air rushed in. A young army sergeant stepped inside. "The pilot's ready," he said. Andy had heard the airplane engines start some time ago, and now, with the door open, the sound was a roar.

"Check your gear one more time," Hepworth shouted above the noise. Raul was carrying the radio equipment, but Andy was packing a .45 caliber handgun, a knife, a flashlight, enough food for a couple of meals, a medical kit strapped over one shoulder, and a British Sten gun over the other. He was also carrying money in his pockets, as well as in his stockings and his underwear. Some of it had been sealed in waterproof wraps. He would bury those once he reached the farm where he and Raul were supposed to set up their base of operations so they could dig the cash up and use it as necessary. All the money had been "aged," left on a floor at the OSS offices to be walked on for a day or two, and the bills were in small denominations—the kind of money a peasant might possess.

Andy checked all his equipment, touching each item, but there was really no need. He had accounted for everything many times that evening as the team had waited for the moon to rise. "You don't have anything from London in your pockets, do you?" Hepworth asked.

Andy had heard the stories of silly mistakes—a book of matches or a British cigarette lighter, even movie tickets that men had forgotten to discard before they left. But he had nothing of that sort, so he walked out with the sergeant and then ducked as the draft from the airplane's propellers hit him. The Whitley bomber had once been fitted with a bellygunner bubble, but that had been removed. The opening now served as an entrance to the craft, but it would serve later as the "Joe hole" through which he and Raul would jump. The men who were dropped behind the lines were sometimes called "bodies," sometimes "Joes," and that was the reason for the name Joe hole.

Climbing up while loaded with equipment and with a parachute strapped to his back was not easy, so the sergeant cupped his hands for Andy to step on, and then hoisted him up. Raul followed, and then the sergeant pulled himself up, dropped the plywood cover on the hole, and latched it shut. A few minutes later the airplane taxied a short distance and then raced down the runway and took off. Within seconds the belly of the bomber was cold. Raul and Andy sat on the metal floor, uncomfortably bracing themselves with their hands as the airplane jostled and vibrated. The sergeant pointed to a red light overhead and shouted above the noise, "It goes yellow when we get close, green when it's time to drop."

Andy and Raul knew that. The sergeant knew that they knew, too. It was merely something to say. But after that, nothing else seemed worth yelling to one another. The sergeant did disappear and return with what Andy thought for a moment was coffee, but when he saw that it was hot chocolate, he was cheered. The stuff was warm going down, and the paper cup warmed his hands.

The channel crossing was actually a short trip, but time seemed to stretch. Andy was no longer thinking about the big picture. His mind was on the jump itself—going out the hole into dark. He prayed a few times, in quick little thoughts: "Help me to do this, Lord."

When the airplane finally banked and turned, Andy saw the yellow light come on and felt his body tighten. He and Raul were to drop into a farming area just south of Orléans. They would pose as peasant farm laborers on a farm outside the city, but the target of their surveillance would be the German garrisons in and around the city: the railroad yards, an ammunition dump, and factories that were producing bullets for the German war effort.

"This is it, boys," the sergeant yelled. "Ten minutes." Andy looked at Raul, who nodded, but Andy could hardly swallow, his mouth was so dry. The turn continued—and then the sound of the engines quieted and the plane began its slow, gliding descent. The sergeant unlatched the plywood cover and lifted it back. With the hole open, a rush of air hit them, fierce and cold.

Andy waited five minutes or so, and then, when the sergeant pointed to him, he scooted across the metal floor closer to the hole. He found himself thinking that he couldn't go through with this, but he kept sliding forward and extended his legs into the hole. The wind grabbed at his coveralls, whipping them, freezing his legs. Each time Andy had done this, he had had the feeling he was jumping into a hurricane.

The sergeant checked the static line one more time and then hooked Andy up to it. All Andy had to do was jump; the line would open his parachute. "We're going to swing around one more time and level off," said the sergeant. "Then it's time to go."

Andy waited, bracing against the powerful draw of the air on his legs. The turn was agonizingly slow. Then he saw, without looking up, the little blue-green light come on, and at the same moment the sergeant yelled, "Good luck! Jump!"

Andy thought he would take another breath first, but his body reacted to the word, and suddenly he was dropping into a tremendous gust of air and, in another couple of seconds, falling into nothingness. He could feel himself plunging in no particular direction that he could determine. Then came the powerful tug on his shoulder straps and the sudden stop, as though he were suspended in air, no longer falling.

He looked below, saw nothing, and worried that he would hit the ground before he could see it. But then he spotted the lights—five narrow shafts, straight up. Four of the flashlights made a rectangle, and the fifth made a center, a target. The trouble was, Andy was drifting out of the target area. He pulled the lines the way he had been taught, but the current was still carrying him away. He seemed to have time, seemed to be descending slowly, but suddenly he saw the outline of trees under the moonlight, jumping up at him. He held his feet together and felt limbs lash at his body as his legs drove through the tree. Just when he thought he was going all the way through to the ground, his shoulder gear grabbed hard again and he was stopped, still hanging in the air.

Andy's first concern was to get down, but he didn't know how high above the ground he was. What he did know was that his right shoulder had taken a powerful jerk and he was feeling intense pain, not only in his shoulder but down his arm and side. He thought of releasing himself and dropping, but he didn't know if that would be safe. He tried to think what he could do, wondered how far away Raul had landed, where the "welcoming committee" might be. He couldn't depend on anyone to help him, he realized, or even to find him in the dark. The thought that a German patrol might have heard the airplane and followed his descent was terrifying. He was dangling with his Sten gun unusable over his shoulder, at the mercy of anyone who found him there.

And then he heard someone moving toward him. He held still and listened. He had heard a whistle, he thought. Then he heard it again: three short bursts and a longer one—Morse code for V, for "Victory." Or at least he thought that was what he had heard. He waited. The next time the signal was clear—and close. He tried to whistle, blew out mostly air, and then tried again. Suddenly there was a voice. *"Monsieur de Londres?"* the voice said.

"Yes. Yes," Andy said, forgetting himself. But then he added, quickly, *"Oui, oui. C'est moi."*

"I can see you," the man said in French. "Are you hurt?"

"A little, I think. My shoulder could be injured." Andy was surprised that his French felt so natural. He hadn't been sure he remembered the word for "shoulder" until it had left his mouth. "Can you help me down from here?"

"Yes, I'll help you. Your feet are almost touching."

Andy had known that by then, from the sound of the man's voice. He released the shoulder harness and suddenly dropped a foot or two onto the ground. He grabbed his shoulder immediately and knew what was wrong. *"Monsieur, je—"*

"Roger. It's the name I'm using now."

"Yes, Roger. I'm known as Armand. You must pull on my arm, quick and hard. I was hurt in football once, the same way. It's what my coach did."

Roger came closer, but he surprised Andy, not by taking hold of his arm, but by kissing him on each cheek. "I greet you," he said. "I honor you that you have come here to help us."

"*Merci*. But take hold of my arm, and when I tell you, pull hard."

"Yes. I have done this before."

When the joint snapped into place, another sharp pain struck, and the ache didn't go away. But Andy could move his arm now. "That's good," he said. He was still trying to catch his breath, and his head was full of the pain. "Can you pull the parachute down from the tree? We need to bury it, along with my outer clothing."

"Yes, yes. We know this. I brought a shovel."

"What about Raul—my partner?"

"Others are searching for him. We saw both your parachutes in the moonlight."

"And the weapons?" Andy knew what he had to worry about, but the pain was interfering with his thoughts.

"We saw the other parachutes. There are many of us. We'll find everything."

"You've done good work," Andy said. "I saw your lights. I'm sorry I couldn't reach the target."

"Don't worry. It's difficult to allow for the wind. We knew it would be. We were ready."

"Have you done this before?" Andy was taking off his helmet, using only one hand.

"Yes and no. You're the first agents to come to us, but we've had supplies dropped. We know what to do."

"What about the Germans? Don't we need to hurry?"

"Yes, of course. We saw no one tonight, and heard no trucks, but we must always be careful."

Andy couldn't see the man well, but could tell that he was wearing black, that he had a mustache, and that he was stout, or maybe bundled up against the cool air. Andy was beginning to shake, more from the pain than the cold, he thought. He struggled out of his coveralls, but his shoulder made that difficult. Roger tried to help, and that only made things worse. Still, Andy wanted to get to a place where he felt safe, so he forced the coveralls off his shoulder more quickly than he wanted to, and then helped with his good arm to pull at the parachute. But he wasn't much help, and Roger finally took over, yanking hard, throwing his weight against the line. He eventually climbed into the tree and pulled again, but the chute was caught firmly, up high, so he cut the lines and then jumped down. "There's nothing we can do now. I can send someone back to climb higher into the tree. But for now, we must leave it."

Andy had already begun digging as best he could, with one hand. But Roger had a little shovel strapped to his side, and he dug in the packed earth. In a minute or two he opened up enough of a hole that Andy could throw in his coveralls and helmet, and then they kicked dirt and leaves over everything and ran off across a plowed field—the target Andy had missed. Andy felt the damp earth catching in the *sabots,* and he knew already that he wasn't going to like wearing those things all the time.

Andy saw figures in the distance moving across the same field from a different angle. He felt a momentary pang of fear until he saw Raul, his slim, dark silhouette moving along with two other men. He changed his angle and so did Roger, and as the groups converged, Andy was surprisingly relieved to see Raul. "We did it," Raul said. Andy couldn't see his face well, but he heard the laughter in his voice. After all the tension of this long day, the sound was good.

"Did anyone find the rifle containers and ammunition?" Roger whispered.

One of the men said, "Yes. They're in the truck and gone already." That relieved Andy, too. Things had started out fairly well, all things considered.

*   *   *   *   *

Andy and Raul spent the rest of that night at Roger's farm, not far away. They slept in a hayloft in the barn. Roger said it was safer there. If any Germans had heard the airplane and were searching, they usually checked the houses first. The barn was close to a wooded area. If Andy and Raul heard vehicles approaching during the night, they could make a dash out the back way and into the trees. Andy wondered about the cold, and worried about the pain in his shoulder, but Roger went into the house and came back with blankets. As it turned out, Andy lay still on his back, and the pain wasn't so bad that way. He was so tired, having hardly slept the night before, and having put in such a tense day, that he fell asleep immediately and slept pretty well. In fact, morning came much too quickly. When Roger came into the barn and called to Andy and Raul to come with him to the house, Andy actually wished he could stay where he was a little longer.

But inside the house Andy smelled sausage, and he was surprised to see Roger's wife frying eggs. He had heard that eggs were in short supply in France. He and Raul stepped into the kitchen, a nook of a room with a big iron cookstove, a sink on the wall, and only a small cabinet for food. But it was warm and clean, and the smell of the food was wonderfully comforting.

"You won't get this kind of food in the cities," Roger said. "The Germans are taking everything away from us and shipping it to their own country. People in the cities rarely have enough to eat. But we eat better on the farms, even though *Les Boches* take most of our crops."

Les Boches. It was the name the French used for Germans. It could only be translated as something like "cabbage heads."

"Good morning," Raul said to Roger's wife. "Thank you for getting up so early to cook for us."

"It's not early," she said, smiling a little. "It's the usual time for us." She was a trim woman, almost delicate, but her clothing was coarse and worn. She was wearing a heavy sweater over a dark skirt, both patched and frayed. She looked like a woman who had worked plenty in her life. The skin around her eyes and along her neck was as shabby as her clothing, and her teeth were stained dark.

"She's called Micheline," Roger said. "That's not her real name, of course. Be careful not to learn our real names, if you can help it. It's not good for any of us to know one another, should we be apprehended."

"How bad is the pain in your shoulder?" Micheline asked.

"I'm trying not to move it much. It's not too bad when I'm careful."

"I'll make a sling for you."

"That would be helpful," Andy said, and then he asked, "What gives you the courage to hide us here?"

It was Roger who answered. "They've taken our country from us, *Les Boches.* If we are not to have it back, life is not worth very much. You two are the courageous ones. You've come to help us."

"It's my country too," Raul said. "I'll say no more than that."

"I've lived here as well," Andy said.

"I hear it in your French," Micheline said. "I thought you might be Englishmen, or Americans, with schoolboy French. But you both speak well. This will help you."

"My French is too correct," Andy said, "because of the way I learned it. Our leaders have taught me to speak in dialect as best I can. I'll be better as I listen to the people here."

"Say as little as you can to the Germans," Roger said. "That's the best way to get by."

Andy and Raul sat down at a small wooden table, and Micheline brought them each a huge omelet, with sausage, and slices of dark bread. Andy ate more than he had eaten in one sitting in a long time, and he was embarrassed. But the food was wonderful; he hadn't had the stomach to eat the day before.

The four were finishing, sitting back, talking about the plan for Raul and Andy to be moved on to Olivet, closer to Orléans, when Andy heard a tapping on the back door of the kitchen. Roger got up immediately and opened the door. A man slipped in quickly—Raphael, one of the men from the night before. He was wearing the same tattered black coat, but his face was flushed now, probably from riding his bicycle.

"They must hide," he said, breathless. "*Les Boches* are searching. They're coming up the road, stopping at all the farms. Jacques thinks that someone reported the sound of the airplane last night."

It was hard for Andy to imagine that French people would report such things, but they lived in fear, under pressure from the Germans, and collaboration was the easiest way to get by. Andy had heard, too, that the Germans gave rewards for such information, and many people were in desperate need.

"What about the parachute?" Roger asked. "Did anyone go after it this morning?"

"Jacques sent some men back there last night. But they couldn't find the right tree in the dark. The Germans might have discovered it blowing in the wind this morning."

Andy felt the fear again. His shoulder was a giveaway—not just the injury, but the bruises he had taken a look at this morning. His instructors at Beaulieu had warned him that Germans, when they caught a suspected agent shortly after parachuting, knew to take off the man's shirt and check for bruises from the harness. Andy's would be worse than most—and would last for some time.

"Should we go back to the barn?" Andy asked.

"They're here!" Raphael said. He was looking out the side window. "A whole truckload of them."

"Come with me," Roger said. "Quickly."

Roger hurried to a hallway outside the kitchen. He pulled back a threadbare rug that ran the length of the hall. "This isn't the usual thing, this entrance. And there's no telling from outside that we have this cellar. It's the best place to hide."

Andy wondered. He had been warned in training that a hiding place with no back exit was simply another name for "trap." But there was no time to consider other options. Andy could hear doors slamming outside, and he knew that men were piling out of the truck. So he and Raul climbed down the ladder into the cellar, and Roger shut the door over them. Suddenly everything was black. Andy felt his way along the rock wall carefully. The musty smell of decay, like rotten potatoes, was so thick around him that he thought for a moment he would vomit.

"Work your way back here," Andy whispered to Raul. "We can sit down against the wall." That seemed to make sense, that they should be as far from the door as possible, but he knew very well, once the door came open above, there would be nowhere to go.

"Do you have your pistol?" Raul asked.

"Yes."

"If the door opens, let's grab the first man by the foot, drag him down and kill him, and then get out of here. We can come out shooting."

"We wouldn't have a chance."

"But they'll torture us before they kill us, if we get taken in. We might as well kill some of them first."

Andy understood the logic, but he didn't want to think of any of that happening. He was praying again. He could soon hear the noise of men walking above them, the big hobnail boots of the Germans pounding like hammers. He could hear the muffled talk, too, even some loud commands. He caught a few words, heard a German say in French, "I don't believe you. You're lying to me."

But he couldn't hear the reply, which must have been softer. What he did hear was furniture moving, doors shutting hard, more and more of the tromping back and forth, sometimes directly above them.

Andy tried to breathe normally, knew that this was the first great test of his courage. But he wasn't very brave, he realized. He thought of the painful shoulder and what a sadistic Gestapo agent could do with it.

The noise upstairs continued for ten minutes or so, then stopped abruptly. Another quarter of an hour must have passed before the door to the cellar finally came open. "You can come up now," Roger said.

Andy and Raul climbed the stairs. Andy blinked as he came out into the sunlight, which was bright as he walked into the kitchen again. "Something just happened here," Roger said. "I don't know how to explain it."

"What was it?" Raul asked.

"The German captain came into our kitchen. Micheline had put the plates in the wash pan and tried to cover them with soapy water, but he reached in and counted the plates. Then he said, 'They're here. There are too many plates.' Micheline told him, 'Two of those were from our dinner last night,' but he didn't believe her. 'Where's your root cellar?' he demanded, and I told him outside. We do have another old cellar by the barn. He went out and found it half fallen in, and he came back and demanded to know whether there was a cellar in the house. I said there wasn't."

Andy looked at Micheline, who was breaking down now. She sat down at the kitchen table and covered her face, but tears began to drip between her fingers. "I was so frightened," she said.

"It's all right. God is with us. I know it," Roger said. He stepped next to Micheline, patted her back, and then rested his hand on her shoulder.

"The captain said, 'All these farmhouses have cellars. Show us where yours is. Do it now or I'll shoot your wife first, and then you.'"

"And you didn't tell him then?" Andy said.

"No. It was no use. It's the way the Germans operate. Once he had found you, he would have killed us anyway. I told him the water table was high here, and there was no cellar. It's true in a way. That cellar is often wet."

"Did he believe you?" Raul asked.

"No. That's the miracle. He told his men, 'There's a cellar here somewhere. Pull up all the rugs until you find the door.' But then he walked outside, I suppose to see what was happening in the search of the barn. A man was about to pull up the rug, the one covering the cellar door, and I said to him, 'I don't know why your captain doesn't believe me. There's no cellar in this house.'

"The young man looked at me and said, 'He doesn't believe anyone.' And then he walked out the front door. The others followed him. It's not like a German to ignore an order. I've not seen it happen before."

Andy thought of his prayers.

"But we must move you very soon," Roger said. "The captain told me that some of his men had spotted the parachute in the tree this morning. He knows that something was dropped, if not someone. He told me that he would keep searching, and if he found out that I had helped you, he would kill us both. And after he killed us, he would kill ten of our neighbors."

"Would they really do something like that?" Raul asked.

"It's been done. I can tell you that. I'll contact Jacques, our circuit leader, as soon as I can. By tomorrow, at latest, I'll find a way to move you out of the area."

Andy hadn't been brave down in that cellar. He knew that. But he had seen bravery now. He saw it in Roger's face, but even more in

Micheline's. She must have been terrified, but she had faced the German captain and said what she had to say. And the German must have believed her, in reality, or he never would have taken his men on to the next farm.

CHAPTER 9

ANDY AND RAUL slept in Roger and Micheline's barn again that night. But Andy was not as tired as he had been the night before, and his shoulder was bothering him more. Micheline had made a sling for him and secured it tight so that his arm was immobile. That was probably good, but with the restriction, he found it harder to relax and find a position that was comfortable. He had no idea how serious the damage was and really wished that he could get some medical attention, but he saw no way that could happen for now.

As Andy lay in the hayloft, trying to rest, hoping to sleep, he felt as if he were realizing for the first time what he had gotten himself into. He knew now that tedium was going to be a big part of his life. All day he and Raul had sat in the barn, ready to run to the woods if the Germans returned. They hadn't dared to set up their radio. Germans monitored radio signals and had mobile equipment in trucks that could home in on the source of the broadcast. With suspicions running high right now, it would be suicide to contact London from this site. But that meant there had been nothing for him and Raul to do all day but wait—and Andy had never really liked to wait.

Now, lying in the prickly hay, he wondered how many nights he would spend like this. As a boy, he had liked to sleep under the stars, but he had also enjoyed the night he got back into his own bed at home. But

OSS agents had no home; they had to be ready to move quickly and hide where they could. He had hated the terror that morning when the Germans had been so close to finding him and Raul, and he certainly didn't want to go through anything like that again, but he also wondered how many days like this he could stand—just waiting.

Andy sensed Raul's tension, too, and he was quite sure that he wasn't sleeping, but it was Raul, finally, who asked Andy, in French, "How bad is the pain?" They had vowed always to speak French so they would be in less danger of responding in English in some situation when they shouldn't.

"The pain isn't terrible, just annoying. But I can't seem to sleep."

"Do you think the Germans will keep looking for us?"

"Yes."

"If they come back, they'll pull up the rugs this time, won't they?"

"Yes. I would think so. And then they'll know Roger was lying. We can't stay here much longer."

"Roger said he would find a way to get us out of the area. I think we have to do that first thing in the morning."

"Yes."

Five minutes passed, maybe more. Andy could hear scuttling sounds in the barn. He hoped mice were making the sound, not rats, but he didn't really like the idea of either one. Out in the desert at night, he had been frightened of snakes, but he had never told his friends that, and he didn't like to admit to himself now his dread of rodents running over him, touching his face.

"I've been thinking about my family," Raul said. "I don't think I considered them as much as I should have when I agreed to do this."

It was one of the things Andy had been thinking too. "I know."

"Do you have a big family?"

"We're not supposed to talk about that."

"I know."

Again some time passed, and then Andy said, "I have three sisters and a brother, all younger than I am." It felt better to say it. He was tired of being a stranger to everyone around him.

"You live in the West, don't you?"

"Yes."

"You're religious, aren't you?"

"Yes."

"I have two sisters, no brothers," Raul said. "My mother worries about me. I'm her only son and I'm the youngest."

Andy could hear the scratching sounds again—all below, he thought, not in the loft. But the sound reminded him of summer nights when he had sometimes slept at the old house at the family farm rather than walking back into town after working all day. All of it, the smell of the hay, the breeze making the trees outside creak and rustle, even the sound of the mice, felt familiar to him. A wave of homesickness struck him without warning. He suddenly wanted to go home, and he wanted to stay there. He lay there for a time, listening, breathing in the smell, and he tried to tell himself that he would return someday, but he didn't believe it. Home was gone. He had heard those Germans today, and something told him they were too formidable, too many, too committed to finding him. Fate had given him some time, but the very closeness of the enemy had told him that he couldn't be that fortunate again.

"I think my mother guessed what sort of thing I was getting myself involved in over here," Andy said. "I told her nothing, but that's the very thing that made her suspicious."

"It was the same for me. My father and I aren't very close. I'm not sure he thinks much about anything, let alone about me, but I know my mother is worried, and I have no way to reassure her now."

"That's what bothers me too. I told my parents I couldn't write for a while, but I know how hard that's going to be for them."

"You have a girl back home, too. I've seen you read her letters. That's got to make things even harder."

The barn was tighter than those back home, built of brick, but the doors were open at both ends of the loft, so the breeze passed through. Andy listened to a chirping sound—a cricket or locust of some kind—not quite like anything back home. The air was different too, moist and dense with the smell of manure. "I know you live in Utah," Raul finally said. "I've seen the address on your letters sometimes."

"And I know you're from New York somewhere."

"Someday we'll get to know each other—really get acquainted. You know what I mean?"

"We know each other," Andy said.

"Maybe. But I'd like to know you by your name—and have you know mine. I know you played football in high school. And I know a few other things. But someday I want to talk to you the way friends talk."

"We will."

But Andy didn't really think so. Maybe Raul didn't think so either; he said nothing more.

After a time Andy could tell by Raul's breathing that he was asleep. Andy finally slept too, if not very deeply. When he awoke, his shoulder was stiff and throbbing. This extra burden—the pain—was not something he had counted on, and the preoccupation interfered with his concentration on the job at hand, even reduced his resolve.

But Roger came to the barn early, and Micheline fed the men again. While they ate, Roger told them his plan. He had made arrangements with a wine dealer. The man took a trip to Orléans twice a week, passing through Olivet, and would be going today. The man was not part of the local Resistance circuit, but he hated the Germans, who often confiscated his wine—or demanded bribes—and left him struggling to feed his family. "We'll meet him on the road between here and town," Roger said. "He'll have two empty barrels on his wagon. You two will get inside, and we'll replace the tops. We'll leave the barrel uncorked, so you have air, but it won't be a comfortable ride—especially for you, Armand."

"That's all right," Andy told him, but it wasn't what he was thinking.

"We have to get you out of the area. The Germans have never stopped searching. They know that an agent landed in that tree, and they believe he hasn't gone far. They're watching all trains and busses, and they're stopping people in town, checking their papers. My guess is, they'll be sweeping through the farms again. Moving you in the barrels is a gamble, but keeping you here is a bigger one."

"What if they find your cellar and know you lied yesterday?" Raul asked.

"It's no use talking about that," Roger said, but Andy saw him glance at his wife. She seemed older today, the color gone from her face, the wrinkles around her eyes more noticeable. He knew that she hadn't slept, that she had been thinking about all the possibilities this day might bring. No wonder so many of the French chose to collaborate with the Germans.

No one ate as much this morning. Yesterday's breakfast seemed days ago now, and Andy felt bound to these good people in a way that he hadn't expected, having known them for such a short time. After breakfast Andy kissed Micheline on her cheeks. She patted his shoulder and said, "I'm sorry I couldn't do more for you."

Andy wanted to say that she had put her life in jeopardy for him, but that wasn't exactly accurate and he knew it. They had all put their lives on the line for things that were too complex to describe at the moment. So he merely thanked Micheline, and then he and Raul followed Roger through the woods to a dirt road. They waited again—much longer than anyone expected—and Andy's shoulder continued to ache. When he finally heard the plodding of horses and the crunch of wheels on the hard-packed dirt, he was relieved that something was finally about to happen.

Old Anselme, the wine merchant, stopped his horses in the place that had been agreed upon, and Roger whistled from the woods. A return whistle sounded and the men hurried to the wagon. "Move fast," Anselme said. "Germans are everywhere today, checking everyone."

Andy jumped onto the back of the wagon. Anselme didn't get down, didn't help. Andy realized that he was not a young man. "Which barrels?" Raul asked.

"The ones in the front of the wagon. Crawl over the top of the others."

But that was not so easy for Andy, with one arm useless. Raul helped him onto a tall barrel, and by then, Roger had scrambled across the other barrels to the two with loose heads, both of them surrounded at the front. He and Raul helped Andy step into one of them—not without pushing against his shoulder more than he would have liked—and then, when he tried to sit, he realized that that wouldn't work. He could only kneel. "How long will we be in these things?" he asked.

"How long to Olivet?" Roger asked Anselme.

"If we're not stopped, an hour, maybe a little more. If the Germans stop us, it could be longer."

An hour on his knees, the wagon jostling, knocking his shoulder against the side of the barrel. It didn't seem possible. But staying was clearly not an option, so Andy hunkered down, having to bend his neck more than was comfortable, and Roger replaced the lid. All was dark inside, and the smell of the wine was overwhelming.

Andy heard the sound of the other barrel head being dropped into place, and then he heard a muffled, "God bless you!" and in another moment, the wagon began to roll. Andy felt the pressure on his knees already. He wondered how bad the pain would get before the trip ended.

Andy prayed again—prayed for patience and strength. He prayed that he and Raul could get to a safe house this day, that he could survive the pain, and that he could get help for his shoulder before the day ended. He decided that was all he could think about for now: surviving this day. But he was forced to think about his knees, his neck, the over-powering smell. He told himself stories—or let himself see them. He remembered a day one summer when he was fifteen—Flip's age now. Whisper and Adele had been sitting on the porch at his house when Andy had come home from working on the farm. They had said they were bored and wanted something to do. So he'd told them he would take them swimming in the irrigation canal. He was dirty, his hair and clothes full of hay and dust, but he had gone into the house and slipped on a swimsuit and then pulled on his jeans. The girls had done the same, Whisper using one of Adele's old swimsuits. They had walked to the ditch, and Andy had dived in first. Adele had worried that the water was too cold, but Whisper hadn't hesitated. She'd dived in and then come up close to him, treading water, looking at him, smiling. She was thirteen or so, skinny, flat chested. But he remembered her face that day, freckled and shining, her hair plastered down. It was the first time the thought had crossed his mind that she was pretty: those green eyes, her creamy complexion, her smile. And she was so thrilled to be with him, close. He had always known that, and yet it hadn't mattered to him. That day, it was like a moment of awakening. Afterward, he had shut his eyes to it again for quite some time. Still, it was something good to think of now, that freckled face. The thought passed too quickly, so Andy pursued it, rehearsed the details in his mind, the things they had done and said that day.

There were other good memories, but the pain forced its way into his head and fought against any other thoughts. Andy kept trying to guess how long the wagon had been moving. There came a time when he allowed himself to hope that half an hour had passed, but he knew better. He told himself to assume that only half that time had gone by and then to be happy if he was surprised; then the wagon pitched and Andy's shoulder took a blow. He had tried to use his other arm to brace against that, but there was no way to protect himself fully without pressing his bad shoulder hard against the barrel, and that hurt too much.

He tried to think of new pictures, old memories, but nothing worked very well, and when he thought that the time had doubled, he told himself that that was only half an hour, and he was probably not halfway. The pain in his knees was gradually becoming worse than that in his shoulder, but in truth his entire body ached—his thighs, his back, his neck. And the heat inside the barrel was becoming an equal misery.

Then the wagon stopped. He wondered whether his estimates had been all wrong and Anselme had actually reached Olivet. The wagon rolled ahead again, stopped, then repeated the motion twice more. Then he heard voices. He heard Anselme name his destination. And he heard muffled responses. He felt the wagon tip a little, and he knew that someone had stepped onto the back. He heard some knocking, perhaps barrels moving. This had to be Germans, checking the wagon, searching for him and Raul.

But the talk quieted, and after a time Andy heard some laughter. Not long after that, the wagon moved on. Andy felt the pain again, but it wasn't as bad as before. His mind had found new worries for a time, and his body was becoming numb. Andy had lost all sense of time by now; he only knew that there seemed no hope of ever stopping. But then the wagon did stop, and this time he heard someone on the wagon again, climbing over the barrels, then prying at the lid and popping it off. The air flooded into the barrel like cool water and Andy realized how badly he had been sweating in the muggy heat. He tried to stand but couldn't, and then someone had hold of his bad shoulder, and Andy gasped. "No, no. Not that shoulder. I'm injured."

"*Pardon*," the man responded, then grabbed the other shoulder, under the arm, and helped pull Andy up.

When Andy was standing, he felt the pain stab through his knees, but he tried not to show what he was feeling. "*Merci. Merci,*" he told the man.

"You must hurry into the house," the man said. Andy glanced to see that someone else had opened Raul's barrel, and Raul was climbing out. Raul helped Andy—all three men did—pulling him by his arm, his jacket, his belt. He thanked them again, walked over the top of the other barrels, jumped down onto the wagon and then to the ground, each landing sending pain through his knees and his shoulder again. But he was out of that barrel and he was alive.

Andy was heading for the house, a brick farmhouse, dark red, when he thought of Anselme. He turned back. "*Merci, mon ami,*" he said.

"Yes, yes. It's good."

"How did you get past the Germans?" Andy asked.

"I drained off a little wine for each of them. They were happy with that. They didn't suspect me."

Andy laughed and thanked Anselme again, and then he walked on to the house. A woman greeted him at the door. She kissed his cheeks and said, "I understand you've been hurt."

She was a sturdy woman, dressed like most of the peasants in dark clothes that seemed too heavy for the weather, but her eyes were keen. "Yes. My shoulder," he said. "It could be broken. I don't know."

She laughed. "You smell like a drunk. Did you drink that barrel dry before you got in?"

"No." He laughed too. "But I smelled enough to get drunk, I think."

"I have some brandy you can drink, not smell. It may help the pain a little. My son has gone to locate a physician, but he may not be able to come for a time. He's one of us, but we have to be careful about being seen together too often."

"I understand."

"I'll get the brandy. You and Raul can rest in the living room for now.

We have an attic where you'll sleep. My husband is not well. We're spreading the story that we're hiring two workers to help on our farm. But it won't make sense to hire an injured man. We'll have to add something to the story. That you fell the first day. That you're not much use yet, but we've kept you on. Something of that sort."

Andy had lots of questions. He would have to adjust his cover story to fit this circumstance, but for now, he was alive, and the woman seemed confident. That made him feel better. "Never mind the brandy," he said.

She stared at him for a moment, confused.

"I don't drink wine—or any kind of alcohol."

It was a moment before his words seemed to register, and then she laughed. "What do you mean? Not at all?"

"No. Not at all."

"That's not healthy," she said, sounding like a concerned mother.

"In my case, it's what's best." And he let her decide what that might mean.

"All right. Go sit and rest. My code name is Francette, but you'll need to know, our family name is Bertrand. If people were to stop here, you would naturally know our names, and that's what you should call me—Mme. Bertrand."

"I am Armand. You need not know my actual name."

"You're a handsome boy. And far from home. Does your mother worry about you?"

Andy smiled. "You can be my mother now."

"I'm not quite so old as that," she said, with some flirtation in her eyes.

"Be careful what you say," a man, apparently her husband, said. He laughed too. He had been listening to all this, saying nothing. He was one of the men who had helped Andy from the barrel. The other one had already left. The man extended his hand, and Andy used his left hand to give it something of a shake. "I'm Felix Bertrand. In our *réseau,* I'm known as Gaston. Some in the circuit know who I am, but be careful not to spread my name to those from other towns. It's best to use *Gaston* at any of our meetings."

Andy thought he had come, at least in part, to train Resistance circuits, but his impression was that these people seemed to know plenty about what they were doing. When a member of a network was caught, if he or she knew the names of the others, there was too great a chance that all the names would come out under torture. Code names were a protection. What impressed Andy, however, was the courage of these people who lived such precarious lives. He knew he had to be less self-indulgent about his own worries.

*   *   *   *   *

Raul had set up his radio in the attic, and soon after their arrival in Olivet, he broadcasted a quick coded message that he and Armand had reached their secondary safe house and all was well. He didn't bother to let London know about the difficulties they had faced. As it turned out, Andy's shoulder improved steadily. In a week, he was moving his arm pretty well, and in another week the bruises were healed.

What Andy was anxious to do was to send a message to headquarters that would be of some tactical use. The OSS had picked the Orléans area because there was a sizeable German presence there. It was an area where Raul and Andy could learn something about troop movements, order of battle, numbers of tanks, and the like, but it was also an area where considerable sabotage could be done when the time was right. The plan was not to attack too forcefully and alert the Germans, but to do a little damage to communication lines and railroad tracks from time to time, and let the Germans think that the attacks were random and disorganized. Some of the locals wanted to assassinate German officers, but that kind of action often brought brutal retaliations on innocent citizens, and when that happened, locals hesitated to support the Resistance. So it was better to move slowly for the present, to wait for the day when an invasion would begin, and only then to move the fight into the open.

For now, the most important duty for Andy and Raul was to gather information. Some of that they could do themselves, but they would also work with Resistance forces to recruit and organize more members, and then to train new recruits to gather and report intelligence.

For two weeks Andy and Raul had stayed close to the farm. Raul had done some work around the place, since Felix Bertrand—Gaston—really had been sick that winter and was still not back to his full health. Andy tried to do a few things on the farm too, and was gradually able to do more, but he and Raul had to be seen a little more all the time so that locals were accustomed to having them about. They also wanted to observe the area and gain some personal knowledge of German facilities. They began to walk into Olivet from the farm from time to time.

One day they caught a ride with a farmer on his way to Orléans. They saw the German camp, noted some of the insignias on German uniforms, and walked past the train yards. Andy had asked Gaston lots of questions and had picked up information about German troop strength, but Gaston could only guess, and Andy wanted something more specific to report. "Let's go sit in a bistro and look at the German uniforms," Andy said. "We can get some idea of how many separate units are stationed here."

"That's a good idea," Raul said. "I could use a cool beer right now. I drank too many warm ones in England."

"Gaston says that alcohol is often not available."

"Yes, well, it's worth a try."

Andy wished for something cool himself. The day was warm and humid. The air reminded Andy of his time in Maryland and Washington, D.C., the year before. His denim clothes were heavy and hot, but Gaston had told him that they were exactly what a French farm worker would be wearing, even in the summer.

Andy and Raul found a shabby little café in town and sat down at a table. Raul whispered, "No luck. The people at the table we passed were drinking coffee. I don't see any beer or wine anywhere."

Andy smiled at that and said, "Let's order mineral water."

"I don't think so," Raul said. "No peasant worker would pay money for water. And who knows? It may be something else you can't find with the war on. Let's play it safe and order what other people are drinking."

Andy nodded, and when the waiter came, he said in a quiet voice, "Just a cup of coffee."

But Raul said, "I suppose you don't have any real coffee?"

"Of course not," the waiter said. "It's made from chicory."

"All right then. I'll have a cup. But it tastes like puke."

Andy didn't think such talk was wise. Raul should have accepted the *ersatz* coffee and said nothing about it.

As the waiter walked away, Andy looked around. There were maybe forty people in the café, most of them German soldiers. They were talking, laughing, paying no attention to Andy and Raul, but the idea was frightening, to sit among the enemy. Raul had to be more careful. "Don't say so much next time," Andy told him. "Let's not draw attention to ourselves."

"Are you frightened?" Raul asked.

"Of course I am."

Raul smiled. "It makes me excited. I'd like to cut a few throats."

Andy shook his head at Raul. It was the wrong time even to whisper such a thing. Andy had chosen a table next to four young soldiers who were talking rather loudly. Andy and Raul had taken a crash course in German during their training, but it was mostly book learning, and Andy soon realized that he understood next to nothing of what the men were saying.

The chicory coffee came, and Andy tried a taste, but it was as disgusting as Raul said it was. Still, it didn't break the Word of Wisdom, and he needed to look natural, so he kept taking sips.

"This isn't getting us anywhere," Raul said after a time. "They all have the same markings on their uniforms, and I can't understand anything they're saying. They aren't going to speak French unless someone speaks to them."

"Do we dare ask them anything?"

"I don't think so. It's not what a farmer would do."

Andy nodded. He knew that was right. "But how are we going to gather information?"

"We'll rely on our people. That's how it's supposed to work anyway."

Andy knew that. But there had to be other ways. In training, the teachers had constantly advised the students to be inventive, flexible, to use their ingenuity to get the job done.

Andy noticed two Germans coming toward him. He wondered what they wanted, and he felt his heart accelerate, but he looked away. One of the soldiers said, in French, "May we take these two chairs? We want to join these men." He pointed to the next table.

Andy nodded, trying to assume the manner of an uneducated worker, but he said, "You speak good French."

"Thank you," the soldier said. "I lived in the Alsace growing up. I spoke both languages."

It was a strange moment for Andy. This German, this enemy, was congenial, friendly. He seemed like anyone he might have met back home. "No beer today," Andy said, trying to keep the conversation going.

"Yes. I know. It's a hardship." He laughed. The other soldier took a chair and set it at the next table between two men who had slid their chairs apart.

"A Frenchman without his wine—that's worse," the German said to Andy.

"Yes, of course. And no real coffee either."

"It will all be better someday. Don't worry about that."

"Have you been here long?" Raul asked.

But he had sounded a little too outgoing, friendlier than Andy thought a French peasant would be in the circumstance.

"I'm new here, but my friend was here all year. He likes it fine. He tells me I will too."

The soldier turned to go, but Andy wanted something more. "How many are here now? It seems a great many."

Suddenly the look on the soldier's face changed. "You must have some idea. You live here."

"We're new here. We came to work for a farmer outside of town."

"Then let me give you some advice. Don't ask questions. There is no reason for you to know our numbers. I won't ask for your papers, but I should."

Andy saw the remarkable change in the young man, the intensity in his eyes. He wondered which was the real man—the friendly one or the one trained to be so careful. "I meant nothing," Andy said.

The soldier smiled again. "I'm sure you didn't. It doesn't matter. Thank you for the chair."

He joined the others.

"Let's go," Raul whispered.

"No. Drink your coffee. Take your time." And Andy lifted his own cup to his lips, sipped at it again.

They waited ten more minutes that way, and then they paid the waiter and left. When Andy got outside, he realized he was shaking. He was still thinking of those pleasant blue eyes that had suddenly turned so hard. Andy knew he had a lot to learn.

* * * * *

That night Andy and Raul met with some of the local Resistance forces in a home on the edge of Orléans. There were eight men and a young woman seated on a couch and on some wooden chairs brought in from the kitchen. Andy knew how dangerous this was, to gather people this way, but they all seemed relaxed, as though they had grown accustomed to their danger.

Andy took the lead at the meeting. He described the kind of information that he needed. Some of the men said they had sources to gather information, and Andy encouraged them to feed it to him and Raul, but not to take chances that would get them caught. A man called Xavier worked in the Orléans rail yard and said he could report specific information about troop movements and shipment of arms.

Then the young woman, who used the code name Simone, said, "I thought you came here to begin the fight."

There was sarcasm in her voice but a bit of playfulness in her eyes. She was a pretty young woman, maybe a little older than Andy. She had rich brown eyes and softly curved cheekbones, smooth as porcelain. She had been watching him the whole time, seeming curious as well as entertained—as though she were sizing up Andy and Raul and wasn't entirely convinced that they knew what they were doing.

"If we get ourselves killed, we won't be of any help to anyone," Andy told her.

Simone was sitting on the big couch, but she was slumped down, looking casual. She folded her arms now. "I guess I don't understand," she said. "I thought heroes died for great causes."

"I'd rather *live* for one," Andy said, and now he smiled.

"Very nicely stated," Simone said. "But this organization of yours—the one that sent you to us—does it have any *men* working for it, or only boys like the two of you?"

"That's enough, Simone," Gaston said. "These men didn't have to come here."

"That's fine," Simone said. "But I want to know, when do we get more weapons? More explosives? When do we start blowing up trains and killing Germans? All this talk of information is nonsense. We have a war to fight."

"Don't worry. We'll fight one. Have some patience and—"

"That's all we've had so far, and France has shamed itself. We need some people brave enough to throw *Les Boches* out of this country. I'm not afraid to die, if that's what it takes."

"We brought more weapons," Andy said. "They were dropped with us. We have to find a way to get them to you. In time, you'll all have what you need. This war can't be won in a day."

Simone was smiling again. "No. But someday it has to start, in earnest. I hope some *soldiers* are coming."

"You'll find out what we can do," Andy said, the same words he had used in his first OSS interview. He liked staring back at her, letting her feel his commitment. He realized that he probably had been too frightened so far. He rather liked Simone's call to arms. Maybe it was what he had been needing.

CHAPTER 10

BISHOP GLEDHILL WAS sitting in his office at the bank on an October afternoon. He was working on a talk he felt he needed to give in his ward. Flip had forced him to think a good deal lately about the people who were interned at the Topaz camp. He thought he understood that his ward members had a hard time right now thinking about Japanese people as anything but a brutal enemy. It wasn't easy to send sons away to fight a war, maybe to die, and then make a distinction between the people who had attacked Pearl Harbor and the ones who had come here from California. War seemed to demand simple categories. It was much easier to invent an adversary—one that barely seemed human—and then cheer when that caricature of a person died in the newsreels, his airplane crashing into the sea. Bishop Gledhill heard lots of hateful comments these days, most directed toward the enemy in Japan, and some toward the people at Topaz, but all of that hatred, as far as the bishop was concerned, was wrong.

Bishop Gledhill had written a few things down, and he had read the Sermon on the Mount once again, but mostly he had sat and stared at the wall. The Stewarts had lost their son on some little island in the Solomons a couple of months back, fighting against the Japanese. They were doing their best now, their faith tested to the limit. Old Milt Stewart hadn't been regular about coming to church most of his life, but since young Milton—"Buddy"—had been killed, Milt had come every week. He was surely doing that for Rayona, who believed in a celestial kingdom and was focused on the hope of seeing her son again. The bishop had talked to her about eternal increase, that Buddy would still have a chance to have children, and she would be their grandmother, but Milt had sat staring at his battered, overworked hands as the bishop and Rayona had talked, and Bishop Gledhill wasn't sure the man believed in any of that. Now, was he supposed to look at Milt, sitting on a back row of the chapel in his twenty-year-old suit and his work boots, and say to him, "I want you to love the next Japanese folks you see in town"?

But there were things that had to be said. The bishop had heard about a nasty incident the week before. Some of the Japanese people from the camp had ridden into town in the back of a truck and gone into Service Drug. They had been spending the bit of money they made at their jobs at Topaz, buying a few personal items. They had been polite, probably overly so, since they were always aware what people thought of them. Brother Johansen, at the store, didn't mind having them shop there, but Huey Thompson, from east of town, had made a big ruckus, used a lot of filthy language, and told a couple of nice little Japanese ladies to get out of the place. Huey couldn't have *read* the Sermon on the Mount, let alone understood it, so the bishop didn't worry so much about him. What bothered him were some things said at the barber shop. Mel Eakins, a good man and a high priest, had been waiting his turn while the bishop was getting his hair cut. "Maybe Huey shouldn'ta cussed and carried on like that," Mel had told the men in the shop, "but I don't think he was wrong. We shouldn't ought to be taking those Japs' money. They wouldn't be sitting out there at that camp if there wasn't a reason. They side with their folks back in Japan, and that's where we ought to send them just as soon as this war is over."

Everyone had looked at the bishop. He had only said, "Mel, it's not as simple as that and you know it," but then he had decided to wait and say something more in sacrament meeting, maybe even take a fair share of the time this week. But the words weren't coming. He looked up briefly and saw Dale Kramer standing in his open doorway, his hat in his hand, his face white. "What's happened?" Bishop Gledhill asked.

"It's Dale Junior. We got a telegram. He's missing in action."

Bishop Gledhill got up and walked to Brother Kramer. He put a hand on his shoulder and asked, "Is that all the telegram said?"

"His ship went down out near New Guinea somewheres. Some from the ship was picked up, but he wasn't."

"He might be found yet, Dale."

"I know. But you know what people say: MIA just means KIA, only they make you wait to find out."

"Not always. I've seen cases where another telegram comes, maybe just a few days later, and it turns out he's been found."

"Try to tell that to Sharon. She says it's worse not knowing. She's carrying on real bad—crying right out loud and saying she can't stand it, having to wait."

"It is a hard thing, Dale. I've seen it before, and it's as hard as anything that happens—except maybe seeing boys come home all mutilated, body and soul."

"I don't know. I guess I'd take him any way I could get him, if he could just come back to us."

Dale Kramer was a thin man, taut as a stretched rope. He'd worked hard all his life, and his wife had given him six daughters, one right after another, and then finally this son, Dale Junior. Dale had tears on his face now. He stood with his hat in both hands, and Bishop Gledhill could see how hard he was fighting himself not to break down altogether. His hair was thin on top, his scalp white, but his cheekbones and his nose were browned deep from many days in the sun. He had never done anything but farm and raise those kids, but the bishop knew his joy—teaching Dale Junior to ride a horse when he could hardly walk yet, showing him how to shoot a rifle, watching him bag his first deer over in the low cedars east of Delta. Bishop Gledhill never thought of Junior without picturing the day the boy had approached him in church and said, "I got my deer, Bishop. A nice four point." He couldn't have been more than fourteen. And now that was what his dad was likely remembering too—all those things he had taught his son, and the boy gone, never to come back.

"Do you think you could ride out and talk to Sharon, Bishop? I don't know what to say to her. The Relief Society found out, and Sister Stephens come over. She's with her now. But Sharon don't want to hear a thing any of us tells her."

"Sure I'll come, but Dale, there's not much to say. You know that better than anyone."

"I guess. I just thought maybe you'd know something." He was turning the old brown hat, holding it with all his fingers, nervously working it round and round.

Bishop Gledhill heard the sound of his clock ticking, the one on the wall behind him—something he rarely noticed. He knew he didn't have time to do this, but he also knew he couldn't say no. "Well, let's ride out to your place," he said. "Let me call Belle first." He rang up central and asked Alice to put his call through, but the phone rang two shorts and one long, several times, and Belle didn't answer. She was probably outside.

On the way to the farm in Dale's old truck, Bishop Gledhill kept thinking that Sharon was right; that was the problem. Not knowing *was* harder, and most of the MIAs did turn out to be dead. All the things Sharon believed would come back to her soon, and she would deal with this, but telling her what she already knew might not do a bit of good today. Sharon was as faithful as anyone around, but pain like this was like a toothache from head to foot, and nothing helped much until time took a little of that sharpness away. Dale drove slowly, the way he always did, and he had apparently filled his quota of talk for one day. The bishop sat with his window down, air passing over him. It felt cool on his sweating forehead, but in reality, the fall day was still warm and dry.

By the time they reached the farm, Sharon wasn't crying. She was sitting quietly, her hands gripped together, a handkerchief wadded up in her fingers. Belva Stephens was sitting next to her, wise enough not to talk too much. Sharon stood when the bishop walked to her, and she let him take her in his arms. "Give it to the Lord, Sharon," he said. "That's all you can do for now." Sharon sobbed. She clung to the bishop for a long time and cried against his shoulder. The bishop looked over her shoulder and watched Dale, who had come over to them. He was looking stoic, broken, but finished already with his own tears, just those few. Death was one more field to plow. Nothing was ever easy for a man like him, farming out here in this alkali ground.

"Why?" Sharon finally asked. "I don't understand why."

It's what the members always asked the bishop. They understood that mortality was a test, that hard things were supposed to happen. They understood when someone else in the ward went broke on a farm, or when someone got cancer. It all made sense when it happened to other people—part of God's plan for us—but when the bad things came home everyone seemed to look at the bishop with the same innocent eyes and ask why. He always knew what they meant: "I thought the Lord loved me, and now this."

"It's not a good question, Sharon," Bishop Gledhill said. "It doesn't lead anywhere. Things just happen. But you're not alone. All over this world mothers are asking the same thing right now."

That didn't matter—not today. It would matter later, though; the bishop knew that. Sooner or later, Sharon would decide she had to be as strong as other mothers. She would begin to think about her daughters, her grandchildren, her husband, and she would do what she had to do. It was a process he had watched many times. But for now, he had learned, it didn't do a lot of good to talk theology.

Belva Stephens was a big woman with arms like a man's. She had worked hard all her life too. When Bishop Gledhill had called her to be Relief Society president, Belle had said, "Oh, Ron, why her? Belva's as prickly as a Joshua tree."

Bishop Gledhill hadn't answered. As far as he was concerned, God was the one who had chosen her. But he thought he knew why. She had grit in her, and that was what the women needed these days. Most of them had made do during the Depression. "Use it up, wear it out, make it do, or do without," the saying went, and these women could do that, but as he watched them send away their sons, he knew they would have to hold on in a way they never had before. Sister Stephens was a no-nonsense woman who wouldn't cry a lot with the women; she would help them keep going. These were the granddaughters of women who crossed the plains. They had it in them to wage this war, to be mothers of stripling warriors, but they would need someone like Belva, someone who would keep walking and not lie down and whine halfway to the valley. All over town, in the windows of Bishop Gledhill's ward members, were blue-star flags—"blue-star mothers," the women in those houses were called. That sounded pretty at the Fourth of July picnic, when patriotic talk was needed, but when sons died and blue stars turned to gold, those symbols didn't mean so much. What worked was getting up the next morning and doing the wash, and Belva was the type who would help a woman do just that.

"Bishop, is he dead? That's all I want to know. Then I'll do what I have to do. But I can't wait. I can't wait for days and months and years, and just not know."

"I wish I could tell you, Sharon."

"But tell me what you feel? I think maybe he's still alive. But that's what I want to believe." She finally let go of the bishop and stepped away. Her face was awash in tears, her eyes red, the color all gone from her lips and cheeks.

"I guess the Lord's as likely to tell you as anyone. You're his mother. But my experience is, the only thing that works is to say, 'I accept. Whatever comes, I'm ready.' My mother lost a child—my little sister, just four months old—and sometimes she longed for life to end, just to hold that baby in her arms again. But that didn't help the rest of us. I was a little boy myself, and I needed a mother. You've got your grandkids to think of, and two daughters getting by without their husbands right now. It's tempting to fall apart and forget about the rest, but that's not the kind of woman you are, Sharon."

Belva Stephens stood up at that moment. She didn't say a word, but the motion seemed to say, *That's right. Here I am.*

"Oh, Bishop, I can't think straight. I—"

"Your daughters will be coming over soon," Belva said, "and all the kids. Why don't we get some supper started? That'll give you something to do."

Sharon pulled her apron to her eyes and wiped her face. "That's right," she said. "I've got to stop this before they all get here."

And that was answer enough for the moment. "Bishop, I'll be all right," Sharon said. "You go on now. I'm sorry you had to come clear out here."

"That's all right, Sister Kramer," the bishop said. "After this all settles down just a little, you might want to talk some more. Let me know if I can help that way."

"Oh, Bishop, there's nothing to talk about really. I know everything that you can tell me. I'll just take this a day at a time. There's nothing else to do."

"I think that's right. But just when you think you're doing okay, it will hit you, and if I can help you through some days like that, it's what I'd like to do."

Sharon hugged him again, cried a little more, then wiped her tears away one more time and went with Belva to the kitchen. The bishop and Dale walked out to the truck, and Dale drove back to town. On the way, he said, "It scared me the day Dale Junior joined the navy. I never liked the idea of all that water."

"It's better than crawling in the mud, I guess," the bishop said.

"Maybe so. But dirt is something I understand. Water, I never have liked."

The bishop knew what he was thinking: his son, at the bottom of the ocean. It did seem worse, somehow, worse than lying on the ground, even with a bullet in him. But the bishop was thinking about his own son, had been this whole time. It was all very well to tell Sharon to buck up, but he wondered how he would react if the same news came about Andy.

"I always wanted a son," Dale said. And that was all he managed to say all the way back to town. Bishop Gledhill didn't say anything either. He knew that Dale had cried once and didn't want to do it again.

By the time Bishop Gledhill got back to the bank, Whisper had closed it up for the day. He hardly knew how he would get by without Whisper, who looked after everything when he had to leave. But he was worried about her. She had said more to Flip than she had to him, but he knew she was upset about a letter that Andy had sent. She was afraid he was trying to wiggle his way out of his commitment to her. Bishop Gledhill didn't think that was likely, but he wondered what it did mean. Belle had believed all along that he was heading into some kind of dangerous duty, and that did seem likely. There had to be some reason he wouldn't be able to write for "quite some time," as he had written. For the moment, however, it bothered the bishop to see some of the spark gone from Whisper's eyes. This war was hurting people in so many ways.

The bishop used his key to step inside the bank for a minute. He thought of calling Belle again, but then decided he might as well just walk home and talk to her. There was no question she was going to be upset with him. He had promised to leave the bank early so he and Belle could drive up to Salt Lake in time for the play Adele was performing in that night at the University of Utah. He hoped there was still time to make it, even if they were a little late. He locked up the bank again and walked home, striding out, waving to people along the way but managing to avoid conversations.

When he opened the door, Belle had already stepped into the hallway. She was wearing a house dress, not one of her nicer dresses, so she had obviously given up on going. She didn't say a word. She only stared at him. That was the worst of the possibilities the bishop had considered.

"Dale and Sharon Kramer's boy has gone missing in action, Belle. I had to—"

"I heard about that already."

"Could we still go? We might miss the first act or something, but—"

"I called Adele half an hour ago. I told her we wouldn't be coming."

"How long does the play run?"

"It's only tonight and tomorrow night, and you told me already you can't go tomorrow."

The bishop nodded. It was true. There was a meeting tomorrow night that he really couldn't miss.

"Did you tell her what happened—why I couldn't make it?"

"Of course I did. And you know what she told me?"

Bishop Gledhill shook his head, but he actually had a pretty good idea.

"She said, 'I didn't ever expect you to come. Dad always puts everyone else ahead of his own family.'"

"Belle, that's not true. Adele always interprets everything that way. What was I supposed to say to Sharon Kramer? 'Your boy's in the bottom of the ocean, but I can't come out today—I've got a play to go to'?"

162

"Your *daughter's* play, Ron."

"I know. But the woman was going all to pieces."

Belle stood for a time with that hurt look in her eyes that the bishop hated more than anything, but more firmness than usual in the way her jaw was clamped. "Your daughter is missing in action, Ron. You better catch on to that one of these days. This meant a lot to her, that we had saved our ration points and had enough gasoline credits to drive all the way up there. I talked to her on the phone on Sunday, and I promised her we really would make it this time. But even then she was saying, 'I won't hold my breath. Dad will find something he has to do.'"

Bishop Gledhill hung his hat on the hall tree. "She looks for reasons to get her feelings hurt."

"I know she does. But she needed this tonight."

"Let's go right now. We can get there by intermission, at least. We can take her some flowers backstage, and I'll talk to her about what happened to Dale Junior."

"Ron, you already made your choice today, and she knows it. It was the right one for the Kramers, but it was the wrong one for Adele, and it's too late to pretend that it didn't happen." Belle stared at him for a few seconds, and then she said, "I packed a dinner for the drive. You can eat that. It's sitting on the kitchen table." Then she turned and walked to the back of the house, stepped into the bedroom, and shut the door.

Bishop Gledhill stood for a time, his hands in his pockets, and then he walked into the kitchen and sat down at the table. But he didn't eat anything. He was feeling what he felt so often: that he couldn't live up to all the requirements of everyone who needed him.

*   *   *   *   *

On Friday evening, Lamar, Jeff Jones's cousin, took Whisper out on her first date since Andy had left. He drove her to Fillmore in his pickup truck, where they went to a church dance. He was a year younger than

Whisper and clearly nervous around her. He was quiet, and not very interesting when he did talk, but he danced pretty well. He had a fun group of friends, so his own quiet manner didn't seem that much of a problem. But after the dance, back in the truck and driving out across the desert, neither he nor Whisper could come up with much of anything to say to each other. Finally, Whisper said, "You have a nice group of friends."

"Yeah, they're pretty good. But most of my close friends are in the war. Two of those guys there tonight—Freddy and Gerald—both came back wounded. That's why Gerald limps."

"He told me that." Whisper had danced with all the boys in the group, and she had learned a little about each.

"The other guys are all like me—on deferment so we can keep our farms going. But I just can't do that much longer."

"What do you mean?"

"I can't stand the way people look at me—like I'm some kind of yellowbelly, here at home when their sons are gone." He had had trouble looking at Whisper all evening, but he was glancing now, as though he wanted reassurance.

"But we have to feed the troops," Whisper said. "You're doing your part for the war effort."

"Sure. That's what my dad always says, and it's hard to get farm help, but I think he just wants to keep me from leaving, and I don't feel right about that. He has a weak heart, he says, and can't work out in the sun all day. That's all well and good for him—but no one stares at *him* when he walks down the street."

"I think if you can stay home, you should. You ought to be happy you've got a good reason."

"That's not how I think about it. I want to join the navy, or maybe the marines, and fight in the Pacific. I've put my dad on warning. I'm not waiting much longer before I go in and sign up."

It was a warm evening. Lamar and Whisper had cracked the windows, just to let a little air into the truck, but the air was rushing, rattling the windows and seeming to shake the whole truck. It was an old Ford with faded paint and worn-out seat covers. It smelled like dirt and manure. But all that was what Whisper expected, was used to. She knew Lamar was like her—from a family that had scratched its way through the Depression and was doing only a little better now, with the government buying up beef and the prices better. The truth was, Andy's family made her feel uncomfortable at times, simply because they were accustomed to having more. She always wished, whenever Andy was home, that she were able to buy a few more clothes, so she wouldn't have to wear the same things night after night. She actually could have had a little more for herself from her wages at the bank, but she helped her parents by paying rent and buying some of the groceries.

"I just think everyone should give what they can to get us through this war," Whisper said. "In your case, raising alfalfa and feeding cattle is what you're expected to do. The draft board wouldn't give you a deferment if they didn't think so. I have a cousin in Ogden who works for the railroad. He has friends who work at that defense depot up there. They all have deferments."

"That's fine. Maybe that's what they want. But I don't want to tell my kids someday that while everyone else was fighting, I was hiding out on my farm. Besides, I want to see a few things. The farthest I've been away from here was up to Salt Lake, and I've only been there twice."

"That I do understand. I've thought of joining the WACs or something like that, but my dad won't even talk to me about it."

Lamar laughed and shook his head. He was holding the steering wheel with one hand, leaning half against the door, even turned a little. He was going pretty fast, too, and that worried Whisper. His talk about going off to war seemed to be bringing out his confidence. "See, my dad is exactly like yours," he said. "I don't think he's so worried that I'll get shot as much as he is about me being in the service. He thinks I'll start to smoke and swear and run around with women. I tell him I could do that right in Fillmore if that's what I wanted to do, but he says it's different out there in the world. I tell him, 'Well, if it is, you must not trust me very much. I guess I won't forget everything I've been taught the first time I leave this valley.'"

Whisper listened to the buzz of the tires, the vibrations in the car, and she looked out at the blacktop, lit just ahead. It seemed like all of life was that way now—a long path she couldn't see the end of. She didn't blame Lamar for wanting to get away. "What about after the war?" she asked. "What do you want to do then?"

"Dad wants me to have the farm. My brothers don't care a thing about being farmers, but it's what I know, and it's what I'll probably do. That's the funny part. I want to get away, but then I want to come back. I guess I just want to see a few things before I settle down here forever."

"Sometimes I think I'd like to move to Salt Lake, or maybe California. Things are so much the same all the time here. I'd like to know what other places are like."

"Sure. But I still think I would always want to come back, somewhere around here."

"I guess maybe I would too, but I'd like to try something else, just so I could compare."

There was a long silence, and Whisper realized she had said the wrong thing. It was almost as though they were discussing the possibility of meshing their lives, but she hadn't meant that at all. Her future probably was here, but it was with Andy. Still, she knew for sure what Lamar was thinking when he said, after a moment, "I want to settle down here and raise a nice family. That's my goal in life: run the farm, marry a beautiful girl, and just be happy with her, raising kids and taking them out hunting and fishing and things like that."

He had glanced at her, sort of nodded, when he had said "beautiful," and Whisper had known immediately it was time to change the subject. But she wondered. Maybe Lamar wouldn't be so bad. Maybe she had made a mistake to attach her heart to one idea: having Andy. He was out there in the world, seeing pretty girls, meeting people who had been places and knew things. He was probably laughing about Whisper now, telling his army buddies that he had had a girlfriend back home, but she was just a country girl who hadn't been to college or anything else. Whisper had been reading lots of books lately—anything that looked interesting or worthwhile at the public library or borrowed from friends in town. Somehow, when Andy came home, she had to show him that she wasn't stupid, that she did know a few things. She liked that Lamar would accept her without worrying what she had read, but that was just the problem. She wouldn't grow an inch if she settled for someone like him.

"You know what I said about a beautiful girl? About marrying one?"

"Yes."

"Well, I don't mean just beautiful on the outside, and all that. I mean a wonderful girl in every way."

Whisper didn't say a word.

"You're the prettiest girl I've ever seen, and good as gold too."

"Well, that's nice of you to say." And then she changed the subject. She didn't want him to say another word of that kind. He knew all about Andy, and he ought to know better than to think he could make her forget him. But she did wonder, what if Andy really had forgotten her already? What would she think of Lamar if Andy weren't filling her head all the time?

CHAPTER 11

ANDY AND RAUL were sitting at a little table in the Bertrands' attic. They had set up their radio, and Raul was sending a coded message to London. This was only their second broadcast even though it was October now and they had been in France almost a month. They had collected some general information about local railroad activity and some solid estimates of troop strength in the area. They still had much to learn, but they had so far stayed close to the farm most of the time, keeping to their cover story as hardworking farm laborers. Their intelligence was coming mostly from members of their Resistance network.

Since there were so many German troops in the area, Andy was well aware that security would be tight. Radio signals would surely be monitored by Gestapo anti-espionage units. That meant that broadcasts had to be carefully worded, made as brief as possible, so that Raul would not be on the air long enough to allow their position to be traced. Andy and Raul's cover story was plausible, but the presence of two young men in the area, strangers, could still raise questions. The Germans were gathering up young men at an increasing rate and sending them off to Germany to work. Andy had a doctor's statement that he was recovering from tuberculosis. That tended to be an effective ruse, since German soldiers were frightened of tuberculosis and wanted nothing to do with it. The doctor's statement would also be helpful if Andy needed to travel, but if a Gestapo agent knew the whole story, that he was hired as a farm laborer, the illness may seem to contradict the idea that he had been hired to do strenuous work. "We'll tell them we need any help we can get," Felix had told Andy, but the idea of holding to such a story under interrogation was frightening.

Raul had been on the radio for twelve minutes, according to Andy's watch, when a rapping noise sounded on the attic door. "Detection truck," Francette called.

Andy jumped to his feet, almost in a panic. They had to get out. Detection trucks could pick up radio signals. Operators in the trucks used a triangulation method to locate the origin of the signal. If the truck could be seen on the road, heading toward the house, that didn't necessarily mean that the operators had an exact bead on them—but it wouldn't take long before they did.

Raul shut off the radio immediately and closed it into a valise. Andy was already pulling down the antenna, which had been sticking out through a little window in the attic. In a case like this, the plan was to gather up the radio and code books quickly and get out. Their escape route was through the back door, across a little pasture, and into the woods. From there, they were supposed to make their way to another safe house. They had practiced the maneuver several times and knew the way well.

Andy hid a few papers under some junk in the attic—information he had noted and included in the broadcast. These were things he didn't want on him if caught. He and Raul lifted the door and hurried down the ladder.

"Hurry," Francette said. "The truck has stopped by the farm down the road, but they'll surely search our house as well. They must know that they're close."

"Search the attic again," Andy said. "Hide anything we left."

"Do they know you have two laborers here? Maybe we shouldn't run." Andy was amazed at how calm Raul sounded.

"No," Francette said. "Our neighbors know. But I doubt the Germans have heard the story."

So Andy and Raul headed out the back door and ran to the rock fence at the back of the property. Raul put one hand on the fence and leaped over, radio in hand. Andy couldn't do that, his shoulder still not entirely healed, but he scrambled onto the wall and then dropped to the other side. In another few strides, they were into the woods and out of sight. They walked after that, and Andy felt less awkward in the heavy clogs he wore. He kept listening but heard nothing. He had no idea whether the truck had reached the farm.

They walked the mile or so through the woods, then sat and watched their new safe house before approaching. Andy and Raul knew the name of the family—Granet—but they weren't certain whether they had met anyone from the house. Only code names had been used at circuit meetings. What Andy knew was that someone could be visiting the house, or perhaps the family had laborers themselves. He didn't want to approach until he felt sure there was no chance of raising suspicions.

The house was in a pretty little glen, just over a hill from the Bertrands' farm. The fall colors, yellow and rust, were beginning to appear along the hillside, and in the valley below a couple of bronze-colored cows were grazing. The house and barn and even the sheds were built of dark brick, like the Bertrand place. Everything looked old and firm, confident and calm. Andy hated the idea that he might be bringing trouble to the people who lived here, whoever they were. He wondered what might happen to the Bertrands if agents found suspicious papers in their house. He had never heard whether anything bad had happened to Roger and Micheline, who had hidden them at their first safe house. He was not sure whether any of the people in his circuit would tell him if something had gone wrong, but he had asked, and so far he was assured that things were all right with them. Still, it was hard to believe that none of these people would pay a price for their bravery.

Andy and Raul waited, thought of holding off until after dark, but then a man walked from the house to the barn, not far from where they were. "That's Pierre," Raul whispered. He was one of the men who had attended their meetings.

Andy had already recognized him, and also realized that he was Simone's father. That wasn't something he had bargained for. He didn't need her disdain. But Raul said, "Let's talk to him at the barn."

So the two left the woods, climbed over another rock fence, and crossed a soggy barnyard where a milk cow watched them without moving out of their way. Andy walked to the barn door, looked inside, waited a moment, and then stepped in. The light in the barn was shadowy and dim, and his eyes had to adjust. But then he saw "Pierre" pitching hay down to the ground from a door at the back of the loft. "Excuse me, Pierre," Andy whispered.

Pierre stopped immediately and turned around. "I'm sorry. My name is . . . ," he began to say, but then he seemed to recognize whom he was seeing. "What is it?" he asked.

"Our safe house has been compromised. We need to stay with you for a time."

"Were you followed?"

"No."

"Do you know that certainly?" He had begun to climb down the ladder from the loft.

"Yes. We waited a long time in the woods. A detection truck must have picked up our radio signal, but the operators were searching the neighborhood."

"That's very bad. But I doubt they'll search the farms on this side of the woods. You should be all right." He stood for a moment, seeming to consider, not looking so confident as he had tried to sound. He was a thin man, handsome in his way, with serious, thoughtful lines in his face. He was wearing bib overalls and a denim jacket, but he looked more like a teacher than a farmer. "Come," he finally said. "We'll put you in our attic for now. We may have to move you again soon."

"Shouldn't we stay here in the barn?" Andy asked.

"I think not. It's a long run to the trees, and in all this mud, you could be followed easily."

So Andy and Raul followed him into the house and scurried up the ladder to the attic. There were no chairs there, hardly room to sit down. There was a dormer, and Andy went to it and looked out, but it led onto the roof, with no way down the side of the house that he could see. He wished that his shoulder weren't injured. Lots of things would be easier if he had full use of his arms.

But after all the excitement and exertion, it was once again time to wait. And waiting was almost all Andy and Raul had done since arriving in France. Andy found that frustrating.

*   *   *   *   *

Five hours had passed and most of Andy's fear was gone—or at least the panic he had felt as he and Raul had made their getaway. But his anxiety never really left him, hadn't since he had landed in France. He wondered how thoroughly the Bertrand place might have been searched, if the Germans had come there, and whether Francette had sanitized the house adequately before the Gestapo arrived. If agents were on to the idea that someone was operating in the area, maybe he and Raul should move on. But they had provided their contact in London with little information. If every OSS agent in danger panicked and got out, adequate intelligence would never get back to London. Still, Andy wondered how long he could take this kind of pressure. Nothing had gone smoothly since this mission had begun.

The attic was too warm; it smelled sour. The family had stored boxes in stacks, and all sorts of household items—pictures, old clothes, pots and pans. There wasn't really room to stretch out, but then, Andy wasn't sleepy anyway. Raul was able to curl up on his side and fall asleep, but Andy didn't try. He found some books and looked through them absently, but saw nothing he really wanted to read. It was early evening when he finally heard a gentle tap on the attic door. "Come down for dinner. There seems to be no search going on." This was a woman's voice, not Pierre's.

Andy shook Raul's shoulder, and then he opened the door in the attic floor. "Come on," he told Raul. "We're going down to eat."

"Good," Raul mumbled. He smiled, looking surprisingly childlike. He seemed to find all this intrigue entertaining—and he *did* love to eat, even though he never seemed to gain any weight.

When Andy reached the bottom of the ladder, he turned to see a woman in her late forties, a nice-looking woman, obviously Simone's mother: the same dark eyes and pretty skin. "You should call me Agnés," she said. "Pierre walked through the woods and talked to the Bertands. The Gestapo didn't search there. But it's better for now that you stay here. Our older sons are married. We have an extra bedroom now."

"That would be fine," Andy said. He liked the idea of a room with a window—a way to get out.

"Come. I fixed something for you. My husband is coming in now. I hope I can remember to call him Pierre."

The men followed Agnés into the kitchen. Pierre soon entered through the back door. "What an afternoon!" he said. "I feared every minute that the Gestapo might appear."

"But you said—"

"I know what I told you. But I never know what to expect from those people. I'm not sure they detected your signal at all. They might have been moving about with their truck, nothing more. We see them out here from time to time."

"I hope you're right," Andy said. "But they might have picked up the signal before we went off the air and just not had time to pinpoint exactly where we were. I suspect they'll be watching this area for a time."

"Yes. Perhaps. But God was with us this time." He pulled off his jacket, hung it by the door, and walked to the kitchen sink. "Let's eat something. Let's say a prayer of thanks. Are you praying men?"

"I was raised Catholic," Raul said. "We prayed in my home. But I . . . maybe you understand . . . haven't stayed too close to those things."

"You'll return now," Agnés said, laughing. "Danger can make a man religious." She looked at Andy. "Isn't that so, Armand?"

"I *am* religious. I do pray."

"You look like a good boy. You never worried your mother, did you?" Agnés had changed her clothes now, had put on a nicer dress—dark blue and made of a softer fabric. Andy could see, though, that it was well worn and a little too big for her. Like many of the French, even those living out on the land, she had probably lost weight since the war had started. She took off her white apron before she sat down at the table, and something in her manner seemed to say that she liked having company, liked the change, however dangerous it was.

Andy smiled. "I suppose I worried her a little at times. Not much. But I must admit, she assumed I was better than I really was."

"Is she French?"

"Yes."

"And Catholic, too, I suppose?"

"No."

Agnés nodded, looking curious. But Andy knew he had said enough.

"Sit down. Sit down. This is simple food—a farmer's dinner—but it will fill you up. I know you're hungry."

Andy and Raul sat at the table on one side, with Pierre and Agnés at the two ends. Another place was set, but nothing was said about that. The kitchen was warm and full of the aroma of Agnés's dinner. There were lamb chops on the table, potatoes and vegetables, and a dark loaf of bread. Pierre said a prayer, thanking God for safety and for the good food.

"This is too much," Raul said, after the prayer. "I know you don't eat like this every night."

"No, no. Of course not," Pierre said. "But we have vegetables from our garden. It's only the meat we don't eat often. Everything is in short supply now with the Germans taking our food from us. We know how to hide a few things from them, so we never go hungry, but that's not the case for people in the cities. Those people are barely getting by. They come here and beg us to sell them a few things, but we can't do it. We can go to prison if we do."

"Tell the truth," Agnés said. "You don't *sell* our food. You give it to them." She glanced at Andy and smiled.

"No. Not often. Now and then I've done this, when I know a man has hungry children, but it's not wise to take such chances."

"It's not wise to have us here either," Andy said. But he loved this kitchen, with the warmth from a big stove, the good smell, the white plastered walls. It was like home, and Agnés reminded him of his mother.

"Of course it's dangerous," Pierre said. "But the Germans have taken everything from us—not just our food. They've stolen *France* from us. We're not the same people. I don't blame those who make the best of things, who fear to resist. But someone has to fight back. Our family hasn't done a great deal so far, but we do a little, and we agreed to let our farm be a safe house."

"When *Les Boches* are finally defeated," Agnés said, "we want to be able to hold our heads up. Collaborators will be ashamed for the rest of their lives. There are so many who are placating the Germans, making a profit off them. Most of the German officers have French mistresses who live very nicely now. But I hate to think what will happen to them when the war ends."

"They won't—"

Everyone heard the front door open, and then, in a moment, looked up to see Simone enter the kitchen. "We have guests, as you see," Pierre said.

Andy stood and greeted her—a politeness he had learned at home.

Surprise had been obvious in Simone's face initially, but now she smiled. "What's this? Our saviors? Our brave secret agents, here to defeat the Germans all by themselves."

"Don't start again," Pierre said.

But Simone sounded playful more than hostile, and Andy had the feeling she liked having guests, the same as her mother. Maybe she liked the excitement. "Excuse me. Welcome to our home. I assume you're on the run or you wouldn't be here."

Andy decided to sit down. Raul laughed and said, "Actually, we wanted to see you. You always make us feel important."

"Just as you deserve." Simone walked to the table and sat down, but as she did, she glanced again at Andy. She was still smiling. She had eyes the color of dark honey, seemingly translucent. She was flushed a little, maybe from walking home, or probably from riding a bicycle. Andy had seen very few prettier women in his life, but he contrasted her in his mind with Whisper, whose beauty was homespun, who didn't toss around sarcastic comments.

Simone took a second glance, and this time she caught Andy looking at her. A full second passed, enough time to become aware of some mutual discovery, and then they looked away, but Andy felt his embarrassment.

"Our daughter works in town," Agnés said. "It's not easy for me to remember to call her Simone. That isn't her name, of course. But I'll try to be careful. I don't want to reveal her name."

The words ended the smiles, and the reality of their danger returned. Andy ate quietly. But Raul didn't seem as affected. He asked the family about the farm and about the history of the Resistance in the area. Pierre talked about the early days after the German victory in 1940, when everyone was still shocked by what had happened. It had taken time for reality to set in and for the French to understand what the occupation was going to mean. In the occupied zone, local police were ruled by the Germans, and local mayors had no choice but to cooperate. Fear itself ruled most of the population.

"Resistance groups, from what I know, are everywhere in France now," Pierre said. "But one network knows little or nothing of another. We're part of the Free French network. We think of Charles de Gaulle as our leader, but we work in isolation, hardly knowing what else is happening around the country. Here in this area, around Orléans, we've sometimes sabotaged railroad tracks or cut telephone wires, but we haven't had the weapons to do more than that."

"We haven't had the courage. That's what we haven't had," Simone said. "We should start killing *Les Boches,* one at a time."

"Yes, and you know what the Gestapo would do," Agnés said. "They've been known to kill ten locals for each man assassinated—or worse. We've heard of cases where they killed everyone in a village—man, woman, and child."

"Yes, and every time they do such a thing, they create more *Maquis,*" Simone said. "The Germans can't keep losing to the Russians in the east and hold enough troops here to keep us under control, not if we rise up in great enough numbers."

"It will happen," Pierre said. "And the Allies are coming before long. But we have to take one step at a time."

"Slow steps are just another form of collaboration." Simone took a longer look at Andy, as though she wanted a sign that he agreed, or maybe to assure herself that he didn't.

Andy decided not to respond. Nothing he could say would satisfy her. The fact was, her father was right. The Allies would be coming, and the Resistance would be committing suicide to push too hard, too soon.

But Raul said, "It wouldn't be wise to start killing now. Armand and I want to recruit more people to your *réseau,* bring in more arms, and then, as the invasion approaches, intensify the sabotage operations."

"Do you know what sabotage is?" Simone asked. "*Sabot* is the name for the shoes we wear here on the farm—wooden shoes like the ones you two are wearing. During strikes, workers tossed them into the machinery as a way to shut down factories that weren't fair to them. It took courage to do such a thing, but it was the right thing to do. You're asking us to wait until the fight is over before we join the battle. I see no courage in that. I want to throw my shoes in the machinery right now."

"Elise, you say that, but . . ." Pierre stopped, obviously realizing that he had said her name. He shook his head and went on. "When the time is right, we'll fight. Charles de Gaulle will announce the signal from London, and we'll know. Good soldiers must follow their generals."

"We could—"

"That's enough!" Agnés said. "We've had this conversation too many times."

Simone—Elise—shook her head in disgust, and once again she looked at Andy, as if to say, *I'll say no more, but you know what I think of you.*

Andy was worried. This young woman was dangerous. She could do something on her own and get caught. Maybe she wouldn't be so brave when Gestapo agents were beating and torturing her. This was not the time to say anything more, but someone needed to bring her under control.

After dinner Agnés said that she needed to do some rearranging to make a bedroom ready for her guests. "Simone," she said, and then looked at Andy and Raul as if to say, *You know her name now, but let's not use it.* "Could you sit with our friends while your father helps me? Can you be that good-natured for a few minutes?"

Simone smiled and looked at Raul. "I'm a very nice person. Ask anyone. I simply have a strong opinion or two." She was flirting with Raul, quite obviously, and Andy found himself a little annoyed by that.

The three walked into a little living room. Andy and Raul sat on a large old couch, deep maroon in color, and Simone sat in a big wooden rocking chair. She turned on a table radio, then tuned it to some band music. "So, my friends," she said, "what can we talk about other than war and sabotage and killing and the filthy *Boches?* Music, perhaps? Are you both good dancers?"

"I'm a *very* good dancer," Raul said. "In America, we do the jitterbug. Have you heard of that?"

"Yes. Of course. We see those things in the movies. But I choose not to dance." She looked toward Andy. "Am I supposed to know that you're Americans?"

"No. You were not supposed to know." Andy was looking at Raul. It was time for the conversation to take a less playful tone, he thought.

"But I did know," Simone said to Raul. "You two are not stiff enough to be Englishmen. I think Armand's name is actually *Gary,* or something of that kind. I think he's a cowboy at home. And you, Raul, you're French. Your parents moved to America and started a restaurant. You're the head chef."

"No, no. That's not true about me." Raul laughed. "But I think you might be right about Armand. He's from the West."

"That's quite enough," Andy told Raul.

"From the West, is he?" Simone said. "I think he's going to go home a war hero, and then become a cowboy in the moving pictures. Like Gary Cooper or Gene Autry." She pronounced the name *Zhan O-tree.*

Andy wanted to be as stern as that Englishman she had referred to, but he found himself smiling, so he decided to change the subject. "What kind of work do you do, Simone?"

"I work in a market. We have little to sell, and what we do have, we have to ration, so long lines of people wait all day long. I stand in one place the entire day and do nothing that makes me think or feel or care. I don't even feel sorry for the people any longer—partly because my emotions are dying from all the sameness in my life, and partly because I detest the people for acting like sheep, being herded about. But I shouldn't say such things. That's talk of the filthy *Boches* again, and I'm not allowed to bring that up."

"We don't blame you for how you feel," Andy said. "We wouldn't be here if we didn't want to defeat the Germans."

"Thank you." She took him in with her eyes. She surely knew that she was beautiful and knew what she did to men when she looked them over that way. Andy didn't like her self-awareness, but he had heard the sincerity in her frustration, and for the first time she had seemed a real person, not just an angry voice. "And what about you, Armand? Do you also like to dance the *zhitterbug?*"

"Not really. I'm not a very good dancer."

"But you dance?"

"Everyone dances in our country."

"With whom do you dance, Armand?"

"All the girls in my little town."

"A village, is it?"

"You could say that."

"In the West?"

"Yes. I'll say that much, but no more."

"And some pretty girl is waiting for you to come home, so she can marry you and bear your children."

It wasn't a question—more of a prediction. Andy was still smiling a little, but he offered no answer.

"I'm right. I can see it in your eyes. She's the prettiest girl in your vil-lage. She likes to cook and keep house, and she never talks of *killing* any-one. She has eyes as blue as the sky—and the sky, of course, is much bluer in America. She kisses you at her door when you take her home, but then she says, 'Just that one kiss. That's all we decent American girls allow. And I'm a *very good* girl.' Am I correct?"

Andy couldn't help grinning. He sat for a time, trying to think what to say.

"Please, tell me. Have I touched on the truth?"

"No. She has red hair. Green eyes. And freckles."

"Like Ava Gardner. But still, only one kiss?"

"Sometimes two."

"How wonderful for you. Two kisses. I think you miss those kisses now, so far from home."

Andy tried to stop smiling. This had to stop.

"I suppose there are no young women like me in America? I think you've never known a woman like me in your entire life."

"I know *I* haven't," Raul said. "But it's the way a woman ought to be, if you ask me."

Simone didn't look at Raul. She was still studying Andy. She was sit-ting with her slender legs crossed, her shoulders held high, knowing full well that her body was perfect. Her lips were parted just a little, almost as though she were whispering to him, *You'd trade that green-eyed girl for me right now and I know it.*

Andy had begun to take long, smooth breaths just so she wouldn't see that she was reaching him. "Western girls aren't afraid of much," he said. "You might be surprised if you met some of them."

"Yes, I can tell your young woman isn't afraid at all. Two kisses, not one. That's more than enough for a man like you, I'm certain."

Andy took one more long breath, pretended not to pay much attention to what he had just heard, then looked at Raul. "Maybe we should help Pierre and Agnés," he said. "They shouldn't have to work so hard just to get a room ready for us."

But this made Simone laugh.

CHAPTER 12

I T WAS WINTER now, January 1944, and Andy and Raul had been operating around Olivet for almost four months. Some things had gone very well. The two had blended in pretty well and were accepted in the village as local farm workers. They made an occasional excursion into Orléans and spotted troop insignias, estimated strength and movement of units, observed train and truck traffic, and picked up information about behavior of the German troops toward the locals. They had also built their Resistance circuit into a sizeable force. Recruiting had to be carefully handled, and Andy and Raul had little to do with the actual contacting of potential informants and saboteurs, but their core people had managed to reach inside factories and railroad yards, to find and enlist locals who worked for Germans directly, and to recruit some of the barbers, bartenders, waitresses, and prostitutes who served the Germans. Most valuable were live-in mistresses, who often acquired information no one else could. These women were hated by most French, and some of them, perhaps out of the guilt they felt, wanted to prove that they were still loyal to their country.

Andy knew that all this intelligence, gathered by dozens of OSS and British SOE agents across the country, was providing an overall picture for analysts in London, but he also knew that 1944 would surely be the year when the great invasion would have to begin. Some had expected the attack the year before, but now everyone knew, including the Germans, that the time was soon at hand. Andy had seen the buildup of troop strength in England, with hundreds of thousands of Americans arriving, and surely the Germans knew about that. What Andy was also sensing from brief communications with headquarters was that it would soon be time to step up the intelligence work and the acts of sabotage. Andy and Raul had developed a plan to slow train traffic through the Orléans area when the invasion came.

Germans were bolstering their defenses on the French coastline, but they couldn't weaken their control over the cities and towns and let Resistance groups gain power with locals. Therefore, they were tightening security around their camps, making ever more harsh demands on local leaders, and retaliating viciously against any acts of belligerence. Undercover groups were continuing to restrain themselves, for now, but when the invasion started, the Germans would have to rush troops to the focal point of the attack. If those troops were slowed by several days in reaching the front, and if lines of communication could be disrupted, time could be bought for the Allies to gain a foothold, and once that western front was opened, the war, in all probability, could be won.

In the fall of 1941, Hitler had seemed on the edge of taking Russia, but since that time, Russia had been steadily pushing the Germans back toward the homeland, and all the while Stalin had been pleading, sometimes demanding, that the Allies open up a second front to relieve the Russians from carrying most of the fight. Hitler, it appeared, would be overwhelmed if he had to fight an equally powerful enemy from the west. Andy knew that once the Germans had to deal with an attacking military force, the *Maquis* would be able to fight more openly, so he hoped that time would come soon.

Andy and Raul knew they also needed an occasional show of strength to demonstrate to the French people that Resistance groups were gaining in power and numbers. Too many acts of sabotage could bring down retribution from the Germans and set back the development of their *réseau,* but now and then the people had to know that the *Maquis* were at work, biting at the hamstrings of the German jackals. The Resistance people themselves needed to strike now and then as well, just to know that they were more than an intelligence organization, that they were fighters.

And of course, no one had pushed harder for such actions than Simone. Andy and Raul had not stayed at Simone's house long before they had returned to the Bertrands' farm. But Andy saw Simone at meetings, and sometimes he and Raul sneaked through the woods with their radio equipment and made their broadcast to London from Pierre and Agnés's farm. It wasn't safe to establish any sort of pattern with their radio transmissions, so using another site was only wise. But always, when Andy and Raul visited, Simone wanted to know when the fight would begin. Andy became more anxious to strike a blow, but he wasn't sure how much of his motivation was a desire to feel that he was a man in Simone's eyes, not the frightened boy she accused him of being.

One night that winter, after he and Raul had made their radio report, they lingered and chatted with the family. After a time Simone said that she needed to go to the barn for something and wondered if Andy was brave enough to go with her "for protection." All this was said playfully, and certainly with some flirtation, but Andy took the challenge and walked to the barn with her. It was cold outside, but a little warmer in the barn. Once there, Simone seemed to have little purpose, although she did throw the milk cow a little hay. She used a wooden pitchfork, showing that she had grown up around animals and certainly knew how to pitch hay, but she leaned on the handle after a time and looked at Andy. "What will you do when you go back to America?" she asked.

Andy pushed his hands into the pockets of his trousers. All this felt natural to him, the fecund smell of the animals, the hay, Simone acting more like a farm girl than she ever had before. She had carried a lantern with her and hung it on a post, and the light fell across her face now, shadowing her eyes. He looked back at her more directly than he usually did, feeling less self-conscious. She was wearing a simple farm dress, dark, with no collar, but fitted from the waist up. She had walked out into the cold without a coat, and he could see the glow of her skin at her neckline, could see her chest slowly rising and falling as she was perhaps a little out of breath after the effort with the pitchfork.

"I'm not sure what I'm going to do. Home seems distant to me now." He wasn't supposed to answer her questions, but more than that, he now had trouble thinking about his old life. He hardly knew how to think about the future. "I'll go back to my little town. That's the only thing I'm sure of."

"You studied at a university before you came here, didn't you?"

"Yes. But I've never told you that."

"Still, it's clear to me."

He watched her and forgot to respond for a moment. It was difficult for him to think of anything but her skin, the curves of her cheek and neck, shadowed in the lamplight. She was breathing more gently now, but he seemed to feel the pulse of her, a kind of rhythm that was also running through him. "I might decide to be a farmer," he said, aware that he had to say something, to stop looking at her that way.

"You're not a farmer. And you're not an Armand. It's a comical name for you."

"Why?"

"Raul is French, but you're not. You're an American boy, completely."

"My father was in France in the first war. He met my mother here and took her back with him to America. I'm half French."

Andy wondered what implications she might find in his words. He knew he was saying things with his eyes and with a hint of a smile that he couldn't seem to hold back. Sometimes he half liked Simone, and sometimes he didn't like her at all, but this was not about liking. It had more to do with danger. She was just so beautiful.

Simone smiled a little too. "I've done enough farming in my life already," she said, as if to say, *You won't entice me to America by saying you're a farmer.*

"My father owns a bank," Andy said. "It could be mine someday, if that's what I choose to do." It was so stupid, implying some sort of counter offer; Andy had to stop this.

"A banker? Such an important man. And will you be very rich someday?"

"I could try, I suppose. I've never had much interest in money."

"What *are* you interested in?"

"A quiet life."

"And that pretty girl with freckles on her face?"

"You remembered that."

"Oh, yes. Green eyes and freckles, you said. Is she *very* pretty?" But they both knew the real question: *Is she as pretty as I am?*

Andy didn't answer. He wasn't sure of the answer at the moment. He enjoyed a few more breaths, both his and hers, and then he decided to stop this. He looked away.

"Tell me your name," Simone said.

"No."

"Please. You can tell me. I don't want to think of you as Armand."

"You might be a spy. A collaborationist. I can't trust you." He felt himself returning to their game. He actually took a little step toward her.

Simone leaned the pitchfork against the wall of the barn, pulled down the lantern, then walked past him, her shoulder brushing his arm as she passed. She walked to the door without a word, and Andy thought she was heading back to the house. But at the barn door she stopped and turned around, and he walked closer to her than he should have. "Tell me," she said. "I want to know."

She took a bigger breath. He felt himself reach deeper for his own air. She was waiting, and he wasn't sure what he was going to do. "Andy," he finally said, and stepped back.

But the name made her laugh.

"It's André, really. French. But even my mother calls me Andy."

"It's perfect," she said. "You're French but not French. Nothing's more American than *An-dee*—like Andy Hardy, in the movies. It's a silly name, if you want my opinion."

"I don't want your opinion."

"But you're not André any more than you're Armand. I'll have to call you Andy."

"Don't ever use that name."

"I won't *say* your name. But now I'll have a name to use when I think of you."

"You mean you think of me sometimes?"

Now he really had flirted, and they both knew it. He saw the satisfaction appear in Simone's eyes. "Whenever I ask myself why our circuit never *fights*, that's when I think of you. Now I'll know it's *Andy* who's afraid, not Armand. And that will sound as it should. It's such a little boy's name." She turned then and walked from the barn. Andy was left standing there, surprisingly shamed.

And maybe that had something to do with what happened over the next few days. He and Raul developed a plan to break into an Orléans railroad yard. A rail company employee who had been recruited to their Resistance circuit agreed to leave a gate unlocked to get them inside the yard. Andy had received a parachute drop of weapons and ammunition. As part of his supplies, he had ordered light-sensing detonators that could be attached, along with explosives, to the underside of a train engine. When the train passed into a tunnel and the light suddenly failed, the sensor would set off the explosives and disable the locomotive. A disabled train inside a tunnel would be a major predicament for the

Germans. The train route would be blocked for days as the wreckage was cleared and the tracks repaired.

Andy and Raul planned to take two local underground men with them so that the circuit could share in the glory at the next meeting. Maybe Simone was the most vocal, but all the local *Maquisards* needed to know that Andy and Raul weren't afraid to act.

So on a cold night, when German guards were likely to seek out the warmth of their guard station, Andy and Raul—along with two young men code-named Gautier and Luc—stepped through the unlocked gate and moved it back into place. They were wearing black, and they had darkened their faces. Andy and Raul had received a tip from their insider that a large freight train carrying supplies and ammunition to German troops was sitting on track number four. It was mostly loaded and would be departing in the morning. The matter was actually quite simple: get to the train, attach the device, which could be done in less than a minute, and get out. The problem, of course, was that German guards with flashlights occasionally walked through the train yard, and they carried automatic weapons. Because nothing had happened in the yard for a long time, the guards were said to be lax, and they would sit and talk, even sleep, in the guard station, but one never knew when they would decide to have a look around.

It was almost four in the morning now, and Andy hoped that the guards were dulled by the cold and the lateness, half awake if not asleep—certainly not prowling about. Andy crouched and ran along the fence, his three friends behind him. At a spot far from the guard station, he ran to a train, climbed over the coupling between two freight cars, then looked to see whether anyone was moving about. He waited for a minute or so, listened carefully, and then moved across two empty tracks to track number four. He let his team catch up, alarmed to hear how loud their footsteps were in the cinders around and between the tracks. He huddled close to the others and whispered, "We're making too much noise. I'm going to move very slowly along the train toward the locomotive. Follow me, but take careful steps. Keep your knives ready."

Andy was carrying a pistol on his belt, but it was nothing he wanted to use. If he fired the weapon he would have guards running at him from all directions. So he carried his double-edged stiletto at the ready, and he moved with careful steps, setting his foot each time and then slowly shifting his weight. The only trouble was, the longer he and his partners were in the yard, the more likely it was that a guard might come by on patrol, so he picked up his pace slightly and made it to the coal car behind the engine.

"I'll move to the other side of the engine," Andy whispered to the others. "Raul and I will keep watch, one on each side. Once I'm in place, Gautier and Luc, you move under the locomotive and work as fast as you can. If I tap on the engine with my knife handle, stop everything and hold still."

Gautier and Luc knew the procedure, and they had practiced attaching the device without light. Andy climbed over another coupling and then moved along the side of the locomotive. He soon heard the subtle crunch in the cinders as the other men moved into position. He hoped they hadn't been loud enough to alert anyone. He still held out hope that all the guards were in their station, sound asleep.

But almost immediately Andy saw a shadow moving toward him on the platform parallel with the train and one track over. Andy gave a quick tap, and everything under the train fell silent. The guard, or whoever it was, wasn't walking fast, wasn't even using his flashlight, so it seemed unlikely that he had heard anything. But he kept coming, easier to see now as he passed the guard station, which was casting some light from a little window.

Andy saw the silhouette of the distinctive German helmet, even saw the barrel of a rifle, but the rifle was slung over the man's shoulder, not ready. Andy hoped that if he remained silent, crouched low alongside the engine, the man would pass on by. That seemed to be happening until the guard drew close, but then he stopped. Andy was holding his face low, but he could see the man's legs out of the corner of his eye. Everything held for a moment and Andy tried to think what he could do if the guard climbed down from the platform.

Suddenly a light flashed, and for a moment Andy thought the guard had turned on his flashlight. Actually, he had only struck a match to light a cigarette, but in that instant, Andy's muscles had reacted and he had jerked just a little. Now he looked up enough to see that the guard hadn't used the match, hadn't lit his cigarette. He was holding still, probably staring down at Andy and wondering what it was he had seen. Andy expected the flashlight to come out next, and he thought of making a move, but he couldn't get to the man and kill him without making a lot of noise. He gambled, decided to wait. Maybe the guard didn't have a flashlight with him. But would he light another match?

The guard reversed himself and walked back the way he had come, moving faster now. He was going for help, perhaps, or maybe going back for a flashlight. Andy waited a few seconds and then he whispered, "We've got to get out of here." He heard the men scramble out from under the train, and while they did, he waited and watched. The guard had heard them too. He had stopped and turned around. Andy knew at any moment he would yell for a backup, and so Andy, on impulse, called out in French, "Guard, can you help me?"

"Who is it? What are you doing there?"

"I'm supposed to start these repairs, early, but the door to the locomotive is locked up tight."

"You shouldn't be working now. How did you get in here?"

But he was walking back along the platform. "It's what they told me to do," Andy said.

"This is not right." He was getting close now. "Come up out of there."

"I only do what I'm told," Andy mumbled, trying to assume some of the peasant manner he was learning. He walked to a ladder, held the knife low as he climbed to the platform, then slowly approached the guard, as if reticent, his head down. Suddenly he released himself like a spring and drove the knife upward, under the man's ribs. The guard let out a grunt of surprise; by then, Andy had jerked the knife back and driven it in a second time. He was on the man as he crumpled, grabbing at his throat with one hand and ramming the knife into his ribs one more time. As the man hit the platform, Andy found his mouth, gripped it, and waited for a long, last breath. Then he rolled the man off the platform. His body thumped like a bag of grain in the cinders below, and then everything was silent.

Andy wanted to run, but he didn't. He climbed down from the platform, returned to the locomotive, climbed under, and found the explosive device on the ground. He attached it to the train in a few easy motions, and then he climbed out and hurried back across the tracks. Outside the fence he found Raul and the other men waiting by a ditch, where they had all agreed to meet if they were separated.

"What happened?" Raul asked.

"I killed the guard. I attached the device. Someone will probably find it, once they discover the body, but it was worth a try."

"You really killed him? Are you sure?"

"Oh, yes."

Andy felt a slap on his shoulder. "That's good. That's one for us," Luc said.

"Yes. Now let's go."

* * * * *

They crawled into the back of an old charcoal-powered truck Gautier drove to make deliveries of produce from local farms. He was often seen on these roads, so he could move about without suspicion. He covered the other men with canvas and drove them over the bridge that crossed the Loire River, back to Olivet. It was getting light when Andy and Raul made it back to the Bertrand farm.

At first Andy worried about being stopped and inspected. When that didn't happen, he wondered about the explosive device, whether anyone would find it and remove it. He hoped that it wouldn't be spotted and that the sabotage would work. But something else was beginning to fill his head—more a sensation than a thought. He hadn't known the human body could be penetrated so easily. He kept feeling the knife slide into the man, through the guard's wool coat and through his skin, his flesh. But it had slipped in softly, smoothly, with more ease than into the straw-filled dummies back at Camp X. Andy hadn't hesitated. He had merely done what he had been trained to do, and in only a few seconds it had all been finished.

It didn't take much to die.

The guard had appeared much older than Andy, maybe forty or more. As he had struck, Andy had seen the outline of a plump cheek. A thick hand had flashed into view, then had dropped. That was all. Fairbairn had made the Germans seem smarter, more dangerous. This guard had been a small man, plump and comfortable, not much of a warrior at all. And in a few seconds, dead.

Andy and Raul cleaned the black off their faces and put on their work clothes. They ate breakfast with the Bertrands and then went about their day. They didn't report their actions to London for a few days. After a killing of this kind, and the possible discovery of an explosive device, local Gestapo agents would be on high alert and probably watching for radio traffic.

Later that week Andy did get word that a train had exploded in a tunnel west of Orléans. It was something to report to their Resistance circuit and to OSS leaders. Andy felt good about the success—finally felt part of the war in a real way.

Still, a hundred times a day, he heard the sound as the knife cut through the wool, felt the sensation up his lower arm as the blade glided through the man's fat and flesh. He wasn't sorry he had done it, but aware—every minute of the day, aware. He had killed a human being with his hands and rolled him into the cinders. Then he had calmly placed the sensor under the locomotive and walked away. He was a soldier now. He hadn't panicked when the time had come. He had done what he had to do, just as he had once promised Chambers that he could do.

But everything stayed in Andy's mind. The guard had grunted and gasped, and he had left his last breath on Andy's hand. Andy found himself washing carefully every day. He had found a bit of blood on his coat sleeve when he had come back to the farm—just two small spots. It was an old, ugly coat, with lots of stains on it, and these dark spots were hardly different from dozens of others on the frayed edge of his sleeve. Still, he rubbed dirt into them, and once tried to wash the stuff out with hot water, but the spots wouldn't come out.

Andy waited another week, and then he asked some of the Resistance leaders from around the Orléans area to meet at Pierre's farm. It was dangerous to assemble. People had to find excuses to be moving about in the countryside. On the other hand, members of the *Maquis* needed to get ready for the invasion. He needed to establish a better system of circulating messages, and that was one of the things he wanted to discuss with the leaders so they could respond quickly when the coded signal for action came from England.

What he found was that word about the destroyed locomotive had made its way through the system. The leaders knew that Andy had killed a guard, and they were well aware that the Gestapo had stepped up its spot checks for papers around the railroad yard and factories. More guards were stationed around the facilities, and one *Maquisard* had been caught in a neighborhood with no explanation for his presence there. He had actually been delivering a handgun to a new member and had been able to ditch it before being interrogated, but he had finally had to claim he was selling black-market goods as a way of giving the Gestapo something they could pin on him. He had spent some nights in jail, but he hadn't given up any information. Still, this news brought some solemnity to the meeting. Simone was at the meeting because it was at her house, but even she seemed to sense that the fight was beginning. She said she liked that, but Andy could see some hint of concern in her eyes—a reaction he hadn't expected.

After the meeting Andy and Raul waited as the leaders slipped out through the wooded areas one at a time and found their way to hidden bicycles or vehicles to make their trips home. Simone sat down next to Andy on the living room couch. There were others in the room, but she spoke quietly to him. "So—Andy—they tell me you killed a man."

"Don't call me that."

She laughed. "I didn't think you could do it."

"What? Kill? That's what I came to do."

"I'm glad you figured that out."

But Andy found no humor in this. He was tired of her games. Nothing seemed the same to him these days. He kept trying to think of home, of the desert and football and going to church with his family. But it all seemed as though he had made up his own history, that none of it had ever existed.

He thought of church sometimes—of Sunday School and the things he had been taught there. But it was hard to remember what he had thought then, what he had felt, hard to fit this new reality with the one he had known back then. The guard had had stubby little fingers. Andy saw them sometimes when he shut his eyes—just a quick image as the man's hand had flown up, then dropped. It was a strange thing to remember, but the image was easier to recall, seemingly more pressing, than anything he could remember back in Delta.

"Did the guard discover you planting the device?"

"Not exactly."

"Why did you kill him?"

"He walked close to us. I think he spotted me. He was going back to get help. Or at least I thought he was. So I called him back and I killed him."

"Called him back?"

"I made him think I worked for the railroad."

She was looking at him curiously. "This bothers you, doesn't it?"

"No. I had no choice."

"But you're too kind, too nice. It's hurt you to take a life."

"No. It was easy. I don't know how to tell you how easy it was."

She stared at him for several seconds. "Walk outside with me," she said.

Andy got up, almost as though he had been commanded. He wasn't actually feeling much for Simone tonight, was hardly aware of her prettiness, but he thought he knew what she wanted.

Outside, Simone held his hand and led him back to the barn, where it was dark this time, without a lantern. She stopped and turned to him, took hold of his other hand. "Andy, it's all right. It's what we have to do."

"It was easy. I caught him by surprise."

"It's all right, Andy. You had to do it."

"I know. I don't regret it."

But now she was wrapping her arms around him, kissing him, and he kissed her back. He pressed against her, kissed her more passionately than he had ever kissed Whisper. Then she stepped back, took hold of his hand, and began pulling him down to the hay. He started to go with her and then stopped. "No," he said. "I can't do that."

"What? Why not? Because of her?"

"I don't know."

"Andy, it doesn't matter. You can go back to her. Let's just take this pleasure. We might all be dead before much longer."

"I can't." But he wanted to. And he didn't know exactly what held him back. He only knew that too many things had changed lately; he had to keep hold of some part of himself.

CHAPTER 13

FLIP HADN'T SEEN Tom all winter, not since they had brought in the hay the previous fall. But it was planting time now, and Tom had agreed to come back to help put in a big vegetable garden at the home in town and then to plant a few acres of corn at the farm. It was an April day and the weather had finally warmed some; the sky was broken up by some lumpy clouds but bluer than it had been in a long time. It was still fairly cold, but Flip loved being outside, and he really liked having Tom around again. Tom would soon be graduating, but he said that it was not a big problem to get away from the camp high school when he wanted to. So he rode into town on the camp truck nearly every day, sometimes in the morning but usually early in the afternoon. Flip joined him most days when he got home from school.

Tom had plowed the garden with the little tractor the bishop kept in town, and then he and Flip had run strings and hoed furrows. They were planting a row of peas late one afternoon when Flip looked up to see a man approach, walking tentatively, looking about. He stopped and looked at Flip, and Flip knew the whole story immediately. The man was a hobo, dressed in overalls and a dirty army coat that looked a little too heavy for the weather now. There were still some of these men around, just not so many as there had been before the war. They rode the railroads, jumping open rail cars, sometimes piling off in a place like Delta to look for food. The Gledhills didn't live all that close to the rail line, but Flip knew what a lot of people in town told the men: "Walk on over to the white house on the corner, two streets from here. The bishop's wife will feed anyone." Some of the men who showed up reported that was what they had been told. And it was true. Belle baked extra bread once a week, and she kept baloney and cheese around. When the men knocked at her back door, she made them sandwiches. She had even been known to brew coffee for them when that was what they said they wanted. Bishop Gledhill laughed about the coffee and was glad that Belle would take the time to feed people, but he did have one rule. He didn't want them coming into the house when Belle was there alone. He doubted that any of them would cause trouble, but he also knew that Belle was just a little too trusting. Flip always noticed that she talked to them like they were her neighbors, not "bums."

"Someone said I might be able to get something to eat here," the man said as Flip walked toward him. He looked a decent sort, fairly clean except for his battered coat and a muddy pair of work boots that were ripped open in some of the seams. He had shaved within the last few days, though, and somewhere along the way had washed his hands and face. He sounded like a country boy, maybe even Southern.

"Step onto that porch and knock on the back door. My mom will give you something."

"Much obliged," the man said, and he pinched a shabby felt hat, raised it off his head, then set it back down.

Flip paid little attention after that, but a while later he glanced up and saw that the man was sitting on the back step, eating a sandwich. Next to him on the step were another white-bread sandwich, an apple, and a glass of water, all laid out on a cloth napkin. He was making short work of it all, chewing hard.

The sun was still going down fairly early these days, and the light was waning now, the red of the sunset almost gone. Flip and Tom finished planting a row, Flip dropping seeds and Tom pushing dirt into the furrow with a hoe, and then they walked toward the shed behind the house, where they would leave their tools for the night. They were almost to the door of the shed when the man said, "Hey, what's going on around here?"

Flip looked over at him. "What?" he said.

"Is that a Jap you got with you?"

Flip couldn't think what to say for a moment.

"I sure hope he's a Chinaman, because you sure are treating him like he's some kind of cousin of yours."

"Take your sandwich and get out of here," Flip said. "You have no right to come on our property and talk like that."

"And what have you got? The right to love Japs?"

Flip started toward him, but Tom grabbed his arm. "Don't," he said, and he pulled Flip back. Then he walked on by, heading straight to the man. "Hi. My name's Tom Tanaka. I'm actually an American."

Tom held out his hand, but the man didn't respond. He had gotten up when Flip had told him to leave, and now he gathered up his second sandwich and his apple.

"My parents moved to this country from Japan," Tom said. "Where did your family come from?"

"We ain't Japs, if that's what you mean."

"I suspect you're European. You look like you could be Scandinavian."

The man didn't seem to know what that meant. Either that, or he was confused by the whole conversation. He looked past Tom to Flip. "It ain't right. This here's the enemy. I'd rather shoot this little cuss than stand here and talk to him."

"Actually, I'm joining the army this summer," Tom said. "I'll be fighting for America. Why aren't you in the army? Are you 4-F for some reason? You look healthy enough to pack a rifle."

The man was already moving, and he kept right on going. Tom was laughing. "Don't let the guy bother you," he told Flip. "It's not worth it."

"You shouldn't have to put up with that kind of stuff," Flip said. And it really did bother him. Flip had missed Tom all winter, and he had enjoyed these days together. Flip had a few friends at school, but no one who could talk to him about the things Tom understood. He was always telling Flip how to handle high school next year, how to improve himself at sports, even what to say to girls. Flip had wished all his life that he'd had a brother a little closer to his own age.

He also knew what his friends would think if he ever admitted thinking that way about Tom. Flip and Cal had been helping each other out lately, collecting tin foil and combining it into a big ball. There was a contest coming up, sponsored by the county. The person who gathered the most foil for the war effort would win a savings bond worth $18.50, and worth $25.00 when it matured in ten years. But it was going to take a lot of tin foil, and the stuff was hard to accumulate, removing it from chewing gum wrappers and cigarette packs they found here and there. Neither one alone had much of a chance to win, so they had decided to put their collections together.

Cal had come over a few days before with a pocketful of foil to add to the ball Flip was keeping for them, and Cal had run into Tom working with Flip in the backyard. Tom had been friendly with him, asking him all about himself, but Cal had given quick answers and seemed nervous. The next day at school he'd said, "Flip, I don't know how you stand it, working with that guy. He tried to act like he was some old pal of mine."

"That's just how he is," Flip had told him. "He's friendly with everyone."

"Well, he oughta figure he's just lucky we don't spit in his face—not act like he's a regular guy."

Flip came close to telling Cal that he *was* a regular guy, but instead, he said, "He wants to join the army and fight for America. And he's going to do it as soon as he turns eighteen."

"Yeah, sure, that's what he says."

"No. He means it. He's going to do it, too."

Cal had taken a long look at Flip, and then had let the whole matter drop, but a couple of days later, Charlie Nash saw Flip in the hall before school and said, "Hey, Flip, Cal tells me you're startin' to love that Jap you work with. What's going on?"

"Lay off," Flip said. "All I told Cal was that the guy wants to join the army. And it's true."

"So what are you, buddies with him now?"

"No. Dad just hired him to work for us. There's nothing wrong with that." But later, Flip wished he had said something different, maybe, "He's a better guy than you, Charlie, if you want to know the truth."

*   *   *   *   *

Whisper was nervous. She had been trying for a week to work up the nerve to talk to Bishop Gledhill, but she had put it off. She knew she had to say something now, though; it was only fair to give him ample notice. So she stepped into his office just before it was time to close the bank on a March afternoon. "Mr. Gledhill," she said, "could I talk to you for a moment?" She usually called him "Bishop," but she thought it was more proper to call him "Mister" when she had a business matter to discuss.

"Sure, Whisper. Come in," Bishop Gledhill said. He pushed some paperwork away as though he were happy to do so, took his reading glasses off, and looked up at her. He was smiling, maybe because she had called him "Mister." But he must have seen her seriousness, because she watched his smile disappear. "Is everything all right?"

Whisper had not intended to cry. She had promised herself she wouldn't. But his question sounded far too affectionate. "Oh, Bishop," she said. "I don't know how to tell you this."

"Sit down. You can tell me anything."

She did sit down, and she pulled a handkerchief from her skirt pocket. She wiped her eyes and told herself she had to act more professional. "I've decided it might be best if I take a different job. Doctor Noorda needs someone to run his office, and I told him that I could do that for him."

She didn't want to look Bishop Gledhill in the eye, but she glanced now to see his reaction. He looked troubled more than upset, the lines in his forehead turning into creases. "Are you just thinking you need a change, or . . . is it something else?"

"A change would be good, I think. That's probably the most important thing."

He continued to watch her. "But not the only thing, apparently."

The heat from the furnace never seemed to make its way all the way back to this office. That didn't seem to bother Bishop Gledhill, but Whisper found herself shivering. She folded her arms tightly against her middle and looked past the bishop as she said, "Andy hasn't written me for a very long time, Bishop. I think he's changed his mind about me. It's going to get more and more awkward for me to work here if he's decided he doesn't want to marry me. I think it would be better if I worked somewhere else, so things won't get too difficult for both of us."

"But Whisper, he hasn't written to us either. You know what he said—that he wouldn't be able to."

"I know." She had to say the rest. "Bishop, I've been dating a fellow from Fillmore and—"

"Is that the Jones boy—Jeff's cousin?"

"Yes."

"So is something going to come of that?"

"I don't know. But it makes me uncomfortable to be going out with him, and him talking marriage, and me here every day, not sure what I ought to do."

"Whisper, that's not a problem for me. You do a wonderful job. I'll never find anyone as good. Every now and then I've thought I ought to hire Adele once she graduates, and the thought scares me half to death. I'd hate to think what she might do to this place." He chuckled. "But listen, maybe this is what's best for you. I'm sure you'd like working for Doc Noorda. You'd learn a lot. He's a little gruff sometimes, but you know that, and you'd probably sweeten him up a little. Could you give me a little time to try to find someone else?"

Whisper knew what he was doing. He was making things easy for her. He had concluded from what she had said that she was going to marry Lamar, and he was letting her escape. She almost wished that he would beg her to wait for Andy. The truth was, she had no idea how she felt about Lamar; she simply knew that she had to start taking his attentions seriously. "I wouldn't run out on you just like that," she said. "I told Dr. Noorda I couldn't start for him until I trained someone here."

For all his cheerfulness, there was always a well of sadness in Bishop Gledhill, maybe from all the burdens he carried. Whisper saw it now, the droop of his eyelids, the quiet in his eyes. "I guess there is one thing I want to say to you, Whisper." He nodded, as if to say, *Now, listen.* "Don't give up on my son too quickly. You know how much I want you in my family. I've already thought of you as my daughter for so long, it would be very hard to change my mind."

Now Whisper's tears came again. For a few seconds she almost gave in to what would be so much easier. She loved this job, the sense she had that she was in charge much of the time, and that she was needed. She looked at the desk and tried to think what to say.

"Do you want to take a day or two to think the whole thing over?"

"No. Like you said, it would be good for me to learn something new. Dr. Noorda said I might want to go up to Salt Lake and learn nursing. I really should do something like that. He said that after a while he could maybe help me do that."

"So do you think that's something you would like to do—be a nurse?"

Actually, she hated the idea. She just wanted to have Andy, and she wanted to be a mother. But if she didn't find a husband, she needed to start thinking about having some sort of work she was trained to do. "Maybe. I'll see if I like working in a doctor's office. I guess nurses are always needed."

"Whisper, I don't quite understand." The bishop had been holding his glasses in his hand all this time, but now he set them down, as though he expected there was still more to talk about. "I'm not sure why you think Andy's lost interest in you."

"I didn't tell you everything, Bishop." She wiped her eyes and tried to get control of her voice. "When he wrote me last time, he said that he didn't want to tie me down. He said that I should consider dating other boys."

"Actually, I did know something about that. Flip mentioned it to me. But I know Andy, and I know darn well what he's up to. He's afraid he's going to get himself killed and leave you back here a widow without ever having gotten married. He was trying to do the right thing."

"That's what I try to tell myself, but I just wonder—maybe he's meeting other girls, and maybe he wishes he never promised me. His letter sort of sounded like that. He didn't say anything about still feeling the same about me."

The bishop smiled. "Now, listen to me. Andy may not be the brightest boy on this planet, but he's plenty smart. No guy in his right mind would tell *you* to kick a rock down the road."

The bishop sounded like Flip. Whisper loved both of them for their loyalty to her, but she wasn't at all sure they were right. They both liked her, but neither of them was wandering around the world looking at all the beautiful women out there.

"Let me ask you this," Bishop Gledhill said. "Are you starting to doubt whether Andy is the right man for you?"

"No. I'll never do that. But Lamar wants to get serious. So far I haven't let that happen, but someday I might have to look for someone else, and if I'm working here, it would be very hard." She wanted to tell the bishop that she had never so much as let Lamar kiss her, but she couldn't bring herself to tell him something quite that intimate. "I don't want to be an old maid, Bishop. I've always wanted a family."

"I know. And I can't speak for Andy, even though I think I know what he would say. And I can't promise he'll come home. I think he probably is in danger right now." He seemed to think that over, and then he added, "But if you need a change, don't let me talk you out of it. Just make your decision based on that—and not about our feeling awkward."

Whisper felt the pull again. She wanted to stay. She loved the bishop and Belle, and she loved Adele and dear Flip. She wanted to be part of their lives. But she could feel something happening, and no matter what Flip or the bishop said, she really believed that Andy would find some way to write to her if he still wanted to marry her. She had to make this break now.

"I think a change will be good," Whisper said.

"All right. But don't stay away from us, Whisper. We love you too much."

Whisper nodded, and she felt an emptiness settle into her chest. But she knew she had to do this.

*   *   *   *   *

Raul was in the Bertrands' attic broadcasting a message, and Andy was standing at the upstairs window, below the attic door, watching for the Gestapo detection truck. Suddenly he saw men rushing toward the house. "Raul, stop! We're in trouble." He pushed the attic door up, shutting Raul in, and he ran downstairs. He had to bluff these men somehow, keep them from searching the house.

But the sound of pounding was coming from the front and back of the house at the same time, and then Andy heard the crashing sound as someone smashed through the kitchen door in back—and a moment later, someone else bashed in the front door. Andy walked to the men who had come in through the kitchen. "What's wrong?" he asked. "What's going on?"

"What is your name?" a man demanded. He was a burly fellow in a leather coat and an officer's cap with an SS insignia in front. "Armand Lefranc," Andy said. "I work here for the Bertrands. They own the farm." He tried to use the dialect, sound like a peasant laborer.

"Search him," the officer commanded.

Two younger men wearing the same kind of long, leather coats grabbed Andy, spun him around, and slammed him face first against the kitchen wall. Andy turned his head and avoided getting his nose smashed, but the side of his head hit hard and he almost lost consciousness. The men jerked his denim jacket down and off, and then they ripped at his pockets. "Where are your papers?" one of them shouted at him.

"In my coat."

One man held both hands against his shoulders, pushing him against the wall. The other grabbed Andy's jacket from the floor, found the papers, and handed them to the officer, who then took his time, apparently studying everything closely. Andy could hear men throughout the house, banging things around, obviously searching for the radio they had picked up on their detection equipment. Mme. Bertrand had apparently come into the house. He could hear someone demanding to know who she was, could hear her faint reply.

"He has a work pass," the officer mumbled after a time. "For farm labor. And a travel pass. It says he's from Tarascon, in the south."

"Yes. I came here to work. The Bertrands needed—"

"And why so far? There's no work where you live?"

"I've suffered from tuberculosis. I came here first to the sanitarium, and then, when I was doing better, I looked for work nearby."

"*Tuberculosis?*" The man holding him let go, obviously frightened. It was what the planners in London had told Andy would happen.

"What work is it you do here?" the officer asked.

Andy turned around slowly. He had the feeling that his papers had passed inspection. The officer was speaking with less authority now. He was a bulky man with a heavy chest, his coat draping over him like a monk's robe.

"I do whatever is needed," Andy said. "We're planting now. And I feed the animals, look after the—"

But Andy heard the shout. "We found a man in the attic. He has a wireless, with code books."

"And who is that?" the officer asked Andy. "Another *farm worker?*"

"It's Raul. Yes, he works—"

"Shut your mouth." He turned to the man who had let go of Andy. "Take him to the car." The man slammed Andy in the chest, drove him back against the wall, striking the back of his head against the hard plaster. Then both soldiers grabbed him and dragged him out of the house. They marched him off the farm, his arms twisted back almost to the breaking point. On the dirt road, behind some trees that blocked the view from the house, were a number of vehicles, including a detection truck. One of the men opened the door to an armored car and shoved Andy in the back, then shut him in.

Andy was trying to think. What could he do? Could he convince them he had nothing to do with Raul and at least save himself? But there was no chance of that. Andy knew what was coming. The Gestapo wouldn't kill him or Raul quickly. They would inflict pain until they got the names of the people in the circuit. The Bertrands were as good as dead, just for harboring them. Andy told himself he would die in the end anyway; he might as well hold up under the pressure and give no names. He couldn't let them kill Pierre and Agnés—and Simone. He thought of the cyanide capsule that was sewn into the cuff of his trousers. He could take it now and die quickly. That seemed so much easier than facing what was coming, but he thought of his parents. He had to try to stay alive somehow if there was any hope at all.

In another minute or two Andy saw the agents drag Raul to another car and shove him into the back. The agents who had manhandled Andy got into the car with Andy, one to drive and the other to sit next to him. The man in the back was a simple-looking young man with no hint of animosity in his eyes. He said rather casually, in excellent French, "It wouldn't be wise to resist in any way." He had a Luger pistol in his hand.

"I don't understand. I work on the farm. I haven't done anything."

The man smiled, looking friendly, and then without any warning lashed with the gun, the barrel gashing Andy's forehead. Andy fell back and covered his face with his hands. He felt the blood run through his fingers. The driver said something in German, seemed to tell the man in back to stop—maybe to keep the blood out of the car.

Andy's mind was spinning. He decided he would get nowhere denying. He would keep his mouth shut for now and take things as they came. It was time to find out what he was made of.

The drive into Orléans was long and silent. Andy let the blood run down his face and only wiped it out of his eyes. The flow gradually slowed, and the pain set in, but he knew it was nothing compared to what was coming. He prayed for courage, and he asked the Lord whether it was all right to take the cyanide. But he didn't feel good about that. He never had liked the idea.

When the car finally pulled up in front of an old Gothic building, Andy got a glimpse of Raul being taken in, two men escorting him. Raul glanced at Andy, then took a second look, obviously surprised by the blood on Andy's face. A moment of understanding passed between them, as though they both knew they would probably not see one another again, and then Andy's escorts hustled him up the stairs and into the building, down an elegant hallway, and into a small room. They threw him inside and shut the door, leaving him alone. The room had been stripped of furniture and floor coverings. There was only a straight-backed chair and four plastered walls. Andy sat on the stone floor, where he had been pushed. He had always known this could happen but somehow had convinced himself that it wouldn't. The idea—the fear—that was building in him was that God wasn't going to protect him, that maybe he was about to die, like so many others.

In a few minutes the officer who had first questioned him entered the room. "Tell me," he said in English, "are you American or British?" He had spoken French until now, fairly well, but his English was even better. It was disgusting to think how bright the man was, and what he was nonetheless willing to do.

Andy pretended not to understand.

"My name is Eberhard. Captain Eberhard. I'm a reasonable man. You can name the members of your circuit and then we will kill you quickly. Or we can do things to you that will cause you to plead for us to end your life. Either way, you will give us the names, and then you will die. So tell me, which way would you prefer?"

Andy didn't answer, but he didn't hide the fact that he had understood. He prayed again, in his mind, that he might be allowed to live, if at all possible. But he didn't feel any surge of faith. So he prayed for what was possibly more important: "Help me not to give him the names."

"All right, then. I'll ask again a little later. I believe you need a sample of our work before you can make a knowledgeable judgment. Sit on this chair and make yourself comfortable until some of my friends join you. They won't be long."

Eberhard stepped out. Andy got up from the floor, but he didn't sit in the chair—mostly because he was nervous but partly, too, because Eberhard had commanded him to do so.

When the door opened, he saw the men who had been in the car with him. The one who had driven was bigger than the man who had struck him with his pistol, but he seemed less enthralled, as though this were all in a day's work. He had reddish hair and fair skin, rather delicate features. He looked like an accountant or a bank teller, not a Gestapo agent. But both men had taken off their overcoats and uniform tunics. They were now in their shirtsleeves. Each was holding a long black stick. The man who had hit him before said, in French, "Would you please tell us your real name. It's required of us, that we report this. I'll tell you the simple truth. The more you tell us, the less we hit you. If you answer all our questions, we won't have to hit you at all. It's very nice for you that way—and actually, better for us. So I'll tell you my name. It's Taubert. And this is Mr. Hegemann. Now you tell us your name."

"Armand Lefranc. I told you already."

The stick flashed so quickly that Andy didn't see it coming. It smashed his nose and sent him reeling backward against the wall. And then a rain of blows followed, across his head, his neck, his shoulders. As he slumped toward the floor, the big man grabbed him and drove the stick into his stomach—point first, with full force—before he let him fall. Andy rolled into a ball on the floor, gasping for breath, and felt their heavy boots pummel him in the back, the head, the ribs.

Andy was choking, drowning, it seemed, out of breath, blood filling his mouth and throat. He hardly knew where the pain was coming from; it filled his entire body. Hegemann, the driver, finally said something and both men stopped kicking. But Andy knew they were only being careful to keep him conscious.

"We're very sorry to have had to treat you this way," Taubert said. "But we asked for your name and you were impolite. Will you tell us now, or should we beat you again?"

Andy could feel his body jerking as he coughed and gasped.

"I think maybe it's difficult for you to speak right now," Taubert said. "Why don't we let you rest for a few minutes, and then we'll stop by again. Maybe you'll be able to say your name by then. To stop us next time, however, it will take not only your name, but others."

The men left, and Andy continued to cough. For a time he lost consciousness; when he came around again, the pain in his body was much worse. Only his breathing had improved. Now he wanted the cyanide. He didn't really care whether he should do it or not; he just wanted to die without saying the names. That was at least something. But he knew he couldn't reach that far, knew he didn't have the strength to rip the thread loose and get the capsule. He needed a little time first, and then maybe he could do it.

But the door opened much sooner than he expected. He didn't look up. He merely tried to pull himself in a tighter ball, to be ready for the next blows. But it was Captain Eberhard this time. "Sir," he said in English. "You're a young man. A young American, if my guess is right. And I'm not sure this war, here in Europe, should matter so much to you. Why don't you tell me your name now? What can that hurt?

Andy didn't answer.

"Well, then, let me give you something to think about. These two fellows you were chatting with before, they love to play with electricity. It's a hobby with them. They like to hook wires to men like you—hook them to very tender parts of you—and find out how much voltage you can take before you beg them to stop. Or sometimes they choose tools of various kinds. They like to see how far they can stick things into a man—using whatever entrances are available, or sometimes making new ones. It's a nasty business. I can't stand to watch it, to tell you the truth. I have to wait outside."

Andy hadn't known he could hate anyone this much. He thought of coming up suddenly and grabbing the man by the neck, squeezing the life out of him—taking him along if he had to die himself. But he couldn't move, couldn't do it, and the truth was that he was terrified.

"There is one other possibility. Are you interested in staying alive?"

Andy wasn't going to answer. He wasn't going to grovel.

"Here's a thought. How would you like to do a little work for us? We could set up your radio again, and you could broadcast the information we provide for you. You could mislead your friends in London just a little and save your life. And most important, I won't have to send Taubert and Hegemann back in here."

Andy didn't say anything, but he was thinking this one over. He had been told that if he were forced to "play back" false information, he could negate the effect by using a code that would let headquarters know that everything he said was false. His mission was ruined anyway. Maybe this way he could buy some time, do no actual damage, and find some way to escape. Or was it worth it? In the end, they would still kill him. Maybe he might as well get this over with now.

"No answer?"

Andy was still thinking.

"All right then. I'll have Taubert and Hegemann bring their little generator in. In a few minutes you'll wonder why you ever turned my offer down. But I won't make it again."

"All right," Andy said in English. "I'll do it."

"Well, now, what a fine gesture. But tell me one more thing. What *is* your actual name?"

Andy wasn't thinking well. "William," he said. "William Johnson."

"That's not very believable, Mr. Johnson, but that's all right. It's a name we can use. And maybe, after we become better friends, you can tell me all about life back in America. You *are* an American. I can hear that in your accent. Isn't that true, Mr. Johnson?"

"Yes."

"And if I ask you where you're from, you'll tell me Chicago or New

York, I'm certain—and not the truth. But I'll take the one bit of truth you've offered so far—that you're an American—and we'll build on that. So rest a little, and one of these first days we'll put you back on the radio. Isn't that right, Mr. Johnson?"

"Yes."

"I suppose you know that you still have to give us all those other names we need. But we'll talk about that a little later. You take a good rest. You've had a hard day."

"What about my partner?"

"Oh, my. I don't know. The man is not feeling very well at the moment. I hope my friends didn't get a little too rough with him. I tried to stop them, but they're so enthusiastic about their work."

Eberhard left, and Andy wondered whether he had done the right thing. Since he had agreed to cooperate, what would they do with Raul? Torture him all the more? Maybe the Gestapo knew about false codes and would know what he was up to. But it was not wrong to stay alive, not if his people in London knew what he was doing. And he hadn't given up the names.

Still, he wondered. Why had he agreed? Was it really only to stop the beating—and the electricity? What would he do next time all of that started? Andy thought of praying again, maybe at least thanking the Lord for this little respite, but the truth was, he wasn't feeling very grateful.

CHAPTER 14

ANDY WAS SITTING in a grim little jail cell. He had been there a month now, and three times he had been hauled out to broadcast false information to London. He only hoped that Headquarters understood his coded warning on the first broadcast; he didn't dare repeat it and take a chance of being discovered in his deception.

He had gradually recovered from most of the effects of the beatings, but his injured shoulder had been wrenched again. That pain never really went away, but it was worst at night when he tried to sleep and every move sent shocks of pain into his neck and down his side. Almost as bad, however—at least after those first awful days when his whole body had been filled with pain—was the grinding boredom of sitting in a cell alone. He was in Olivet, he thought, but he wasn't even sure of that. He had asked, but the German guard—who had clearly understood him—had only stared at him and said nothing. It was as though providing him with an answer would be a comfort, and no comfort of any kind was allowed.

This month of confinement had changed Andy, reduced him, anesthetized him. He slept on a bunk made of planks, with one blanket, no mattress, no pillow. There was a toilet in the cell with him, so he never left the room other than on those three occasions when he had made his forced broadcasts, and then he had merely been marched to an upstairs room in the same building. He had seen no one but Captain Eberhard and a couple of nameless Gestapo agents. He asked them about Raul but received no answer. He heard sounds in the jail at times, in another part of the building, and he thought there were other inmates, but he had no idea whether Raul was somewhere in the same jail.

What Andy had time to do was think, and yet, clear thought was almost impossible. He knew he was stalling for time by playing back the information the Nazis scripted for him—and he hoped he was doing no harm—but he also knew his usefulness would play itself out, and then he would be killed. That knowledge, that his life was over, didn't frighten him any longer; in fact, it seemed to strip him of all feelings that made him human, including fear. There was no escape from the inevitability of his situation. Maybe the Allies would make their European landing soon, but he was certain that Eberhard would order him killed when that happened. That was how things worked. This was war, and the idea of mercy would never enter Eberhard's mind.

Sometimes Andy thought of home and wondered what his family and Whisper would feel when they found out he was dead. He didn't like to think about that, but he found it difficult to feel the anguish he thought he should. People at home didn't know what he knew. He was being handled by men who cared nothing for his life, who hated him for no reason, who found no regret, maybe even pleasure, in administering pain. But Andy wasn't sure he was all that different. He had slipped a knife into a man's ribs, taken his life quickly and cleanly. It was what a soldier did.

Andy tried to pray sometimes, but he couldn't feel anything that verified the things he had thought he believed. He hadn't become an atheist. That was a belief, and he couldn't muster anything that assertive. He hadn't exactly given up on the idea of a life after death; he merely couldn't feel it. He lived with a constant sense of nothingness, and it was hard to imagine that anything else was ahead for him.

Andy told himself over and over that he had to perform one act of sacrifice, of goodness, before he died. When Eberhard decided it was time to end this whole game, Andy had to accept the torture that would come. He had to refuse to give up the names of the Resistance people he knew. In many cases he knew only code names, but he often knew where people lived, sometimes where they worked. He could hold all that back and possibly save some lives. The problem was, he knew what he had experienced the last time he had been beaten. He hadn't been far from the breaking point, and the agents had never used the torture techniques he had heard about: electrical shock, crushing of testicles, fingernails jerked out with pliers.

Andy had decided back in London that he would never break, no matter what, and now, as he spent his days sitting on his bunk or pacing about in his cell, he wanted to believe he could die for his friends. In the end, he was afraid he might succumb to the torture, but if he did that, all the things his family had taught him—all the principles Christ preached—just didn't hold up. Maybe a person pushed to the limit always cared more about himself than anyone else. But he didn't want to accept that, so he vowed that he would make this sacrifice before he died: He would give himself over to the pain and take everything the Gestapo could inflict upon him. When he doubted himself, he tried to picture the Bertrands, Pierre and Agnés, and all the others who had put them-selves in danger for his sake. And he thought of Simone—Elise. He wanted her to live.

One afternoon Andy was pacing, trying to awaken himself. He was weary of the constant lethargy. He came to a stop when he heard a key in the outer door. When his cell door opened and Andy saw Eberhard, he felt a kind of relief. *Something* would happen now. Even if he only made another broadcast, at least he would move outside the cell for a short while. But Eberhard was alone, and that had not been the procedure when Andy had been taken upstairs.

"Hello, my friend," Eberhard said in English. "It's a beautiful day. It's very sad that you can't see it. Too bad there's not a window in this cell so that you can look outside and see the blue sky."

Andy didn't speak. He hated these games Eberhard insisted on playing.

"I would take you out for a nice stroll if I could, but I'm afraid my commanding officer is not pleased with you." He waited, as though he expected Andy to ask why, but Andy refused. "The trouble is, he has the opinion that you have signaled your leaders somehow not to believe your transmissions. We are not receiving the responses we hoped for."

Andy waited. Things were about to change, and that was just as well. He noticed the smell of the place, the rancid odor of decay and sewer that he had found sickening when he had first entered this cell. Maybe the air had stirred when the door had swung open, and that had enlivened the odor, or maybe Andy was coming back to life. He suspected that this was the day he would finally face himself.

"So, I'm sad to say, we won't be broadcasting again. My leader says we must have those names from you now—the people in your Resistance circuit. I told you from the beginning that it would finally come to that."

Andy stared at the man. He wondered who he was, really, whether he had ever been a kid like himself who kissed his mom when he went off to school each morning. There was something so deeply perverse in him now. Had Hitler or fascism or the war brought this irony into his every word and action, or had it always been there, even when he was a boy, just waiting to find a vicious outlet?

"I'll make this very simple. Tomorrow I'll come back. I'll give you a sheet of paper and you will write down every name you know."

Andy couldn't resist saying, "And then what?"

"Well, now, that is the question, isn't it? I sincerely wish I could promise you some nice future if you simply give up the names, but that wouldn't be honest, would it? The question is whether you want this to be simple and easy or very, very difficult. You met my men before. They carry out their duty with great enthusiasm. Last time they only cuffed you about a bit, but this time . . . well, I suppose you can imagine some of the possibilities. As you lie awake tonight—since I'm sure you won't sleep—think about some of the worst things that can be done to the human body. With truly creative people, the variations are endless, and I have men who like to experiment, like to search for the most exquisite pain. It's really quite sad, how much they enjoy it."

Eberhard smiled at the thought. He turned slowly around, as though he were surveying the room, perhaps asking himself how he would like to be confined here, but at the same time daring Andy to attack him. "My friend," he said, looking away, "I would recommend the easy way. Think about the names tonight and then write them down. Every one of them. Oh—and include your own. We also want to know that. For our records, you understand. We like to be tidy about those things."

"No. I won't give you anything."

Eberhard faced Andy. He was still smiling. "You won't last an hour, Mr. *Johnson.* Your partner didn't. He told us everything we asked of him. But my leaders are not easily satisfied. They think you might know more. And don't try to deceive us. We have your friend's list. We'll know if you are lying."

Andy wondered. Had Raul actually broken, or was this a way to make it seem less important that Andy give up the same names?

"Your partner thought he was a *tough guy*—as you say in America. He also told us no in the beginning. And then he broke as my men pulled his head from the water the third time. But there are worse things than drowning. It's frightening, but it doesn't hurt nearly so much as . . . well, I'll let you think overnight about the many possibilities. You are not a hard man. You won't last long."

Andy didn't speak again. He only tried to tell the German with his eyes that he was harder than Eberhard thought he was. He tried to deepen his commitment, promise himself. He would not give in. He wouldn't give this man the satisfaction. He was going to die tomorrow, so he might as well die with that much sense of triumph.

When Eberhard left and Andy sat down on his bunk, he felt some pride in his resolution. He would die with his honor, no matter what Raul had done. But his chest was shaking, and another fear had penetrated deeper than the idea of the pain. He looked inside himself again and tried to find faith in the idea of a heaven. Maybe after the pain, there would finally be peace—and then a better place for him. But it still didn't seem so; he couldn't muster any hope. The truth was, he had come to doubt that humans deserved a heaven. Eberhard was proof of that, but so was Andy. He had stuck a knife in a man without the slightest hesitation. He told himself over and over that he had done it for freedom, as a defense against the evil Nazis, but he knew that he had actually stabbed the man to save his own life. Back home, he had known lots of good people, but they weren't at war, weren't pushed to the limit.

Tomorrow he would die, and maybe that was the simple, dark end of things. When he was a kid and would go on a trip with his parents, his mother would tell him to go to sleep in the car so the ride wouldn't seem so long, but every time he shut his eyes, he would wonder what he was missing, what might be worth looking out the window to see—even crossing the Nevada desert to California, where everything was the same for hundreds of miles. So he would always open his eyes and take another look. He hated more than anything, now, the idea of not existing.

He thought of the things he would never experience: especially being a husband, a father. He had thought so many times of sleeping next to Whisper, getting up to have breakfast with her, coming home to her at night. He thought of Elise, too. He thought of turning her down that night and hated to think that he would never know a woman that way.

Everything was being taken away from him, but maybe someone would know that he held out and didn't give up the names. Maybe there was some inspiration in that—the idea that humans really could do the right thing. He wanted that to be important—worth the torture. He wanted to believe that the idea of goodness wasn't entirely an invention.

Andy slipped to the floor, got on his knees. He had promised his father he would never stop praying. He asked God to let him feel something. He wanted the hope that there would be some part of him alive when the suffering ended. He didn't get an answer, but he found himself crying, moved by a stirring inside him. He wasn't sure what that meant, but it was better than what he'd been feeling. He got up. He decided not to sleep. He would hold onto what life he could for as long as he could. And yet, he was exhausted. He had no sooner made up his mind not to sleep than he felt the need to lie down and rest a little, and he fell asleep immediately.

When Andy awoke, he didn't know what time it was, but he heard a voice and realized that the jailer was at his door. The jailer was bringing his evening meal: black bread and cheese and a couple of slices of German sausage. That meant Andy had slept only a couple of hours. He still had the night ahead of him. He had no appetite, but he ate anyway. It was something to do. It was something to taste.

And then he paced. He now actually wished that he could sleep again so the endgame could begin, but when he lay down, his mind wouldn't shut off this time. He watched the light fade around the loose door and in the slit in the middle, the one used to pass his meals through. He heard the sounds diminish from other parts of the jail. He sat at times, walked at times, but his nervousness kept mounting. He tried not to imagine the things they would do to him in the morning, but images kept coming to him. He told himself there was only so much pain a body could take, and then it could get no worse. He would pass out, perhaps, or even if they kept him awake, that kind of pain could last only for minutes, not hours, and he could stand that. What difference did it make how much pain he felt? It would end, and then he would find out whether anything else existed. If there was a God, and Andy had to answer to him, he wanted to say that he had died saving lives, not taking any more.

At some point he drifted into a restless sleep again. He was half conscious when he heard a noise out front beyond the outer door. He sat up before he was fully awake, aware that he was hearing something new, some chaos he had never heard in the building. He heard grunts, then something heavy moving, scraping—furniture, he thought. And then someone was using a key in the outer door.

When it opened, light flooded in through the slit in Andy's door. "Armand," someone said. "Where are you?"

Andy couldn't speak for a moment, still so surprised, but the man called again, and Andy said, "I'm here," in English, only then realizing that the man had called to him in French.

"We're getting you out of here. Which door is it?"

Andy hurried to the door, bent, and yelled through the opening, "Here. Straight in front of you."

The man rushed to his cell, and by then Andy had remembered the voice. It was Xavier, one of the leaders in his circuit. There were others behind him. And one man had keys. "Which key is it, Armand? Do you know?" Xavier asked him

"Give them to me." He reached through the opening, and the man handed him the ring of keys. Andy had watched the jailer use the keys when he had returned to his cell each time. He knew the key to look for. "This one, I think," he said, and passed it back through the slit in the door.

Xavier fumbled with the keys, took what seemed a long time to turn it in the lock, and then the door finally swung open, but as it did Andy heard the grind of an engine outside, tires sliding in gravel, and someone from the outer office yelled, "*Les Boches.*" At the same instant there was gunfire outside.

Andy stepped from the cell. There were two other men, dressed in black, and one of them put a pistol in his hand. "There's no back way," Xavier said. "We'll have to fight our way out." By then Andy was hearing automatic fire, people shouting, bullets striking walls. He tried to push past the others and run out first, but Xavier was already moving. He charged through the outer office, where bodies were on the floor, and ran outside with Andy behind him. But the gunfire had stopped. Xavier and Andy ran across the yard to the front gate. Andy saw two men on the ground near an armored car—Germans, he thought.

Someone called to Xavier near the front gate, and then two more people in black clothes appeared, and the four ran together. Xavier turned the corner at the end of the wall and ran down an alley. Andy was suddenly bursting with power, and he had to hold himself back not to run past the leader but to follow. He heard the reverberation of a truck engine behind him at the end of the alley, and the popping sound of rifle fire—lots of bullets flying, sparks flashing off the cobblestones. He heard a bullet ricochet off a building next to him, and he veered to the other side of the alley and ducked down against a rock wall. By then he realized that one of his Resistance friends had gone down, was lying in the middle of the alley on his face. Andy ran back to him, but Xavier was shouting, "They're coming up the alley. We have to go."

Andy wasn't going to do that. He dropped down next to the man. He rolled him over and felt for a pulse in his neck, and then in the dim light, he saw who it was. Elise.

Andy was paralyzed. He knew, not through his fingers, but with his eyes, that there was no life in her.

Xavier was suddenly there, grabbing at Andy. "Come with me. Now," he demanded.

"She's dead."

"I know. Come on."

Bullets were buzzing again, snapping as they flew by him. And Andy did run. Xavier led him down some stairs and into a basement, through the building, and then out the other side, and from there across a street and into another alley. They ran until Xavier couldn't run anymore, and then Andy walked with him fast, but he didn't care what happened.

Eventually they reached the edge of town and then ran again, this time into the woods, and when Xavier wore out again, they sat down and tried to breathe.

"We can't stay here long," Xavier said between breaths. "They'll bring their dogs. They'll search everywhere, and they'll shut off the roads. There's a safe house I can get you to, but we'll have to walk all night and stay in the woods. We can't take a chance on any of the roads."

"How many died back there, Xavier?"

"I don't know. There were six of us. Some might have run in other directions."

"Why did you bring Elise?"

"Simone?"

"Yes."

"You know how she is. She wanted to come. She wouldn't take no for an answer."

"You shouldn't have taken such a chance. Not any of you. Not for me."

"You came here for us. We had to stand with you."

"It wasn't worth it. Not if five are dead—or even just Elise."

"Armand, we knew a man who worked in the jail. He told us what was going on. They were going to torture you in the morning, and you might have broken. You might have given up all our names."

"Code names."

"Yes. But you know things about us. One thing would have led to another. You would have broken. Everyone does."

"I think Raul gave them what they wanted to know."

"No. They were too severe with him. They killed him before he told them much of anything."

So Raul was gone too. Andy had to take a long breath and let that sink in. Then he said, "I would have held out. I was ready to die."

"You may yet die, Armand. We probably all will. But we had to break you out if we could."

Andy tried to think whether he could believe that. He tried to tell himself that he would fight furiously, that he would avenge Elise's death, but he didn't feel the rage he wanted. He was still too stunned by her limp face. He thought of what she had offered him and his refusal. It seemed, now, that he had done the wrong thing.

Andy was leaning his back against a tree, breathing the rich smells of the forest. He would get up again and he would walk. But Elise was back on the cobblestones, her blood puddling around her. He had loved her, he supposed—had fallen in love for an hour or so, in any case. He didn't know what that meant, what that changed in his life, but his sense was that he had not been true to Whisper and he had killed Elise.

Xavier got up, so Andy did too, and they walked all night. But Andy was longing for the numbness he had felt back in the jail.

CHAPTER 15

ADELE WAS HOME, and her parents were worried. She had finished her requirements for her teaching degree during winter quarter and begun her practice teaching in the spring, but she had hated the experience and after two weeks had quit and come home. She didn't want to be a teacher. "Those little kids drove me crazy," she told Bishop Gledhill. "They never shut up, and I don't know how to keep control of them."

The bishop knew better than to offer her much advice. She wouldn't listen anyway. What concerned him, though, was that she had started to talk about going to California to look for a job. He suspected that he'd better say something before she made her mind up and got stubborn about her decision. He arrived home from the bank one afternoon in late April, after she'd been home a few days, to find her sound asleep, flat on her back on the living room couch with a *Life* magazine resting on her chest. "Adele," he whispered. "Do you have just a minute? I wanted to have a little chat with you."

Adele's eyes fluttered open. For a minute she seemed not to comprehend what he had said to her. She brushed some loose hair away from her eyes and ran her hand over her mouth, where a bit of saliva had dribbled onto her cheek. She looked like a boy, with her hair so short and messy. That was something else the bishop didn't like, that short hair, and he knew she kept it that way because he had once expressed his opinion about it. "Oh, Dad, not right now," she protested. "I'm sleepy."

"It's five o'clock, honey. I don't see—"

"I was up very late last night, and then Mom insisted that I get up at the crack of dawn."

"You were still in bed when I left, and I didn't leave until almost eight o'clock."

"Oh, Dad. I need to get out of here. You and I are going to drive each other crazy."

That was exactly what Bishop Gledhill feared the most—that she would take off one of these days, so he was careful to sound light and friendly when he said, "Oh, come on. We're not *that* different. Sit up for a minute and let's talk."

Adele let her eyes go shut for a moment, as though she were making an effort to be patient, and then she slowly swung her legs over the side of the couch and sat up. "Don't tell me what a bad person I am, okay?" she said. "I already know. I'm lazy and weak and irresponsible and I'm wandering through life without a plan. No one knows that better than I do."

The truth was, the bishop was a little surprised by her admission. He was never sure she realized how unfocused her life actually was. The only trouble was, she wasn't expressing any desire to do anything about it. It all seemed a joke to her—or too much of a bother to worry about. The girl actually loved her weaknesses.

"I won't ask you, then, what your long-range plan is. But I've been wondering, what are you going to do next? Like, say, tomorrow?"

"Don't worry. I'll get a job. I just wanted a little time off right now."

"Are you thinking you want to go back and finish a degree in another subject?"

"I don't know, Dad. I don't think so. At least not right away." Adele had sat up straight at first, but now she was slipping down, letting her legs stretch out in front of her. She had no shoes on and she was wear-ing jeans with a big white shirt that she had probably sneaked out of Andy's room. It was huge on her, but she had rolled up the sleeves and let the shirttail hang to her knees. It was wrinkled now, after she had slept in it. Actually, she had worn it almost constantly since she had arrived home. Bishop Gledhill hadn't said a word about that, but he really didn't like to see girls in blue jeans. He had accepted the idea that they wore slacks sometimes these days, but blue jeans and boys' shirts—which way too many girls were wearing these days—seemed to him much too sloppy and unbecoming.

"So when you say that you'll find a job, are you talking about going back to D. Steven's again, or—"

"I don't know. I haven't decided."

"Well, then, why don't you work for me? Since Whisper left me, I haven't found anyone who can take over the office the way she did. The Culver girl can type and take care of customers, but she's way too timid to step forward and make a real go of the job. You could do it, though. You've got the confidence when you put your mind to something. You could learn a lot, too. After a while I could put you pretty much in charge, the way I did with Whisper."

"Dad, that sounds so boring to me."

"Not really. Whisper enjoyed herself at the bank. Everyone in town comes in and out, so you get a chance to talk to lots of people. And that's something you could learn from—meeting the public, taking care of cus-tomer needs. You may never work out of your home again, once you're married, but skills like that are always useful. It's the kind of thing that can really help a woman when she serves as a Relief Society president."

Adele let her eyes roll. "Dad, sometimes I wonder if you even know me."

"Why do you say that?" he said, but he was thinking that she was probably right.

"I'm not sure I'll ever get married. I may be working 'out of the home' all my life. And think about *me* as Relief Society president. Can you imagine the damage I could do?"

Bishop Gledhill could see that look in her eyes—the one that said, *Don't push me. I'm going to live my life my own way.* He knew he had to be careful or she would start making vows. It would be just like her to pop off with some flat statement—"I'm definitely not getting married"—and then make that her new claim, especially if he showed any signs of concern.

Bishop Gledhill looked toward the living-room windows, watched the sheer curtains billow gently with the breeze. It was nice to have some windows open. It was a pretty day, the temperature in the seventies, and the smell of earth was in the air. The bishop had walked home feeling rather happy, just from the goodness of it all: the tea roses blooming in Sister Handley's yard, clusters of cherry blossoms still showing in his own little orchard in the backyard. It was a day to be happy, but he couldn't quite manage that, with no word from Andy for such a long time and Belle so worried she hardly talked anymore. And now this silliness with Adele. "Why wouldn't you get married?" he finally asked, trying to sound only vaguely interested.

"Dad, I dated half the boys at the university and I never got serious with a single one of them. A couple of them wanted to marry me, but they also wanted to *own* me. They wanted to take me home, stick an apron on me, and expect me to cook three meals a day, scrub the kitchen floor on my hands and knees, and tell them how wonderful they were every morning at breakfast. Maybe some woman might want fourteen kids and a husband to tell her what she can and can't do—but I don't."

"I don't tell your mother what to do. I never have."

"You don't boss her around. But you expect your breakfast on the table at 6:30, and you expect her to live by *your* schedule. You're the most important man in town and everyone knows it. Mom's job is to keep you going, wash your clothes, press your suits, fix your meals—and take care of your kids. I'm not saying she's not happy with that, but it's not what I want."

"What *do* you want?"

"Ahhhh. The question again. And I have only one answer: *I— don't—know.* That's my problem. I only know what I *don't* want."

"Adele, you'll fall in love one of these days, and you'll get married and have a baby, and then instincts will come out in you that you haven't experienced yet."

"That's what I'm afraid of." She smiled. "Dad, if I do that, I'll end up in Delta, Utah, land of lizards, for the rest of my life. And I'll never know anything else."

Bishop Gledhill sat back in his chair and folded his arms. He did remember having felt that way once. "I think when we're young, we imagine there must be something better somewhere—you know, that the grass is greener. But look at your brother. When he came home for Christmas he told me he wanted to come back here and never leave again. I'll bet that's what he's thinking right now, too, that he wants more than anything just to come home."

"You're worried that he's dead, aren't you?"

That was Adele. She never came at things sideways. "I'm worried," he admitted. "I wish we would hear from him."

"Mom's worried that she's lost him and she only has me and the other kids left. She loves us, I'm sure. But not one of us will ever be what Andy is to her. I think it's pretty much the same for you too, actually."

"Adele, look at me." He waited for her head to rise, her eyes to engage. "That is *not* true."

She didn't look convinced. "Well, anyway," she said, "that's not the point. If Andy went away and found out he wanted to come back, it must be a good thing to go away—just to find it out for myself. I know you don't want to hear it, but I'm heading for California one of these days."

"Oh, Adele, why is it all the kids around here have such a fantasy about California? It's not all Hollywood, you know."

"But there are lots of jobs there right now. I know I could find work in an office or something, the same kind of work I'd be doing in your bank. I could learn all those same things you want me to learn, but I could do it in a new place. I just want to try a few things in my life. I'll probably settle down someday, exactly the way you want me to, but first, I want to try my wings a little. I don't see why that's such a bad thing. Why is it, every time I bring it up, you and Mom have such a fit?"

The big grandfather clock rang out its 5:15 chime, a sound so familiar to Bishop Gledhill that he rarely noticed it anymore. But it reminded him now that he had come to love sameness, the comfort of things that were familiar and expected. He didn't blame Adele for feeling otherwise, but her talk scared him. "Honey," he said, "I think I understand everything you're saying to me. But here's what I fear. In the next few years you're going to make the most important decisions of your life. I want you to marry a good man, and marry in the Church. I want you to go to the temple and be sealed, and I may be a little self-serving here, but I want you to give me some grandchildren. I know that all sounds dull to you, but I promise you, those are the things that will make you happy in the long run."

"I can go to church in California. There are lots of Mormon boys in the service down there. Maybe I would meet someone while I was there—and come home married in the Church, just the way you want."

"But will you, Adele? You skipped church way too much in Salt Lake. Your bishop called me twice about your not showing up. I'm afraid you'll get to California and quit going altogether."

"Dad, I'm an adult. If I quit the Church, that's my decision. And I can do it right here in Delta as quickly as I can anywhere. I know plenty of people in this town who don't go to church."

"I know that, Adele. But if you're here, maybe you'll find a local boy who—"

"Dad, they're all gone. They're in the service. There's no one around here even to go out with."

"They'll be coming home. And then you'll have lots of boys to date. They'll be ready to settle down then, too." He saw the look on her face, the resistance, and he knew he had to give up the sales job, but this was all so hard for him. He felt the breeze in the room again, watched the curtains rise, hold for a second or two, and then drift back.

"Yeah, this is some exciting place," Adele said. She wrinkled up her nose. "Every time the wind blows, I smell manure. I always forget about that when I'm up in Salt Lake for a while."

"It's a good smell, if you ask me," he said, smiling. Then he softened his voice and hoped she would hear his concern, not his censure. "Adele, I wouldn't worry about you leaving if I thought your commitment to the Church ran a little deeper. What I don't think you understand is that if you're here with us, you're not so likely to wander away from the things you've learned. I know you don't like to hear that, but it's true. And if you marry into one of the good families here, you can put down roots and raise a fine family. That's the greatest joy in life."

Adele laughed. "Oh, sure. I notice that I've brought *you* a lot of joy. That's all I need, some kids just like me." She laughed harder. "No thanks."

"Adele, look at me." She was leaning back, her eyes focused past him, but when he waited, she did look at him. "When Andy was born I was happy to have a boy, but I hoped our next child would be a daughter. As far as I'm concerned, there's nothing quite so beautiful in this world as a little girl in pigtails. When you were born, the nurse brought me into the room where your mom was and I held you half the afternoon while your mom was resting. I didn't think I'd ever seen anything so beautiful in my whole life. Parents don't learn to love their kids—the love just comes when the child does. There's no way I could love anyone more than I love you, and there's nothing in this world more important to me than my two sons and my three daughters."

Some of the defensiveness seemed to leave Adele's face. She smiled a little. "But Dad, you have to trust me. You have to let me try things my way for a while. If I never do, I think I'll struggle forever, wondering what I might have experienced."

"It seems that way, but we all grow up, and when we do, we start to think differently."

The telephone had begun to ring. In a moment, the bishop heard Belle say from the kitchen, "Sister Crowther, he's busy for a few minutes. Could I have him call you back?" And then a few seconds later, "Oh, dear. Was he badly hurt?"

The bishop glanced at Adele, took a moment to decide, and then called, "Let me talk to her, Belle." To Adele, he said, "Don't go away. Let's finish this."

Adele was back to rolling her eyes, and he knew what she was thinking. So he told himself he would talk to Sister Crowther just briefly and then come back to this conversation. But on the phone, he heard, "Bishop, Jack's been hurt. He rolled his tractor into our back ditch, and it landed right on him. Doc Noorda's been working on him, but they're about to put him in an ambulance to drive him up to Salt Lake. Do you possibly have a minute to come down and give him a blessing before they take him away?"

"Well, sure. Of course."

He walked quickly back to the living room. "Adele, it's Jack Crowther. He's been in a bad accident. I've got to run down the street to Doc Noorda's office to administer to him, but I'll be back in ten minutes, no longer. Just read your magazine a few minutes and I'll be right back."

But Adele stood up. "There's nothing more to say, Dad. We're just saying what we always say."

"I love you, Adele."

"I know. And you love the Church, and you love Jack Crowther, and you love everyone in town. There's not a doubt in my mind about any of that." She turned and walked down the hall toward her room. He thought of going after her, but the ambulance would be leaving, and he had to get down to Doc Noorda's.

*   *   *   *   *

Flip had been riding his bicycle out to the farm every afternoon after school lately—either that or working in the garden in town. When he arrived home from school one day, he found Tom in the garden, hoeing a row of potato plants. "Grab a hoe," Tom told him, and he laughed. "It's good work for an intellectual young man. You can contemplate great ideas and work at the same time—since it takes no brains to do the work."

"Is that what you are, Tom, an intellectual?" Flip called back. He was already walking toward the shed to grab a hoe.

"No. I meant you. You've spent the day learning the great truths of the universe. Now you can spend some time in deep thought—you know, assimilating all your ideas."

Flip got his hoe, then walked back and stopped at the end of the row that Tom was working on. "I'll tell you how intellectual I am. I got back an English paper today with a C+ on it."

"Above average. Not bad."

"Tell my dad that. My English teacher says I use too many run-on sentences, but I don't see how I possibly could. I don't even know what a run-on sentence is." He grinned. "I just pile up words until I figure it's about time to throw in a period."

"Well, I happen to be an ace with punctuation. Before you leave today, let me show you."

"You write for the newspaper out there, don't you?" Flip had set his hoe in place, ready to get started, but he hated hoeing more than almost anything he knew, and he was happy to put off the job as long as he could.

"I've written some articles before. But not lately. A lot of guys don't agree with what I have to say."

"Like what?"

"You know how I feel about things."

"What things?"

"Flip, let's hoe. I need to at least get the potatoes done before dark tonight."

So Flip hoed. And he did think. But he didn't think about anything he had learned at school that day. He thought about the same thing he always thought of these days: His brother. And Whisper. It had been more than six months since Andy had written, and the tension was getting worse around his house. Mom had talked Dad into writing the army to ask about Andy, but there hadn't been any reply. No one said it, but Flip knew that his whole family was wondering whether Andy was still alive. It just didn't seem that he would go that long without writing, no matter what he was doing or where he was.

Flip had come home one afternoon and found Mom and Chrissy sitting at the kitchen table, both of them crying. His heart had almost stopped. But no word had come. Chrissy admitted later, when Flip asked, that she had asked her mom what she thought might be happening to Andy, and Mom had broken down and sobbed. She had told Chrissy, "Your dad says the army will tell us, if something happens, but I don't know if that's true."

Chrissy had cried again, and told Flip, "We just can't lose him, Flip. I don't think I can stand it if we do."

Flip hadn't cried, not in front of Chrissy, but he had gone to his room and hidden out for a time. He had gotten down on his knees—which he didn't always do the way he should—and prayed that Andy would be all right and that the family would get a letter from him soon. He had felt a little better after that, but then he had made the mistake of asking Adele what she thought, and Adele had said, "Something isn't right. We might as well get used to it. A lot of other families are having to do that—but in our family, we always pretend everything is all right, whether it is or not."

Flip knew that Adele was frustrated and unhappy right now, but it was almost as though she wanted something else to be wrong, to take some of the attention away from her. Flip liked Adele at times; other times, he could hardly stand her. She was the center of the universe, in her mind, and once she finished thinking about herself, there wasn't much effort left over for anything or anyone else. She had taken on a style that brought attention to her for all the wrong reasons: for being outspoken, too fancy, smart-mouthed, and she had chased boys long before they had taken much interest in her.

For Flip, a world without Andy hardly seemed worth living in. For as long as he could remember, Andy had been his hero. Half of Adele's problem was that she was Andy's little sister, a decent student, but only halfhearted about most things she did.

When Flip came home each day, he didn't ask whether a letter had come. He merely looked at his mom and knew that one hadn't. He saw the same thing going on with Whisper, too. Lamar Jones couldn't make it over from Fillmore very often—not with gas so hard to come by—but she went out with him whenever he did come over. That worried Flip, but still, he knew Lamar was strictly second-string material. There was no way that Whisper could compare Lamar with Andy and pick Lamar. Flip just worried that she would decide she had to settle for *someone* if Andy didn't care about her. But Whisper was afraid now, the same as everyone else. For a time she had been upset about the letter Andy had sent, convinced he didn't really love her, but now she was just scared he was dead. Flip had watched the life go out of her, a little more all the time. She was working for Doc Noorda, but when Flip asked her whether she liked that, she could hardly say anything. It was like trying to ask someone with a toothache whether she was having a nice time at the movies.

Flip was pretty much the same way. He wasn't working very hard in school and he knew it. He had written that C+ paper in about 45 minutes rather late one night when it was due the next morning. He had done a little research for it, but he couldn't remember about doing footnotes right, so he had just stuck something at the bottom of the page. The teacher had turned every footnote into red pencil marks, and she had split about half his sentences up, then written "run-on" out to the side. The truth was, Flip didn't care. And even his dad only seemed to go through the motions of admonishing him when he didn't do as well as he could.

Flip had practiced basketball hard the previous fall, and he had hoped to make a showing on the ward team, but he hadn't done much better than the year before. He could dribble better, even shoot better at practice, but in a game he always seemed to go to pieces. Since the season had ended he had decided to give up on basketball, and he wasn't going out for football that fall. He had grown a little, but not enough; he knew he'd get murdered on the football field.

Flip and Tom worked their way slowly along the same row, gradually coming nearer to each other. Sweat was soon running off Flip's forehead. The afternoons were getting pretty warm now. He straightened his back for a moment and wiped his shirtsleeve across his forehead. He had forgotten to wear a hat and he really needed one. "Don't you get lonely staying out at the farm by yourself?" Flip asked.

Tom straightened too, then put his hands on his hips and bent backwards to stretch his back. "Yeah, I do. But at least I'm not all crowded in, the way I am at the camp."

Tom had mentioned the crowding before, but Flip had never been exactly clear about the conditions at Topaz. "How crowded is it?" he asked.

"We have a room that's twenty feet long and sixteen feet wide. Five of us live in it—my parents, me, and my two little sisters."

"One room?"

"My father and I built some partitions out of scrap lumber and blankets, but it's still like one room. And there's two more families in the same building. We can hear everything they say, and they can hear us."

"I'd hate that."

"You don't know the worst of it. We sleep on metal cots, and they squeak when you move on them. I know everything *everyone* is doing— if you get what I mean."

"Oh, man. That's terrible. I've been out around there, and I've seen all those barracks, but I thought each one was a house for one family." What Flip remembered were flimsy, rectangular buildings with tar paper on the outside, no siding.

"The wind blows right through those places. When we get a big dust storm, everything inside gets covered with sand. We've got a potbelly stove, and we can usually get enough coal, but once the wind gets blowing in the winter, nothing keeps you warm."

"But I don't get that. Can't you complain to the government and get them to come in and fix things up better?"

Tom laughed. "Yeah, sure. Have you heard anyone around town getting themselves all hot and bothered about the poor Japanese people out at Topaz?"

"No. Not really." The truth was, Flip had heard people say that the Japs had a good deal. They lived at the camp with no rent, got three meals a day, and then got paid when they worked. A bus would bring internees into Delta sometimes and allow them to shop at the local stores. People in town claimed that all the internees had big wads of money and could buy anything they wanted. But Tom had told Flip that top pay was $19 a month for full-time work, and the people who came into town were usually buying for everyone in their block of houses.

"Besides, the worst thing we can do is complain. People hate us, and the only way we'll overcome that is to prove ourselves. Or at least that's how I look at it." He bent and began to chop at the weeds again.

"What do the others think?"

Tom stopped, still leaning forward. "We better just hoe, Flip."

"Are some people getting mad?"

"Sure they are. Wouldn't you be mad?"

"Yeah, I guess. But you never seem very upset about anything."

Tom stood and drew in his breath. "I wrote a column for our newspaper for a while, and one time I said that all us young guys should join the army. It used to be that the army didn't want us, but now that the Four-Four-Two is doing so well, the government says we all have to sign up for the draft. So I wrote, 'Let's all volunteer, and let's show our stuff.' But some guys feel the other way. They figure the government stuck us out here in this desert and took away our rights, so why should we fight wars for a country like that?"

"But you disagree with that, right?"

"Not exactly. I'm just saying that we can't buck the system. We might as well show people that we're good Americans. After the war, maybe things will get better."

"But are some guys sore at you for saying things like that?"

"Yep. You got it. They're fed up, and I don't really blame them. But if our people start any trouble—riots and stuff like that—the government will tromp down on us all the harder. So to me it doesn't make any sense."

"Everyone around here says you were put out there for your own protection—so people wouldn't get mad and beat you up and stuff like that."

Tom laughed. "Think about it, Flip. Does that make sense? If someone was after you, wanting to beat up on you, do you think the cop ought to put *you* in jail for it? Those guns out at the camp aren't pointed *out*—you know, to stop all the bad guys who want to hurt us. They're pointed *in*, at us. And you must have heard what happened last year. An old man took his dog out for a walk, got too close to the fence, and a guard shot him—killed him for no reason at all."

"Well, yeah, I knew about that. But around here people say he got warned and everything, and he wouldn't go back where he was supposed to."

"He didn't speak English, Flip. He was an old man. How could someone think he deserved to be *killed,* just for walking in the wrong place? He didn't try to break out."

Flip thought about that as he went back to his hoeing, and after a time he said, "It's really not right, is it? You didn't do anything wrong, and yet it's almost like a jail out there."

"Let's just hoe, Flip. If you go back into town and tell people I said things like that, it'll just throw fuel on the flames."

"But it's not right to make you live like that. I don't think most people have any idea about it."

"It's a lot worse than what you're seeing, Flip. We're getting by for now. But look at what we're facing in the long run. When we found out we had to be 'relocated'—as the government likes to call it—we had to walk away from everything we owned. We tried to sell as much of our farm equipment and furniture and everything as we could, but we got next to nothing for it. I told you before that we rented our house, and then the guy never has sent us the rent money. Well, it's worse than that now. Friends of ours wrote to us the other day and said that the guy has moved his family out of the house, but they've taken most of our furniture with them."

"You mean they just stole it from you?"

"You got it."

"Have you told the police?"

Tom laughed hard this time. "Yeah. We told the police. And they're wringing their hands, just feeling awful about it."

"But aren't they? Don't they have to do something about it?"

"Flip, we're *Japs*. We're the enemy. The police don't care what happens to us. I left a lot of stuff in my house—things I don't want to lose. But I'll probably never see any of it again."

"Can't you get permission to go down there and salvage what's left?"

"Flip, you don't know *anything,* do you? You figure truth and justice always win out—just like in the movies—and people all look out for each other, the way your dad looks out for people in his church."

"They should, Tom."

"Oh, sure. They should. I'm a Christian, Flip. You know that. My dad had us all join the Methodist church. I think he was trying to show we were good Americans, as much as anything. But I've been hearing all my life about the way Christians are supposed to behave, and I gotta tell you, I don't run across many people who pay a lot of attention to that stuff. I made the mistake of being born the wrong race in this country."

Flip didn't want to believe any of that, but he couldn't think of a single argument on the other side.

"Think about this, Flip. We've got a German American as our camp director, and we're all in the camp because we're Japanese Americans. Explain that one to me."

But Flip couldn't. He felt sick. A lot of things weren't the way they were supposed to be; that was what he'd been finding out lately.

CHAPTER 16

ANDY WAS BACK IN England. After his escape from jail in France he had had no hope of returning to his work in the area around Orléans, and he no longer possessed papers anyway, everything having been taken from him by the Gestapo. He had hidden out for a few days at a safe house near Olivet, and then a Lysander airplane had flown in from England, landed on a grassy field several miles south of town, and lifted him out of all his trouble. He had suddenly realized, somewhere over the channel, that he had actually survived, and at the same moment he had felt an uneasiness he didn't want to think about. A few hours later he had been dropped off in London and left to catch up on his sleep in a little flat that the OSS kept for agents returning from or heading over to the continent.

Sleep had come easily that night, but he had awakened early the next morning, too nervous to go back to sleep, and had gotten up. There had been a few canned goods, C-Rations and the like, in the little kitchen, and he had managed to fix something for himself for breakfast, although he wasn't hungry and didn't eat much. He knew that someone would be there to pick him up in the afternoon, but the morning looked tedious, with not one thing to do.

There was a lot to think about, but Andy had already learned at the safe house that thought was his worst enemy. One of the reasons Andy was alive was that Raul had died so soon. Raul was the radio operator and would have been the logical one for Eberhard to keep around to play back phony intelligence to London. It was clear that Eberhard had lied to Andy. Raul hadn't given up any code names or descriptions. Andy knew that because none of the members of the local circuit had been arrested.

But Raul was dead. Andy was still having a hard time getting used to that. Elise was dead too, and others. Andy had learned that two of the men who had helped break him from the jail had also died, and another had been arrested and could be dead by now. The Bertrands had been jailed, and chances were high that they would be executed. Andy didn't know why he was in England resting in a comfortable room while so many others had died. It was not a good thing to think about.

Andy felt only half alive himself, but when he leaned his head back on the couch and shut his eyes, he didn't like what happened. It was what had kept him awake most of the time at the safe house. He saw the things he wanted to forget: the bodies he had jumped over as he had run from the jail; Elise's face, pale and limp; even the stout little man with the flabby cheeks, the one he had stabbed.

He also remembered, though he tried not to, something one of the Gestapo agents had said to him during his beatings: "You Americans, you think you're so much better than Germans. But your airplanes are bombing all our cities, killing as many civilians as you can." Andy knew that was more or less true. Americans and Brits were destroying every city in Germany. Of course, the Germans had tried to do the same to England. All of that looked different to him now—different from the way he had thought of it when he had signed up, when he had gone through his training. It wasn't that he didn't believe the Germans had to be defeated, but the war now seemed to him an immense conflagration, as though the whole world were burning up around him. It was hard to think about the politics: He could only see the results of what humans were doing to one another.

Andy knew what he had to do. The night before he had quickly written out a message and asked his driver to send a telegram to his parents. The note had said simply, "Sorry I couldn't write. I am fine. Will send letter soon."

Now he needed to write a letter and tell his family something more, but he wasn't allowed to say much more than what he had said. He stalled for a time, but the stillness was worse than writing might be, so he found some stationery in a drawer, sat down at a little kitchen table, and wrote a quick letter. He told his parents he had been in a situation that had kept him from writing, and he was sorry, but they needn't worry about him. He was in London, and he was getting some rest. Then he asked about people back home and managed to say a few things about London weather—anything to make the letter seem normal.

But that letter was easier than the other one he needed to write. He stared at the paper for a long time before he tried a couple of sentences, tore the sheet up, and started over. In the end, he wrote:

Dear Whisper,

I don't know what you must think of me by now, since I haven't written for such a long time. I can only tell you that it wasn't my choice. As I told you last fall, I was going into a situation where I simply couldn't write. That's all I can tell you. I hope you can understand.

Whisper, I told my family that I'm all right. In many ways, that's true. I haven't been wounded or sick. But you need to know, I'm not the same person I was when I last saw you. I can't say anything that would explain that, and I'm not sure that I ever will be capable of explaining how much I've changed. I doubt that I will ever be the person you once knew, and I feel sure that I would be a great disappointment to you if I came back home.

What I'm trying to tell you, Whisper, is that you need to go on with your life. I said something like that last fall, but I said it then because I felt selfish about asking you to wait. Now I know that you wouldn't ever want to be married to me, so it's better if you move ahead with your life.

I know you want to know whether I still love you. I can only say that I love my memory of you. I love to think about us, the way we were, and how the world looked to me then. But that's not enough to build a marriage on. I'm not sure what I believe anymore. All the things I used to trust in just don't seem true anymore. I keep praying that I can be the guy I used to be, but I don't feel much hope of that. To be honest, I haven't really kept my promises to you. I don't mean that the way it might sound, but I couldn't look you in the eye ever again, not without feeling ashamed. So all this is my fault and you can just put the whole thing behind you.

Whisper, I'm sorry. I'm really sorry. I wish you great joy in your life. I know you'll be happier this way in the long run.

Andy

Andy had no idea whether he should send the letter. There was no way she could understand what he was saying to her. But it was hard to remember how people thought back home, how they felt about life. He thought of writing to Flip, too, but he couldn't do it. There was nothing he could say to the boy. For his sake, it would surely be better if Andy never returned home.

Andy leaned forward with his forearms on the table and tried to pray. He wanted to know whether he should send the letter. But he received no answer, and he didn't feel worthy of God's attention anyway. He knew what he had felt toward Elise. He also knew what he'd found inside when his civilized self had been stripped away. He doubted he was much worse than other people, but that was just the problem. He wasn't better, either. The real truth was, he and Eberhard were cut from the same cloth.

Andy was being picked up at 1400 hours and would be spending the rest of the day at Headquarters, debriefing. He would probably return to the offices for another day or two, completing his report on conditions in France and detailing his entire mission. After that, he wanted to get back to the war somehow. He knew why, but he didn't like to say the words to himself.

For now, he didn't want to sit in this room any longer, so he dressed in a Class A uniform that had been placed in the closet for him. He left the flat and walked the streets of the Mayfair district, not far from Headquarters. Life continued there. He found pockets of destruction, but Londoners were amazing people who simply went about life, doing what they had to do. It was true that the dark days of the blitz had long since passed, but he had seen what Brits could do, facing an enemy that could strike suddenly, without warning, and he told himself he had to be more like that. These people weren't whining and complaining about their loss of innocence the way Andy felt himself doing. They accepted the reality they had to live with and did their best to survive it. Andy posted the letters, but then he wondered whether he should have. Maybe he should have sent Whisper on her way without saying quite so much. But it was done now, and he told himself he had to take the next step in his own life: He had to deal with what was, not with the world he had believed in as a boy.

So he walked briskly, looked about himself, and then returned to the flat in time to catch his ride. His first interview was with his commanding officer, and he knew what he wanted to say when he got there. Not two minutes into the conversation, he told Colonel Wilson, "I want to go back, sir. Drop me into France as soon as you can get a new cover story ready. Just put me down in a different region where I won't see anyone who knows me. All the signs tell me that the invasion is coming very soon, and I want to be there when the action starts."

Colonel Wilson was not an impulsive man. He considered everything before making a decision. "I talked to the men in the airplane crew that picked you up in France, Lieutenant Gledhill. They said you weren't in very good condition."

"That was before I'd had a good night of sleep. But I feel better this morning."

"Were you tortured while you were in jail?"

"I was beaten, but that was weeks ago. They were just getting ready to ratchet things up when the *Maquis* broke me loose."

"How long were you in their jail?"

"About a month."

"My impression is, from reviewing your messages from France, nothing went all that smoothly for you. You faced pretty much constant pressure the whole time you were in the country. Isn't that true?"

"Yes. I guess so. Doesn't everyone?"

Colonel Wilson leaned back in his chair. He didn't wear a uniform, didn't even let it be known around London that he had military rank. He was a gray-haired man who might have been forty or sixty—Andy couldn't tell—but he was like Chambers, the man who had first interviewed Andy. He had the haircut, the suit, the manner of an Ivy Leaguer. "Pressure, yes. But some drop in, reach a safe house, and never have any major problems. Very few have been arrested, and most who have are dead now, or still being held. You're one of only a handful who has made it back after being worked over by the Gestapo. In most cases, we wouldn't even consider sending you back—probably couldn't."

"I'm all right. I can go. My experience will help me do a better job this time."

"But why would you *want* to go?"

Andy took a breath. He didn't really need this. "I was sent in to help the Resistance get ready for the invasion. I didn't finish my job. I want to go back and have another shot at it." He drew in some more air. He didn't want Colonel Wilson to hear any emotion in his voice. "I think I'll always feel that I didn't really accomplish anything, if I don't go back."

"You seem nervous to me."

"I probably am, a little." Andy realized that he had been rubbing his hands together, moving about in his chair. He folded his arms now and leaned back. Wilson had a cluttered desk with all kinds of paperwork spread around on it. Andy wondered how a man like that thought—a man who saw the war as paperwork. How would Andy himself feel if he only received intelligence from others and could sit here and move chess pieces on a board?

"Anyone would be nervous," the Colonel said, "but—"

"It's only going to make things worse to sit around here. I want to get back into the action. If you don't want me anymore, I'll go make the jump with my Airborne unit."

"No. There are reasons that can't happen now."

"They're ready to go. That's why. And I don't have the final training."

"I didn't say anything like that."

"I know. But I'm sure it's true. Send me back to France before I miss the whole thing." But Andy felt himself leaning forward again, gripping his hands together. His fear was that he would be stuck here on a desk, and he would have to think too much, the way he had the last twenty-four hours.

"Sometimes, when a guy loses his partner, he wonders, 'Why him and not me?' He figures he won't be able to live with himself if he doesn't go back and put his life on the line again. I think guys like that almost want to get themselves killed."

"Hey, I'm a country boy. My mind isn't that complicated. Maybe I just like the thrill."

"Don't try to con me, Gledhill. I know your background."

Andy shrugged, didn't say anything.

Wilson sat and thought again, so long that Andy almost demanded to know what was going on. But finally he asked Andy, "Do you know about the Jeds?"

"The what?"

"The Jedburghs." He pronounced it "Jed-burrows."

"Sure. Some of them trained with us in Beaulieu. They're dropping into France as three-man teams: one American, one Brit, and one Frenchman."

"Well, that's the idea. It doesn't always work out that way, but you're right, they are three-man teams. They're more involved with sabotage than with intelligence, and they're going to be crucial at the time of the invasion."

"Put me with them. If those guys are going in fresh, I've been there long enough to know the ropes. I could be a big help to them."

"We have a team almost ready to go, and one man has gotten sick. You could take his place. You would have to work very hard for a few days to get ready, but then we could include you in the drop."

"Okay. Let's do it, sir. I'm ready."

"I think you're not, actually. I think you'll get yourself killed if you don't calm down. But I also think we need you, and we don't have anyone else who can step in this late in the game."

"Would I command the team?"

"No. We normally send only one officer, but in this case there's a captain, another American, going in. But he doesn't speak French, and we need someone who does. That's why we thought of you."

"I don't know why I'm sitting here. I better get where I need to go— and start my training."

Colonel Wilson sat still for a long time again, and then he finally said, "I have no other choice. I don't think you ought to go. I think you should spend a month in a hospital and then maybe go home. But I'm going to send you. Just let me say, I don't want you to get these men killed. We're not losing many teams. We've done better than anyone ever expected, but you need to get your nerves under control or you'll make mistakes, and you've already learned what happens when mistakes happen."

"We didn't make mistakes!" Andy stopped himself and tried to get his voice under control. "We just got caught. We had some bad luck. You send enough people over there, with the Germans looking for them all the time, and some are going to be found." Andy needed to believe that.

He didn't want to think that anything he had done had gotten all those people killed.

"I know what you're saying. From what I've read, you did a good job. If I didn't think so, I wouldn't send you. But if your trainers find you too nervous, I'm going to call this whole thing off. I'll be asking them every day."

"Don't worry. I'm fine." But Andy was still holding his hands together so Wilson couldn't see them shake.

* * * * *

It was Friday, June 2, when Flip came home from school and found out that a letter had come from Andy. He read it before he had to hurry out to the farm. Mom had called Whisper, and she said she had gotten a letter too. So after dinner Flip decided to walk over to Whisper's house, just to see how she was feeling about that. He had promised Andy he would drop by and see her, and he had done that now and then, but probably not as often as Andy had expected. What he hoped tonight was that she would be a lot happier than she had been lately. She had felt relief along with the rest of the family when the telegram had come, but since then her worry had set back in. He knew she'd been wondering what Andy would say to her when he finally wrote.

When Flip reached Whisper's house, he saw her sitting on the front porch. He stopped on the sidewalk and said, "Hi, Whisper," just to surprise her.

"Oh, hi, Flip," she said, but she didn't sound as happy as he had expected.

He walked up the sidewalk toward her porch, pausing at the steps. He didn't like what he saw in her face. Suddenly he was afraid to ask about her letter. "I thought I'd walk over to the baseball park and watch my friends play," he said instead. "Do you want to walk over with me?"

"No, thanks."

"I've been working out at the farm after school every night."

"I know. Adele told me that. I'll bet you're about worn out."

"Oh, I don't know. Kind of, I guess. Now that school's getting out, I'll be out there all day. That's worse—especially the way it's warming up now."

"Adele told me that the Japanese boy is a hard worker."

She was just saying things. She wasn't looking at him. Flip felt sick. "Yeah, Tom works hard. And the funny thing is, Adele likes him now. He comes in to eat with us some nights, and he makes all my sisters laugh."

"Well, that's good."

"What's wrong, Whisper?"

She finally looked straight at him. She tried to say something, but stopped and cleared her throat. By then he could see tears glistening in her eyes.

Flip walked up on the porch and stood closer to her. "What did he say to you, Whisper?"

"Sit down, Flip," she said, so he sat next to her on the love seat. But she didn't say anything more. The sun was setting and the air was glowing. The undersides of some clouds off to the north were turning orange. It had been a nice day, but Flip could feel the change coming, the breeze turning hot, even in the evening. Before long it would be too hot to sit out here.

Whisper was wearing a white cotton dress with little red polka dots. Flip glanced to see the golden light on her face, in her eyes. He could never get used to how pretty she was. It was almost more than he could stand to see her this unhappy. He wondered what Andy had said to her this time.

"He told me not to wait for him—to marry someone else."

"Whisper, he said that before, but I told you, he's only trying—"

"It wasn't the same this time. He said he's . . ." She stopped, pressed her hands to her cheeks, then wiped away the tears, but more were coming. "He meant it this time, Flip. He doesn't feel the same way about me anymore."

"I don't believe that for one minute," Flip said, and he couldn't hide the anger he felt toward Andy. But then he added in a softer voice, "Whisper, my dad said he's probably been through a bunch of stuff. He could be spying or something like that. That's why they won't let him write. I know exactly what's going on. Andy's afraid he's going to get killed and he doesn't want you to be all sad and everything."

"Flip, he said some other things—stronger things. He doesn't love me anymore."

"Yes he does, Whisper. I *know* he does." Flip turned and looked into her eyes. He wanted to take hold of her hand, or even put his arm around her, but he never in the world could have done it. He leaned a little closer and said, "Listen to me, Whisper. He loves you, and he always will, and he's coming back to you. I promise you."

"He said he's not even the same person he used to be. He doesn't feel the same."

Flip sat back and stared at the clouds again. He had been so happy all afternoon, just knowing that everything was okay. How could Andy do something like this? He had to know how much he would hurt Whisper with a letter like that.

"Don't say anything to your parents, Flip. They'll just worry all the more, and right now it's better if they feel like everything is going to be okay."

"You ought to write Andy and tell him he's the stupidest guy in this world, and he ought to be thankful you've waited this long, the way he's treated you. I'd like to get hold of him right now. I'd slug him right in the jaw."

Whisper smiled. "Thanks, Flip. That's what I've been thinking all afternoon. I cry for a while, and then the next minute I want to slug him with both fists. My whole life I've been waiting for him to care about me, but he never really has. I think he thought he loved me for that month he was home, but I don't think he really did."

Flip didn't believe that. "He'll come around, Whisper. He needs to get home and get back to normal. That's all."

"I can't plan on that anymore. Lamar wants to marry me, and I've got to decide if I want to marry him."

Flip shifted toward her again. "Whisper, you can't marry that guy. You know you can't."

"Maybe I can, Flip. He treats me like I'm the best girl in the world. He's going into the navy this summer, but he wants to marry me before he leaves and then have me join him wherever he's stationed after he gets his training. I could see a little bit of the world, maybe, and then after the war, we'd move to Fillmore. He's got his dad's farm he's going to take over."

"And you'd be sitting over there in Fillmore wondering about Andy back here in Delta, once he comes home."

"No. I'd be raising kids and keeping house. I wouldn't have time to worry about that. And I'd never have to wonder whether Lamar loved me or not."

Flip folded his arms. "Sounds like you've got this all figured out."

"Oh, Flip, don't be mad at *me*. It's Andy who broke his promises—to both of us."

"I don't trust anybody anymore."

"Come on, Flip. Why would you say that?"

Flip got up and walked to the rail of the porch. The color of the clouds was already fading away, and dark was coming on fast. He stuck his hands into his jeans pockets and stood stiff. "It just seems like everything is wrong in this world."

"Like what?"

Flip wasn't sure he knew. But he felt as though he'd had his eyes opened lately. "For one thing, while Tom is stuck away in a prison camp, people are stealing things from his house back in California. He's an American, the same as we are, and no one cares about that. He's in a prison because he's Japanese, and that isn't right, Whisper."

"I don't know. I don't think our government would do something like that if there wasn't a good reason."

"I don't believe that anymore. Tom's a good guy. He's just like us. But I hear what people say about the Japanese—all the names they call them and everything."

"People do hurt other people, Flip, but most of the time they don't even know they're doing it. They just don't think."

"Everybody looks out for themselves. If they want something, they just take it. It's not right to break into Tom's house and take his stuff—and then figure it's all right because he's just a Jap."

"No, it's not right. But most people wouldn't do that."

"I don't know, Whisper. I'm not so sure about that anymore." But he was thinking mostly about Andy, breaking all his promises to Whisper.

CHAPTER 17

LONG BEFORE DAYBREAK on June 4, 1944, Andy dropped into France with a three-man Jedburgh team led by Captain Delbert McComb. A master sergeant named Evan Roberts, a Welshman, was the radio man. It was a clear night, and the team made an uneventful landing in a farmer's field near the little town of Malaunay, just outside Rouen. Andy had learned in a last-minute, top-secret briefing that the Allied invasion of France was planned to occur "very soon." His team could not be told the day or place, since they would be making their drop ahead of the invasion and could be caught and tortured, but what they were told was that Hitler had kept troops in reserve, ready to rush to the point of invasion, and McComb's team was going in to join with Resistance forces to do everything they could to delay those troop movements. Once the invasion began, they would receive additional information about which roads, bridges, or railroads they should sabotage.

The team also had an immediate assignment to be carried out on Sunday, June 5, so they slept one night at a safe house and the next morning approached a German army post in Rouen. Captain McComb and Andy were wearing French police uniforms. Sergeant Roberts waited with a car, two streets away. The plan was to bluff their way inside, leave a satchel full of plastic explosives at a headquarters communication center, and get out before the timer detonated the bomb.

Andy, of course, would do all the talking. The captain would use his rudimentary French only if he absolutely had to. McComb was from Georgia and had a way of making every word he spoke, in any language, sound like it had an extra syllable or two. He was a big guy—six-two or so, with a massive upper body. He looked like a weight lifter, and yet something in his face, his jaw, spoke of insecurity. Andy had the feeling he was trying to convince himself that he was as tough as he looked.

The two walked directly to the camp gate, where a stout young guard in a field gray overcoat stepped out the door of a guard house. The weather had changed overnight, and now a blustery wind was sending a drizzle of rain into Andy's face. He turned and bent his head sideways so his officer's hat protected him a little better. "We have arranged to meet with *Oberst* Kammer," Andy said. "He is expecting us."

The guard, Andy could now see, had a ghastly scar across his right eye, the eyeball itself obviously made of glass. The good eye stared at Andy, squinted, full of doubt. "I know nothing of this. Show me your papers."

The guard spoke French quite well. Andy was glad of that, since he knew almost no German. He and McComb handed over their fake identification papers along with a forged letter, supposedly from a French general. The guard studied the papers carefully, then walked inside and picked up his telephone. He talked for quite some time before he came back and said, "*Oberst* Kammer isn't available this morning. Why did you come on Sunday?"

"Look at the letter. He agreed to meet us this morning. I'm certain he will be here. This is an intelligence matter of the utmost importance."

"Wait here," he said, and went back to his telephone. Andy had the impression that he was mostly annoyed that he had to deal with something out of the ordinary on a wet Sunday morning, not that he considered McComb and Andy a threat. When he stepped back outside, he said, "The sergeant in Kammer's office knows nothing of this, and he's not to contact the colonel this early."

"But this can't be," Andy said. "I tell you, this is a matter of *great* importance. If we are not allowed to relay our crucial information to the colonel, we'll report you and the sergeant as responsible."

"It's not my fault. There's not one thing I can do."

"Then let us talk to the sergeant."

The guard stared into Andy's face for a time and then said, again, "Wait there." He went back to the telephone. When he returned this time, he said, "Another guard is on his way here. He'll take you to the office, but I must search you first."

"Of course. We are carrying no weapons."

"What's in that valise?"

Andy held his arm up and showed the man that the valise was chained to his wrist. "Top secret papers. I cannot open it. You know that already. Everything was explained in the letter."

"You're not going inside with that. You'll have to leave it here."

"That isn't possible."

"Then you'll have to wait. The sergeant will try to contact *Oberst* Kammer and find out whether he knows about this. But only after nine o'clock."

"That is simply unacceptable. Time is very important in this matter. Tell me your name, and tell me the name of the sergeant who won't contact the colonel."

By then, another guard was approaching the guard station. He had an MP40 machine pistol slung over his shoulder. Andy had practiced using one during his training—along with most other French and German weapons. The guard with the wounded eye stepped to the other German, and the two turned their backs to the rain and conferred for a time. Finally the man from the guard station looked back at Andy and said, "Go with this man. Talk to the sergeant in Kammer's office. This shouldn't have to be my problem." He stepped back toward Andy and said, "Open your coat."

He patted Andy up and down, did the same with McComb, then turned them over to the other guard. Andy and McComb walked in through the gate and followed the guard with the machine pistol to the first building, an old brick structure that the Germans had taken over for their headquarters. Andy had studied the floor plan of the building, provided in England, and he had memorized the details. If he could get inside the building and leave his valise virtually anywhere, his job would be finished. The chain actually snapped off his wrist and wasn't locked, and the lift of a lever alongside the handle set off a timer that would allow them ten minutes to leave the building and get far enough away. The problem was, there was not much chance he could leave the valise without anyone noticing. They had hoped that few people would be in the office on Sunday morning and that elimination of the sergeant might be all that was necessary. The question was, would this guard with the automatic weapon stay with them the whole time?

The guard stepped inside first, and then motioned for Andy and McComb to follow him. The sergeant was sitting at a desk. He stood up and offered a halfhearted salute, saying something in German. "I speak little German," Andy said. "Do you speak French?"

"Yes. A little. But I cannot contact *Oberst* Kammer. This is impossible."

"We will wait then," Andy said. His hope was that the guard would leave, and then McComb, who had bragged about his killing skills, could take out the sergeant.

"You may wait if you like," the sergeant said. "But the colonel does not come this morning. You will not see him."

"He will come," Andy said. "We made arrangements. I don't understand why he didn't tell you." Andy took a seat close to the desk, and close to the inner wall—a good place to set off the bomb. That much had worked out well. But then the door opened and another guard stepped in, a big, rough-looking man. He spoke to the sergeant, who nodded. Andy didn't understand much of what the guard said, but he surmised that the guard at the gate had sent a second man over, just to be careful. Now Andy knew that he and McComb had a problem. For the moment, the best plan was to wait, but if the guards had been instructed to wait until he and McComb left the post, nothing was going to get better.

Andy glanced at McComb, who gave a little nod. That seemed to mean that he, too, wanted to sit tight for a time. McComb had taken a seat across from Andy, where he could get to the sergeant directly, without a desk in between, but the two guards were standing close to the door, and both had weapons slung over their shoulders.

The office was austere, with only the desk and a few chairs, a filing cabinet, and an old wooden clock on the wall. The sergeant soon busied himself with some kind of paperwork, and the guards stood like statues. The clock ticked loudly, the seconds gradually piling up, but after fifteen minutes or so, nothing had changed. Andy kept glancing at Captain McComb, and eventually he realized that he was trying to say something with his eyes. Andy was holding the valise on his lap. McComb looked at it, then looked at the floor next to the desk. He repeated the motion, over and over, only with his eyes, not moving his head.

Andy had no question about what he meant, but he also saw the problem. He couldn't set the valise down without drawing attention to himself, and he couldn't unhook the bracelet without raising questions. And if the guards suspected something, everything could go to pieces. Andy's thought was that they would do better to abort the mission, but he had gotten to know McComb pretty well in the last week or so, and the man thought he could do anything. Clearly, he didn't want to leave without getting the job done—and he was the commander. Andy did understand that knocking out communication centers was important to create havoc for the Germans at the time of the invasion, but he also knew their other sabotage work might be equally important, and local Resistance leaders needed help and organization to make that happen. Andy and McComb really needed to get out of this place alive.

Andy shifted his weight and lowered the valise to his side. He wanted the guard to think he was only trying to get the thing off his lap. He let his hand hang by the side of the chair for a couple of minutes, and then he said to the sergeant, "What do you think? Couldn't you make your telephone call now?"

"Not yet." He turned and looked at the clock. Andy knew the guards would look too, and he used that moment to reach across himself and release the bracelet. But it rattled as it slid down the leather valise and hit the floor, and when he looked up, he could see that both guards were watching him. So he rubbed his wrist, as if to indicate that he was tired of keeping the chain on. The guards clearly knew that the valise was there, though. They would never let him walk out without it.

After a couple of minutes, McComb suddenly stood, and rather than risk his bad French, merely motioned with his head. Andy saw disaster coming. "We cannot wait any longer," Andy said to the sergeant. "We'll return later."

That made no sense at all and Andy knew it. The sergeant looked confused. And then, when Andy turned toward the guards, the one who had led them inside pointed to the valise. Andy glanced at McComb, tried to get some sense of what the man wanted him to do, saw no indication, then reached for the valise. He said to the sergeant, "These are important papers. I'll leave them here. When *Oberst* Kammer comes in, be certain he reads them." He pulled up the little triggering device and set the valise on the chair.

But the sergeant looked to the guards and said something in German. The big guard stepped to the chair and picked up the valise. "No. You must not open that," Andy said.

The guard was hefting it by then. Andy heard the word *schwer,* and he knew the man was saying that the valise was heavy.

Suddenly McComb was moving. "Get the other one," he said. A knife flashed, and McComb drove the blade into the big guard's ribs. Andy spun to the other guard, who was trying to swing his machine pistol off his shoulder. Andy reacted exactly as he had been trained. He drove the base of his hand into the man's nose, heard the bone crack, saw the blood splatter, then grabbed his chin and the back of his head and, with brutal force, snapped his neck.

The guard dropped like a bag of sand at his feet. Andy looked up to see McComb jumping over the desk. The sergeant was fumbling for a sidearm, but McComb was on him, knocking him to the floor, and then the knife flashed again and Andy heard a cut-off scream, a gurgle in the man's throat.

McComb pushed the man to the floor, then turned toward Andy. "Put the bomb back on the floor, against the wall," he said. "Let's go."

Andy moved the valise to the base of the wall, but at the same time, he was saying, "We've got blood on us."

McComb seemed to have thought of that too. He was pulling off his big overcoat. The blood was on the front and on the sleeves—and it was on his hands. "Cover your hands with your coat," he said. "Walk out normally. Don't run."

Andy had his own coat off by then, and the two stepped outside. They walked back to the guard station. "We'll be coming back later," Andy said to the guard.

"Where are those other guards?" the man wanted to know.

"They walked that way." Andy motioned with his head, pointing away from the administration building. "They said they wanted breakfast." He kept on walking.

"Wait there," the guard was saying.

"I told you, we'll be back." And they kept going. Andy glanced back to see the guard looking perplexed, but he wasn't pointing his rifle, so the two kept going.

They walked to a corner and turned, and as they did, McComb started to laugh. "Not bad, huh?" he said. "Two against three, and we took 'em, no problem."

"Where did you get the knife?"

"I keep this little baby in my boot. Don't you have one?"

"If the guy had searched us carefully, he could have found it!"

"Hey, I wasn't walking in there without a way to protect myself. Those guys had automatic weapons."

"If that guard heads to that building right now, we'll have people after us in another few seconds."

"He won't. He doesn't dare leave his post. When they'll look for us is when those explosives go off. And we'll be gone by then."

Andy could see the car down the street—a beat up old *Citroen* that a Resistance circuit member had provided for them. There was no one on the street, so Andy and McComb picked up their pace, ran the last few yards, and jumped in the backseat. Evan sped away. "What happened?" he asked. "Why were you down there so long?"

Andy was still a little too nervous to tell the story, but McComb said, "I killed two Nazis, my first day on the job. And Gledhill got him one. We left that bomb in the office. It should be going off any minute."

Andy hoped so. He hoped no one would find it first. If the building blew, fewer men might die when the invasion took place. He and McComb might have saved some lives. He had talked to himself a lot about that during the previous few days. He had to keep his thinking straight during this mission—just do his job and let the rest go. He only wished that McComb would shut his mouth and not sound so thrilled with himself. Andy had made up his mind: He wasn't going to think about anything this time. He was simply going to do what he had to do. But McComb was going to test his ability to do that.

* * * * *

On Monday night McComb's team met with the leaders of the local Resistance circuit. By then, they had a surveillance report that the bomb they had planted had never gone off. McComb was furious about that. Before the meeting started, he told Andy, "They didn't pack that thing right, that's what I'm thinking."

"Maybe someone got to it in time, saw the lever, and pushed it back down. Or someone might have thrown the thing into some basement, so it didn't do much harm."

"Or maybe you never did pull the lever up all the way."

"I did. I know I did. But when that guard picked it up, his hand might have hit it. He might have knocked it back down."

"Didn't you look at that when you set it back on the floor?"

"I'm not sure. I can't remember. Everything happened fast."

"Don't tell me something like that, Lieutenant. You're the guy who's been here. You're supposed to know how to handle all this. I wasn't impressed by anything you did in there this morning, if you want to know the truth. You looked nervous, and you gave away the whole thing by the way you tried to get rid of that valise so fast. I expected you to pull it off a whole lot slicker than that."

"I don't think the lever was pushed down, Captain. If it had been, I'm sure I would have noticed."

"But you don't know for sure, do you? And that worries me a whole lot. I need men I can trust. In another few days the real shooting is going to start, and when that happens, it won't matter whether we can speak French or not. Roberts and I can handle this thing by ourselves."

Andy didn't reply. What was he supposed to say? But he didn't like this guy, hadn't from the first.

"I did like your work on that guard. You didn't have a knife and still you took him out so quick, I hardly knew what had happened. That's something I can respect. But from now on, you gotta be thinking every second. That's what this duty is all about."

Andy didn't say a word, but he told the man with his eyes that he resented this entire conversation. Captain McComb didn't seem to notice.

When the captain started his meeting, Andy translated. The *Maquisards* had gathered in a circuit member's house—not the safe house where McComb's team was living but one not far away, on the edge of Malaunay. Members had come in through a back entrance, arriving, according to plan, at different times. There were eight men in a cellar, with a single lightbulb hanging in the middle of the little group. The smell of dust and mold was powerful, and something was affecting Andy's allergies, making his eyes itch. The men stood in a half circle, with McComb, Evan, and Andy in front.

"You don't need to know our names for now," McComb said. "You can call me Captain, since I'll be your leader."

Andy should have been surprised by McComb's statement, but he wasn't. Jeds were supposed to train and support Resistance groups, not lead them. It had become clear in discussions from the moment of landing, however, that the local leaders expected McComb to take over. And of course, he was only too happy to oblige.

"I'll tell you more before long," McComb said, and Andy translated. "Let me ask you first, did you listen to the radio messages from London last night, and did you understand what you were being told?"

The men were all nodding, and one of the younger of them, a skinny boy code-named Alfred, smiled knowingly and said, "It all begins now."

"Yes. That's right. Two of the coded sentences I hope you recognized were signals for the Resistance uprising to begin all across France. Another indicated that Plan Green and Plan Violet are to start now. We're going to start cutting telephone lines and blowing up railroad tracks."

Andy and McComb had listened to the broadcast the night before. Andy had felt chills go through him when he had heard: "It's hot in Suez," and "The dice are cast," both indications that the sabotage should begin. For over six minutes similar short phrases had been announced, many of them meaning nothing, others, all-important to particular circuits.

"We already cut some telephone lines last night," an older man said. "It's very dangerous for us to be together tonight."

"I know that," McComb said. "We won't be here long. But there are things I need to know, and I wanted to make you a solemn promise that before this summer is over, you'll have France back in your own hands and we'll be marching right down Hitler's throat."

Andy translated and the men nodded resolutely. But Andy could see that they were seasoned men who knew better than to accept the words at face value.

"Let me just say that we aren't afraid to face any danger with you. Yesterday we walked into a German army post and killed three armed men with our bare hands."

Andy translated the words even though he thought the description sounded arrogant—and not exactly true.

"We hoped to blow up a communication center, but we didn't get the job done. I'm not sure why. We set the explosives, but they didn't go off. Maybe something went wrong with the bomb. But all the same, we did our part, and we didn't back down when we were outnumbered and had to face men with weapons. We'll get that building another way, another time—and soon."

Some of McComb's idioms were not easy for Andy to translate, but he did his best. What bothered him more was that he saw no way to knock out the building with all the Germans on high alert. That was just McComb spouting off. So Andy said the words but didn't use McComb's cocky tone of voice.

"You have to know, the invasion is coming now. I've asked Alain's group to return here at midnight. The rest of you, wait for word from me."

He spent the rest of the time gaining information. He asked about numbers of circuit members, found out what targets had been attacked earlier, and questioned the men about their experience and the experience of their own groups. He compared their weapons and ammunition report with what he had been told in England, and he checked to see whether the additional weapons that had come with his own team's drop had been distributed.

The *Maquisards* seemed sure of themselves, confident, well organized. Andy was impressed with the work others had done to get them ready—and with the preparation they had done themselves.

"All right, then," McComb said at the end. "Don't all leave at once. Let's not get picked up at this point. I'll see you soon, and I'll fight to the death with you, if that's what it takes. I'm not French, but I hate the Nazis as much as any of you. This world won't be a safe place until we kill them all."

Again the men nodded. One man said quietly, "*Vive la France*," and the others repeated the words. But they didn't shout. And they left as quietly as they had come.

McComb and Andy and Evan didn't have far to go, so they planned to leave last, but they climbed from the cellar and sat in the kitchen. The man of the house was code-named Vincent. He was a little fellow with a sparse beard. He had told his wife, he said, to stay away during the meeting. He didn't want to bring her into danger. But he said it with a tone that implied that he was brave himself and wanted to protect his woman. He seemed as impressed with himself as McComb was, and the two began to drink wine together and talk, Vincent speaking English fairly well.

Andy and Evan, after a time, moved into the living room and took more comfortable seats. "Andy," Evan said when they sat down, "don't let Del bother you. He thinks he's the only guy who knows how to do anything."

"I don't care," Andy said, and he felt the truth of his own words. He was mostly just glad that McComb was in charge and he didn't have to be. "He's probably not such a bad guy, once you get to know him."

"No. The better you get to know him, the more you'll hate him." But Evan was laughing, and Andy wasn't sure that he was entirely serious. Andy had spent only a few days with these men, training hard and working on cover stories, memorizing maps and plans and strategies, but Andy and Evan had rarely had time to talk. "Evan, what were you doing before you got caught up in all this?" he asked.

"I was just a little Welsh sergeant with no more brains than to volunteer for something that sounded exciting. I was shocked when they took me. It seems to me they were scraping the bottom of the barrel."

Evan was a small man, half a foot shorter than McComb, and yet he was firmly built, and Andy had seen that he could pack a wallop when he used all his force. When the two had practiced hand-to-hand fighting, Evan had given Andy all he could handle. "What did you do before the war?" Andy asked.

"I was learning bricklaying. And I didn't like it much. Too much of the same thing all the time. I did sing in a men's choir in my hometown, and we traveled about just a bit, and that added a little fun to my life. I had a sweetheart, too, and I left her for the war. One of my good friends picked up where I left off, and he's married her now. He was taller, better paid, better-looking, but other than that, I don't know what she saw in him." He laughed rather loudly. "Have you got a girl back home yourself?"

"I don't know."

"What? You had one, but she's going out with your best friend now?"

"No. I had one, but I told her that she'd be better off to look for someone else."

"My goodness. Why'd you tell her that?"

Andy tried to remember, tried to decide what he could say to Evan. "I told her that I wasn't the man she fell in love with. I've changed too much."

Evan was sitting in a handsome chair, upholstered in deep-colored flowers. He looked almost too small for such a massive piece of furniture. "We've all changed," he said. "So has she, I have no doubt. That's what life does to us. But that's no reason to cast her aside."

"She's a sweet girl, Evan. I'm not the man for her—not now."

"I doubt you're right about that. You're not the hard man you think you are. You're not like Del."

"I don't know what I am anymore. What about you? Are you glad you volunteered?"

"I think I'll like bricklaying just fine if I manage to get back to Cardiff. A little sameness might suit me now." He smiled, and his little mustache arched with the motion, seeming comic.

Andy nodded. He thought about Delta. He told himself over and over not to expect to see the place ever again, but now he had lived through another situation he probably shouldn't have. He was sometimes tempted to find hope in the idea that he wouldn't make it, that the odds would finally catch up with him and he could just escape everything he was trying to deal with. But the stronger impulse was to find a way to live. At least he wasn't so nervous now; he wouldn't have much time to think, starting tonight.

CHAPTER 18

THE JED TEAM'S FIRST assigned mission was to knock out a railroad
bridge north of Rouen, near Barentin. Andy and his partners knew
that the great invasion would be under way that morning. The blowing
of the bridge was set to coordinate with the invasion. All through the
weekend bombs had been dropping on France, reports coming in from
up and down the coast. What Andy didn't know—no one in France
knew—was where the Allied forces would land. But knocking out rail
lines and bridges would hamper troop movement regardless of the destination. If railroad lines were cut, the Germans would have to move their
men in truck convoys. With ammunition, arms, and supplies also
needed, roads would be congested, and that would be the job for the
many Jed teams that would be dropping into France over the next few
days: Delay those convoys.

McComb's team, code-named "Arthur," would attack with a group
of twenty-four local *Maquisards*. Technically, a man named Léon Rabetet
was the leader of the circuit and in charge of the operation, but everyone knew that McComb was in command. The problem, of course, was
that the Germans recognized the vulnerability of the railroads and were
guarding the bridges and trestles. The targeted bridge was a fairly short
span, built of brick, over a little ravine. Rebuilding the structure would
be difficult and would take a good deal of time. But according to local

observers, the Germans were well aware of the danger and had moved a platoon-sized force into place, half at each end.

Andy was convinced that more Resistance troops should be called in for the attack, but McComb argued that he didn't plan to overpower the Germans. He would strike with surprise, slip a team in, set the explosives, blow the bridge, then escape. More troops would only complicate matters. So the march had begun about 0230 hours, and by 0500 McComb had moved his men into place along a hillside at one end of the bridge. At the same time, a three-man explosives team was wading in the river, silently moving toward the target. At first light, McComb would make a knocking sound, clicking the stock of his rifle with a little stone. The men on the hill would stand up and fire on the guards at one end of the bridge. "We have the upper ground and the cover," he had told Andy. "We can pick them off from up here and keep them busy while our demolition men set the explosives."

"But the Germans have mortars," Andy told him. "If we don't take them out fast, they can zero in on us."

"I've thought of that," McComb said. "When they go to the mortars, we'll move through the brush, down the hill, and fire from closer range. They'll be firing up at the hillside, and we'll be in their faces."

Andy knew that small units could strike and pull back, but this sounded more like a frontal attack. A lot of men could die. And if the Germans were smart, they would have troops at the base of the bridge, not just at the ends. The demolition men could get picked off, and the whole operation would be a bust.

But things started well. When McComb signaled the men, Andy raised up, aimed carefully with his carbine, and dropped one of the guards standing near the end of the bridge. At the same time, two other Germans fell. Most of the German troops, however, took cover in the brush on either side of the bridge. Return fire soon began, and it was automatic fire, ripping through the foliage. Andy heard one of the

Maquisards cry out that he was hit, and he worried that others were going down.

Andy saw Germans from the other end of the bridge run to the aid of their comrades, some of them taking hits and falling under the fire. Two Germans also appeared on the road and tried to set up a mortar tube. Both went down, but a tube set up in deeper cover thumped, and a shell dropped into the underbrush not far from Andy. He heard another *Maquisard* scream with pain.

"Tell 'em to start down the hill," McComb yelled to Andy, and Andy gave the command, even though he doubted that enough German troops had been taken out. He worked his way forward and found a place where he could see the bridge. Two men had set up a machine gun and were beginning to fire. Andy leaned against a tree, took aim, and squeezed off a round that caught the gunner full in the face. Blood flew from his forehead, and he fell backward. The other man took over the gun, but Andy took him out the same way. And then he ran farther down the hill.

Andy could see other men working their way through the woods, but he couldn't see McComb. Then he heard a Sten gun, firing on automatic. He knew that had to be McComb. The guy had apparently made it to the road and was taking on the Germans face-to-face.

Andy hurried to get there to back him up, but machine-gun fire and mortar shells were ripping the woods now. Andy dropped down. He thought it might be time to give up the effort and pull the men back. But suddenly there was a huge explosion, the sound cracking like a thunderbolt and rumbling up and down the valley. Debris was flying, dropping into the woods. A huge cloud of dust filled the whole valley, and Andy couldn't see, but he heard McComb yell, "We got it. Fall back. Fall back."

Andy yelled the command in French and then climbed hard up the hillside. All fire had stopped for the moment. Andy kept scrambling through the trees, up the steep incline, watching for others. He was worried that he didn't hear or see much movement. The idea now was to retreat out of the valley and deep into the woods at the crest of the hill. Then the men would split up and work their way individually or in small groups back toward Malaunay or the other towns where they lived.

But when Andy reached the designated meeting point, no one else was there. He waited a couple of minutes before he saw another man stumbling toward him. The man's dark shirt was covered with bright blood, spilling down his chest and onto his denim trousers. He was holding his shoulder, and blood was running through his fingers. Andy got hold of him, eased him down, and then found a bandage in his rucksack. He was applying pressure to the man's shoulder when McComb showed up, helping another wounded man, this one with shrapnel in his thigh. McComb worked on him, and by then Evan and two others arrived. Evan's shirt was torn, and blood was running down his arm. A few more showed up after that, but only eleven out of twenty-seven.

"Some of them just didn't find their way back here," McComb told Andy. "I don't think we lost as many as it might look like."

"What about the demolition guys?" Andy asked. "Where are they?"

"They might have ended up on the other side of the river. They'll find their own way back."

Andy doubted that.

But McComb was grinning. "We got the job done," he said. "One whole end of that bridge went down. No train is getting through there for a while."

Andy was thinking about the price they had paid. They might have lost sixteen men, and three more were wounded—one quite badly. How could local Resistance leaders continue to recruit soldiers if word of this got around?

McComb seemed to know what Andy was thinking. He was still kneeling by the boy with the wounded leg, but he turned and looked at Andy. "Think about it, Gledhill. We got boys landing on beaches somewhere. If they get thrown back, we'll lose this war. We just stopped a railroad line that could carry German troops to the front."

"I know. It was a good operation. I just hope you're right that some of our other men are alive and making their own way home."

"Look, we did what we had to do—we took out that bridge. These French boys are fighting for their country; they know the risks."

Andy didn't look at McComb. He was still compressing the bandage against the wounded man's shoulder. He was a young man with a family; Andy knew that much about him. He hoped the bleeding could be stopped. "I told you, it was a good operation," Andy said. And then he asked the *Maquisard,* "Is that morphine starting to help?"

"Yes. It's starting to." But Andy could still hear the strain in his voice.

* * * * *

Andy walked with McComb and Evan most of the morning, staying in the woods, watching carefully before they crossed any roads. A little before dawn, they made it back to their safe house near the village of Le-Petit-Quevilly, but they had no time to sleep. They met with an informant, a man named Julien, who had been watching movements around the German army base in Rouen. A mobilization was about to get under way. Julien had heard a German soldier in a bistro complain that his company was to move out before nightfall and he could see no way that everything could be ready by then. Another convoy was getting ready to move out that afternoon. It would probably pass through the village, heading south.

"South?" McComb asked. "Why south?"

"The Allies have landed on the Normandy coast," Julien said in English. "In the Carentan Peninsula, west of here. The Germans have to cross the Seine and then turn to the west."

Andy had actually expected that, but McComb had argued that it would happen north, in the Pas de Calais.

"Well, we've got to slow those convoys." McComb had established a system for spreading word. "I sent our men home this morning," he told Julien, "but we need to assemble again, here. Get your runners out. Tell the leaders we need more men, new men, and we need them here as soon as possible—no later than 1500 hours." Then he looked at Andy. "You and Evan go find some spots where we can stop those trucks—three or four places, over a mile or two distance. We've got plenty of explosives, and the road runs through some pretty thickly wooded areas just south of here. We'll knock down trees on the road. We'll get them stopped and then ambush them."

That was a technique that instructors in London had talked about, but Andy worried that the team wouldn't have enough men. Still, Andy and Evan set off through the woods, staying off the road. Evan's wound wasn't serious, but his arm was bothering him and he had lost a fair amount of blood. He was slower than usual, less talkative. They found some spots a couple of miles south of the village where big trees hung out over the road, forming a canopy. It would not be difficult to drop them across the road, and some were big enough to require a great deal of work to remove.

By the time Evan and Andy had made it back to the farm where McComb had stayed, a few men had gathered, but only nine so far. One of them was a quiet little man named Victor who had fought the night before. When Andy walked into the house, Victor was dozing in a chair in the living room. He awakened and looked up, still looking weary. He was a man of at least fifty, the owner of a little café in town. He had fought in World War I, but he seemed too kindly to do what was being asked of him now. "Victor," Andy asked, "do we know what happened to the other men last night? Did any of the others get back?"

"I don't know," Victor said. "I tried to sleep a little, and then they came for me again."

McComb stepped into the room. "We found out a few things,"

McComb said. "None of the demolition guys came home. I'm thinking something went wrong. That blast happened sooner than I ever expected, and I have a feeling one of the pouches went off early. It might have killed those guys."

Andy thought of Reginald, a boy of seventeen or eighteen. He had looked so thrilled when Captain McComb had assigned him to go with the other demolition men. He was strong and able to climb, McComb had said. But maybe he had made a mistake and killed himself and the other men, one of them his uncle.

"It's something that happens in war," McComb said. "It might have been a mistake, but it worked, and in the long run, those three lost lives will save a lot of others." McComb was staring at Andy, almost daring him to disagree.

It was Victor who said, "Reginald's mother didn't want him to go. She was afraid this would happen. She lost her brother, too."

Andy translated the words for McComb, but he didn't respond. Instead, he said, "We did get some other men back. The one with the scar under his eye—whatever his name is. He's here, and he wasn't there last night. And he said he walked back with two others. I just hope we get a lot more men in here today."

"They come," Victor said in English. "But who dies today?"

McComb walked over to him. "Listen, you can't think about that," he said. "If you feel too old, if you can't do this, go home. But don't go with us into battle scared you're going to die."

Victor stood up. Andy wasn't sure how much he had understood, but he said, "Yes. I scare. But I fight."

"That's fine," McComb said. "But let's not whine anymore. Let's be men."

Victor didn't say anything, but his look expressed the disdain he felt for McComb.

During the next hour, men kept gathering. Another of the missing men arrived, and that meant that twelve had died the night before, at worst. Others might have been wounded and found their way somewhere to get help. The numbers sounded a little better, but Andy still remembered the faces of some who had died. He doubted that McComb did. He also wondered how many they had left in the woods who might have been patched up if they had been able to return and find them.

By 1500 hours, thirty-three men had gathered. With rain pelting down, McComb asked Andy to lead him and the other men through the woods to the ambush site he and Evan had chosen. He left Evan behind to collect any latecomers and join them two hours later. "I don't know when those trucks are going to be moving out, but the first thing we gotta do is get there ahead of 'em," he told Andy.

So they hiked to the spot, and then McComb deployed the men in the trees along one side of the road. He placed them back in the woods far enough to find cover, but in spots where they could get a clear look at the road. McComb and Andy chose the trees that would be dropped and helped set the explosives themselves. Then everyone waited. McComb had told the men to stay with him this time, so they could harass the convoy, perhaps for several days. If they could shut down the first trucks, others following from Rouen or from farther north would be held up on the same road. "We can't get away with this forever," he had told Andy. "Sooner or later, the Germans will have to send enough troops after us to clear us out. But we can hold things up for at least a couple of days."

Hours passed. Sunset was late this time of year, but the heavy clouds darkened the woods and added to the soldiers' concealment. Evan showed up with two more men, bringing the Resistance forces to thirty-five, plus the three Jeds.

McComb had sent a man well up the road to spot the convoy and signal its approach. He didn't want to drop the trees until shortly before the trucks showed up. That way there was no chance that word could get back to the German leaders in time for them to find some route around the blockade, maybe on country roads or across fields.

But the trucks didn't come. Andy wondered whether there was any chance that the convoy had gone some other way, but no one could think of any other road they could take without traveling well out of their way. So the men curled up in whatever makeshift manner they could, no one digging into the ground but curling up under trees, some wrapped in blankets. Everyone was soaked through, so there was no keeping warm.

Andy hadn't slept at all when they had gotten back to town the night before, and he was miserably tired, but with the cold, and with rain dripping on him through the stand of hardwood trees, he was too uncomfortable to drop off. He was reminded of his first days in France, when he had learned that the romantic life of an OSS agent was a few minutes of excitement followed by days of boredom. But just when he had decided that the convoy had delayed its trip until the next day, he heard McComb say, "Okay, we got the signal. They're coming. I just told the men to go ahead and detonate the explosives." Andy yelled to the men to plug their ears, and soon after, there were two big explosions and a pair of giant maple trees crashed across the road, one from each side, their limbs tangling together.

The noise—and the fear—brought Andy back to life. He could see *Maquisards* hiding not far from him, now alert and ready. The men all had their instructions. They should wait until the convoy was stopped and allow plenty of time for the Germans to survey the situation and discuss what they were going to do. As long as the convoy was bogged down, the men should sit tight, but once the Germans began to work on the trees and find some effective means to get them out of the way, McComb would fire the first shot. The men were spread out all along the road, and dark was finally coming on, which would give the Resistance men all the more advantage. Andy told them, according to

McComb's instructions, to pick out a man and be ready. When the first shot finally rang out, they should take out the German they had targeted, and then they should shoot up everything in sight for a minute or two. They could shoot into truck tires, at engines on smaller vehicles—anything that would inflict damage and delay. After the barrage of fire, the men were to fall back into the woods, then work their way farther south to the next sabotage site. Andy had described the chosen spot to them, and all of them knew where it was, so they didn't need to march together.

Andy had no problem with the plan, but he wondered how quickly the Germans would return fire, and how fast they might organize patrols to start searching. McComb seemed overly confident that the Germans would fall into confusion and disarray. But Andy knew that many of these German soldiers were highly experienced. A lot of them had come back wounded from the eastern front and had been sent to assist with the French occupation as a recovery assignment, but they were men who knew what they were doing, and certainly they knew something about ambushes.

Andy kept watching the road, and finally, over a hill came the first headlights. The trucks were rolling slowly, with an armored vehicle out in front. The car approached the trees, slowed even more, and then stopped. For a time, no one got out, and Andy knew what they were guessing, that the fire might come as they stepped from their vehicles. But it wasn't long until headlights turned off and men started piling out of the back of the troop trucks. They clearly had been instructed to get out and take up defensive positions if they were blocked in some way. Andy watched the numbers of men jumping out and hunkering down in the low areas on either side of the road. There were eight trucks, and certainly well over a hundred troops, and they were not easy to see. Andy knew that his Resistance men were about to grab the tail of a tiger.

After the troops were all deployed, two officers got out of the armored vehicle and knelt down too, ready with their weapons. After a couple of minutes, though, they stood and walked to the trees that were blocking the road, mere shadows on such a dark night, clouds covering what light there might have been from the moon. Time kept passing, but Andy's heart was beating hard.

Eventually, the officers seemed to decide that a truck could be brought up to push the trees to the side, but that meant moving the armored car and then bringing up not a troop truck but a heavy truck that was probably loaded with supplies or ammunition. Several troop trucks had to be moved to one side on the narrow road, and then the big truck crawled up close. But the bumper was too high, and that brought on more discussions. Men moved about, and the officers smoked cigarettes, apparently concluding that no attack was coming. At least half an hour went by before another armored car came up the road, driving around the bigger vehicles. The man who drove it stopped close to the tree and hefted a big chain out of the back. He soon discovered that there was nowhere to wrap the chain all the way around the tree, so the soldiers did some experimenting, finding a limb to link to, and then hooking the chain up to the truck. But nothing went easily. The chain wasn't really quite long enough, and it kept slipping. So the truck would pull until the tree angled in against the front bumper, and then the chain had to be taken off and reattached to a higher point on the tree. It was a grim sort of comedy. Eventually the first tree was far enough out of the way for the trucks to get past, but there was no way to get it all the way off the road, and that meant the second tree was an even bigger problem.

More discussions followed, and then the officers settled in and smoked again. Many of the soldiers were standing or leaning against trucks. Some had gotten back inside. The rain had mostly stopped, but the cold hadn't let up, and Andy wondered how much longer all this could last. After another hour he saw that a tank was moving along the road, passing the trucks. The Germans had probably sent for it all the way from Rouen. But this would work, and it wouldn't take long. Andy got ready.

The tank approached and stopped, and a man opened the hatch and looked out. He was talking to the officers when Andy saw his head explode. It took him a second to realize that McComb had fired his first shot. Andy opened up with a Sten gun, ripped into a row of men who had been sitting by their troop truck. And then he fired into the big supply truck, hoping to set off an explosion if there was ammunition inside. That produced nothing, so he raked the soldiers again, and then he heard the first bullets fly back at him. He crawled for twenty yards or so, scurrying on his hands and knees, his rifle in his hand, and then he jumped up and ran, staying low, getting deeper into the woods as fast as he could. He ran hard through the bracken, fighting the limbs and bushes that he could hardly see, but he felt better as he got more of the foliage behind him. He eventually broke out into a little clearing and spotted a man in black, like a shadow, running in the same direction. "Let's turn south now," he said, and he heard a grunt in return. They ran into some denser woods and then slowed to a fast walk.

"I killed some of them," the man said. "They were just standing there and I shot them down."

"They had decided we weren't there," Andy said.

"Such fools. They had no idea how to move those trees."

Andy knew, however, that although a tank would take out the next blockade quickly, no tank could keep up with a convoy, so the troops would be delayed again when the next trees went down. The Germans would be ready this time, though, and he hoped McComb would take that into account.

Andy kept walking with the man he'd met. His name was Sabastien, he said, "and that's not a code name. I'm a soldier now. I'll use my real name." After a time they found another man moving in the same direction. It took them half an hour or so to reach the next ambush spot, and they knew that the convoy would be moving again soon. McComb was there ahead of them. "All right, that was perfect," he told Andy. "We slowed 'em down about four hours, I figure, by the time they get here."

"We can't stay so close to the road this time," Andy said. "They'll pile off and come looking for us immediately."

"Hey, I know that. I'm way ahead of you. I'm putting a couple of snipers in trees. We'll let those guys search around for a while. And then, just when they think they're all right, and they've got their tank in position, we'll take out a couple of their leaders. German troops don't know what to do without their commanders. I should have taken out those officers last time, but the tank came up and blocked my view."

"Well, it worked out fine," Andy said. "But it could be sunrise by the time we get finished with this next ambush. If we stick men in trees, how are they going to get down and get away without being spotted?"

Andy could see that McComb hadn't considered that possibility. He looked away for a few seconds and then said, "They'll be here pretty fast. If our men see the first light coming, I'll tell them to fire away and then get out fast. That'll put the idea in the Germans' heads that we're still out here, and they'll spend some time looking for us. But I want you to move everyone out, except for the snipers, as soon as we're all here."

McComb kept most of his troops well back in the woods for the time being, but he sent two men up to the road to drop some more trees. It wasn't long until the explosions sounded. When the men came back, they said these trees hadn't dropped as precisely as the time before, one falling mostly sideways so it only blocked about half the road, but the Germans would still have a mess to clean up. McComb sent Andy and the men on their way at that point to set up the next ambush. To his credit, he stayed behind to act as one of the sharpshooters himself.

Andy considered the next move as he led his men through the woods, and he and Evan talked about the possibilities. They decided to work from the opposite side of the road this time.

Andy got his men set up and left someone to spot McComb and the other sniper when they showed up on the other side of the road. After a time the sound of McComb's Sten gun rang over the valley, and then a terrific volley of small arms fire followed. It was only about fifteen minutes before McComb showed up. He had been running hard and was out of breath, but the man was in great condition. "What do you think we ought to do this time?" he asked. He sounded excited, almost like a kid playing a game.

"Where's Louis?" Andy asked.

"I don't know. Maybe they got him. I never saw him once I dropped out of the tree. He fired his weapon, and that's all I heard. But the good thing is, I know I took out at least one of those officers from the armored car. I saw him go down. The other one might have just ducked, but he hit the dirt too. The thing is, though, we've got to think about the light this time. We've got to go about this a little different."

"I know," Andy said. He was looking to see whether Louis was approaching, but he saw no one. "Evan and I were thinking we could hit them hard as soon as they get out of their trucks, and then we'll fall back along a trail up here as fast as we can go. They're not going to chase us too far, not on a trail where they know we can set up an ambush."

"And that's just what we'll do," said McComb. "Let's go find a spot. We'll run back there a couple hundred yards and then slip off into the trees. When the Germans come tromping up there, we'll cut them down, and when that unit doesn't come back, their officers won't send anyone to chase us next time."

"But they might send a lot of men. We could get caught in our own trap. If we shoot up the first men who come up the trail and don't get away, they could overpower us."

"We can take the first bunch and then scatter back into the woods. We'll get a whole lot more of them than they can get of us. Come on. Let's go find the spot." McComb had already caught his breath. He walked hard, and Andy, who was in good shape himself, had to push himself to keep up. McComb chose a spot, and then he and Andy walked back to the men and got them in place. Another wait began—but not nearly as long this time.

The convoy approached the downed trees faster this time. The men piled out immediately and ran for cover. The Resistance men fired in a massive volley, and then they jumped onto the trail and ran hard up the hill. McComb let everyone run past him and brought up the rear, whispering intensely all the way, "Go hard! Come on. Go faster!"

Andy had been assigned to lead. He found the ambush spot and quickly placed his men. They climbed onto some high ground overlooking the path and hunkered down in the underbrush. "Don't fire until I do," McComb said, and Andy repeated the command.

Only a couple more minutes passed before Andy heard someone on the trail. A German patrol was coming, all right, but they weren't running now. They were moving carefully, expecting trouble. McComb let them keep coming, let most of them pass by his post, and then he shot down the last guy. What followed was a massacre. In a few seconds, all the Germans were down on the trail or in the brush on the other side of the trail, where they had tried to run. Andy could hear them gurgling, moaning. He could see blood on the leaves of the brush, could see a hulking soldier, flat on his back, not moving.

"Wait. They might have sent more," he told the men. "Sit tight." But it became clear after a time that this patrol—twelve men, as it turned out—had been the only ones sent, and the plan had worked perfectly. McComb was the first to walk out of the brush and survey the situation. He walked along the trail and three times fired his sidearm into German bodies—men he apparently thought were still breathing. Finally he said, "We got every one of 'em," and he laughed. The other *Maquis* joined him on the trail, and some of them laughed too, slapped each other on the back. Andy understood that. The French had been pushed around by German troops for years now, and finally they were getting some pay-back. They had no regret.

Andy stepped onto the trail and looked at the dead soldier he had seen before. Blood was running from his mouth. He was an ordinary-looking guy, a corporal, with a day's growth of beard and a uniform jacket that was frayed around the collar. He had been around this war for a while and probably knew, walking up this trail, that some officer had made a mistake to send him up there. His face was pale already, and blood was pooling in the crook of his neck where a big chunk of flesh had been torn away. Some of the men moved from body to body, pulling everything out of the soldiers' pockets, taking their pistols. Andy walked off the trail and looked up into the tall trees. A flying flash of blue passed his eyes. The bird didn't care what had just happened here. This was just another day as far as it was concerned.

Victor stepped up next to Andy and said, "Some of those Germans were just boys."

"I know," Andy said.

"All right, let's move out," McComb was calling. "We've got to get ahead of them again and stop them all day long."

He headed up the trail and turned south once more. The game would continue.

CHAPTER 19

WHEN FLIP GOT OUT of bed he could hear a man's voice in the living room, mellow yet dramatic—and he realized that he was hearing the radio. He walked down the hall and into the living room and saw his dad leaning forward with his elbows on his knees, listening closely to every word. He looked up at Flip, continued to listen for a time, and then said, "I think this landing is going to hold. It's afternoon in France, and they got a lot more men on shore today."

The invasion had started on Tuesday, June 6, and now it was Saturday morning. Flip liked knowing that the boys were holding on, and he loved to read the *Deseret News* from Salt Lake, or the *Millard County Chronicle*, which came once a week, and to study the maps and see the progression of the war in the Pacific or in Italy. Now he hoped that the lines for the new front would spread quickly across France and into Germany. And yet, he also worried that the war would soon end. He wanted to get there. He had seen boys come home from the war on furlough, or wounded, and he had heard the way people talked to them. If they came into the bank, or walked into sacrament meeting on a Sunday, everyone would shake their hands and thank them for serving. The ones who had been in a safe place, maybe here in the States, would always say they hoped they could get to the fight sooner or later, but the ones who had seen action would say very little. They didn't have to. Everyone knew they were heroes.

"Do you think Andy is part of it?" Flip asked.

"I don't know, son. Airborne units did drop in behind the lines that first day, and it's possible that Andy's back with the Eighty-Second, but he didn't say anything about that. Maybe he wasn't allowed to say."

"I don't get that. And how come they told him he couldn't write to us again?"

"I don't know, Flip. He's obviously doing something secret. I know they send spies in before an invasion like this."

That was what Flip thought too, and he knew it was what his mother had decided. The idea scared Flip. At the same time, Andy had obviously done something secret before, and he had made it through. If he did that again, he would come home the biggest hero in Delta: a spy. Flip could imagine the stories Andy would be able to tell his grandkids someday, while Flip would be talking about going to high school and not doing one thing worth mentioning. Flip couldn't speak as much French as Andy, but he could get by if he had to. He sometimes imagined driving his dad's car over to Fillmore to the recruiting office and telling one of those guys, "Look, I know I'm still a little below the age requirement, but don't you need guys who can speak French? I could be a spy, if that's what you're looking for—and I look young enough, no one would ever catch on." But he knew they wouldn't go for it, and besides, all that was going to be over soon. France would for sure fall to the Allies if this invasion really took hold.

Flip could smell bacon in the kitchen. He walked in and said, "Good morning, Mom."

She glanced at him with that look of worry that was always in her eyes now.

"He made it last time," Flip said.

She smiled a little. "I know. Thank you, Flip. You know what I'm thinking, don't you?"

"It's what we're all thinking."

"Marjie Burton got a telegram yesterday. Her son Grant was killed the first day of the landing."

"I know. I heard. Everyone at the bank was talking about it yester-day."

Grant was one of those guys no one paid much attention to. He had worked at the Texaco station before he'd gone in the army, and he would fill up your car and wash your windows and everything, but usually not say a word. He was good with cars, and he was polite, but mostly he was just Grant. Now everyone who came into the bank was talking about him being such a "fine young man." "He paid the ultimate price," they would say. "He died for all of us." Someday Delta would put up a memorial to this war, the same as for the first one, and Grant would have his name on it. It almost seemed, for Grant, it was better to have his name on a plaque than just to be the guy who worked down at the Texaco station.

After breakfast, Flip rode his bicycle out to the farm. He and Tom didn't always put in a full day on Saturdays, but they needed to fix some fences, and they had decided to leave that work for this morning. Flip wasn't too excited about that. It seemed like all he did was work these days. But at least he was with Tom. He hardly had any other friends any-more. Some of the guys his age were dating girls quite a bit, and almost all of them were playing baseball most nights. Either that, or they got together and threw a football around. Pretty much all the guys he'd grown up with would be on the team again in the fall. Flip had actually grown about an inch in the last few months, and he was hoping that he was about to get his growth, finally, but he knew better than to go out for football. Every time he saw the guys his age—the boys he'd gone out into the desert with when he was a kid, hunting for arrowheads and topaz, and shooting BB guns—they now talked mostly about sports, and sooner or later, someone always made some crack about Flip's trying out for water boy, or going out for cheerleader with his sister. Chrissy was going to be a cheerleader in the fall, and she never had cared much about sports. Nowadays, though, she was talking about football all the time—or about the football players, anyway.

At least when Flip was with Tom, he didn't have to listen to any of that kind of stuff. Tom could talk about all kinds of things that kids around Delta knew nothing about: California, jazz music, and everything about the war. When Flip arrived at the farm that morning, he found Tom sitting on the front steps of the old house. He was lacing on his boots. The first thing he said was, "Have you heard the war news this morning?"

"Yeah," Flip said. "It sounds like we've got us a good toehold, anyway."

"Yeah, I know. I've been listening too."

But Flip could hear disappointment in Tom's voice. "Don't worry. It's going to take a long time to take Germany. You can still get there."

"It takes a lot of months to get through boot camp and all that other training you have to go through. It can be the better part of a year before you get to the fighting."

"Not so much anymore. They'll be sending men over a lot faster—you know, to be replacements for men who get shot. I hear guys talking about that stuff down at the bank when I go in there. And at the barber shop."

Tom pulled the knot tight on one of his boots, and then he looked up at Flip. "One thing's for sure. The war's going to be over before you can sign up."

Tom said it like that was a good thing, and that bothered Flip. He knew that Tom thought he was just a kid. So he said what he'd been thinking lately, just to see who had guts and who didn't. "I've got an idea, Tom. I thought about it all day yesterday."

"Hey, be careful, man. You think that long, you could hurt something. I try to keep my thinking down to two or three minutes, tops." He looked up and grinned. He seemed to know that he'd made Flip mad.

Flip squared off in front of Tom, his hands on his hips. "No, I'm serious. I thought up a way we can maybe make things right—I mean, about the stuff people are taking from your house in California."

"All right, brain man, tell me how I'm supposed to do that." Tom leaned back, with his elbows behind him on the porch.

"My mom and dad are driving up to see my dad's brother in Ogden this next weekend. They're leaving on Thursday morning and they won't be back until Sunday night. While they're gone, why don't we drive our old truck down to Berkeley and pick up your stuff? We could get back before they come home."

"Are you crazy? If I got caught out on the highway, they'd throw me in jail just like some guy who broke out of prison."

"But that's only if we got picked up. Why would that happen? We could drive straight out across Highway 50, right through the middle of Nevada. The cops don't even bother to go out there."

"You still pass through Reno, don't you?"

"Sure, but we'd just mind our business and drive slow, and then we could get to your house, maybe at night, load up your stuff, and head back across the desert again."

"I don't think that old truck would make it—especially over the mountains."

"It needs a couple of tires, but I think Raymond, down at our dealership, could find me some used ones. We might have to take some extra water, in case the radiator heats up, but other than that, it always runs."

"Flip, you're crazy. We can't do something like that. They'd throw *you* in jail, too."

"Naw. I'd tell 'em I'm just young and stupid, and you talked me into it." He grinned.

"That's about right. That's what they'd think, too. They'd probably get me for kidnapping."

Flip liked that it was Tom doing all the backpedaling, and that he, Flip, was the one not afraid to take a chance. But he wished that Tom were more interested. He liked the idea of driving all day and all night, if that was what it took, and getting whatever was left at Tom's house. He even liked the idea of doing something he wasn't supposed to do. Someday he might have a story of his own to tell.

Tom sat up straight and asked, "How would we get enough gas?" He actually did sound as though he were thinking this over.

"I've thought about that. I could fill up with Dad's gas stamps the first time. He lets me do that when the truck needs gas. But I was thinking, Whisper's dad has plenty of coupons. He has a car, but it's been broken down for about a year now and he hasn't fixed it. I could talk to Whisper and see whether there's some way I could get some of his stamps."

"Those things expire after a while."

"I know they do. But he must have quite a few that are still good."

"What's Whisper going to do, steal them from her father?"

"No. I could pay her something for them. And she wouldn't have to say who she sold them to."

"That's black market, Flip. Another crime. You really do want to be a jailbird, don't you?"

"Fine. If you don't dare do it, it's no skin off my nose. Let's just get to work."

Tom laughed. Then he stood up. "Hey, look, I wish it would work.

You're a good guy for thinking of something like that. But I don't want to get you in a bunch of trouble. You've got nothing to gain from this."

"I'd see California. And I'd feel like I *did something* for once."

Tom was still smiling. He was wearing an old, gray, long-sleeved shirt, but he hadn't buttoned the cuffs. Now he started rolling up one of the sleeves. "What are you talking about, Flip? Don't you find enough stuff to do?"

"You know what I'm talking about. I *can't* do much of anything. There's nothing I'm good at."

Tom started on the other sleeve. "What do you want to be good at? Driving across Nevada at night?"

"No." Flip decided he didn't want to talk about this. "Where are we going to start on the fence?"

"Out behind the barn. Your dad wants to put some calves in that field out there, and we've got to get the fence in shape to keep them in." He turned and walked back to the front door of the house. "Just a sec," he said. He jerked at the old screen door, which resisted and then popped open, as always. He was gone for a minute or so, and then showed up wearing a straw hat and holding a pair of gloves. "Did you bring gloves?" he asked.

Flip pulled a pair out of his back pocket. "Sure."

The boys walked to the pasture beyond the barn and then followed the fence, inspecting it. Tom finally repeated, "What do you want to be good at, Flip?"

"I don't know. Anything, I guess."

"What about school? You get good grades, don't you?"

"Not so much lately. No one cares about that anyway."

"Mostly, you want the guys at school to stop giving you a hard time. Right?"

"I guess."

"Then just look 'em in the eye and *be* somebody. I can jitterbug better than almost anybody, and I write for the school paper, and I play baseball. But all that doesn't matter much. I just know I'm an okay guy, and everyone knows I know it."

"What about when you walk through town and everyone stares at you?"

"I don't like it, but I look back at 'em. I say, 'Hello, sir. How are you? It's a beautiful day, isn't it?' And they nod and tell me it is. My mom and dad can't do that. They walk around with their heads down, and they move off to the side and let people go by. But I don't. I've got a right to the sidewalk, same as anyone else."

Flip pulled his gloves on and hoisted a wire. "We can just nail this one back up," he said. "I don't think it needs to be stretched."

Tom nodded, but he didn't look at the wire. "You're going to get tall someday, Flip. That'll take care of itself. But you gotta start thinking tall now. You're probably thinking I'm cocky—that's what people say about me—but a guy can be two feet taller than me and I can still look him straight in the eye. That's what you gotta do too."

Tom *was* sort of cocky, and Flip liked him least when he tried to talk so big. But he knew what the guy meant. That was why he wanted to get to the war. For now, though, he wanted to get in that truck and do something not one of the guys around town had ever done. He half liked the idea of getting caught and getting his fanny thrown in jail.

"How would we take off without your sisters knowing what was going on?"

"What?"

"You heard me."

"Would you really go?"

"I don't know. I'm just asking."

"I'd tell my dad I was going to stay out here at the farm the whole time he's gone—you know, so I don't have to ride my bike back and forth. My sisters never come out here. They'd never know I was gone."

"Could you really get some tires?"

"Raymond has recaps down at the garage. If he didn't have any used tires, he'd let me take a couple of those. I'd just tell him it was for the truck at the farm."

"You have to apply for tires. The ration board can only give out so many a month."

"Yeah, but Raymond would work something for me. I'd just tell him I had to have them to keep the farm running."

"And what would Raymond say to your dad?"

"I don't know. He might say something sometime, and I'd just say the truck needed tires. My dad knows it's true."

Tom had grabbed the strand of wire, but he was still looking at Flip. "Even if Whisper gave you some stamps, we'd still have to buy the gas. I'm not sure I have enough money for that."

"I've got some money saved up—enough for that, anyway."

"You'd spend *your* money to drive me to California?"

"Yeah. Why not?"

"But I still don't see Whisper letting us have her father's stamps."

"Maybe not. But I could ask her. Do you want me to?"

Tom shrugged. "I don't know. It wouldn't hurt anything to ask."

"Do you want to go, then?"

"No. I don't think so. I'm just thinking."

"You're thinking about all your stuff—and somebody walking off with it."

"Yeah. I think about that all the time."

*   *   *   *   *

After dinner that night Flip walked over to Whisper's house. When he knocked on the door, she asked him to come in. "Why don't you come out here?" Flip said. "I wanted to talk to you about something."

She stepped out, but she said, "It's still awfully hot out here, Flip. I think it's a little cooler in the house."

"I know. But I need to ask you something." He glanced at her quickly, the way he always did—embarrassed to look at her very long.

She walked to the love seat and sat down. The sun was still fairly high in the sky, and the air was so hot and dry it felt brittle enough to crack. "I used to like summer so much when I was a girl," Whisper said. "I'm getting so I hate it now."

"I like it better than winter," Flip said. "The wind about takes the hide off my face when I walk over to the school in the winter."

"Delta's too hot *and* too cold. And the wind never stops. There have to be better places than this to live."

"I don't think Fillmore's any better."

"I don't either."

Flip could remember a time when Whisper thought everything was wonderful; he hated hearing her sound so unhappy.

"What did you want to talk to me about, Flip?" He could tell that she wanted to get this over and go back in the house.

"Your dad must have some gas stamps he doesn't use now, with his car broken down."

"He does. We wish we could sell them, but it's illegal."

"If someone could really use them, for—you know—something worthwhile, do you think you could let him have a few?"

"Me? They're not mine. You'd have to ask my dad."

"Yeah. I guess. But I think maybe he wouldn't—you know—be so willing as you would."

"Flip, just tell me what you're talking about."

He glanced at her again. She was wearing a faded green house dress with little yellow flowers. Her hair looked a little messy, her face expressionless. Life was going out of her these days; Flip noticed it more all the time. He felt his own enthusiasm die. He knew what she was going to say. "You know my friend Tom?"

"Yes."

"You know how I told you that people were stealing all the stuff in his house in Berkeley?"

"Yes."

"I just think that's really wrong, don't you?"

"Of course."

"It seems like if me and him could drive down there and get his stuff before it's all gone, that would be the right thing to do."

"You want to *drive* to California? And you want our gas stamps?"

"You're not using them. What could it hurt?"

"Well, you're right about one thing. Dad would never give them to you."

"Why? Don't you think it's the right thing to do?"

She actually smiled just a little. "Oh, Flip, you *do* come up with things. Why don't you walk in the house and tell my dad you want to use his stamps to drive a Jap home to get his belongings—a Jap who's not allowed to go to California. My dad is a nice man, but he thinks too many Japs are running around outside that camp as it is."

"I know. I know what people say. But I know Tom, too, and he's going into the army as soon as he can. He wants to kill Germans. I think he'd go fight the real Japs if they'd let him."

"Flip, that's great. I'm glad you like him. And I don't have anything against Japs. The ones who come into the bank are nice as can be. I'm just telling you that my dad won't give you any stamps."

"But you could maybe sneak some. He's never going to use them. You told me that yourself, that you'd probably never get enough money ahead to get your car fixed. So he probably doesn't even look at those stamps."

Whisper laughed, softly, and shook her head. "You're talking to Whisper Harris, Flip. I don't do things like that. You know me."

"Yeah. I kind of expected you to say that, but I thought I'd ask." Flip was disappointed, in a way, but maybe relieved, too. He liked to think about doing things, and taking big chances, but he never really did any of them. And this was probably the craziest idea he had ever let himself think up. It had scared him all along.

He glanced again at Whisper. She was sitting back, her eyes focused on some distant place—maybe the gray sky that seemed to be drooping in the heat, like everything else. He knew that every day was tedious for Whisper right now. "Things are still going good in France," Flip said. "I heard some people say the war could be over by Christmas. Even my dad says, with the Russians coming from the east and us from the west, we'll finish off the Germans inside a year."

Whisper nodded.

"I think Andy's going to make it, and I think he'll come home and be himself in hardly any time at all."

"Could I go with you?"

"What?"

"I won't give you the stamps unless you let me go with you."

"Me and Tom?"

"Yes."

"Whisper, you wouldn't do that. We could get in a lot of trouble. We could end up in jail."

"Would we see the ocean?"

"Not exactly. I looked at the map, and we'd be across that big bay from San Francisco. We'd see that one bridge that crosses over the bay, but not the Golden Gate."

"Would we see any palm trees?"

"I don't know if they have them up in that part of California. But we'd see Reno, and the Sierra Mountains, and we'd cross down through Sacramento. They probably have some palm trees there."

"I'll give you all the stamps you want if you'll let me go."

"Whisper, my dad would kill me if I got you in a bunch of trouble, and Andy would never forgive me."

"Andy doesn't care, Flip. It's time we both faced that. Andy doesn't love me, and my choice is to marry Lamar or be an old maid and live in this town the rest of my life, doing the same things every day."

"Come on, Whisper. You're the prettiest girl in—"

"You don't have a driver's license and Tom doesn't either. You need someone with a driver's license."

"We're crossing on Highway 50, out where no one goes. We don't need one."

"You might. If we got stopped somewhere and I had a driver's license, we might just say that Tom works on our farm in some town we could name. But if you're both out there without driver's licences, you're in a lot more trouble."

"Where would you say you were going, Whisper? Your dad would have a bunch of questions."

"When would we leave?"

"Thursday night, probably, so we can drive through the desert when it's not so hot."

"I'll figure something out."

"Are you serious, Whisper?"

"Yes. I want to do this."

Flip hadn't expected this. He wanted to be excited that she would go, but he had actually never been so scared in his life.

CHAPTER 20

ANDY HAD SPENT four days following the same German convoy. After
a time, the Germans had brought in more tanks to lead out. The
tanks could push fallen trees aside quickly, but they were slow, and they
held down the pace of all the trucks behind them. McComb had
changed his tactics in response to the new situation. He had made contact with another Resistance circuit and brought in more men. He had
even managed to locate a couple of mortar tubes. The plan now was to
attack the flank of the convoy, fire into the trucks, knock out tires or
blow up truck engines, and then get away fast. This had continued to
slow the progress of the convoy, but seven *Maquisards* had gone down in
the battles: two killed and five wounded badly enough to be out of
action.

Gradually the road was being bogged down with more convoys heading the same direction, and that was good, since more troops were being
delayed, but it also meant more enemy soldiers were annoyed and ready
to hunt down the sabotage groups. They were chasing the *Maquisards*
farther all the time and sending bigger units.

McComb kept making his little speeches. The boys in Normandy
were getting stronger, but every day these backup forces could be kept
out of the fight, more Allies would get ashore. He believed the next few
days would still be crucial.

Then word came that the Germans had almost completed a stop-gap repair of the railroad bridge near Barentin—the one that McComb's group had blown up. Trains would soon be running again if something weren't done. McComb turned the convoy over to forces in the area and led his own men back toward the bridge. They spent a long day marching, hidden in the woods, and then slept for a night while Andy and another man hiked closer to do reconnaissance on the bridge. Andy had slept very little since all the action had started, and he had hoped to sleep that night. But he followed orders, walked through the woods to the bridge, and saw that the Germans had used timbers to build a well-crafted repair. The rails were not yet reset, but that appeared to be all that was left to do.

When Andy got back to camp, McComb was sleeping, so he didn't bother him. He lay down in a grassy spot, curled up in a shelter-half, and fell instantly to sleep, but he didn't sleep long before McComb woke him. "What did you find out?" he was asking. "You were supposed to let me know."

Andy rolled onto his back and pushed the canvas off him. He could hardly think what McComb had asked. He rubbed his hand over his face, tried to wipe away some of the dampness, but he felt wet all the way through—as much from sweat as from the moisture in the air. Sometimes he thought that if he could spend one quiet night in a bed, he would actually come back to life. "We've got to blow that bridge again, right away," he finally said. "They'll be getting trains across it before the day is over."

"Let's go now then. Let's hit them before sunrise."

Andy knew that was the right thing to do, but he also knew how tired the men were. He hated the thought of rousting them out again. But he sat up. "All right," he said. "I couldn't tell how many troops are there. They had a patrol at each end, but there are probably more camped nearby."

"I doubt they've added any more men since we hit them last time. They're getting spread pretty thin trying to watch all their bridges and still get all the men they can shipped to the front."

"Maybe we should hit a different bridge this time—farther up or down the same line."

"This one is already half gone. If we can blow out the other end of the thing, they won't be able to fix it again. Besides, they expect us to hit a different one, not to return where we've been before."

Andy wasn't at all sure of that. He only knew they were down to about twenty-three or twenty-four men, including the Jed team, and if most of a platoon was still covering the bridge, McComb was flirting with disaster one more time. He was brave and, Andy now realized, pretty smart—and he was willing to gamble with his own life as much as with anyone's—but he had lost a lot of men already, and he didn't seem to worry about that.

"I want to hit with all our men on one side of the river. This time I want *you* to set the explosives. If we'd done it right last time, we wouldn't be going back now. Take one man with you and swim the river. We'll shoot them up enough to pull their guards to the side they've been reconstructing; then you climb up under that bridge and blow out the other side."

"I'm not that much of an explosives man, Captain."

"Who is? You've had the same training I have. Take Evan with you. The two of you know that stuff better than these French guys do. That's why we got messed up last time. I never should have sent the men I did."

Andy had thought McComb considered "last time" a great success, but he didn't say that. He only got up and said, "Not Evan. He hates the water, and he's too short to wade out very deep."

"Okay. I'll get you another man."

"I need to get things ready."

"How long is that going to take?"

Andy was wondering how much he remembered from his explosives training. He knew he couldn't make a mistake or he would get himself killed. "Twenty, thirty minutes."

"Do it in fifteen. We've got to get these guys up and going by then. We've only got a couple of hours until the sun comes up."

So Andy prepared his plastic explosives in the dark, while a man named Georges held a flashlight for him. An hour later Andy and Georges were wading into the river. The water was actually quite shallow, and they walked much of the way, until they hit a deeper, swifter current and set out swimming for a few yards. Andy had never considered himself a great swimmer, and now he had to struggle to keep the explosives, detonator, and fuse out of the water. The current took him well downstream. Georges got across more easily and then hurried down the bank to grab the explosives from Andy and help him out of the water. They were half a mile below the bridge, so they weren't worried about being spotted, but they would have to hurry to get to the bridge by 0430, when the shooting would start.

So they hiked hard, without speaking, slowing their pace only as they drew near to the bridge. Andy led Georges away from the river and into the trees, and then they edged along through the underbrush, staying in the shadows. There was still a fairly full moon in the western sky, which helped Andy see the bridge, but that same light added to the danger as he tried to get close. The rest of the team would be facing similar problems as they tried to get into position.

Andy was still twenty yards or more from where he wanted to hunker down when the gunfire started, sooner than he had expected. Maybe someone had spotted the team and fired on them. In any case, a few rounds pinging in the night turned quickly into a barrage of fire. Andy allowed a minute or so; then he touched Georges on the arm, and the two dashed out of their cover toward the bridge. But bullets whipped through the air, cracking as they flew past Andy's head. And suddenly Georges was down in the sand on the bank of the river.

Andy dove to the ground, into the shadow of some overhanging trees. "Georges. Georges. Are you all right?" There was no answer. Andy crawled back to him, slithering in the sand, never lifting his head. When he reached Georges, he felt for his neck and tried without success to find a pulse. He cupped his hand over Georges's mouth and nose but felt no life, no breath. Andy was on his own.

He raised his head just enough to peek out from under his helmet. There were two men at the base of the bridge, watching, looking left and right, holding their rifles ready. Andy was carrying the explosives in a rucksack. He wondered whether the explosives would blow if hit by a bullet. He decided to act, not wait to find out. He pulled his rifle strap off his shoulder, slowly, trying not to be seen, and then he raised up enough to aim. Another bullet cracked past him, but he fired, and one man went down. The other one slipped back into the dark, under the bridge, but Andy came up running, firing. He saw the man step out to challenge him and then drop into the mud by the river.

Andy kept going. He figured there were other men across the river, maybe under the bridge, but he couldn't let his men who were attacking the bridge take such a big chance for nothing. He was almost to the foot of the bridge when bullets flew, smashing into the brick, spraying chunks at him. He ducked into the dark under the bridge, felt for something to grab hold of, and found a wooden support. He knew he had to get high under the arch of the bridge, and that was dangerous, but he climbed through the wooden supports that the Germans had used in their reconstruction. He had no idea whether he could be seen. He pulled himself up quickly, frantically, and then he slipped his rucksack off, slipped his hand in, and pulled out the packet of explosives. He pushed the whole package under a strut, against the brick. Then he found the detonator, forced it into the soft explosive, covered it over, and packed it tight. He had prepared a long fuse attached to the detonator. But now he knew that the fuse would allow too much time for someone to cross the river and detach it, so he pulled a knife from a sheath on his belt and cut the fuse much shorter. He climbed back down through the supports a little way, letting the fuse string through his hand. When he was ready to drop, he pulled a lighter from his pocket, lit the cord, and leaped feet first into the river.

He heard the first bullet before he hit the water. He wanted to go down, find some cover in the stream, but the water was only knee deep. He slumped low, heard another crack of gunfire, and then came up diving toward deeper water. But as he did, he felt a bullet rip at his thigh. He kept fighting his way until he found the stronger current, and then he let the water take him, whisking him downstream. He rode it as best he could, all the while fearing that he would take a bullet in the head, but then came the thunder. The concussion from the explosion bashed into him, sent him under the water. Seconds later, debris pounded the water around him, a piece of brick or mortar striking him in the cheek. After just a few more seconds, everything was quiet, and he swam harder, afraid of the current now, worried that he lacked the energy to swim out of trouble. He kept kicking, reaching, and then, feeling that he was in slower water, he reached down and found the bottom. He slogged through the mud for a little way, swam a little more, and finally pulled himself up on the shore. He looked back and saw the strange silhouette, the two ends of the bridge standing like sentinels with nothing between.

But he was remembering his leg now. He sat up and felt for the wound, but there was only a sting when he pressed it, so he didn't worry. He got up and walked into the woods, hiking hard to find his men. Moonlight was filtering into the trees, and he could see pretty well. He forced his way through the bracken until he found a trail and was able to move faster. The team had to get clear of the area fast. McComb had warned Andy that they wouldn't wait for him. Everyone would scatter, work their way through the woods, and assemble a couple of miles away at a spot near a farmhouse that everyone knew. Andy could catch up with them there.

So he hiked in the dark, under the trees, and he felt some satisfaction that he had gotten the job done—and lived. But he also thought of Georges, back there on the bank of the river. He wasn't very old, still in his twenties, Andy figured, and he was married to a pretty young woman with dark eyes. They had children, at least two. Today she would be one more woman who would find out her husband was gone.

Andy didn't find McComb where he was supposed to be, and he decided they must have kept moving. Perhaps they were being chased. But as the sun came up, he saw no one else, no German patrols out searching. So he headed for the safe house, back near Malaunay. If McComb wasn't there, Andy would hide out, and he would rest, dress whatever wound he had, and sleep. McComb would have to come find him. He had no idea where to look for the guy.

Andy was almost back to the village when he spotted one of the *Maquisards* walking in the woods ahead of him. He was holding one arm, which was wrapped up in a bandage. "Anton," Andy called to him, and the man turned and looked back. "Are you hurt?" he asked.

"Yes. A little. What about you?"

Andy had checked his wound by now and found it was nothing. A bullet had torn at his trousers and broken the skin along the front of his thigh, but it hadn't penetrated. "No. I'm not hurt. Where are the other men?"

"We were walking back to our homes—to get some rest. But we saw some men from Malaunay. They had bad news. There's a tiny village not far from the bridge. It's called Cléres. After we attacked the bridge the first time, the Germans went there and attacked the people. We've heard there was a massacre. The captain took most of our men there, to Cléres."

Andy had heard of Germans exacting retribution in that way, but he had always hoped those were merely rumors the French people spread, not something that *anyone,* even Nazis, would really do. He hoped this was only a rumor now, but he felt ill. If the Germans had taken revenge on this little town, it was revenge for what Andy and McComb and their men had done.

"It's their way of scaring our people, so they won't fight," Anton said.

"Yes. I understand. But what was the captain planning to do? Why did he go there?"

"There are other houses—farms outside the village. The captain said he would go defend them."

Andy wondered whether that was wise. If the Germans came, they might come in force. But he had to give McComb credit—the man didn't back down. So Andy asked for directions, reversed himself, and headed back in the direction of the bridge. He found the town, but he didn't find McComb.

Andy walked through the village, a tiny place, just a couple of dozen homes. The houses were locked up, and no one was in the streets, or in the little market in the center of town, or in the tiny school. Andy kept walking on into the country. Anton had said that McComb was worried for the safety of the farmers. He and his men would be somewhere in the area.

On the edge of the village Andy saw a cemetery filled with old, mossy gravestones leaning in all directions. At one end of it, down a little hill, several men were digging, already knee deep in a wide hole. Andy walked into the cemetery toward the men. Some of them looked up at him, but their faces were hollow. And then Andy saw, beyond them, a long row of bodies, wrapped in sheets or blankets, stacked two and three deep—dozens of them.

"Are these the people from Cléres?" he asked.

One of the men—a farmer, Andy guessed, wearing an old coat and a beret—looked up from his shoveling and said, "Yes. Certainly."

"How many were killed?"

"Everyone," the man said. "I didn't count." He went back to his digging, clearly not interested in answering Andy's questions.

Andy looked back to the row of bodies, noticing that at the end was a shorter bundle, seemingly wrapped in a pillowcase. He walked around the grave the men were digging and stepped close to the little shroud. By then he could see that all the bodies on that end of the stack were small. But this smallest bundle, not more than two feet long, had to contain a baby. A revulsion was building up in Andy—rage. And then he saw a little hand protruding from one of the wrappings. It was pale, almost blue, but the little fingers were perfect, like those of a newborn baby. Someone had gunned down this child, killed it in cold blood.

"How could anyone do this?" Andy asked himself out loud. "What's wrong with these Nazis? They're not human." He had been looking for hatred all this time; suddenly it was there for him and it felt good. It was what he had always needed. The Germans had to be stopped, had to be punished. They deserved to be destroyed so they would never come back to haunt the earth again. There was something wrong with a people who accepted orders to this degree, who committed massacres, who acted entirely without conscience. He had heard all this in his basic training, but he hadn't *felt* it until now.

Andy left the men who were digging and walked again, walked until he found a farmer outside his barn. He asked the man about McComb. The farmer pointed down the road. "They were here," he said. "They went on to the next farm."

"I saw the grave they're digging in Cléres," Andy said. "I saw all the bodies."

The man nodded, grim-faced. "My brother is one of them," he said. "His whole family. Three children, almost grown. They had one more

306

son, and he's been taken off to Germany to work in their factories. If he ever gets back, he'll find out he has no one."

"Did some of the people escape?"

"Yes. Some were not home, not there. Some ran to the woods. But the Germans arrived suddenly, and they came from all directions. They pushed the people out of their homes and off the farms to the center of the village, and then they shot them down with machine guns. After, they stabbed them with bayonets, just to be sure they were dead. I helped wrap the bodies. It was the only thing we could do—give them that much respect. But we have to bury them all together. We don't have coffins for all of them. A priest came and blessed them. But what does that matter? I've lost all my faith in God."

"Don't stop believing," Andy said. "You'll need your faith now." But it was only something to say, not what he was actually feeling.

"They're not human, *Les Boches,*" the man said.

"I think you're right about that," Andy said. "I'm sorry. We blew up the bridge to stop the Germans from getting to the battle. We didn't know it would cause this."

"Don't tell me that. You would have done it anyway. That's what this war means. Killing. Everyone killing. And there will be much more before it's finished. Who will bury them all? Where are there graves big enough? I wish someone would bury me. I don't want to see any more of this."

"But we're here to—"

"You're here to kill. There are always reasons to kill, and wars never stop. I'm sick of it all."

Andy nodded. "I'm sorry," he said. And when the man didn't respond, he added, "I must go," and he walked on down the road. He told himself that Hitler was the worst man who had ever lived. He had to help stop this enemy—the ones who had killed that baby. But the man's words kept repeating themselves in his head. There *were* always reasons to kill, and wars *didn't* ever stop. There would always be other Hitlers and people willing to take orders from them.

Andy found McComb at the next farm. His men were sleeping in the shade behind the house. McComb was sitting up, leaning against the back wall of the house, his rifle across his knees. "You need to sleep," Andy said.

McComb nodded. "You too."

Andy looked around and realized that not enough men were there. "How many did we lose?" he asked.

"Five more. Three dead, two wounded."

"I saw Anton. He told me where you were."

"Is he the one with the bullet in his arm?"

"Yes."

"He's not so bad. The other one, the guy with the big mustache, he's shot through the chest. I don't think he'll live. Some of our men carried him to a doctor they knew in one of these towns, but I doubt they even got him there alive."

"Georges is dead too. He never made it to the bridge."

"So you set it off yourself?"

Andy nodded.

"It didn't take long. How'd you get it to go up so fast?"

"I used a short fuse. I just lit it and jumped in the river."

McComb looked up and stared at Andy for a time. "You're more of a man than I ever thought you were, Gledhill."

But Andy didn't believe that. If he had learned anything from this war, it was that he was less of a man than he had once thought he was.

CHAPTER 21

BY THURSDAY FLIP had worked everything out. He had managed to get two fairly decent used tires, with wheels, from Raymond, and he put them on the back of the truck. The front tires were in pretty bad shape too, but he still had the old tires off the back, so that gave him two spares. Flip figured four of the six tires would hold out long enough to get to California and back. He had filled up a canvas bag with water and draped it over the front of the truck. If the radiator overheated, they would have an extra supply. He also bought a gallon of oil. He told Raymond that his dad wanted him to make a run down to Beaver to pick up a calf, and that was why he needed the extra supplies. Raymond wasn't the sort to ask a lot of questions, nor to say much to Dad about all this. If he did, Andy figured he might have to come clean someday, but by then he would have gotten Tom to his home and back, and he would just have to take his punishment.

Flip had driven the truck into town to get the tires put on. He had no driver's license, but farm boys drove plenty, and the sheriff didn't pay much attention if they ran into town on an errand once in a while. But as Flip was driving out of the garage, he almost ran down his friend Cal, who was walking along the street with Reggie Porter. They jumped back, and then they laughed. Flip rolled down the window. "Hey, sorry about that," he said.

Cal stepped up to the truck and rested a foot on the running board. "Are you still working out on the farm every day, Flip?"

"Yeah. Looks like I'll be out there most of the time, all summer."

"Is that Jap still helping you?"

"I think it's the other way around. Mostly I'm helping him."

"What are you talking about?" Reggie asked. He was a year older than Cal and Flip, but Cal was playing ball with him this summer, and Flip had seen the two of them palling around together lately. "You hired a *Jap* to work for you?"

"He's Japanese American. He grew up in California. He's a good guy."

Reggie looked shocked. Neither he nor Cal seemed to know what to say.

"Well, I gotta get going," Flip told them.

"Did your dad make you work with him?" Reggie asked, as though he were trying to find some explanation that would cancel out what Flip had just said.

"Yeah. Sure." But then Flip knew what he needed to say. "I like the guy, though. We're friends now."

Reggie turned to one side and spat on the sidewalk—maybe just to stop looking at Flip for a moment. But when he looked up, Flip could see the disgust in his face. Reggie was a big kid; he was a lineman on the Delta High football team. His dad was the sheriff and a guy who didn't mind saying that he didn't like having eight thousand Japs camped just a few miles from town.

But it was Cal, not Reggie, who said, "Flip, I wouldn't say that to anyone else. Guys will say you're a Jap lover."

"Let 'em say what they want. Tom's an American, the same as the rest of us." Flip let out the clutch and the truck jerked, hesitated, then lurched ahead again. The truth was, Flip wasn't much of a driver, but he shifted into second, popped the clutch back out, and the truck jumped again before he drove it on down the street. If those guys didn't like what he'd said, what would they think if they knew what he was about to do? He decided he didn't care.

Flip drove back to the farm, parked the truck near the house, and looked for Tom, who was trying to get the garden in good shape before they headed out for California.

* * * * *

It was about 10:30 when Whisper arrived at the farm. Tom and Flip had made a bunch of sandwiches by then, and they had filled about twenty Mason jars with water. Flip heard Whisper at the screen door at the front of the house, calling softly, "Flip, are you there?"

"Yeah. Come on in." He walked toward the front door just as she stepped in from outside. "Are you ready?" he asked.

"I guess so," she said. "I've told more lies this afternoon than I have in my whole life. But here we go."

She looked surprisingly pleased with herself—flushed from the walk and the heat, but maybe also from the excitement. She had pulled back her hair and pinned it up, but some strands had gotten loose and were twisting around her ears. She was carrying a little leather suitcase. She was movie-star pretty, but she was wearing a pair of brown slacks. Flip had never seen her in slacks before, except when she wore jeans to work in the garden.

"What kind of lies did you have to tell?" Flip asked. "I've told a few myself."

"I told Doc Noorda that my friend Arlene, over in Fillmore, got hurt in an accident and I needed to sit with her a few days. Then I told my parents that Doc Noorda gave me some days off, so I was going over to spend the weekend with Arlene. It's almost the same story, so it should hold up all right. But I hope the doctor doesn't run into my parents and ask them if my friend is recovering all right."

"How did you say you were getting over there?"

"I said Lamar was coming after me—and he couldn't come until he finished up with some things he had to do in Fillmore. I waited until my parents were getting ready for bed, and then I said, 'Okay. Here he is. I'm going.' And I ran outside."

Flip walked back to the kitchen, Whisper with him. Tom turned away from the sandwiches he had been wrapping up in waxed paper. "Look, we can call this off right now. I know you two don't usually lie— and I hate to see you do it for me."

"I wish I were," Whisper said. "Then I wouldn't feel so guilty. But I'm mostly doing it for myself. I'll repent when I get back, I guess." She smiled again.

Tom had met Whisper when he had walked into town with Flip one night. Flip had seen her out in her garden and taken Tom over to say hello. Afterward, Tom had said, "Wow! That girl's *hot stuff.* Your brother's gotta be the luckiest guy in town."

Flip could see that Tom was taking another good look at her now. "Well," Flip said, "if nothing else, this is going to be an adventure. Let's get going."

Whisper actually giggled. Flip figured she might have some repentance in her plans, but she didn't seem to be feeling a whole lot of regret so far.

They carried their food and water out to the truck and put Whisper's suitcase in the back, and then they piled in up front. Flip was driving for now, with Whisper in the middle and Tom by the other window. The night was still pretty hot, but the air felt good when it started to flow. Flip drove into town, turned left on Main Street by Service Drug, and then chugged on through town. No one else was on the street, but some cars were parked here and there, mostly by the pool hall and the cafés. Tom was wearing a floppy old hat that he wore when he worked in the sun; he pulled it down low and turned his face away from the window.

Whisper slumped down so no one would happen to see her leaving town with Flip and some other guy.

In only a few minutes they had crossed the railroad tracks and were out onto Highway 50, heading past the farms of Hinckley. After that there was nothing but open space. Flip knew better than to push the old truck too hard. He got it up to forty, then forty-five, and heard enough whining to figure that was fast enough. It would be a long night at that pace, but if the old thing held together, he figured they could make it to Berkeley in about fifteen or sixteen hours—maybe as many as twenty, with some stops. If they could get to Tom's house by evening on Friday, they could load up what Tom wanted, sleep for a little while, and start back Saturday early. If everything went well, they could be back home by Sunday morning and Flip could show up for Sunday School and priesthood meeting. If he didn't make it, he would just tell his sisters that he'd slept in by mistake. They wouldn't be that surprised—and they would never bother to walk all the way out to the farm to check on him.

Flip had been nervous all day, but as the truck rolled out into the dark, leaving the town behind them, he was suddenly elated that he was doing this. There was some pretty good moonlight making lumpy shadows of the greasewood out on the desert flats, and the air rushing through the windows felt good. It occurred to him for the first time that Tom and Whisper were actually his best friends now, and the three of them were breaking free. Flip had been telling himself all day that his lies were not wrong because what he was doing was right—but the truth was, he felt a little like Clyde, and his Bonnie was sitting next to him. He knew he liked that a lot more than he really should.

"Hey, we're on our way," he said, and laughed. "We're roaring down the old highway, lickety-split. Only 649 miles to go."

Whisper laughed. "What in the world am I doing?" she said. "I just don't do things like this."

"Pardon me, boy, is that the Chattanooga Choo Choo," Tom began to sing, and Whisper joined in. Flip couldn't sing worth anything, and he didn't remember words to songs very well, but he tried to sing with them.

Tom knew every line, and he belted it out, loud and true. He had a good voice. Whisper knew most of the words too, and she added a little harmony. Flip laughed as much as anything, but he tried to keep up.

Whisper said, when the song was finished, "How about 'Oh Susanna.'" So they sang that. And then Flip started, in his monotone, "Deep in the Heart of Texas," and they sang that too.

For the better part of an hour they kept singing: "I've Got a Gal in Kalamazoo," "I've Got Spurs that Jingle Jangle Jingle," "Don't Fence Me In," "Mairzy Doats," and a lot of others. Flip was amazed at how he felt; he thought he had never been this happy in his whole life. He could feel the air cooling a little, could smell the alkaline desert, and sometimes Whisper would grasp his arm, lean close, and sing into his ear. Maybe she was trying to teach him the tune—or the words—or maybe she was just having as much fun as he was, but he would glance at her and she would smile, and Tom would always have another song. He would start each time with, "Here's a good one," or, "Do you know this one?"

Eventually they sang "For Me and My Gal," and that seemed to lead to "I'll Be Seeing You." Flip, by then, was mostly just listening. He could hear the emotion in Whisper's voice and knew she was saying something about how she felt about Andy being gone—and everything that had happened to her.

Tom seemed to sense it too, and he let her sing "Dancing in the Dark" mostly by herself. When she finished, there was quiet for a time, and Tom didn't suggest another song. Instead, he said, "Flip tells me that you're waiting for his brother."

"I was," she said, "until he told me to get lost. Now I'm not waiting for anyone. I'm just waiting."

Flip had never said anything about any of this to Tom. He wished

Whisper hadn't brought it up. He wanted her to ignore what Andy had written to her.

"What is he, crazy?" Tom asked.

Whisper laughed, but then she said, "Why do you say that?" as though she wanted someone to tell her how beautiful she was.

"Any guy would have to be nuts to let you get away."

She took hold of Flip's arm again. "That's what Flip says too. I wish his big brother felt the same way."

She was wearing perfume. Flip kept catching whiffs of it, especially when she leaned toward him that way.

"So what are you going to do?" Tom asked. "Have you got another fish on the line?"

"No. She's got a rabbit," Flip said. "About as good-looking as some we've seen smashed on the road out here."

Whisper laughed and slapped Flip's shoulder. "There's a boy from Fillmore who wants to marry me," she told Tom. "But Flip doesn't want me to marry him. Maybe I'll marry Flip, and then I'll raise him up the way I want him. He'd treat me better than Andy. That's for sure."

"That's a good idea. Flip's the best guy in the world," Tom said. "He's six feet tall inside. He just doesn't know it. I think you ought to wait for him to get out of high school and then tie the knot."

"They'd put me in jail for kidnapping," Whisper said, and laughed.

"You can hear crickets out there," Flip said. "Have you noticed that?"

But Tom and Whisper laughed. "I'm sorry. I won't tease you anymore," Whisper said, but then she said to Tom, "Flip's been my best friend since his brother left. I don't know what I'd have done without him."

Insects kept clicking against the windshield, some of them flattening to yellow slime. Flip stared out at the blacktop in front of him, which careened toward him through the light of the headlights. "How about 'G. I. Jive'?" Flip said. "Do you know that one?"

Whisper leaned close and whispered, "I'm sorry, Flip. I really won't tease you again."

By then Tom was singing "G. I. Jive." Whisper sang with him, lots more songs. But Flip wasn't enjoying everything as much as he had at first.

After a time, Whisper asked, "What about you, Tom? Do you have a girl?"

"I have a dancing partner. I don't know if she's my girl or not. Her name's Kumiko. I call her Kimmy. Everyone does. We dance in talent programs out at the camp, and we enter jitterbug contests. We usually win, too."

"Do you think you might want to marry her, once the war is over and life gets back to normal for you?"

"I don't know. I'm joining the army in a couple more months, if I can. Then who knows what might happen? She says she'll write to me, but I think we're mostly just friends."

"What do you mean you'll join *if you can?*"

"My father doesn't want me to join. At eighteen, I can join if I want, but my mother says I shouldn't do that, not if he doesn't approve."

"I thought you told me you were joining, no matter what," Flip said.

"Yeah. I might. But my mother says it's wrong to defy my father."

"Aren't you old enough to decide for yourself?" Whisper asked.

Tom didn't answer for a time, but finally he said, "Japanese children aren't supposed to defy their fathers. But I don't know if we're Japanese anymore. It's hardly like we're a family now. We eat at a dining hall, but I eat mostly with my friends, and my sisters with theirs. Father spends his days with the other men his age, and they talk all day about what's wrong with us kids. Every time I get near him, we start to argue. Then my mother cries. It's a mess. I wish he would give in and let me go, just so my mother wouldn't be upset. But I might have to go without his permission."

"Why do you want to join the army?" Whisper asked.

"Because all these poor *hakujin* can't win the war without me." Tom laughed.

"What's that?"

"*Hakujin?* That's what Japanese call white people. We think we're the best fighters. Look what the Four-Four-Two has done. They've been winning more ribbons than anybody."

"He wants to prove he's loyal," Flip said.

But Tom said, "It's not just that. I want to be part of this country. If I help win the war—even if I only do a little—maybe for the first time, I'll feel like I'm a regular guy. You know what I mean?"

"I guess so," Whisper said. "But it seems like you are a regular guy. Why do you have to prove it?"

"Don't ask me. Ask your *hakujin* friends. Ask yourself."

"You told me you were a regular guy," Flip said. "You know, back at your high school in Berkeley."

"I know. It's what I try to tell myself. But the truth is, I never forget for a single minute that I'm Japanese—and no one else forgets it either."

Things quieted after that. Flip listened to the rumble of the old truck rolling over the pavement, the tires whining. He was getting a little tired already, and a sign a mile or two back had said that it was still 62 miles to Ely, Nevada. Flip knew they'd have some mountains to climb before getting there. After that, it was more than 300 miles across Nevada to Reno. He wished he could make the old truck go a little faster, but when he tried to push it toward fifty, the shaking got scary.

The distance of the trip was finally settling into Flip's mind. He was starting to realize how far they would be from any kind of help if something went wrong with the truck. Out beyond the headlights there was just nothing but dark. For the first time Flip wondered whether he shouldn't turn back before something went wrong and they had no way to get home. He had promised to look out for Whisper, not get her into a mess.

* * * * *

Whisper leaned her head back just to shut her eyes and rest for a few minutes. She hadn't realized she had drifted off until she felt the truck shaking worse than before. She opened her eyes and said, "What's that noise?"

"The truck's just working hard to make this climb," Flip said. "I think this is the worst one until after Reno."

Whisper felt a little frightened. She had assumed that Flip had known what he was talking about when he'd said that the truck would do fine as long as they didn't drive too fast. She hadn't thought much about mountains. The longest road trip she had ever taken was a drive to Ogden, in northern Utah. Once, making that trip, her dad's car had broken down—wouldn't start when they were ready to head back home. But her dad and uncle had pushed the car to a filling station down the street and gotten some help. She hadn't realized how many miles could go by out here without a sign of life except for the jackrabbits that scooted across the road in front of the headlights. Towns were far apart, and only a few cars had passed them, moving fast. Only two had come toward them from the west, at least while Whisper had been awake.

"Up here a ways," Flip said, "why don't you take over driving, so someone with a license drives into Ely. We need to find an all-night gas station, if they have one, and fill up before we head out across the rest of Nevada. It's at least a hundred miles before we can get gas again, and maybe longer if the stations are closed in these little towns."

"What will we do if we can't get gas?" Whisper asked.

"We might have to hole up in Austin or Frenchman or somewhere like that until a station opens. But it's almost two now. By the time we get over there, it won't be so long until morning."

"Are we making pretty good time?"

"Not quite as good as I hoped, but we're doing all right."

"Is Tom asleep?"

"No," Tom said. "I can't sleep sitting up like this. Flip, I'll drive after Ely. You need to get a little sleep for a while."

"Okay. When we make the summit up here in a mile or two, I'll pull over and let Whisper take her on in to Ely, and then, outside of Ely, you take over."

But Whisper had picked up a change in Flip's voice. His confidence was slipping. She thought she heard the same thing from Tom. Maybe it was the shaking of the truck. Maybe they were just getting tired. But they had been at this for only three hours or so, and they had forever to go. She didn't want them doubting themselves already; she was doing enough of that herself.

They made it over the top of Connors Pass, and then Whisper drove into Ely. They found a filling station open and bought gas. Tom pretended to sleep, hiding his face under his hat. "You driving all night, lady?" the attendant asked.

"We might," Whisper told him.

"Don't fall asleep."

"I won't. My little brother can drive for a while and help me out."

"Sure. But some people drift off anyway. It happens pretty often out here."

"I'll be careful."

"There's no gas at night until you get to Fallon—but it'll probably be morning by the time you get to Austin, and there's a station there. If this old truck gets that far."

"It'll be okay. It's a good old truck," Whisper said.

"Good for what?"

But Whisper didn't answer him. He was a man of thirty or so, with a wedding ring on, but she could tell that he wanted to keep talking to her.

He had stepped up on the running board to wash her windshield, but she had seen the way he had let his eyes run over her.

Whisper drove out of Ely and crossed another pass before Eureka. The truck was working hard, she could tell, but it kept going. She liked doing the driving, just feeling a little more as though she were in control. If they could keep going, make it across the desert—and through the night—she knew she would feel better.

And then she felt something happen. The truck pulled hard to the right and some kind of noise, a flopping sound, quickly got worse.

"Blowout!" Flip said from his sleep, about the same time that Whisper realized what it was. She had already let off the gas, and now she guided the truck to the side of the road. "I'm not surprised," Flip said. "That right front tire was the worst one. We'll put one of those spares on and we'll be all right."

"Have you got a good jack?" Tom asked.

"I don't know how good it is," Flip said. "But I've got one."

Whisper's stomach jumped when she heard that, and it clenched tighter as the boys struggled, first to get the truck jacked up, and then to break loose the lug nuts. She could hear them out there talking about the troubles they were having, finally expressing relief when they managed to get the wheel off, and then some satisfaction as they got the spare on. Whisper kept watching for cars, afraid that someone would come along and ask too many questions, and at the same time feeling abandoned on such a lonely road.

When Flip jumped back into the truck, he said, "Sorry that took so long, but everything's fine now. That's a better tire."

Whisper hoped so.

Tom had walked around the truck. He stepped up on the running board and said, "Whisper, why don't I drive for a while now? I'm wide awake after busting those lug nuts loose."

"Do you know how to drive?"

"I haven't driven for quite a while, but don't worry, I know how."

"The clutch on this thing is a little tricky," Flip said.

Tom was laughing. "Hey, there's not a lot of shifting out here in the middle of nowhere."

So Tom took over, and Whisper moved back into the middle, but she didn't sleep. Tom made a start like a jackrabbit and then got rolling, but he seemed to wander about on the road. She hoped he wouldn't get off into the gravel and turn the old truck over.

But he settled down after a time, and Whisper felt a little better as they got some more miles behind them. Eventually she could see a little light in the sky, and that made her feel even better. She knew the sun would get too hot in time, but at least they wouldn't be out there in all that blackness.

Whisper took over the car again just before Austin, and as it turned out, a station was open quite early, so they got some more gas. Flip admitted that he had hoped to be pretty close to Reno by morning, but she could feel that he liked to have light, too. His voice was taking on more life again. "Anyone want a sandwich for breakfast?" he asked.

"Not while I'm driving," Whisper told him, but Flip and Tom ate baloney sandwiches and drank warm water.

Whisper kept the truck running steadily, and she liked the progress they were making, but she was surprised how fast the heat came on. Heat waves were soon shimmering off the road, and the air flowing into the cab of the truck began to get uncomfortable. She longed to get to California, where the temperatures were always supposed to be so nice. She knew the ocean didn't come for a long time after they made it over the mountains, but in her mind, California was all sea breezes and softness. If they could just get Nevada behind them, this long night would be worth it.

But Whisper had begun to notice an odd smell, like a dribble of stew burning on a stove. She was about to say something to Flip when he said,

"I think the truck's heating up. You might drive a little slower. We need to be careful in this heat."

Whisper slowed a little, but the smell was already getting stronger. She drove maybe five miles, everyone silent. Whisper kept sniffing and noticing that the smell wasn't getting any better. Then there was a sudden hissing sound. "Okay, pull over," Flip said, "but don't turn the engine off. We're boiling over, but we've got water."

Whisper pulled to the side of the road and kept the engine running. The boys got out again, and Flip used an old glove he found in the back of the truck to take the radiator cap off. The steam shot into the air when he did, and a smell like burning rubber filled up the truck. But he poured the water in from the canvas bag, and everything calmed down pretty fast. "Get a couple of those bottles of water," he told Tom, and he poured that water in, too.

When he came back to the truck, Whisper said, "Should we go ahead?"

"Sure. We're all right now."

"Won't it boil over again?"

"I don't think so. I think the radiator might have a little leak. The water might have gotten down too low, and that's why it heated up. We should be good for a while now. In Fallon, we'll check the radiator and refill our water bag."

But the truck had not been going fifteen minutes before Whisper caught the smell again, and so did Flip. "Don't let it boil this time," he said. "Pull over." And once she did, he told her to shut the engine down. "Let's let it sit for a while. Once it cools down, I'll add some more of these bottles of water, and then we'll go as long as we can."

"How far are we from Fallon?" Tom asked.

"I'm not sure," Whisper said. "There hasn't been a sign for quite a while."

"It's less than twenty miles," Flip said. "We can limp in there and have someone check out the radiator. Maybe it's sprung a bigger leak. But they can plug those." Flip got out and looked under the hood. When he came back after a while, he said, "There's no water running out on the road. If we have a leak, it's not a bad one."

Whisper didn't say it for a time, but finally she couldn't help asking, "Flip, do you really know much about these things, or are you just sort of guessing?" The heat in the truck was getting terrible, and Delta was three hundred miles behind them—maybe more. The trouble was, Tom's house was about the same distance ahead of them.

"Well, with cars, everything's always a guess. Let's get into Fallon and see what a mechanic tells us."

But she could sense that he was trying his best to be a man, to know, to assure her when he wasn't really very convinced himself.

They all got out of the truck and sat in its shade. Flip kept saying that the water wouldn't take too long to cool, but Whisper wondered about that. They were still waiting when Whisper heard a car approaching from the west. She stood up and looked. Gradually, she could see that it had a red light on top, and she didn't know whether she was glad or scared to see that. "It's a sheriff," she said.

Tom dashed into a little stand of mesquite by the road. By then Whisper could hear the tires of the car crunching in the gravel next to the road. She walked to the front of the truck.

The car stopped on the wrong side of the road, its hood facing the front of the truck. A big fellow with a short-sleeved shirt and burly arms got out of the car. "You broke down?" he asked.

"Yes, sir," Whisper said.

Flip walked up behind her. "We just overheated," he said.

"Where you tryin' to get to?"

"California," Whisper said.

"Where to? Clear to the coast?"

"Yes."

"You sure this ol' truck will make it?" He pulled a big blue handkerchief from his back pocket and wiped his forehead.

"We just need to nurse it along into Fallon," Flip said, "and then have someone take a look at it. We filled it up with water once, and we still have some jars in the truck, but I thought it might be best to let it cool off for a while."

"That won't do no good. The heat's getting worse out here every minute. This ol' wreck will heat up just as soon as you get going again."

Whisper felt sick. They really were in a mess.

"I can take you into town, and you can hole up for the day. The only chance you've got is to wait until night, I suspect. I don't know if this thing'll climb out of Reno over them mountains."

Whisper looked at Flip. She was thinking of Tom, hiding a few feet away. She didn't know what to do.

"Maybe if you could take us into town to get some more water, we could make it into Fallon," Flip said. "It could be that the thermostat's just stuck."

"Sure. That could be. But I still wouldn't run again until night. Did she do all right before the heat come on?"

"Yes," Whisper said.

"Well, let me run you into town. It's ten miles or something like that. Then we'll bring some water back. We should be able to get it that far."

"You go, Flip," Whisper said. "I'll wait with the truck."

"No, lady. I'm not leaving a pretty young woman out here. You don't know who might come along." He tucked his thumbs into his wide leather belt. There was a pistol in a holster strapped to his side. He sounded nice, helpful, but Whisper kept watching his eyes, and like the man at the filling station the night before, the sheriff was letting his eyes roam over her body. "Both of you come in with me and get in out of the sun—maybe get yourself something to eat—and then I'll drive you back out here."

Whisper looked at Flip. He nodded, and the two walked to the sheriff's car, but then Flip said, "Just a minute," and walked back to the truck. Whisper knew he was whispering something to Tom without looking toward him. She wondered how long the poor guy would be stuck out there in the heat.

CHAPTER 22

ANDY WAS ON A train with Captain McComb and Evan Roberts. They were heading south, wearing French business suits and carrying counterfeit travel passes that designated them as salesmen in the clothing industry. Before leaving England they had been told that they might be called upon to help with a second invasion on the south coast of France, and now McComb had received orders that his team should leave the sabotage work to the local *Maquisards* and do similar work as this second invasion began. They would then join forces with a fairly large operational group—twenty men or more—who would be dropped into southern France from England.

Ideally, the three men would have separated on the train and drawn less attention to themselves. The problem was, neither McComb nor Roberts spoke French well enough to cover themselves. It was important for Andy to bluff them through if problems came up. Security was tight now, but the three had made it onto the train without much difficulty. Their papers were excellent forgeries, and the guards at the train hadn't probed. The three had found seats in a compartment with two German officers, which made Andy nervous at first, since he was carrying a Sten gun broken down in his suitcase, but he did what he had been taught. He boldly asked one of the officers to let him put his suitcase under the man's seat. The officer wasn't exactly affable, but he complied and even said in French, "It's not a problem."

Andy breathed more easily. He was sitting in a compartment with eight seats, four facing forward and four backward. The officer across from Andy was a sallow, pale-eyed man of forty or so, who looked as weary as Andy felt. No one inspecting the train, French or German, was likely to ask to see a bag under his seat. The man soon shut his eyes, and Andy watched the loose flesh under his chin quiver with the vibrations of the train. It was strange to think that under slightly different circumstances, he and Andy might fight to the death, Andy perhaps going after that throat. The German was a captain, but not SS—just a field officer in an infantry company. Andy wondered what the man thought of the war now. Was he giving up, only hoping now to get home alive? Or was he still committed to Hitler?

The captain's jaw gradually fell slack. He was clearly exhausted, and that made him seem human, normal. Andy wondered whether such a man could have massacred those women and children back in Cléres. Could all of these Germans do such things, or only the SS fanatics? Andy wasn't sure those were good things to think about. He knew that McComb, sitting next to him, was longing to put a bullet through the captain's skull. Andy had felt that way when he had seen the bodies in Cléres, but looking at this man now, he couldn't seem to call back his outrage.

What Andy needed was sleep. He had never had much success sleeping on trains, but he leaned into the corner by the window as best he could and tried to rest. He had seen so many brutal sights in the last week—broken bodies and ruined lives—that he didn't know how to take it all in, and he didn't want to. He wanted to escape it all for a few hours. He did drift off, actually comforted by the clicking, the jostling, the vibration of the train, but only in short snatches. When he awoke he would watch out the window and see that farmers were still at work in their fields, that the shops in small towns were actually operating, that people were going about their lives. It was strange to think that humans could seek normality even when battles were going on not far away. What Andy knew, of course, was that fighting would soon come to this beautiful Rhône Valley, and these people would see the killing.

Andy watched a woman out in a muddy field. She was wearing a dark dress, a scarf over her hair, and tall rubber boots. She was holding a shovel, leaning on it to rest, and as the train passed, she gazed at it intently but showed no sign of any reaction. Andy thought of his summers in Delta, back when he was in high school, working out on the farm all day. Trains had passed his farm, too, and he had always looked up and waved. And then, after his day in the hot sun, he had walked or ridden his bicycle back into town so he could play baseball in the lingering light of those summer evenings. When the light was finally gone, he and his friends would gather at the drugstore soda fountain. Whisper had usually been part of all that even long before he had considered her his girlfriend.

A memory came to him. He had been there in Service Drug, sitting at the counter, laughing and talking with a couple of his friends from the baseball team. Three girls had walked in: Adele and Whisper and someone else—one of their friends. Andy had turned to look at them, to say hello, and his friend Howard had said, "Wow. When did Whisper Harris get to be so pretty?" Andy had looked around a second time, and it was as though he had never seen her before. She had always been all legs and arms and freckles, but she really had changed lately—"developed," his mom would have called it. Whisper saw Andy looking at her, and she smiled. That was all that happened. He didn't even remember talking to her. But the image was there: Whisper in a little tan dress with white trim, her hair in a ponytail, her face and arms summer brown. He wished now that he could go back to that moment, start from there, and never know a thing about stabbing people, about the slaughtering of women and children. If he had never killed anyone, never met Elise, never felt what he had felt these last few months, he could have stayed in Delta, married Whisper, managed the bank, and not known the darkness that filled him now.

Andy realized that he hadn't prayed for a long time, that he hadn't expected ever to pray again, but he found himself saying something that was half a prayer now. "Let me be me again," he said in his mind, not sure whether he believed there was someone to hear him. He looked across at the German officer again. Sleeping, his jaw loose and jiggling, he looked harmless, no different from those French farmers outside the train window, or from the men around Delta. Andy had concluded at some point that Whisper would know what he was if she ever looked at him again, and she would turn away in disgust. But maybe it wouldn't be that way. Maybe the war would end and people would revert to their former selves. Maybe he and this German captain could go home and forget any of this had happened. Andy shut his eyes and tried to feel some sense that *he* was still inside his body, but he couldn't find anything he remembered.

Andy slept some more and arrived in Valence late in the day. He thanked the captain and walked off the train with him, hoping to say something to him just as German inspectors stopped him to check his papers. He figured it couldn't hurt to appear to be on good terms with a German officer. But as Andy walked along with McComb and Evan and approached the main hall of the station, several lines formed. He didn't like what he was seeing. Andy stopped and turned to McComb. "They're inspecting baggage," he said. "We'll never get these suitcases past them."

McComb nodded. "That men's room over there. We'll have to dump our weapons." McComb hurried ahead, and Andy and Evan followed. A man was leaving as they stepped in, but no one else was inside, so McComb shut the door and locked it, and then Andy and McComb dumped their Sten guns in a rubbish can, and all three got rid of their pistols. Andy grabbed a good deal of toilet paper, bunched it up, and spread it on top to cover the weapons.

"Dump your knife, too," Andy said. "If we don't make it through with our papers, they'll search us thoroughly."

McComb wavered for a moment, but then he said, "No. I need something."

Andy thought he was crazy, but he knew better than to challenge McComb. "Okay, let's hurry. We've got to get out of this train station before someone discovers all these guns." He led the way out of the toilet toward the inspectors. "Stay together," he whispered. They all got in the same line, and they set their bags out on a table and opened them for inspection. A woman looked through them quickly, then slid them down the table. Each man retrieved his own bag and stepped into another line. But as Andy reached a French guard and handed over his papers, another inspector grabbed Evan's. "Where are you going?" the man asked.

The inspectors were members of the French *Milice*—the collaborative police force. During the time of the Vichy government in southern France, it had become a brutal force, as vicious as the Nazis themselves. Andy wondered what they were thinking now, with Allied forces advancing in Normandy, threatening to overpower the Germans. These men would certainly be in a dangerous position once the French took back control of their own country. But Andy saw no sign of self-doubt in this man's face. He was shorter than Andy and not strongly built, but his eyes were steady as stones. "I'm staying here in Valence, calling on customers," replied Andy.

"What is it you sell?"

At that same moment, a taller, stouter Milice officer was asking Evan, "Where is it you are going?"

Andy leaned over and said, "We're all together, we three. We're meeting with other salesmen from our company."

"He can answer for himself."

330

"Of course. It's just that all of the answers are the same. I thought I'd save you a little trouble. By the way, what time is it? Was the train a little late?"

The inspector ignored Andy and looked at Evan. "What is it you sell?"

"Hats for men," Evan said. "And other clothing."

He had worked on these lines. He knew enough to answer simple questions. The problem was, his accent was not very believable. "Where are you from?" the man asked.

Andy's inspector was saying, "How long do you plan to stay here?"

"Just three days," Andy said, and then, to the other man, "His French is not very good. He was raised in Canada and returned to France only a few years ago."

But that made little sense, and Andy knew it. French people who moved to Canada usually continued to speak French. The inspector was staring at Evan's identity card. "These papers say you are French, not Canadian."

"He is French. His father worked in Canada, that's all. He went to English schools. He speaks French, of course, but he does have a curious pronunciation."

The man with Andy's papers suddenly commanded, "Step forward. Listen to my questions, and let that man answer for himself."

Andy was pulled ahead, and now McComb, who had been standing behind Andy, was left to a third inspector. McComb was worse than Evan in these situations. Andy couldn't think what to do. He began to cough. "I'm sorry," he said. "I've suffered with tuberculosis. I still have a terrible cough sometimes."

"Tuberculosis?"

"Yes. I'm sorry." He set off coughing again, bit his lip, hard, and then spat blood on the floor. He turned back toward McComb. "Do you have my medicine?" he asked, stepping toward him. Andy no longer carried the medical papers he had used on his first drop into France, the ones that identified him as having had tuberculosis, but he knew the disease frightened most guards. It was the first ruse that had occurred to him when he saw things falling apart, but the problem was, McComb didn't know what Andy had said, and of course couldn't really respond anyway. Andy's only thought was that the two had to stay together somehow, so they wouldn't be questioned separately.

"Medicine," Andy said, between coughs. McComb seemed to catch the idea and started feeling his pockets, as though he were looking for it. Andy thought maybe his trick had worked. Both guards stepped back, clearly not wanting to be close to the coughing, but the third man was saying by then, "This isn't right. How can this man be a salesman? He speaks no French."

The little man who had first talked to Andy said, "Take these three inside. Question them carefully. Check their papers again." He waved for the other two to take them away.

Andy tried some more coughing, spat again, and the inspectors kept their distance, but they pointed to a door not far away and commanded Andy and McComb and Evan to head that way. Andy knew they were in trouble. They had known that traveling by train could be dangerous— not something Jeds usually did—but it was the only way to get quickly enough to where they needed to be. Inspections were hit-and-miss these days, and in many train stations they could have flashed their papers to a guard and walked on through. What Andy hoped now was that these guards wouldn't think to separate him from McComb and Evan, and that somehow he could bluff for all three of them.

The guards led the men into a small room and had them sit down, the three in a line, Andy in the middle, on straight-backed wooden chairs. The guards took McComb's papers and looked them over carefully, and then they looked at Andy's and Evan's again. A big, heavy man seemed to outrank the other, or at least he took command of the procedure. "I don't understand this," he said. "You say you are calling on customers, but you are also having a meeting. Which is it?" He had a loud, rough voice, and spoke in a crude dialect Andy didn't recognize.

"Both," Andy said. "We're here for a meeting. But I sell in this area, so I'll be meeting with customers after the meeting ends."

"Do you understand that France has been invaded? Who will be buying suits now, and hats?"

"Life goes on. We'll push the Americans and British back into the sea, and soon hats and suits will be selling better than ever."

"I don't want you to say another word." The big man pointed at McComb with a stubby finger. "*You* answer me. Where will you stay here in Valence?"

This was one of the questions they had anticipated, and they had learned the name of a hotel from their *Maquisard* friends. McComb named it now: "*Hotel du Parc.*"

"And what is the purpose of your meeting?"

McComb didn't have a chance. Andy said, "We must learn about the new—"

The finger swung back toward Andy. "I asked *him*. Don't speak again."

McComb tried to repeat the sentence Andy had started, but he couldn't end it, really couldn't even get the first part right.

"You are no salesman. You speak no French."

"Empty your pockets," the other guard said, stepping forward as though he wanted to make a show of his own authority. He was a much smaller man, with a narrow face and sharp nose. His voice was rather high-pitched even though he was clearly trying to make it sound as strong as his partner's.

There was a small desk in one corner of the room. Andy stood and walked to it first, and McComb and Evan got the idea and followed. They emptied their pockets, and then the policemen patted them, checked their coat pockets, and made them take off their shoes, which they checked inside and out. They looked through their wallets, looked carefully at their money, searched through all their belongings.

"Open your mouth," the smaller man said to Andy, and he looked inside, peering carefully. Andy was glad now that his dental work had been redone, as much as he had hated the process at the time. The policeman checked the others the same way, and then he had all three remove their suit jackets, and both guards carefully checked the sewing.

Andy thought he could see some of the sternness leaving the smaller man's face. He turned his back, lowered his voice, and said something to the big fellow. Andy had the feeling he was wavering, probably because the forged papers were so perfectly done, and because the dental work, the clothes—everything—checked out all right. Andy knew he had to explain away one last matter. He laughed and said, "I understand why you're surprised at us. My friends don't speak French well. But you know how it is these days. It's difficult to find men to travel as salesmen. We don't earn much with business so slow. My friend from Canada could find no other work, and our company doubted him at first. But he works hard, and he goes where they send him. He does all right. And Noel, here, he came to the company because he was Girard's friend. He grew up in Canada himself. He's just getting started with us."

The policemen, frankly, didn't look like geniuses, and Andy thought they might be buying all this. But the big man turned to the other. "It's still not right—to be a salesman and to speak so little French. And look how many cigarettes that one had."

Andy was stunned. He hadn't thought of that. McComb had pulled two packs of cigarettes out of each of his pants pockets. They were French cigarettes, but cigarettes were hard to come by these days. The truth was, the men had plenty of money with them, and McComb, a heavy smoker, had paid plenty to buy a supply in Malaunay. Andy hadn't known that he had stuffed four packs in his pants. That was something the men had been warned against doing.

"Where did you get all those cigarettes?" the big policeman asked.

"He smokes too much," Andy said. "But I can't smoke now—not with tuberculosis—so I buy them for him and he pays me back. I don't know how he does it on his income."

"I don't either. You tell far too many lies, my friend. I don't believe any of this. If you have tuberculosis, where's your card for that?"

"The doctor says I'm recovered. Mostly, I am."

"Were you in a sanitarium?"

"Oh, yes. Of course."

"Where was it?"

"Near Rouen. That's where I live."

"There's no sanitarium there. You know there isn't." The man stepped closer.

Andy stared directly back at him. "Of course there is. It's on the edge of town, on the road to Duclair. If you know Rouen, you should know it."

Andy had followed procedure again, always to stay with a story, show no sign of doubt or weakness. But the policeman was staring hard at Andy. "I lived not far from Rouen for several years. Duclair is nothing more than a village. There is no sanitarium there."

Andy didn't blink. "You're playing games with me," he said. "I think I know where I've been better than you do. Make a telephone call if you have to. You'll learn what's there."

"It could be," the other man said. "Their papers seem to be in order."

"It's not good enough. I say we take them to the jail. Others who have more time can question them further."

The narrow-faced man shrugged. "If you think so."

"I think so."

So the two policemen gathered up the Jed team's possessions, along with their identification papers, and dropped everything into three large envelopes. Then the big man put his hand on the handle of his pistol, still in its holster, and said, "Come with us. Leave your baggage here." He led the way, the other guard following. They all walked outside into the muggy heat of the late afternoon, and McComb, Andy, and Evan were forced into the backseat of an old *gasogene*-powered car. The big man had to fire up the burner, get the charcoal going, and let it heat for a while, but the other officer got into the car, then turned halfway around. He had pulled out his pistol now, and he was directing it toward the men. "I have some advice for you," he said. "You should tell me who you are right now, not wait. Once we turn you over to our interrogators, you will eventually admit the truth. Tell me and you can save yourself a great deal of misery." He smiled. "Tell your *Canadian* friends what I've told you," he said to Andy. "I don't think they understand me."

Andy, of course, could only say, "They understand much better than they speak. I tell you again, you have the wrong idea about us."

"Here's what I think. You're not clothing salesmen. You're selling products on the black market. The trouble is, my partner thinks that you're spies. If we turn you over to our leaders, and that's what they suspect, I hate to tell you what might happen. So if you're working the black market, I would admit to that right now. You'll be punished, of course, but you may be able to save your lives."

Andy considered the options. At Beaulieu he had been trained that admitting to some smaller crime was often a way to avoid the roughest kinds of interrogation. But a new set of lies would be difficult to construct, especially with no time to talk to his partners. He decided it was better to stick with their story. "We sell clothing, sir. Mostly hats. I don't know what else to tell you."

"And where are these hats you sell?"

"What? Do you think we carry all those around with us?"

The man laughed. "It doesn't matter to me. Say what you want. But give some thought to what our men can do. We're taking you to our headquarters on the other side of the city. There are men there who specialize in interrogation—if that's what you prefer to call it. Germans, not Frenchmen. At this moment, you think you know what pain is. But before this day is over, you'll learn more than you've ever imagined."

Once the charcoal burner was going, the strange gurgling sound intensifying, the big man got into the car and released a hand brake. The car eased forward and chugged down the street. Andy was sitting in the middle, with McComb behind the man with the gun and Evan behind the driver. Andy realized that their best chance of surviving would be to do something now. Careful interrogators would pick Andy's story apart. He thought of grabbing for the man's arm, but wasn't sure what would happen if he did that with the car moving. His sense was that if he grabbed, he would probably die, but Evan could grab the driver and choke him, and if the car didn't crash, maybe Evan and McComb would survive. It seemed unlikely that all three could get out of this. It wasn't a great plan, perhaps, but Andy knew for certain that he would rather die right now than face the torture that was probably coming.

Andy decided to make his move after they had driven for a few minutes and the policeman might have begun to relax. As it turned out, the driver took a route around the edge of the city, and they passed through a wooded area. This was probably the time to do something, but by then Andy realized that McComb also had something in mind. He had worked his hand slowly toward his vest pocket. The men had been told in England that European guards rarely thought to check vest pockets, where watches were normally kept, but which were often empty. Andy thought he knew what McComb had there: a tiny pen gun, the size of a short pencil. It would be like him to have one and not to have admitted it to Andy. The gun fired only one bullet, but if fired point-blank into the back of the policeman's head, it would kill him. If McComb did make a move, Andy had to time things perfectly, grab for the man's arm just as McComb was raising the gun.

Andy watched out of the corner of his eye as McComb managed to get the little gun out, but then he had to pull out a little triggering device, and he had to do it with one hand. The trouble was, McComb had moved his hand down low, and Andy couldn't see what success he was having with the device. The car had left the wooded area and was passing a farm with a rock fence, but as the road curved and the car slowed a little, suddenly McComb's hand came up. Andy saw it just in time and lurched forward to grab the policeman's arm.

Andy heard the pen gun fire; at the same moment, the policeman's pistol went off. It took Andy a moment to realize he hadn't been hit. The policeman was slumping in the front seat. As Andy had pictured the attack, Evan would grab for the driver, but it wasn't happening. He reached for the man himself and wrenched his head back. As he did, the car went out of control, slid sideways, and slammed hard into the rock wall. Glass flew, and Andy felt the powerful impact as he was thrown across Evan into the side of the car. Black whirled through his head for a time. He was still in a blur when he felt someone pulling on him. Pain was shooting through the shoulder he had hurt on his first jump into France. The pain seemed to bring him back, and then came the realization of where he was and what had happened to him. McComb was screaming at him, telling him they had to get out of the car.

"Come on, Gledhill. Are you all right?" McComb jerked hard on his arm, seeming to pull the joint out of its socket.

"Let go! Don't!" Andy screamed. But he worked to pull himself off the floor in front of the backseat, where he now understood he had landed. As he sat up, he could see that the driver had been hurt in the crash, that blood was running from his head. But he was moving, moaning. Andy slid back and finally glanced toward Evan. But Evan was pushed back into the corner against the door, his face covered with blood. Andy realized that the bullet from the policeman's gun must have struck him. One eye was gone, along with most of his face.

"Come on, Gledhill. Now."

Andy slid across the seat and out the right side. By then McComb was opening the front door. He looked inside, then grabbed the policeman's pistol, which had fallen onto the seat. He reached into the car and shot the driver in the head. Then he stepped back and shot the other man—the one he had shot before. "Let's go," he said.

"What about Evan?"

"He's dead."

"Are you sure?"

"Look at him."

But Andy didn't have to do that. He knew. "We need our papers," Andy said.

McComb knew that too, and he was already searching. The envelopes had flown off the seat onto the floor. He reached over the dead man and grabbed them. "I've got them. Let's go," he said. He ran around the car to the rock fence; using one hand, he vaulted over it. Andy had to climb onto the fence and jump off, but then he raced after McComb, up past a farmhouse, across a pasture, over another wall, and on into the woods.

CHAPTER 23

T HE SUN WAS finally going down as Whisper drove the old truck out
of Fallon, Nevada. It had been an exhausting day for Tom. The sheriff had driven Whisper and Flip into town and bought them lunch. After they had eaten, he had left them at the diner, promising to come back in "just a little bit" with a container to haul some water back to the truck, but he had been gone over two hours. That made sense to the sheriff, of course, since he didn't think the old truck should head out again until dark, but it meant that poor Tom was left sitting out there in the heat all alone, not knowing what was going on. The sheriff finally drove Flip and Whisper back to the truck, filled the radiator, and then told Whisper to drive slowly while he drove behind.

That, of course, made for a dangerous situation for Tom. Fortunately, he could hear the conversation, so while the sheriff was walking back to his car, Tom dashed to the truck and jumped in the back. But when they all got to town and took the truck to a little gas station so a young fellow with about six layers of grease on his hands—and two or three on his face—could work on it, Tom had to stay in the back, and he had to stay down, out of sight. The mechanic did discover, as Flip had hoped, that the old thermostat in the engine wasn't working—was stuck so that little water could get through it—and he replaced it. He charged Whisper a dollar and a half, which seemed more than fair, but he was eyeing her the whole time as though he thought she might abandon her journey and settle in Fallon just to make him a happy man forever. Flip was amazed at the effect the girl could have on men, and the truth was, he didn't like this greasy little guy looking at her like that.

Once the truck was repaired, Flip filled up the water bottles—and sneaked a bottle to Tom—and then they waited at the diner again and drank a cold soda pop. But Tom was still in the truck all this time, and by the time they drove out of town and got him into the cab, he was suffering. "I need more water," were the first words he said. He drank a whole jar before he said anything else.

"I brought you a root beer. It's still kind of cool," Flip said.

"Oh, man, hand it over. Is there anything to eat?"

"Sure. We've still got baloney sandwiches."

The sandwiches looked as though they had been baked. The bread was dry and the meat was shriveled up. But Tom consumed two with his root beer, and came back to life rather quickly. "Man, I thought I was going to melt out there in that brush, but at least I could move around a little. In the back of the truck, I had to stay still the whole time. And that garage was almost as hot as the desert."

"I didn't know what to do," Whisper said. "I thought about telling them that you worked for us, or something like that, but after the story we told the sheriff, that didn't make any sense."

"Hey, I'm glad you didn't say anything. I don't think that sheriff would have taken a liking to me. We could have all ended up in the Fallon jail. That's what I was thinking all day: Just wait this out, no matter how bad it is."

"Weren't you scared, though?" Flip asked.

"Yeah, I was a little scared. But mostly it made me mad. That sheriff had nothing better to do than to look after you two all day long, but if he had taken one look at me, I'd be lucky if he didn't shoot me."

Whisper said softly, "Tom, he was a nice man. He wanted to help us out. Before the war, he probably would have been nice to you, too. It's just the way people think right now."

"I know all that, Whisper. But maybe he wouldn't have been *too* nice to me even before the war. You're white. You've never had people look at you like you were some sort of *rodent.* And you've never treated anyone that way, so you don't think other people are like that."

The truck was running well, the tires buzzing over the highway. The sun was down, but the light was lingering over the mountains to the west. Some of the edge was even coming off the heat. Flip was sitting in the middle, catching the rushing air from the open windows wrapping around behind him from both sides. He felt like the trip might work out okay now. With a new thermostat, maybe the truck would run fine all night, maybe even run the next day in the heat. They were way behind schedule, so they couldn't stop long in Berkeley, but maybe they could take turns sleeping tonight and the next night—and just keep going.

"I'm going to tell you something you need to know," Whisper said, and she glanced over at Tom.

"Okay."

"You're not the only one who feels that way. You don't have to be Japanese to be looked down on."

Flip wondered what she meant. He watched the air whip her hair, saw the sweat on her forehead and upper lip. She didn't look as sweet as she always had before, but Flip couldn't imagine what she would know about people being mean to other people.

"I never had nice clothes when I was growing up," Whisper said. "I never had much of anything. So I felt—I don't know—unimportant, I guess. I made up my mind, if I married Andy, then I'd finally be some-body. But it doesn't work that way. Inside, I'm still the little girl with the hand-me-down clothes and worn-out shoes. Andy can't make me impor-tant. I just have to change how I think about myself."

Whisper was staring at the windshield like she was having a vision, finally seeing things for what they were. Flip didn't want her to feel the way she did, but he didn't blame her if she finally gave up on Andy.

"It's kind of the same for me," Flip said. "You know how everybody makes fun of me—for being short and everything, and not good at sports."

"Sports only matter in high school," Whisper said. "You're good at all the things that matter. You're going to be fine, Flip."

Tom suddenly started to laugh. "Hey, we're something. A Jap and a poor match girl and a midget. But we're pretty good at the criminal life. We're on the run again, just stayin' ahead of the law."

Everyone laughed, and then Flip said, "Yeah, let's stop moaning about everything. We're Bonnie and Clyde, and one more—Baby Face Nelson, or someone like that. Look out—here we come."

Whisper liked that. She slapped Flip on the knee and said, "We're taking control of our lives, boys. What do we care what anyone else thinks about us?"

"That's right," Tom said, and then he started singing "Oh Susanna" again at the top of his lungs, except that instead of saying, "I come from Alabama with a banjo on my knee," he sang, "I'm going to California, some criminals and me."

They sang more songs after that, and the truck chugged on through Sparks and Reno and then on up over the Truckee pass, slow but steady. They rolled on until about two in the morning and were almost to Nevada City, California, heading on down to Sacramento, when another tire blew out. That was not a big problem. Andy and Tom got out and put the other spare on, but they hadn't gone another twenty miles before Whisper, who was still driving, said, "Uh-oh."

Flip felt it at the same time, even though he was half asleep. The old spare they had put on had already gone flat, and *that* was a problem.

Whisper pulled the car off the road and stopped. "What do we do now?" she asked.

"We've got to find someone who can patch an inner tube for us, if that's what's wrong," Flip said. "But that tire might have wore clear through and ruined the tube."

"That other one we took off wasn't so bad," Tom said. "We can get it fixed if we can get to a filling station. That last sign said it was seven miles to Colfax, and we must have come five or six miles since then. Maybe we can walk into town and just roll that tire with us. There could be a gas station open in Colfax."

"I doubt it," Whisper said.

"I know. But we might as well try, and not just sit here. The only thing is, I want to go this time and not sit in the truck. I'll hide out once we get to a station."

"I'll stay here," Whisper said.

But Flip said, "Maybe we better stick together."

"No. I'll be all right," Whisper said. "I want to sleep a little."

"Lock the doors, then."

"Don't worry, I will."

So Tom and Flip set out. Rolling the flat tire didn't work very well, so they took turns carrying it and sometimes packed it between them, Tom walking ahead and holding it up behind him, Flip following. Every method was awkward, but the town was closer than they had expected— probably less than a mile. The only trouble was the one Flip had expected: The only gas station was dark and locked up.

"What are we going to do?" Flip asked.

"I don't know. I sure don't like sitting around here the rest of the night. We've gotta get moving if we're going to make it back to Delta by Sunday. If we could get inside the station, we could use their tools, fix the tire, and leave some money. I worked in a gas station for a while, back in Berkeley. If I've got the tools, I can fix an inner tube really fast."

"I think that's called breaking and entering," Flip said.

"Not if we give them money."

"Oh, sure. Tell that to the local sheriff when he catches us in there."

"Hey, are you forgetting?" Tom said. "We've started a life of crime. You can't back out now. Let's just walk around and check the windows and the back door."

*   *   *   *   *

Whisper had curled up on the front seat and drifted off to sleep. She had the feeling she had been asleep quite a while when a noise gradually intruded into her consciousness—a voice. "Hey, are you all right?"

She thought it was Flip or Tom, and she sat up quickly. "Yeah, I'm . . ." But she realized she was looking at someone else—the shadowed face of a man she didn't know.

"You're okay?"

"Sure. I'm fine. I was just getting a little rest."

"I figured someone was broke down out here, and I just thought I'd stop and help if I could."

Whisper rolled the window down just a crack. "It's okay. I'm traveling with my brother and a friend. They took our tire into town to get it fixed. They should be back any minute now."

"There ain't no place to fix it in Colfax, not at this hour. They could be a long time yet."

"Well, that's all right. I need some sleep."

"This ain't no place for a pretty girl like you to be sleeping. I hate to think what could happen to you out here. If you want, I could drive you on into town."

But Whisper heard something. It was the little exaggeration in the way he had said "a pretty girl," and a certain slur in his voice. She was pretty sure he had been drinking, and equally sure he was no one she could trust. "No, thanks. I'll just wait here."

The man was standing on the running board so he could look down on her. The moon was behind him, so she couldn't really see what he looked like, but he sounded fairly young. She could see a stubble of beard on his cheek, and his hair was messy. "I just can't let you stay out here like this," he said. "I wouldn't feel right about it. If something happened to a beautiful girl like you, I'd never forgive myself. Just hop in my car and I'll take you to your brother, where you know you'll be safe. I could run you and him back out here, once you get that tire fixed."

"No. I just want to stay here."

She could see him nod, but he didn't back off. "Some guy could come along, just the way I did, find you in here—and he might not be a guy like me. He might be someone who busts your window and drags you out of there. He could do what he wanted and drive off, and no one would ever have any way to catch up to him."

But this was beginning to sound like a threat, not a warning. Whisper was trying to think what she should do. She could jump out the other side of the truck, and maybe he was drunk enough that he wouldn't catch her. But it was a big desert out there, and no one was anywhere close. If he did catch her, she doubted she was strong enough to fight him off. She felt safer in the truck.

But now he was extending his fingers into the crack that Whisper had opened up, grasping the top of the window glass. "The thing is," he said, "a guy could jerk hard on this glass and it would bust right out. Then all he'd have to do is reach inside, open the door, and he'd have you."

"Please, just leave me alone. Okay?"

"And if he did something like that, the best thing you could probably do is just make him happy. You know what I mean? If you tried to fight him, he'd probably beat up on you pretty bad. But you and him, if you didn't fight or nothing like that, might have an awful nice time together."

"My brother is on his way back by now. He'll be here right away."

The man laughed. "I don't think so, honey. He's waiting for that gas station in Colfax to open. That's how I got it figured. Has anyone ever told you how beautiful you are?"

"Please. Just—"

"Hey, I'm a nice guy. I don't want to force anything on anyone. I'm just thinking, the two of us, we could have a swell time. I got some whiskey. We could take a couple of snorts of that and just kind of relax out here under the stars—get to know each other real good."

Whisper grabbed the handle and twisted it, tightening the glass on his fingers. He yelped and jerked his hands out, and that caused him to fall back off the running board. But when he appeared again, his voice had changed. "All right now, the fun is over. I told you, I don't want to be rough, but maybe that's the way you like it."

*   *   *   *   *

Flip and Tom were walking back. The back door of the old filling station had been warped, and the lock was loose. It hadn't taken much to jimmy it open with a rusty tire iron they had found out back. Inside, Tom had turned on a lightbulb in the back of the shop, removed the old tire, patched the inner tube, and then put the tire back on and pumped it up. The boys had left a half dollar, pulled the back door shut, and then started back, rolling the tire. But the walk seemed longer this time. Flip was feeling somewhat relieved, but Tom's house was still more than a hundred miles away, and he had some serious doubts about the tires holding up all the way back to Utah.

"Maybe we ought to just turn around and start back," Tom said. "I'm not sure all this is worth it."

Flip was thinking exactly the same thing, but that wasn't what he said. "We've come too far to turn around now. We're almost there."

He was looking ahead, watching for the truck, when he saw some movement, shadowy in the moonlight. "What's going on up there?" he asked Tom.

Tom was rolling the tire, and they took a few more strides, but then Flip heard a voice carrying across the desert. "You come out . . ." were the only words Flip heard, but he thought he knew what was happening, and suddenly he bolted ahead. He could see more as he ran toward the truck. A big man was standing on the running board. His fist was raised. "Hey!" Flip shouted. "Get away from her!" He saw the man turn and step down from the running board. Flip kept running, hard. "Get going! Leave her alone."

The man was facing Flip now, but as Flip ran closer, he heard the man laugh. "So is this the brother you been talking about?" he said. Flip slowed, then stopped, facing the man. "He's just a little kid. What's he going to do?"

Flip took a couple more steps forward, was only about thirty feet away. "You'll find out what I can do if you don't get going right now."

The man laughed hard, and then he stepped back toward the truck. As he did, Flip charged him. The guy still had one foot on the running board, the other on the ground, when Flip hit him with a football tackle, square in the ribs. The man was off balance, and he went down hard. Flip was wild by then. He was on top of the guy, straddling his side and pummeling him—right, left, right, left—smashing his fists into the man's face and the back of his head.

But then the guy threw out an elbow and caught Flip square across the nose. Flip was knocked onto his back in the sand, and in another second, the man was on him. Flip felt a blow that hit his arm as he covered his face, another that caught him in the throat, and one in the forehead. He rolled, trying to squirm away, but a fist struck him in the side of the head.

And then the guy rolled off him, and Flip realized that Tom had hit the man with a tackle of his own. Flip jumped up just as the man threw Tom off and jumped to his feet. Tom and the man were squaring off, and Flip stepped up next to Tom. It was two against one, but the guy outweighed the two of them together. "Just try, you two little boys. I'll bust you up, and then just see what I do to your sister."

"Over my dead body," Flip said.

"If that's how you want it."

And then there was a flash of movement and a huge grunt as the man dropped to the ground. It took a second to realize that Whisper had come around the truck and hit him in the back of the head. She was standing over him now, and Flip saw what was in her hand: a tire iron.

The man didn't stir for a few seconds, but when he did, he reached up and touched his head, then looked at his hand. Flip couldn't see the blood on his head, but he could tell by the man's reaction that he must be bleeding pretty badly. He rolled over and got to his feet, and then he started backing away. Whisper faced him and held up the tire iron with both hands, ready to swing it like a baseball bat. Tom and Flip moved up next to her. The man didn't say a word. He just kept backing away, and then he got in his car, started the engine, and sprayed gravel as he gunned the accelerator and came straight at the three of them. They all jumped back, and he roared on past them and on down the highway, heading toward Colfax.

"Do you think he'll go after the sheriff?" Flip asked.

"Not a chance," Tom said. "He's not about to admit that two 'little boys' and a girl beat up on him."

It took several seconds before Flip laughed a little, and then Whisper and Tom did too, but it was nervous laughter. Flip knew they had dodged another bullet, this time a serious one. He really wished they had never started this crazy trip.

"Are you okay, Flip?" Whisper asked.

"Yeah. I think my nose might be busted, but I'm okay." He could feel the pain in his throat, too. The guy had hit him straight in the Adam's apple.

Whisper took hold of his shoulders and turned him toward the moonlight. "You've got blood all over you," she said.

Flip had sort of known that but hadn't really thought too much about it yet.

Whisper was leaning in, looking at him closely. She produced a handkerchief from the pocket of her slacks and began dabbing at his face. The hankie smelled like lilacs. She touched her tongue to it and kept wiping at him, and he felt a vibration go through him. He wanted her to do this forever, hold her face so close to his and attend to him this way.

"You fought for me, Flip."

Flip didn't say anything.

"You put your life on the line for me."

"So did Tom."

"I know. Both of you did. I love you two guys."

But Flip knew what she meant. It wasn't what he wished.

"I say we start back," Tom said. "This whole thing is getting to be too big of a mess. We better head back while we've got four tires that will run for a while."

"I still haven't seen a palm tree," Whisper said. "We've come this far, and I'm not going back until we do. Then I want to see San Francisco Bay."

"We might have to junk the truck down there and figure out some other way to get back to Utah," Tom said. "What's Mr. Gledhill going to say about that?"

Flip had been thinking the same thing, but he knew the other truth: "We're in a mess no matter how you look at it. We might as well drive the rest of the way and get what we came for."

"Well, then, let's get going. But I'm going to have to pay your dad back somehow for running his truck into the ground."

"It was dying long ago. All we're doing is finishing it off."

So the three got back into the truck, and Tom took a turn driving.

Flip knew he needed to get in the back of the truck and dig another shirt out of his sack, but it was still dark, and they needed to see if they couldn't get into Berkeley before sunup.

"Just lean your head against my shoulder," Whisper told Flip. "Try to get a little sleep."

So Flip did lean against her, and he loved the touch of her warm shoulder against his face. He wanted to put his arms around her and slide in close, but he knew he couldn't do that.

*   *   *   *   *

The sun was coming up when Tom stopped the truck in front of his house, just outside of Berkeley. Flip sat up and looked around. He realized he'd been asleep quite a while. "Are we there?" he asked.

"Yes," Whisper said, "and when we were coming through Sacramento, I saw some palm trees."

"Wasn't it too dark?"

"I saw them in the moonlight. That's the most romantic way." She laughed. "And I'll see them better on the way back."

"Did you see the Bay?"

"Sort of. I'll see that better, too."

But Tom was already out of the truck, striding toward the front door of his house. Flip got out and followed him. Tom used the key he had brought with him to open the front door, but when he stepped inside, Flip heard him say, "Oh, no." Flip stepped inside and saw what he meant. All the furniture was gone. There were a few knickknacks and books and papers strewn around on the floor, but nothing else. "They even took the rug off the floor," Tom said.

Tom walked on into the kitchen. Flip and Whisper followed. "They took the refrigerator," Tom said.

Some of the cabinet doors were open, but the shelves were bare. He walked down the hall and stepped into a room. Flip followed. "This was

my room," Tom said. But the bed was gone, the furniture. In one corner was a stack of what appeared to be junk. Tom walked to it and took
a look, but he didn't bother to sort through it. He turned around and
looked at Flip, his face emotionless. "They took *everything*," he said.
"How could they do that?"

"They're a pack of thieves. You need to call the cops."

Tom shook his head slowly back and forth. "You still don't get it, do
you, Flip?"

"What?"

"They thought they had the right. We're just Japs."

Flip didn't know what to say, but he was angry enough to hurt those
people, those thieves, if he only had the chance.

Tom took some more time after that and went through things carefully. He found two albums full of pictures in his parents' bedroom, and
he found a broken doll his little sister had played with as a child. But the
best thing was, in a box of things in his closet, he found his baseball
glove. He found a few other trinkets, things his parents might like to
have, and he told Tom and Whisper, "I guess to me it was worth it. We
couldn't have taken the furniture back anyway, and my mother will want
the pictures more than anything."

Flip was glad to hear that, but he was looking past Tom by then. A
police car had just stopped in front of the house. "Uh-oh," he said.
"We're in trouble."

His first impulse was to run, but he realized it was too late for that.
He looked at Tom, and then at Whisper, and he could see that they all
knew the same thing: There was not one thing they could do.

When the policemen came to the door, Tom opened it and said,
"Hello. Can I help you?"

"We got a report this house was being broken into."

Tom stepped away from the door and motioned for them to come in. "You're right about that. But that was a long time ago. This is my house, and the people who were renting it took everything and left."

One of the policemen, a thin man with a carefully trimmed mustache, nodded a couple of times. "But you're not supposed to be here, are you?"

"I heard they were stealing everything, so I came to see what I could save."

"You're supposed to be in a relocation camp, out in Utah. Ain't that right?"

"I am. And I'm going back, leaving in just a few minutes."

"No. You're going to jail. You're a fugitive. Who are these two?"

"Friends of mine."

The policeman looked at Whisper. "Ma'am, where are you from?"

"Utah."

"Did you help this young man get here?"

"Yes, sir."

"Well . . . I guess you knew what you was getting yourself into. We're going to have to arrest you—for harboring an escaped prisoner and taking him across state lines. I'll let the judge figure out what he wants to do with you." He looked at Flip. "And who are you?"

"I helped him too. You'll have to put me in jail with them."

"How old are you?"

"What difference does that make?"

"How old are you?"

"Sixteen."

"Well, I don't know. The judge might put most of the responsibility on this girl here. Is she related to you?"

"No."

"See, now that's a problem. She shouldn't be hauling minors around, across state lines and everything."

"Did you three come down here in that old truck?" said the other officer.

"Yes," Whisper said.

"That's a miracle in itself. Let's just leave that thing here for now, and the three of you come with us."

The second policeman, a young guy, walked out first, and then the cop with the mustache waved everyone out and followed along behind. Flip was almost to the police car when he stopped and turned around. "This isn't right," he said.

"What's not right?"

"Tom's an American—the same as you are. How can he be an escaped prisoner if he never should've been locked up in the first place? You oughta be looking for the people who stole all his stuff, not taking *him* to jail."

"Look, son, you don't—"

"It's wrong. And all that me and Whisper wanted to do was help out a guy who got his house broken into. We didn't do anything wrong either."

"You tell that to the judge, son, not to me. Now get in the car."

Whisper slipped in first, and then Tom. But just as Flip was about to get in, the policeman stepped up closer. "You little Jap lover," he said, "I ought to bust your head." And then he shoved Flip into the car.

CHAPTER 24

TOM AND FLIP ended up in the same cell—a little holding cell at the county jail. They were both dead tired from two nights of driving, but when they lay down on the hard bunks, Flip didn't fall asleep. There was a bad smell in the mattress—mold, maybe—and a putrid smell from the rusted old toilet in the corner. Two walls of the cell were made of bars, and there were windows farther down a hallway. There was too much light, and Flip's head was spinning anyway. He could tell that Tom wasn't falling asleep either.

"What do you think they'll do with us?" Flip finally asked Tom.

"I think they'll let you go as soon as your dad or someone can vouch for you. Me, I don't know. Maybe federal prison somewhere. What I did, leaving my camp, is a federal crime. They might send me to Tule Lake. That's where they put the internees they consider troublemakers."

"Where's Tule Lake?"

"Here in California, but way up north, almost to Oregon. It's no worse than Topaz—just more guarded. But I've lost my chance to join the army."

"I wouldn't care, if I was you. You don't owe this country anything, the way they treat you."

Flip could hear a dripping sound, maybe in the tank of the toilet or in the sink. He didn't raise his head to look. But it seemed to mark time as Tom was apparently thinking things over. Eventually, he said, "The war's going to end—maybe pretty soon—but I'll have a police record. I thought I would come home from the service, maybe with some medals, and I'd be able to look people in the eye."

"I'm sorry, Tom. I didn't think enough about all that kind of stuff before I talked you into coming."

"You didn't talk me into coming. I'm older than you. I could've said no. But I figured we could pull it off."

"We almost did. We should have grabbed some stuff and left the house a lot faster."

"Maybe. Or maybe the truck would have broken down in the desert and we would have been stuck out there. I knew better than to drive that old thing all the way down here."

"So why did you do it?"

Again Flip listened to the dripping sound, and he knew that Tom was asking himself about that. Flip finally glanced over at Tom, who was lying on his back, his hands behind his head. "To tell you the truth, I probably did it because it was something my dad would never do. He obeys. He bows down to all the *hakujin*. I just wanted to stand up for myself a little—and get some of my stuff back."

"What's your dad going to say about this?"

"He'll be ashamed. He'll have a son in jail, maybe going to prison. I hate to think what it will do to him. Having a son in trouble will shame him in front of all his *Issei* friends at Topaz, and it will shame him to everyone else if he ever comes back here to Berkeley."

"I don't see why. All you did was—"

"There's no way you can understand how a Japanese father has to hang his head when his children give him trouble. It was bad enough when I argued with him back at the camp. He already thinks I'm worthless."

Flip rested his arm over his eyes. "Actually, I kind of do know what

356

you're talking about—you know, your dad being ashamed. My dad's going to be really mad at me."

"But your father hugs you, jokes with you, talks with you—all those things. I've watched you two together. You'll talk things over and then everything will be okay. My father won't talk. I'll just know what he thinks of me."

"I guess we'll talk, but I know what he'll think: *Andy never would have done anything like this.* He knows I'm second-rate, even though he'd never say so. After they track him down and tell him about this, he'll shake his head, and he'll talk to Mom the way he talks about Adele—you know, with worry in his voice. That's pretty much the same thing as shame, isn't it?"

"Not really. You can go back and do all right in school this year—things like that—and he'll forget all about it. Me, I'll be in prison, and my father will never be the same. *Never.*"

Flip wasn't sure. Maybe his dad would let it all go after a while, but not much about the future looked good to Flip. This story would circulate in Delta, and people would all be talking about how he ran off with a Jap to California. There was no explaining that to any of them. Whisper would be hurt by this too—maybe even worse. People talked if a girl was seen with an Indian or a Mexican. A Jap was probably worse. They'd make it sound like she had turned into some kind of floozy.

"I'll tell you what I think, Tom," Flip said.

"About what?"

"About everything. I think there's more things wrong with this stupid world than right. People don't care about being fair. You've got—what?—about eight thousand people sitting out there at the camp, stuck in a desert, living on throwaway food, in houses most people wouldn't put up with, and what do people say about it? Nothing. They just let it happen, and they don't even think about whether it's right or wrong."

"They listen to the government, that's all," Tom said. "They accept what they hear."

"I know. But it's wrong, and it's the way people are. If a guy has different skin, or if he's a little different from other people, they think it's okay to be unfair, or to make fun of him, or anything else they want to do. Almost everyone's that way."

"Sure. But you and me, we're probably that way too. We find people to make fun of."

"Not me. I'm down at the bottom. There's no one to look down on."

"Come on, Flip. *None* of us act the way we should. If some guy's really fat or something like that—stupid or ugly or something—we say things about it to other guys. You know how that is."

"Fine. Then throw me and you in too, but how does that make a difference? At church they talk all the time about how we ought to be, and how we ought to act, and then no one does it. We all just look out for ourselves."

"More or less. Sure. That's just how we're built. It's self-preservation."

"Well, then," Flip said angrily, "we ought to close up Sunday School and start telling the truth."

"That doesn't make any sense," Tom said. "We've all got to *try* to do the right things."

"I don't see people trying very hard, even right after they walk out of church."

Flip really wanted to sleep. He didn't like the way he felt right now. He felt like he'd been walking around all his life accepting what he was taught by his parents and teachers and everybody, and none of it was true. Maybe people thought all that church stuff was real, but it just wasn't. He rolled onto his side and pulled his legs up a little, tried to get comfortable, but there was no pillow, and his neck was in a kink after just a few seconds.

"Flip," Tom said, "I don't want you to take everything like that.

People *can* think about somebody besides themselves. It's kind of hard, but it happens all the time."

Flip rolled back onto his back and covered his eyes again. He tried to think whether he believed that. But it didn't fit with what he'd been seeing. "Maybe some people take a stab at it," he said. "But if you try to do something that's right, you'll find a hundred people—or a thousand—every time, who'll tell you you're doing the wrong thing. That's how come we're in jail."

Tom laughed softly. "Flip, you're just finding out a few things every guy has to figure out sooner or later. You learn about truth and justice and everything when you're a kid, and you think everything's always going to be fair. Growing up is finding out that a lot of stuff isn't that simple."

But Flip wasn't buying that. Maybe people "grew up" and got used to things being all wrong, and they learned to live with that, but that didn't prove a thing. Flip had a brother he had always thought was perfect, and what was he doing now? Treating the nicest girl in the world like she was worthless. And everyone else was running around hurting people's feelings, calling them names, not caring what was fair and what wasn't—and acting like they were wonderful people at the same time. He thought maybe his parents tried harder than most to do what was right, but he also knew what his dad would think of him for trying to help Tom: that he'd done something bad. "I don't believe in one thing," he told Tom. "I think maybe God's about as real as the Easter Bunny. And church is like one of those sideshows at a circus—a bunch of guys just figuring out a way to con you out of your money."

"Come on, Flip. You don't believe that."

"Yes, I do. And that's how I'm going to operate from now on. I know what's up now, and I'm not going to listen to any more lies."

Flip had nothing more to think about after that, and he actually did drift off to sleep, lying flat on his back. He slept for a long time that way, but eventually the bunk was too uncomfortable, and the smell in the mattress seemed to get worse as the night moisture seeped into the cell. He was cold, too, and pulling a blanket over him didn't help much. Somewhere around two o'clock he was fully awake, with no hope of going back to sleep, and his brain had found more immediate concerns to mull over. He wondered how long he might be in jail, and he was worried about Whisper. He wondered how she was holding up in some cell like this, maybe all alone, or worse, with some bad cellmates. He hated to think of her in some dirty place, maybe being mistreated. He never should have gotten her into this situation.

Eventually, a little light came into the jail through a window that Flip couldn't see. His body was hurting so badly by then that he decided to sit up. Tom soon did the same. But there was nothing else to do. Flip didn't know whether he would get a chance to clean up, or what to expect from another day that might be like the one they had spent the day before. He wanted to use that toilet, but he hated the idea of doing it in front of Tom.

Tom didn't say much, and he looked drearier than he had the day before, probably because of the time he had had to think and to let this new reality settle in on him. Breakfast did finally come. It was oatmeal mush with milk, but no sugar, half a grapefruit, and a slice of toast. Flip was actually hungry by then, and he ate it all, but he winced at the grapefruit, which he never had liked. Tom ate it too, and the two speculated about their day, but Flip didn't want to ask about the days that might follow, and Tom didn't bring any of that up either.

Just after breakfast, however, the same jailer who had first put them in this cell opened the outer door and walked in with Bishop Gledhill following behind. Flip stood up and looked at his father, wondered what he was thinking, and wondered how in the world he had gotten there so fast.

The jailer said, "You can talk to him, and then just knock on that door when you want to get out."

"When will the sheriff be here?" Dad asked.

"Pretty soon. I can't say exactly how soon."

The jailer walked out and shut the door behind him, and then Dad looked at Flip again. "Are you two all right?" he asked. He stepped up to the bars and took hold of a couple of them like some jailbird in the movies. He was wearing a white shirt but no tie, and suit pants and suspenders. Flip knew how he thought. He surely had his tie and his suit coat out in the car, ready in case he needed to talk to a judge. Dad had no idea how to meet with a man like that in a sport shirt.

"Sure, we're okay," Flip said. "How did you get down here?"

"I drove all night. They got hold of me yesterday about noon, so I drove your mom home and then headed down here."

"I'm sorry about this, Dad."

Bishop Gledhill looked at him for a moment, confusion in his eyes. "I guess I don't understand. What was this all about?"

Flip tried to explain it all, but Bishop Gledhill still looked baffled. "Why did you bring Whisper?" he asked.

Flip looked at the floor. "Mostly, she wanted to come. She said she wanted to see California. She's the one who had the gas stamps, too—and a driver's license."

Dad was gripping the bars harder, his knuckles turning white. "Did you ever stop to think about all this, Flip? Did you consider what you were doing, crossing that desert in that old truck?"

"This whole thing was my fault, Mr. Gledhill," Tom said. "Flip did it for me, but I'm old enough, I should have known better."

"From what the sheriff told me on the phone, Tom, you're in some pretty deep trouble."

"I know."

"Did you think you could fill up that truck with things and drive clear back to Utah—and not have anyone notice who you were?"

Tom didn't answer for a time. He pushed his hands into his jeans pockets and looked rather shamefaced. Finally he said, "Mr. Gledhill, what people were doing wasn't right—breaking in and taking our things. I thought so much about that I don't think I considered the problems as much as I should have."

Dad nodded. He looked at the floor and thought for a time. "I'll try to talk to the sheriff and see what good I can do."

"Dad," Flip said, "could you check on Whisper, too? We haven't seen her since yesterday. You've got to get her out of here. They're saying it's her fault because I'm a kid and she's a grown-up, but that's not right. It was all my idea."

"Well, now, that's fine for you to say, Flip. But she is an adult—or ought to be—and didn't act much like one. She should've told you what a harebrained idea this was right from the beginning. I'm not very happy with Whisper right now."

"Don't say that to her, Dad. Our family's been tough enough on her lately."

"What are you talking about? I've always been good to that girl. I let her manage my bank and then she walked out just when I needed her."

"Don't you know what Andy's done to her, Dad? He told her he doesn't want her anymore."

"He didn't say that exactly. He just wanted—"

"He did tell her that, and he broke her heart. She's thinking about marrying that rabbit-looking guy from over in Fillmore, and she still loves Andy. We need to be as good to her as we can or we're going to lose her."

The bishop took a long breath. He looked frustrated. "Flip, we can't decide those things. That's all up to Andy." He let go of the bars and slipped his hands into his pants pockets.

"But Andy asked me to keep her for him—and not let her marry anyone else. I *promised* I'd do that." All the emotion of these last few days was finally letting go in Flip, and he heard his voice shaking. He swallowed and looked away.

His dad's voice softened as he said, "Flip, you can only do so much—and you've done the best you can. Right now we have bigger fish to fry. Let me see if I can find this sheriff. I'd like to get all three of you out of here today, if I possibly can. You two rest a little more, and I'll let you know as soon as I can what's going to happen."

So Dad knocked on the door, and when the jailer opened it, he walked out. Tom said, "He's right, Flip. Whisper should have known better, and I did know better, and I still got you involved in all this. You don't have to take the responsibility. It could've worked too; we almost pulled it off."

"No. Not really. The truck never would have made it. I'm the one who should have known that."

"Flip, sometimes you want something to happen so bad, you think you can just *make* it happen. The only trouble is, there are things you can't do one thing about." Tom hesitated and waited until Flip looked at him. "Like this thing with Whisper. You can't make her wait for your brother. She's gotta decide about that. Her and your brother."

"I know." But then Flip said the rest. "I'd give anything in this world to be five years older than I am."

The cell was quiet for a very long time, and the last thing Flip could have done was to look at Tom. But Tom finally said, "Your time will come, Flip."

"No it won't. I'll never be anything like Andy."

"Maybe Andy won't ever be enough like you."

Flip didn't try to argue that, but he didn't see much in himself that would make Andy jealous. He had talked about this subject more than he should have anyway, so he lay back on his bunk and waited. The better part of an hour must have passed, with Tom pacing sometimes, lying down sometimes, and Flip hardly moving. Finally, the jailer opened the door, stepped to the cell, and unlocked it. "You," he said, pointing to Flip. "Come with me."

"What about Tom?" Flip asked as he sat up.

"He stays here."

"But that's not fair. He was just—"

"Don't talk to *me* about it. I don't have one word of say about anything that happens around here."

Flip turned to Tom. "Dad will keep working on it," he said. "We won't leave until we get you out of here."

"You might have to, Flip. I'm pretty sure they'll send me to Tule Lake—or worse. That's just the way it is."

"No. We'll make this right. We won't let them do that to you."

"Come on, boy," the jailer was saying. "I don't think you need to be too sure you're getting out of here just yet."

So Flip followed the jailer out front and then down a hallway to an office where Flip's dad and the sheriff were sitting. It was a ramshackle little place with a broken-down couch and an old metal desk. Dad stood up when Flip came in, and Flip saw immediately that he was frustrated, the color strong in his face. "I just want you to tell the sheriff what you told me—how you came to bring Tom down here."

Flip had stepped just inside the door, but he was only about two more steps away from the desk. The sheriff was an older man with graying hair, rough gray skin, and a soft layer of fat over a big frame. "It was all my idea, sir. I—"

"It doesn't matter whose idea it was."

"Just let him tell his story."

The sheriff let out a gust of breath, then folded his arms. "Go ahead," he said.

Flip told his story again, and ended by saying, "He wasn't running away from Topaz. We were going right back. He just wanted to see if he could save some things that belonged to him."

"No one got in touch with me," the sheriff said. "No one said a word about that house being broken into."

"His dad wrote to someone down here a long time ago. He contacted the police, he said. And no one did a thing."

"I don't believe that for a minute," the sheriff said. "I never heard about that."

Bishop Gledhill cleared his throat. "Sheriff, Tom was worried that the police wouldn't be much help. Some people seem to feel that they can take advantage of the Japanese right now. That might be wrong, but you can see how they might get to feel that way."

"Just maybe some of them Japs shouldn't have been sending signals out to enemy ships, offshore, using mirrors and stuff like that. If half of them people hadn't been spies, maybe we wouldn't have had to round them up, and maybe they could have been sitting at home taking care of their own property."

"I know how you feel, Sheriff. When the Japanese were first shipped up to our area, I thought the same way about them. But a lot of them have been in my bank, and I've sat down and talked to them. Some of those who had some savings have deposited money with me. And they've told me their stories—what kind of people they are and what they were doing before the war. There might be a spy out there at Topaz. Maybe several, for all I know. But my impression is that we've rounded up mostly innocent people. Good people. Americans. All of these kids in Tom's generation are American citizens. *Good* citizens. Tom wants to join the army as soon as he turns eighteen."

"Well, then, he should have kept his nose clean. He's going to be sitting this war out in a federal prison. He broke the law—and he knew that was what he was doing when he did it."

"But he wasn't running away. He was going to turn right around and go back," Flip said again.

"Yeah, and that's what any guy could say who busts out of some jail."

"Well, now, let's think about that," Dad said. "He had permission to be in town with us, and sure, he knew he shouldn't leave the area, but he figured he could hurry down and take some of his possessions back. Can't you see how that wouldn't look like a crime to him?"

"It doesn't matter what it looked like. It matters what it was. For all I know, he was coming to check out some of these defense installations around here. And our shipyards. Then he was going to get word to Japs so they could bomb us."

"Oh, come on, Sheriff. Think about that. We have the Japanese on the run. They're trying to stop us before we occupy their islands. What chance is there of them bombing us now?"

"I don't know that for sure. And maybe this Jap kid doesn't know that either. All I know is that your kid helped him come down here, against the law, and that pretty young lady, nice as she looks, is an adult, moving a couple of kids across the country. That's another crime. I'm willing to let your kid go, since he's the age he is—although I sure wouldn't have to—but I can't let the other two out of here. I already notified the FBI about what I've got here."

Flip felt some panic setting in. "But that's not fair," he said. "I told you, I'm the one who talked Tom into coming here."

"Well, then, I can throw you back in that cell, if that would make you feel any better."

"It would. Put me back."

"Wait a minute," Dad said. "That's nonsense." He stepped to the sheriff's desk and said, "Sir, let's think about this before it turns into a federal matter. Tom wants to join the army. He'll be eighteen in a couple of weeks. You've heard about our Japanese troops in Italy. They've distinguished themselves. You can let the boy fight for his country—or you

366

can send him to prison and make a mess of his life. Why don't you let me drive him back to Utah and I'll have him in the army right away. And let me take the Harris girl. She didn't use good judgment, but she certainly meant no harm to these two boys."

The sheriff stood and looked hard into Bishop Gledhill's eyes. "You go ahead and take the girl," he said. "I'll get her sent up here right now. It's not her I care about. But this Jap boy broke a federal law, and it's not my job to get him into the army. It's my job to enforce the law."

"Sir, you can enforce the law, or you can see that some justice is done. You can ruin a boy's life, or you can help him be the man he wants to be."

The sheriff cursed. "You're talking about a Jap, Mister. I've got a son fighting those little rats out in the Pacific. How do you expect me to tell my kid that I let one off, trying to get back here to California where he don't belong?"

"You might tell your son that you're a decent human being and you decided to do the right thing."

"Get out of here before I decide to keep this no-good son of yours and that Jap-loving girl besides."

Flip had seen his father really mad only a couple of times, and he saw it again now. Bishop Gledhill seemed to get a couple of inches taller. He pointed his finger at the sheriff and said, "My son is a *fine* young man, and his mistake was that he wanted to help another human being—another fine young man. You say one more word about him, or about Whisper—one of the loveliest spirits who ever graced this planet—and I swear, I'll knock you against that wall. And then we can all occupy this jail together."

"Don't think I won't put you there."

"Oh, I don't doubt you'd do it, but I'll tell you something. The Japanese people I know are honorable and they're good—and I have no trouble at all loving them. But I'm going to have to do a lot of work on myself before I can find any love in my heart for you."

"You just spoke your last word. Take your kid and get out of here. And take the girl. But don't open your mouth to me again."

"Fine. But you haven't heard the last from me. I'm going to see that justice is done for Tom, no matter what it takes."

The sheriff was walking away. Twenty minutes later, Flip and his Dad, with Whisper, were driving away from the jailhouse, and Flip was doing what he had tried for two days not to do. He was sitting in the backseat crying—hiding his face, but sobbing. All he could think of was Tom, still sitting in that jail.

CHAPTER 25

ANDY AND MCCOMB had made their way to a safe house, but they had a new problem. One of the guards at the train station had studied Andy's papers. He might remember the false name on the identity card. Gestapo agents in the region had surely begun to look for Andy and McComb as soon as the bodies of the policemen had been found, so Andy's false name, perhaps even McComb's, might be widely circulated by now.

Andy radioed London to let his leaders know that the team had been compromised. Word came back that they should drop their cover stories and fight with the operational group they had intended to advise. *Maquis* leaders had made contact with the OG and could arrange to get McComb and Andy to them. The local *Maquis* boss told them, "Just wait for a day or two. Something is going on, and we're not sure what it is. My suspicion is that the second invasion is about to start, this time in the Mediterranean. Everything is being set up in the south the way it was in Normandy, but we're not allowed to know exactly what's going to happen, or when."

What Andy and McComb soon learned was that the OG had been dropped into the area a few days before. They had received most of the same training as the Jeds, but they fought in uniform and were sent to give leadership to the *Maquis* as much as anything. There would be less surveillance, more open fighting, but the combined forces would still be small enough that most of the fighting would continue to be in hit-and-run operations.

So Andy and McComb waited a couple of days, hidden again in a cellar. As usual, there was way too much time to think. The inaction was almost more than McComb could stand. He spent hours pacing, talking, telling Andy about his exploits back home: his heroism on the football field, his conquests with girls on campus, his drunken brawls with fraternity boys. He wanted to hear Andy's stories, but Andy had few to tell.

McComb also slept a good deal, and Andy wished that he could too. But he often lay awake, even at night, and he thought how different he was from McComb, from most of the men he had met in the OSS. He had been telling himself for a long time that he would never fit in if he went back to Delta, that he would be a foreigner in his own town. But it occurred to him now that he really didn't fit anywhere. So much of who he was came from his family, his church, his small-town way of life. He started trying to picture himself at home again. He was realizing that he might survive after all, and he wondered if he could find a way back to the self he remembered.

When he tried to pray his way back, he couldn't manage it. He said the words, but he didn't feel them. Maybe he couldn't go home. But there was nowhere else to go. He needed to marry someone like Whisper, and yet there was no one else like Whisper, and she wouldn't want him, even if she was still single, once she understood why he couldn't pray.

Finally word came that a code sentence had been announced on the BBC; it was time for the OG to move, and time for Andy and McComb to join them. They didn't have uniforms, but they were guided through a wooded area to the operational group, and the captain who led the group assembled enough pieces of uniforms for each of them to be identified as soldiers, not spies.

Andy and McComb hiked with the OG through the country at night, working their way south. Within a couple of days, Andy watched the group turn more and more to McComb for leadership, just as the *Maquisards* had done in Rouen. McComb had experience in the country now, but more than that, he was forceful, and the group leader, Captain Booker, didn't possess the same confidence. Officially, Captain Booker was still the leader, but he consulted with McComb about everything, and McComb more often than not made the actual decisions. Along with the thirty-two OG soldiers, including Andy and McComb, a group of more than a hundred *Maquisards* had joined with them, and so the little unit had become a force to be reckoned with.

In the Rhône Valley, south of Montélimar, the team set up an ambush and attacked a company of Germans who were marching south. By then, Booker had word that the Allied landing had taken place on August 15, and German units were trying to get to the coast to stop the invasion before it took hold. The OG unit hit the German company from the flank, attacking along a main highway. It split them in half, killed many, and scattered the others. The OG and *Maquis* forces took eleven casualties, four killed and seven wounded, but they knocked out many more of the German forces.

McComb was thrilled. He liked this fighting in the open. Andy was glad to see the Germans in increasing disarray, and he knew this second front was important, but he had gotten to know one of the OG men who had been killed, shot through a lung. Andy had tried to treat him and had been holding a bandage against the soldier's chest when he felt a final vibration, and then stillness. It was just one more death, and Andy was becoming numb to it all, but it still bothered him to hear McComb exulting after the battle. What Andy hoped was that the war in Europe could end quickly now. Some were saying that the Germans would never last until Christmas, that they were on the run. In the next few days, Andy saw some evidence that that might be true. All the movement south turned around, and the Germans began to retreat, sometimes in ragtag little remnants of their former units. Booker, with McComb's guidance, ripped up some of these groups and one day worked over a truck convoy with mortar fire.

Andy had been ready to kill all the Germans he could after the massacre in Cléres, but now, as he watched young men running back to their homeland destroyed, he wondered what the point was of continuing to kill. He knew the war was far from over, and McComb kept saying, "Every Kraut we kill in France is one we don't have to face when we cross the Rhine." That made sense to Andy until he saw the dead Germans lying in their blood on the roads or in the woods. So many of them were kids.

It was true that some German prisoners, when interrogated, remained committed to fight the battle to the end. "We're working on weapons that will turn this war around," some of them would say. "We'll win the war yet." But only a few seemed to be holding on to that idea. Others seemed relieved to be taken prisoner. It was clearly their hope that they would actually be alive when the war was over.

The team kept moving and attacked another German unit on a country road that crossed the Ardeche River. It was another successful operation, this time against a larger force, but afterwards the French and Americans had to hide out for a day to keep the Germans from chasing them down. On the following morning, Andy was eating some of his K-rations as he sat by a little fire and talked to a couple of *Maquisards*. McComb walked toward him and motioned for Andy to step aside with him. "We just got intelligence that a convoy of Germans is moving up that same road we hit yesterday," he told Andy. "The trucks will cross the Ardeche late today. It's a sizeable force with tanks leading the way. We're going to head out now to get there ahead of them and set explosives. We want to blow up a big rock bridge while the tanks are crossing and take out as many of them as we can. We'll force the troops either to rebuild the bridge or to find some other way out of the valley. We figure we can set up on higher ground and make life miserable for them—snipe at them if they try to get across the river and harass them if they look for another route. I want you to—"

"Every bridge we blow now will have to be rebuilt later."

"What?"

"Sometimes we're hurting the French more than the Germans. The people are going to need those bridges."

"Gledhill, let me remind you of something. You seem to forget it about twice a week. We're still at war."

"I know that. I'm just saying—"

"I don't want to hear this. It's a good plan. We'll make a mess out of this unit. We're not only killing them, we're breaking their morale. We need to leave them hopeless, so those who make it back to Germany won't have any will to fight." He pointed his finger into Andy's face. "And *that* will save lives—theirs as well as ours. We need to hit them hard now while they're on the run."

Andy nodded. That sounded right.

"Okay, I want you to get to the bridge. You're as good with explosives as anyone we have. I've got ten men going in with you. You've got to be the one to make sure the stuff is placed right. This is a substantial bridge just south of a place called . . . I don't know how to say it." He held a map in front of Andy and pointed to a place called Vallon-Pont-D'Arc. "We're going to have to run a line, so we can blow the bridge at exactly the right moment, not rely on a fuse or a timer."

"All right. I can do that."

So Andy set out with his men, and for once they weren't walking at night and they actually had enough time to get where they were going. Andy guided his men to set explosives carefully, in spots that would break the span of the bridge between the heavy stone understructures. There was no way the entire bridge could be blown away, but the job of bridging the gaps would be slow and difficult. Andy doubted the Germans could reconstruct the bridge with three breaks in the span and snipers firing at anyone trying to start the job. He thought of blowing only one span, so the French would have less trouble rebuilding, but he knew what McComb would say about that. What he feared was that not enough of the bridge would go down to destroy the tanks.

When everything was set, Andy directed the men in laying a long line to a plunger, and then he instructed them to hunker down and wait. He walked back and told McComb that everything was ready. "All right. I want you to be the one to turn that handle," McComb said. "You have to wait until the maximum number of tanks are on the bridge."

Andy wondered whether McComb was actually the commander now, but he didn't say that. Instead, he said, "I can only blow out the spans between those wide columns that hold up the bridge. It's possible that tanks at either end will get off."

"What are you talking about? I told you to blow the whole bridge out of there."

"We don't have enough explosives. That bridge is solid rock."

McComb stared at Andy as though he were crazy, but he backed off. "Okay. I'll put men in position on this side of the bridge. If a tank gets away, they'll take it out with our bazooka."

"It depends on the tanks, Captain. If they're Tigers, our bazookas can bounce right off their armor."

"So what are you now, an authority on tanks, too? Why is it you question every decision I ever make?"

"You know that about Tigers, sir. We learned that in our training."

"What I learned is that you have to get in close, and the bazookas will work against any tank. At the very least, you can blow a track off and put the thing out of commission."

"Yes. That is right, sir." Andy had rarely called McComb "sir." He knew that there was some sarcasm in using it now, and he also knew that McComb sensed it.

"We'll get our people in close, then. But turn that handle at the right time. I don't know how many tanks they have exactly, and we don't want to deal with any more of them than we have to."

"The Germans don't usually bunch their tanks that way. They might lead with some and keep the rest at the back."

"That's right. So get the ones on the bridge, and then we'll work over the troops and the trucks with mortar fire. We don't have enough men to take them on straight up, but we can hold them down until they get organized. Then we'll fall back and hide out in the woods. Maybe tonight we can come back and hit them again for a while."

"All right, sir. I'll—"

"Look, Andy, don't start all that *sir* stuff with me. That's not the way we've worked together. I think I've got a good plan. Let's just make it work."

"Okay."

"I'll help Booker place the men. Keep a couple with you. You'll be closer than most, and you might have to shoot your way out. That's one reason you better get those tanks."

"Okay. I'll get as many as I can. How far away are the Germans?"

"I don't know. We can't seem to find out anything very definite. But I don't think we're going to be waiting much more than an hour."

Andy hiked back to his site, where the wait was actually three hours, but he finally heard the creaking and rattling of the tank tracks on the pavement. He had two men with him now, both *Maquis.* One was a young fellow named Gilbert, only about eighteen, and the other a man in his forties named Xavier. They were smart men, experienced in sabotage work, but they hadn't taken on troops openly until these last few days. Andy didn't want to get into any "shoot your way out" situations if he could help it.

"All right," Andy said. "This is it. Stay low. Don't show your faces. After I fire off the explosives, we're going to run back up this hill before the Germans can react to us."

"Let's kill some Germans before we make a run," Gilbert said.

"We'll shoot from up above, once we're in a better position, but let's just get ourselves out of here first."

The noise gradually increased. Andy could hear the hum of truck engines along with the crunch of the tanks. He figured most of the troops must be traveling in trucks. Maybe others were marching, as had been reported. But a lot of men could jump out of those troop trucks and throw a massive force against the OG's hundred and thirty men. The Americans and French would have to fall back at some point and then return to their hit-and-run attacks later. He just hoped that the *Maquis,* eager for kills, wouldn't linger too long, and he hoped Booker—or McComb—would call them off quickly.

The tanks finally appeared, emerging from under a canopy of trees, rolling down the road alongside the river. The road swung away from the river, climbed a little hill, and then turned to cross the bridge. Andy watched as five tanks appeared, all Tigers. He doubted that more than four could cross the bridge at the same time. He saw no way that he could get all five.

He found it hard to breathe as he held onto the handle and waited. He would twist the handle when the first tank reached the last span, but everything depended on how closely the tanks followed each other.

And then the tanks all stopped. Andy thought for a moment that the Germans were going to send men to check the bridge for explosives, but no one emerged from the trucks. The tanks sat idling for a few seconds, and then the first one started across—and the others didn't follow. But that only made sense. Andy realized that the Germans were too smart to fill the bridge with tanks. They would put only one in danger at a time. That meant Andy had to make a quick decision. He let the tank roll forward, deciding he would let one across, away from its convoy, and take the second one. He hoped that the men with the bazooka could handle that first one and that the explosives would take another. The team could then shoot up the convoy for a few minutes and get away. The Germans would still be up against the problem of spanning the bridge or being delayed as they sought a new route. They just wouldn't lose as many tanks.

Andy noticed that Gilbert and Xavier were peeking up in spite of what he had told them.

"We've got a problem," he told them. "I'm only going to get one, and the others will be able to open up on this hillside. So as soon as I turn this handle, head up the hill as fast as you can."

He saw some paleness in Gilbert's face, watched him nod. Clearly he wasn't feeling so brave now.

Andy watched the first tank move all the way across the bridge. The second tank waited another ten seconds or so before it started across. The second tank slowly crossed, and again the next one waited. So Andy let that second tank reach the farthest span, and then he set off the explosives.

There was an enormous explosion, with rocks and debris lifting into the air. A dense cloud of dust filled the valley. Andy saw the tank plunge toward the river just before he said, "Run! Run!"

Both men took off ahead of him, and Andy followed close behind. They were concealed by the dust and dirt in the air, and the Germans weren't responding yet. Andy could hear the whomp of mortar fire from the top of the hill and knew that the *Maquisards* were dropping some fire in on the trucks and tanks that were stopped in the river valley.

What Andy hadn't heard was any fire close to the bridge on this side. He wondered what the tank that had gotten across was doing. As he crested the hill, still in the trees, he turned off to the right and ran toward the bridge. But just then he heard a powerful bang and a zipping sound, followed by a clanking noise. He knew instantly that the bazooka team had fired from too far away. The tank hadn't blown. The bazooka shell had ricocheted off it.

Andy kept running hard, trying to see what was happening, but he was still in the trees. When he broke out of the woods he saw the turret on the tank turn, and just then a second bazooka shell fired. But it clanged off the tank and dropped to the ground, failing again to penetrate.

Andy stopped, not quite sure what to do. At least the tank was isolated. If the men got away quickly, it wouldn't be able to follow them through such a thickly wooded area. But the big tank fired at something, and Andy ran left, away from the bridge, trying to see the tank's target. What he saw were two *Maquisards* on the ground, off in the distance, the bazooka still in one of the men's arms. At the same moment Andy spotted McComb, with half a dozen men, running toward the bazooka team. The turret turned a little, then fired again, and all the men went down. Andy wasn't sure how many had been hit; he knew only that they were pinned down and in deep trouble. The tank began to roll forward toward the men. Andy was suddenly running. He knew what he was going to do, but he had no idea whether it would work.

As he ran, Andy pulled a grenade off his belt. The tank was heading away from him, continuing toward the men who were down. Andy hoped that the driver and the machine gunner were watching ahead and wouldn't spot him. He had to get in very close.

Andy heard the tank fire again, and he heard the machine gun pumping fire toward the men on the ground. Andy kept going, reached the tank, pulled the pin, and dropped the grenade onto the tank track near a wheel. He spun and bolted away, ran a few steps, and dove onto the ground. The explosion sounded, and he turned to see the tank twisting slowly sideways, the track broken and fouled up in the wheels. He looked out toward the front of the tank and saw his men jump up and bolt into the woods on the opposite side of the road from him.

Andy was instantly up and running again. He had barely reached the woods when the first bullets cracked around him. A shell from the tank's gun crashed into a tree close by, breaking limbs but missing him. He kept running hard through the underbrush and soon was out of the sight of the tank.

He could still hear mortars and small arms fire, so he made his way to the sound. By the time he reached a pocket of *Maquis,* return fire from the tanks below was starting to rip into the trees above the men's heads. "Fall back. We've done what we can," he shouted.

The men didn't stop firing immediately, so he shouted again, and this time they jumped up and followed him into the trees. They ran hard at first and then, once they felt safe, jogged through the trees, some of them laughing and shouting. "I got my first German," one man close to Andy yelled. "I saw him go down." Another called back, "I put a mortar into one of those trucks. I took out a whole bunch of *Les Boches.*"

Andy was wondering how many of their own men had been caught in the return fire with all those tanks throwing shells into the woods. And he wondered about McComb and his men. It had all happened so fast that he didn't know how many had gone down, or how many had gotten up and away.

He and the men ran to their appointed gathering site and waited. There were almost thirty of them, and in a few seconds, more started showing up. Andy tried to count, tried to see who was missing as more and more arrived, but men were milling about, talking, bragging, and it was impossible to keep track. Booker got there and said, "You did the right thing, Lieutenant. We should have realized that they would send the tanks across one at a time."

"Not necessarily. We've seen the Germans do different things. And it didn't look like a bridge that a *Maquis* group could take out."

"There are quite a few OG teams in here now, though. The Germans are running scared."

In a few minutes McComb came walking in with his men behind him. "Did you lose anyone?" Andy asked.

"No. Two guys were wounded, but they were both able to get up and run with us. And they're doing okay. You saved our lives—every one of us. That's the bravest thing I ever saw a man do."

Andy hadn't thought much about that. He had been scared the whole time, so it hadn't occurred to him that he had been brave. But a surge went through him like few things he'd ever felt in his life. He *had* saved their lives, and he liked the way that made him feel. "I'm sorry I let the tank across. I didn't know what else to do, the way the Germans decided to cross the bridge."

"That was what I would have done. When I saw you let one come over, I said to my men, 'He's doing right. We'll take that one and stop the rest.'"

"But he almost got you."

McComb grinned. "It did get a little hairy there for a minute. But I never once thought of taking a tank out with a hand grenade. And if I'd thought of it, I'm not sure I would have tried. I'll owe you my life forever now." He laughed and slapped Andy on the shoulder. "I'm not sure I like that."

But Andy was feeling that surge again. He had saved some lives. He had done something he could feel good about.

CHAPTER 26

BISHOP GLEDHILL WAS sitting in his office at home. For the third time that week he had called Mr. Schneider, the director of the Topaz Relocation Center. He was waiting now, standing in front of the telephone in his kitchen, holding the earpiece ready while the man's secretary was "hunting him down," as she had put it. Finally, the bishop heard Schneider's deep voice. "Yes?" he said.

"Max, this is Ron Gledhill again."

"Yes, Mayor. How are you?"

"You said you would call me back, Max, and you haven't done it. Have you looked into this case I talked to you about?"

"You mean the Tanaka boy?"

"Yes."

"I called my boss, and he says it's a local matter, in California. We can't interfere with the decision the courts might make down there."

"But of course you can. That doesn't even make sense." Bishop Gledhill took a breath. It wasn't going to do any good to sound angry. Still, he added, rather strongly, "Max, if you can round these people up and stick them in camps, you can just as easily tell that sheriff you want him sent back to you."

"But he broke a law, Ron. He left the camp and went back to his home."

"You know what happened. I talked to you about all of that. With a little luck, he would have made it back and you never would have known he was gone."

"Well, he wasn't lucky, was he?"

"Come on, now. Let's get him back here and get him in the service. That's what he wants to do, and that would be the best thing for everyone, wouldn't it?"

"I'm not the one who can—"

"I don't want to hear that, Max. I really don't." The bishop had been leaning against the kitchen cabinet, but now he brought his weight back to both feet and faced the telephone on the wall. "You must care about these people you have out there, Max. Surely you can do something for a good boy like Tom."

There was a long silence. "It's not as easy as you think, Ron," Mr. Schneider finally said. "But I'll see if there's anything I can do."

"That boy is sitting in a stinking little cell. I think you could make one phone call and get him out. If you'll do that, I'll pay for his bus fare back here."

"I told you, I'll look into it a little more. But I don't think there's anything I can do. He's been charged with federal crimes, and it would take more than a phone call to get all that dropped."

Bishop Gledhill came within a breath of swearing, but he stopped himself. "I'm going to pray for you tonight, Max," he said. "I'm going to pray that your heart will be softened and that you'll do the right thing. And I'm going to pray that someone, somewhere in our government will use the brains God gave him. Someone needs to think about what's best for Tom, best for his parents, best for you, best for everyone. Let's get him in the army."

"I told you, I'll look into it."

Bishop Gledhill thanked Mr. Schneider, although he was almost sure the runaround was not even close to an end, and hung up the phone.

Belle had stepped into the kitchen and was waiting for his conversation to end. "They're here," she said. "They just pulled into the driveway."

"Oh, Lord help me," the bishop said. "One more test of my faith."

Adele had telephoned from California a few days before to say she was coming home for a visit. Her "boyfriend" was driving her up from Los Angeles. Belle had talked to her and asked about the boy, and Adele had seemed evasive. She had admitted that he wasn't a Mormon and that he was "a little older." That was already more than Bishop Gledhill had wanted to hear, but he slowly walked out to the front hall. Belle was on the porch already, hugging Adele, and a fellow who looked over thirty was standing behind her, his hat in his hand. He had slicked-back hair and a thin little mustache, like some Chicago gangster, and he was wearing a navy blue shirt with cream-colored trousers and brown-and-white shoes. Decent, normal people didn't run around dressed like that.

The bishop pushed back the screen door and walked out onto the porch. By then Adele was introducing the man. "This is Rex DeCastro, Mom." She looked at the bishop. "Come on out, Dad. Meet Rex."

"Nice to meet you," Rex was saying by then. "But this can't be your mother. This must be your sister." He laughed in a raucous little flurry, like the sound of half a dozen crows. He shook Belle's hand and then stepped around her to reach out to Bishop Gledhill. "Mr. Gledhill, so nice to meet you. Or should I call you Mayor?"

The bishop shook his hand. "Anything you want is fine. You can call me Ron if you like." But in truth, the bishop didn't expect him to do it.

"Then Ron it is, and I'm Rex. I have a feeling you'll be seeing a lot of me in the future. This pretty little daughter of yours has locked up my heart in chains. She's a wonderful girl. But I guess you know that."

"They don't think so," Adele said. "They think I'm nothing but trouble, and I guess I am. What can I say? I'm the black sheep of the family."

And she did look the part. She was wearing a pair of gray slacks and a tight little brown sweater. She had had her hair bobbed shorter than ever, too, like women the bishop had seen in the movies. He put his arm around her shoulders and whispered in her ear, "You're my little girl and you always will be. So don't start calling yourself names like that."

Adele responded, hugged him tight. He wished that he could just pull her into the house and tell this Hollywood slick to clear out.

"You should've seen everyone stare at us when we drove through town," Adele said. "I made Rex ride up and down Main Street twice, and then up and down Second West—just so people would wonder who was driving the bright yellow Buick. I waved to everyone. Rex did too."

"Well, step inside," Bishop Gledhill said. "It's a little cooler in the living room."

"Boy oh boy, it is hot here," Rex said, and he drew a handkerchief from his front pocket and wiped his face.

"It was over one hundred earlier this afternoon," Belle said. "Probably still is." The bishop could hear how hard she was trying to sound natural, friendly. It was what she always did—tried to make people feel at home.

Everyone walked inside and sat down. Flip was at the farm, and Marie was at work, but Chrissy came in and gave Adele a hug, then shook hands with Rex. "Hey, how many beautiful girls you got around here, Ron?" Rex asked.

"Just one more. You know what they say—'the uglier the bull, the prettier the calf.'"

Rex laughed much too hard. "Now, wait just a minute. I wouldn't say that. You're a distinguished-looking man, if you ask me."

The bishop glanced at Adele, who for a moment did seem a little embarrassed by all this obsequiousness, but she looked away just as quickly, and she smiled at Rex. "I'm worried now," she said. "If that's true, as handsome as you are, Rex, I'm afraid we'll have ugly kids."

The thought of Adele having kids with this guy was almost more than the bishop could bear to think about, and he knew that before the day was over he would have to say just that to her. He wasn't going to let her get any more deeply involved with this fellow—not if he could do anything about it.

*　　*　　*　　*　　*

After dinner that night Adele took Rex on a walk around town. Bishop Gledhill was sure that she was introducing him to anyone she happened to bump into, just as proud as she could be. The girl never had acquired a sense of what people in Delta could tolerate, and she probably never would. At the dinner table, after everyone had eaten, Rex had slid his chair back and lit up a cigarette, without so much as asking whether anyone minded. Since Adele apparently hadn't warned him about that— and didn't say anything then—he puffed away, and Belle had to bring him a little dish for his ashes since there were no ashtrays in the house. The bishop wondered whether he wasn't walking around now blowing smoke at the people Adele stopped to talk to. With that hair slicked back like a wet rat, Bishop Gledhill knew exactly what kind of impression he would make around here—like some huckster trying to sell them a piece of land out in the desert.

Belle was sitting next to the bishop, each in one of the two old metal chairs on the front porch. She had said very little, and he knew how worried she was. "Don't you think she'll see through him before long?" she finally asked. "She must know he's not her type."

"I don't know what her type is, Belle. Sometimes I wonder where that girl came from. If you'd given birth to her at a hospital, I'd guess that they sent the wrong baby home with us."

"She was independent right from the first, Ron. As long as I can remember, she's been saying, 'I can do it myself.'"

"I wish she would say that when she needs some money—instead of, 'Shell out, Dad.'"

"Don't talk so loud. Here they come."

And sure enough, the guy was smoking a cigarette again, blowing the smoke into the air. It was not as though cigarette smoking would shock anyone in Delta. There were plenty of people who rolled their own, smoked out on the farm or in the pool hall in town. But they weren't walking around with the bishop's daughter; *that* would cause some talk.

"Hey, Ron, Belle," Rex said when he spied the two on the porch, "what a beautiful evening to sit out." He and Adele climbed the steps. "That's the trouble in L.A. We don't take time for the simple pleasures. We zip around in our cars, but we almost never take a walk, and we don't sit and just chat. It's too bad."

"How do you get enough gas stamps to run your cars all the time?" Bishop Gledhill asked.

Rex let go of Adele, flipped his cigarette away, and stuck his hands deep into his pockets. The man never seemed to stand up quite straight. "Well, a lot don't. But you know, there are ways. If a guy has the green stuff, he can usually get what he wants in L.A. And there's plenty of that green stuff floating around these days." He pulled a billfold from his pants pocket and gave it a little slap as if to say, *I've got plenty of it myself.*

What Rex was talking about was illegal. Did he know that? And why wasn't he in the service? But the bishop didn't pose either of those questions. He brought up the other obvious one. "What is it you do for a living, Rex?"

"That's what everyone asks me. But it's not that easy to answer. I've got my fingers in a lot of different pies."

"What kind of pies?"

Belle reached over and touched Ron's arm, as if to tell him to be careful of his tone, but he didn't care. He didn't like the sound of this.

"Well, for one thing, I'm involved with a group of investors. We've bought up some nice land south of L.A.—Orange County—we're developing it and selling off the lots. Except that I'm in on the building end, too. I guess you could say I'm a building contractor, but my partner is the one who runs the show. I just provide the dough." He laughed in another flurry, loud enough to be heard all up and down the street.

"Can you get the materials you need to build houses?"

"Hey, Ron, we're talking about Southern California. People are making money hand over fist down there right now. They'll pay what they have to just to get what they want. As a banker, you ought to think about moving some of your money into our area. When the war ends, things are going to pop. We've bought land cheap, and building is going to boom as soon as the government loosens up on materials. I figure, five years after the war ends, I'll never have to work again."

"You don't work now," Adele said. She gave him a slap across the shoulder and laughed.

Rex made a fake move, as if to defend himself, and then danced a little like a boxer, ready to throw a punch. But he was still laughing. "Hey, I work. After my partners bring in all the money, someone has to count it. Ain't that right, Ron? That's all a banker does: count the money all the poor stiffs around town have to pay him every month." But he seemed to realize immediately that "Ron" wasn't laughing. "Naw, just kidding. I work, and so do you. Some people think working in an office don't tire you out the same as work out on the job, but me, I'd rather do something outside and not sit behind a desk all day. After I make my million, I might go out and build some of those houses, just to do something with my hands. I like that best."

Bishop Gledhill decided not to comment. He hoped the conversation would soon end. He looked across the street and saw John and Francine Ellis walking along the sidewalk, probably heading over to the Friday night dance at Van's. He waved to them, but he wondered how anyone could dance on a night as hot as this.

Belle was saying, "California is nice. It's more like the area where I grew up in France."

Rex hoisted himself up on the railing of the porch and sat there perched like a little kid. He asked Belle all about southern France. He wanted to travel, he said, and the war had kept him from doing that. He felt bad that he'd had some back trouble that had kept him out of the war, but he wanted to see the world—and on and on and on. After a time, Bishop Gledhill was watching only Adele, who was leaning against Rex, her hand resting on his leg. He couldn't help but wonder what was going on between the two. He tried to think what he could say to her when he finally had the chance. But that chance came sooner than he expected when Rex said, "Listen, we had a long drive across that desert today. I'm about ready to turn in."

Belle told him to follow her and she would get him some towels and show him where he could take a bath, if he liked, and where he was going to sleep. She and the bishop had talked about what they were going to do with the guy. Rex would sleep in Flip's room, since Flip had agreed to stay out at the farm. Adele was down the hallway, next to where Belle and the bishop slept. Belle had said she wanted a long hallway between the two. The bishop would have felt better with a few hundred miles between them.

"Sit here for a few minutes," Bishop Gledhill told Adele. "We haven't had a chance to talk yet."

"I think I'll just turn in too, Dad. We'll talk tomorrow."

"Just stay for a minute." So Adele took the chair her mother had left, but she immediately began to talk about California, about her job, probably anything to keep the subject away from Rex. The bishop let her talk for a time, but then he finally asked, "How serious are you with this man?"

"Very serious, Dad. We're not really engaged yet, but we're planning to get married."

"So you don't mind marrying out of the Church?"

"Oh, Dad, let's not start in on all that tonight."

"We're not *starting*. I've taught you since you were a little girl what it means to marry in the temple." He crossed his arms, but felt the heat of his body and dropped them back to his sides. This was the second time today he had been tempted to shout at someone.

"But Dad, I feel different about a lot of things now. Around here everyone thinks that Mormons are the only good people. I found out, down in California, there are all sorts of nice people, and they go to lots of different churches."

"Does Rex go to a church?"

"I don't mean they have to *go*, necessarily. Some people are just good. They've learned from their families. They may not be as religious as people around here are, but that doesn't mean they're bad people."

"Does he *have* a religion?"

"He's Catholic. But he's independent in the way he thinks. He believes in God, and he loves nature. He talks a lot about how he feels close to God when he's out in a forest or something like that."

"What forest?"

"I don't know, Dad. I'm not saying that he goes out there to be religious. I'm just saying that he does believe in God."

"Have you talked to him about the Church?"

"Sure I have. Some. He doesn't care if I'm a Mormon. He says I can believe anything I choose to believe."

"So if you marry him, do you plan to be active in the Church?"

"I don't know. It's hard to say. Right now, though, I just want to think a little more for myself. I agree about feeling close to God in nature—more than in church."

"You hate the out-of-doors, Adele. You've *never* spent any time in nature."

"I don't mean it that way. I just mean that I look at a flower and I think, 'That's so perfect, God must have made it.' But in church, those boring talks don't do one thing for me."

This was all so disheartening to the bishop. He had spent a whole lifetime trying to get his kids to feel what he did about the gospel. How could he have failed so completely?

"The thing is, Dad, Rex treats me like a queen. He'd do *anything* for me. I have to make him stop or he'd be buying me presents every day. And he takes me out to the nicest places in L.A. I've seen about twenty movie stars now. I sat three tables over from Deanna Durbin one night in the Brown Derby. But it's not that so much. I want to be happy, Dad, and Rex can give me a happy life."

"Do you think at all about eternity?"

"Look, I know what you're saying. I'm a *huge* disappointment to you. Just figure, all the other kids will do what you want them to, and they'll make you happy in your old age. But I never have liked church; I can't help it."

"Do you ask yourself what the Lord wants you to do with your life? There's more to life than having a good time."

"This is where I came in, Dad. Every time you and I talk, you start in on the same script. If you want me to come home sometimes and be friends with the family, then you'll just have to accept me the way I am. Or if you want, I can just stay away, and then you can disown me or something—and tell everyone you had one kid who went bad even though you tried your best."

"Adele, I love you. That's what this is all about."

"Sorry, Dad, but I don't buy that. If you loved me, you would accept me. Maybe I'd feel different if you hadn't put everyone else in town ahead of your own family."

"Adele, that's not fair. I know I've—"

"Good night, Dad. Tomorrow let's act like we like each other, and then Rex and I will head back to L.A. a little sooner than we planned. That'll be better for both of us." She got up and headed for the door.

"Wait a minute, Adele. Let's just—"

But she kept going. Bishop Gledhill couldn't believe how badly he had handled the situation. One more time he had tried to hold on to her and ended up pushing her further away.

*   *   *   *   *

Flip rode his bicycle into town early the next morning, Saturday, so he could have breakfast and have some time to visit with Adele. But Adele slept through breakfast. Flip ended up eating with his mom and this Rex guy Adele had brought home. He looked like those guys in the movies—the ones who were supposed to be from Hollywood and spent every night in nightclubs throwing around big tips and everything. He had a mustache about as wide as a pencil scratch and teeth all yellow from cigarette smoke. He smelled like smoke too, and that was bad enough until he lit up a cigarette right in their kitchen. Flip had tried smoking a couple of times—usually with "Indian tobacco" that the boys found growing along the riverbanks—but the idea had never occurred to him that anyone would ever pull out a pack and start smoking right in his house.

The guy never stopped talking, either, and he kept saying how rich and important he was. He said he'd invested in a Bud Abbott and Lou Costello movie and "made a killing" on it. He claimed he'd even had dinner with Abbott and Costello a couple of times and said they weren't very funny when they weren't getting paid to be that way. "Bud Abbott's kind of a grouch, if you want to know the truth," he told Flip, "but Lou, I'll tell you, don't ever think he's stupid just because he acts that way in the movies."

Flip let his mother make all the comments. All he could think was that he didn't want this guy in his family. Adele was moving too far away from everyone else as it was, and they didn't need some guy like this coming up to Delta to act like a big shot.

Flip had planned to stay in town all day, but he changed his mind.

He told his mother he would stop by later, but he had a few things he needed to take care of at the farm. He started back, and then, as he passed Whisper's house, he saw that she was out in back working in the garden. He dropped his bike in her front yard and walked around the house. "Hi, Whisper," he said.

She was bent over, but she stood quickly. "Oh, Flip, I didn't hear you walking up. You surprised me."

"Sorry." She was flushed from the work and the bending, and her green eyes seemed a little brighter, maybe even happier, than they had been lately. "I just saw you back here and thought I'd say hello. Are you doing okay?"

"I guess so. But everyone who comes in the doctor's office looks at me differently now. No one will say anything, but I know what they're all thinking: She was a nice girl all her life, and then she took off with a Jap one night, drove to California, and got herself thrown in jail."

"I know. It's about the same for me. Cal told me yesterday I was pretty much the same as a traitor, since I helped a Jap run off. He can't figure out why I'm not in jail still—and you too. He said no one at the high school is going to have anything to do with me this fall."

"It won't be like that. People know you. They know you're not a traitor."

"I'm joining the army. I'll lie about my age if I have to. If I could pass the minimum size requirements, I'd do it today. But I'm growing now, pretty fast. It won't be too long until I'll be tall enough. I've just got to eat all I can and put on some weight."

"Oh, Flip, you don't have to prove anything. The day's coming when people are going to change their minds—and they'll tell you that you did the right thing."

"I don't think so. Not for a long, long time, anyway. For now, I just want to get out of here."

"I know. I feel pretty much the same way." She wiped her sleeve across her forehead. She was wearing one of her dad's worn-out white shirts with the tails hanging out.

Whisper had tied up her hair in a knot in back, but it had mostly come loose. She probably should have looked terrible, all sweaty and dirty, but to Flip, she looked great. He could look at her now, straight in the eye, and not get embarrassed. She was his friend, probably the best he'd ever had. "So are you going to leave?" Flip asked her.

"I don't know. My parents think I'm some sort of a fallen woman because I spent a night in jail—but I guess that will pass if I never again do anything interesting. I need to start producing grandchildren for them pretty soon, I suppose. They think I'm an old maid." She pulled a glove off and tucked a strand of hair behind her ear, then wiped sweat from her forehead again.

"You sound like Adele. That's the kind of stuff she always says."

"The difference is, she follows her whims and I don't."

"She's got herself a *whim* at our house right now. Have you met this Rex guy? If he turned out to be a con man, I wouldn't be surprised. I know darn well he's a liar, and I only talked to him for about ten minutes."

"Really? Adele called me yesterday. She was telling me how swell he is."

"The only thing swell is his head, which is swollen up big as a watermelon."

Whisper smiled. Flip watched her tongue appear, just whisk across her pretty lips. "Flip, you don't seem to like any of the boys Adele and I choose for ourselves."

"I like Andy."

Whisper pulled the other glove off and walked closer to Flip from the row she had been weeding. "Come here for a minute," she said. She took him by the arm and walked him to the lawn, and then she had him sit down with her in the wicker chairs that were out behind the house, under the big horse chestnut tree. "I need to tell you something, and I know you aren't going to like it. But I think you've known for a while that it's been coming."

"You must have told Lamar that you'll marry him. And you're right. I don't like it."

"Why, Flip?"

"You know why."

"Flip, you did your best to keep me for your brother. It's your brother who didn't hold up his end of the deal."

"I know that. But I also know you don't love Lamar. That ought to be kind of important, if you ask me."

"Flip, there are different kinds of love. There's the twitterpated kind—you know, like little Thumper in *Bambi*. That kind of love happens when you're still a kid, but there's the realistic kind that comes along when it's time to settle down, get married, and start a family. I'm twenty-two and I'm still living at home. It's just time for me to go on with my life before I miss the chance to have a family of my own."

"You've told me all that before. But it's not right. No one knows it better than you do."

"It's not how I thought things would be, but that doesn't mean it isn't right."

Flip let her words sink in. He did understand that much. "Everything's different from what they tell you when you're a little kid. America's supposed to be so great—better than other countries and everything—but I don't see what we've got to brag about. There's no justice and all that stuff, not if people have it in for you. And then they tell you at Mutual and in the movies and everything all about falling in love and getting married and always being happy. But that's a bunch of hooey. Look at you and Adele, marrying people who aren't right for you, and even a guy my age can see it. I heard Rodney Parrish arguing with his wife, standing right on Main Street, and she was telling him what a numbskull he was. Then I saw them at church, acting like nothing was ever wrong. That's how it's going to be for you and Adele. You won't be happy, and you'll just let on like you are. I guess that's how it is most of the time."

"Flip, I promise you that I'll always—"

Flip stood up. "*Promise?* Whisper, do you think I believe in promises? You don't. My brother doesn't. 'Promise' is the biggest lie of all. It only lasts until somebody gets some other idea. I made a promise and I've been trying to keep it. So I guess I'm stupid."

"Flip, it's just hard for you to understand. I have to—"

"Why? Because I'm too young? Well, I may be young, but I'll tell you this much. If I had been the one who made a promise to you, I'd keep it forever. I've got more promise inside me than you or Andy will ever understand."

Whisper's eyes filled with tears. "That's probably true, Flip. It's too bad you weren't the big brother."

"But *I'm* too young. Right? It's always the same thing. I don't know why it has to be such a terrible thing to be younger than someone else. It's like someone made up a rule, and just because I'm younger, I can't have any feelings of my own."

But now Flip couldn't look at her. He was breathing hard, shaking a little, and, if he wasn't careful, about to show more emotion than he could live with. He stood for a long time, ready to leave, but still wanting to know what she would say. He finally glanced at her again, and he saw that that was what she had been waiting for.

"Flip, I know what you're saying." She nodded firmly, as though she wanted him to be sure she *did* understand. "It breaks my heart to know the feelings you have. I just don't know what I can do about it."

"I don't even know what you're talking about. I've got to go." He walked back around the house, got on his bike, and took his time riding back to the farm. And when he got there, he didn't do any work at all.

He sat under the cottonwood tree by the stream and tossed pebbles into the water. He was thinking he might set out one of these days, maybe hitchhike, and go back to California or somewhere like that.

*   *   *   *   *

Adele brought Rex over to meet Whisper later that day. Whisper actually thought the guy might be pretty good-looking if he didn't grease his hair down so much, but she didn't like him. From the moment Adele and Rex sat down on her living-room couch, Whisper felt his eyes running over her, never stopping, and when he finally caught her eye, he gave her a quick little smile that seemed to say, "I'm interested; are you?" She had seen that look many times, but not from her best friend's boyfriend. Whisper uncrossed her legs and gave her skirt a tug to get it down past her knees.

"I don't think Rex and I are going to stay around too long," Adele was saying. "I forget how boring this town is until I get back here, and then Dad starts in on his usual questions, wanting to know whether I'm going to church or not."

"It's seemed a little boring to me around here lately too," Whisper said.

"That's because you went and put a little excitement in your life. I can't believe what you and old Flip—and that Jap boy—did."

"Hey, that did sound like an adventure," Rex said. "What's life without taking a chance once in a while?" He was nodding, eyeing her still, smiling too much.

"I like Tom," Adele said. "I didn't think I'd ever like a Jap, but he's as American as any of us—and funny. I don't see why they brought all the Japs out here in the first place. My thinking's changed a lot about things like that. People in California don't have so many rules about everything, the way people here do. And that's how I'm getting to be."

Whisper had the feeling that Adele would believe anything right now as long as it was something different from what she'd been raised with. She had always desperately wanted to be *herself*, but the truth was, she'd never developed any of her own ideas. These days, she was obviously taking in anything Rex told her.

"So is this Jap fellow your boyfriend?" Rex asked. "Because if he is, I don't have a single problem with that. I think people ought to be a lot more broad-minded about those things. I say, live and let live."

"He's not my boyfriend. He's just turning eighteen."

"Hey, rob the cradle. That doesn't bother me either. Do what makes you happy."

Whisper hardly knew how to react to that. She glanced at Adele, who was laughing. "Isn't Rex something?" she asked. "With him, every day is an adventure."

"And the nice thing is," Rex said, "I can afford it."

"Where's your mother?" Adele asked Whisper. "Is that her I can hear in the kitchen?"

"Yes."

"I'm going to step in and just say hello to her. Do you want to meet her, Rex?"

"That's all right. You say hello. I'll do a little *Whispering* in here."

"Hey, you be good. I know she's prettier than I am, but she's taken. So don't get any ideas." Adele got up and walked into the kitchen.

"Is that true?" Rex asked Whisper. "Are you *taken?*"

"I think Adele was talking about her brother, Andy. I was going with him when he left for the army."

"Yeah, I know that, but it sounds like you aren't quite so sure." This was said with a raised eyebrow.

"I need to break the news to Adele. I'll do it when she comes back. I'm going to marry a fellow from Fillmore. His name is Lamar Jones."

"And what about poor old Andy? How's he going to take the news?"

"Actually, it was his idea. He told me quite a while ago that I ought to start looking around. Adele already knows that."

"Oh, brother. I missed my chance. I should have arrived when you were between fellows."

Whisper stared at him. What in the world did he think he was doing?

"Hey, I think you need to forget this Lamar fellow and come to California. You're a beautiful woman. You could be in the movies, and I know people who could put you there. Do you have any interest in trying something like that? We could team up, the two of us, and I'll tell you, your life would never be boring again."

Whisper still couldn't get a word out.

"Hey, I'm just kidding. You know that. Adele's my girl now." He leaned back and laughed, sounding like a wounded bird of some sort. "But oh, my dear, if anyone could make a man waver in his commitment, you would be the one." He laughed again. "And I'm serious about the movies. I know I could get you a part in one of our shows. Come down to California and let me see what I can do."

"No, thanks. That's not something I would be interested in."

"To each his own. But I can sure think of some things I'd like to whisper to you." Again the laugh, and again, "Just kidding. Just kidding."

But later, after Whisper had told Adele about Lamar and their plans, and after Adele had gone back home, Adele called Whisper to say good-bye. She and Rex had decided to start back that night, to avoid the desert heat in the day. Whisper said to her on the phone, "Adele, can I give you a little advice?"

"No, thanks. I've gotten plenty of that already. And I know what you're going to say."

"Adele, Rex said things to me he shouldn't have—while you were in the next room talking to my mom."

"Whisper, he told me all about that. He was just teasing you. That's what he does all the time. But he treats me wonderful. He wants to marry me, and so far, I keep putting him off. But one of these days we'll just run off and get hitched without any big ceremony. Life will be crazy with him, but it's going to be fun."

"Adele, be careful. I don't want to say anything bad about someone you want to marry, but I just have a feeling you could be making a mistake."

"Whisper, I'm sorry, but don't talk to me about mistakes. Lamar is about as exciting as a pile of cow manure, and that's exactly what he's going to have on his shoes every night when he walks in your house. Maybe Rex is unpredictable, but I can see your future, and there's not so much as a hill in the path: just everything as flat as the desert, one day exactly like the next."

Whisper felt the controlled animosity, and she knew that Adele was striking back. She had been doing that for as long as Whisper could remember. "I'm sorry I said anything," she told Adele.

"I'm not. I'm telling you right now, you ought to get out of Delta on the next bus. If things aren't working out with Andy, come to California and I can fix you up with twenty different guys, any one of them a whole lot better than Lamar."

"Good-bye, Adele. Good luck."

"Fine. Marry the guy. But don't tell me later that I didn't warn you."

Whisper was thinking that she could have said the same thing herself.

CHAPTER 27

IT WAS LATE AUGUST, and Booker's operational group had returned to the Rhône Valley, south of Valence. *Maquisards* in the area reported that German forces were encamped near a village west of the Rhône, called Choméric, so the group made a forced march to reach the region. Booker—or, more accurately, McComb—was concerned that the Germans might move farther north before the OG could catch up with them, but Booker's unit reached the area and then began to use their two 37-mm artillery guns to let the Germans know that they were still in trouble. The only problem was, the OG was almost out of ammo for the big guns, and most of the *Maquis* units in the area had been bloodied up and retreated back to their villages. Booker and McComb weren't sure how many Germans were in Choméric, but probably too many to attack. American airplanes were strafing the area on a regular basis, and clearly the Germans were worn down by their race northward and all the harassment they had taken along the way. McComb hoped they could be held down long enough to get more Allied troops into the area to cut them off before they escaped and continued toward Germany.

On the second night the troops were camped in the area, *Maquis* soldiers brought in a captured German *Hauptman*—a captain. His vehicle had overturned while he was making a run up the road along the river under fire. He was limping badly when they brought him in, and his head was bandaged, his face bloody. He admitted that the men of his company were in Choméric, and he had been trying to reach other scattered units in the area. The captain spoke decent French, but he had been unwilling to say very much to his captors, so Booker asked Andy to talk to him and see what else he could learn.

Andy knew enough to get acquainted first, to see whether he couldn't break down some of the man's fear and resistance. So he took the man away from the others and had him sit on some grass where, even with his hands tied behind him, he could lean against a tree. "I hope you know," Andy said in French, "this is a good day for you. You're going to be alive when this war is over, and many of us won't be." He offered the man a cigarette.

"I don't know that for certain," the captain said, but he grasped the cigarette eagerly in his lips and waited for Andy to strike a match and light it for him.

"I promise you, we'll treat you well. The war will be ending before long, I believe, and I don't know about you, but I'm sick of all the killing."

The captain nodded, and Andy saw the weariness in his eyes. "I have seen so much death," he said.

"Tell me your name."

"Lipp."

"*Hauptman* Lipp, how long have you been in the war?"

"Always, it seems. Since 1940," he said, speaking awkwardly, with the cigarette held in his lips. He drew in some more of the smoke, his eyes going shut as he held it inside and then finally blew it out.

"What part of Germany are you from?"

The captain didn't answer for a time, as though he were not sure what he should say, but finally he said, "I'm not from Germany. I'm from Austria." He puffed on his cigarette, holding it in his lips as he spoke.

Andy finally took it from him and knocked the ashes off, then put it back in his mouth.

"So this wasn't really your war."

"That's not how the Germans see it. They gave me no choice."

"Yes. I understand. I suppose none of us would go to war if we had our first choice."

Lipp stared back, as though trying to assess what sort of man he was dealing with. "I started out as a private," he said, "and worked my way up to sergeant. I did whatever they asked of me. I was wounded near Stalingrad and spent three months in a hospital. After that, they made me an officer and sent me here to France. It was supposed to be easy duty."

Andy smiled. "It was, for a time."

"It's never been easy for me. I've hated this war from the beginning."

"*Hauptman,* I . . . but tell me your first name. I don't like all this formality. My name is André—it's French—but in America I'm called Andy."

"My Christian name is Karl, but I've been in the army so long, I hardly know my name anymore."

"Yes, I know the feeling. For a time, back home, I thought I might enjoy this war," Andy said. "I wanted to defeat Hitler, and I thought it would be a pleasure. But I've lost my taste for war, the same as you. Far too many have died already, as you say. The best thing you could do, in my opinion, is encourage your troops to surrender."

Karl took another long look at Andy, as though he were wary about trusting him, but Andy had the feeling that he was taking the option seriously.

"How many men in your company are still alive now?"

"I can't tell you that," said Karl. But after a moment, he added sadly, "The truth is, I don't know for certain. Not very many."

"Fifty? Or . . ."

"More like twenty."

"So many dead."

"Yes. So many. Some of them were no more than boys." He dropped his head, and an ash fell off his cigarette onto his dirty gray uniform. He remained that way, head down, for a long time, and when he looked up, he asked, "Is it possible I could go to them and convince them to surrender? I would like to save their lives."

"We can't just let you go to them. And I'm not sure we can put our men's lives in jeopardy. How many more are there in Choméric?"

"I don't know how many. There are scattered units, remnants like ours, north of town. All of them are running out of food and ammunition. Maybe they would all surrender."

"We have artillery, Karl; we have the high ground; and we have the advantage in numbers. We can destroy your troops. I hope you know that."

"Yes. I understand. But our officers need to know that. Some are stubborn and say they'll fight to the death. But it's mostly talk. I've seen it in their eyes—they no longer believe we can win the war. And I think they want to save their soldiers."

"Where do your troops hope to cross back into Germany?"

"No one knows. We're just running. Some speak of Strasbourg, but others say the Allies will cut us off before we can get there. We've lost contact with our commanders. There's no organization at this point."

All this was what Andy had set out to learn, but he was surprised that the captain was giving up the information so easily now. Maybe he was lying, just buying time so the troops around Choméric could slip away. But Andy didn't believe that. He saw it in Karl's face; the man was defeated.

"Let me talk to my commander," Andy said. "I need to see what he wants to do. If I went with you—with a white flag—would you speak with the other officers and tell them it's time to surrender?"

"Yes. I would make this argument. But I told you before, I can't say how they will react. There are those who would want to grab you and use you as a hostage."

"I understand. Just relax here. I'll talk to my commander."

Andy walked back to Booker, who was sitting on a log drinking coffee from his mess kit cup. He and some other OG soldiers had a little fire going. Andy sat down next to Captain Booker, rocking the log as he did. "What did he say?" Booker asked. "Was he willing to talk?"

"Yes. He told me plenty. He thinks their troops might be willing to surrender. I want to go with him into the village in the morning. There must be at least a hundred Germans down there, and they sound ready to give themselves up."

Andy looked up to see McComb heading their way. Booker looked at the other troops nearby and said, "Men, could you step away? We need to talk some things over here." The soldiers didn't look pleased, but they got up and walked a few paces away, all carrying their coffee with them.

"What did that officer have to say?" McComb asked as he stepped in front of Booker and Andy, his back to the fire.

Andy repeated what he had told Booker.

"I don't trust a word of that," McComb said. "Did he tell you where they're headed?"

"They don't know. They're just clearing out, and they've lost contact with their commanders."

"And you believed that? The Germans have fought hard every step of the way. This guy is lying, trying to get us to back off a few hours so they can slip out of the noose we've got them in."

"We don't have a noose, Captain," Booker said. "We're sitting up here with two guns and only a couple of dozen shells. And we're almost as low on ammo for our rifles. They could have a hundred troops down there, maybe a lot more, and we're under a hundred now."

"They don't know that," Andy said. "I've got this captain believing we have them outnumbered. I let him believe that we could drop shells on them as long as we wanted. If I let him talk to his officers, that's what he's going to tell them."

McComb was like a giant, his big silhouette looming over Andy. He put his hands on his hips, seeming to create wings, and he said, "You don't know what he'll tell those officers. You don't speak German. My guess is, you try to walk into the middle of them, white flag or not, the first thing they'll do is nab you and see if they can't use you to get us to back off."

McComb's voice was as big as his shadow. He had a way of dominating any conversation, his confidence, his presence seeming to devalue any other opinion. Andy knew the power he had over Booker, and he suddenly felt angry. He stood up. "Captain, we have a better chance of taking them prisoner than we do of defeating them. We've got them bluffed right now, but all they have to do is start moving out and they'll find out that we can't stop them."

"We can call in an air attack," McComb said, his voice growing in authority. "Our planes can strafe them the way they've been doing. We can hit them, then move back, the way we've been doing. If we can keep them where they are, that should buy us time to get more ammo."

Andy lowered his voice in response, trying to sound reasonable, not angry. "Captain, I don't think the Air Corps is going to bother with these remnants left down here. They've got larger forces moving all through southern France. What have we got to lose? Let's play out our bluff and see if we can't pick up a hundred prisoners without losing any of our own people. I doubt any OG has done better than that. It's the sort of thing we could be decorated for."

Andy could see that this last argument had been the best one to impress McComb. But Captain Booker said, "I don't know, Lieutenant. I don't want to get *you* killed."

"If we take them on, a whole lot of us might die. If I take their captain with me, and he argues for surrender, they may turn us down, but I don't think they're going to kill me. They're running too scared. They think we're sitting up here with superior troop strength and our guns ready to open up."

McComb turned around and faced the fire. "Andy, you haven't learned one thing about the Germans," he said. "Look what they did in that little town by that bridge we blew. They killed those people—women and children—without a second thought. They're fanatics. They don't think the way we do."

"They're not all alike," he said to McComb's back. "You ought to talk to Karl over there. He—"

McComb spun back around. "Karl? Is that what you called him? Let *me* talk to him. I'll kick his ribs in and then see whether he tells us what we want to know."

"I called him Karl to get him to relax. It's exactly what we learned in training."

"Yeah, well, maybe that's a good technique with human beings, but that man's a German. The only thing he understands is a gun pointed at his ear." McComb looked at Booker. "I'm going to do my own interrogation. I'll take one of our French guys who knows German and we'll talk a little reality this time."

"No." Now Booker stood up. "I think the lieutenant's right. We might as well give these troops a chance to surrender. It's worth a try."

McComb stood his ground for a moment, his arms folded over his chest, but then he let them drop to his sides. Andy knew McComb had made a decision not to fight the man who was actually his commander. "All right," he said. "Then I'm going down there with Gledhill. The Germans won't want to give themselves up to a lieutenant."

Booker thought about that before he said, "Captain, I hate to say it, but I don't think you've got the temperament to pull off something like this. You'd say something to the Germans that would get both of you killed."

"No, I won't. I'll just let Gledhill do the negotiating."

"If he makes some headway, I'll send you down to accept their surrender," Booker said. "But let's go in without a lot of fanfare."

"I'll just be there in case something goes wrong—and so the Germans will take us seriously. I can do that."

Booker stuck his thumbs under his belt, stood for a time, and finally said, "All right. I know where we can get hold of a car—from the *Maquis*. But I don't want a big show of authority—just a couple of officers with white flags, as though we don't have a fear in the world. We'll let 'em think we've got hundreds of troops up here, all over this hill."

"Maybe we better head in there right now," McComb said, "before they slip away in the night."

"No. We'll do it in the morning. We'll throw a few more shells in there now, just to convince them that we can fire at them any time we want to. But I don't want you two down there in the dark when we can't see what's happening to you."

Booker had rarely overruled McComb, but Andy was glad to see it now. He watched McComb, who clearly was on the edge of blowing up, but he turned back toward the fire and didn't say another word.

Andy walked back to Karl and told him to rest, that they would enter Choméric in the morning and see whether there was a way to avoid destroying all his men. Karl thanked him.

"We're going to shell them again, just so they won't try to make a run in the night."

Karl looked up, his eyes distraught. "They haven't slept for such a long time. They've been attacked again and again."

"I know. Let's save their lives tomorrow."

"But I told you, I don't know how some of the officers will react. If they turn you down, I can't promise you that they will let you walk away.

You're putting your own life in danger if you go in there. And they might kill me, if I argue too hard for surrender."

"But you're willing to do it, aren't you?"

"Yes."

"Good. I am too."

Andy went back and had something to eat, then waited for the shelling. After a few more minutes there were four loud *whomps,* and then the sound of the explosions in the valley. Andy thought he heard rubble falling and wondered what sort of buildings might have been hit, how many more soldiers might have been killed. He crawled into a shelter-half he had set up to keep the dew off him, and he stretched out. He had never been more tired in his life, but he couldn't go to sleep. He wondered if maybe his luck would finally run out in the morning. Still, he wasn't doubtful about what he was going to do. He remembered how he had felt after he had taken lives, and how he had felt when he had saved some. He wanted to keep a hundred Germans from dying, along with some of his own men.

* * * * *

Andy was sitting in the front seat of an ancient Renault, holding a white flag out the window. A young sergeant named Wilson was driving. *Hauptman* Lipp was sitting in the back, holding a white flag out his window on the opposite side, and McComb was behind Andy, holding an American flag.

Sentries on the edge of the village stopped the car and kept their rifles trained on everyone inside. Andy said, "Does anyone speak English or French?"

"French," one of the men said.

"We come in peace. As you see, we have one of your officers with us. We would like to speak to your commander."

"Get out of the car."

"We can do that. But bring your commander to us, or take us to him. We don't want to kill any more of you."

"Don't talk to these guys," McComb said from the back. "Make them bring an officer out here."

"I know that," Andy said. "We're just getting out of the car. They're going to get someone."

So everyone got out of the car. The Americans, along with *Hauptman* Lipp, were searched and then told to move in front of the car. A ring of six soldiers, all with machine pistols, stood around them. Ten minutes went by, fifteen, and then Andy saw the sentry returning, and with him was a German major. Andy could hardly believe his eyes. There had to be more than a hundred men here if a major was leading them.

The major—an erect, gaunt man—walked to the circle, told the sentries to move back, and then approached McComb, not Andy. He said, in English, "Why are you coming here?"

"To take your surrender," McComb said. "We're giving you one last chance to save the lives of your men."

But the major looked confused. "Do you speak French?" Andy asked.

The major turned to him. "Yes. Much better."

"Major, we've brought Captain Lipp with us. He has something to say to you."

Lipp nodded. "*Herr Major,*" he said, and then he talked to the man for quite some time in German. Andy could only trust that he was making his case. He thought it would be better for the major to hear the argument stated from a fellow officer.

But McComb was whispering to Andy, "What do you think you're doing? We can't let those two talk. We need to know what's being said."

Andy ignored him and let them continue for a time. Then he said, in French, "There's no reason for any more of your men to die. We have guns, as you know, and we have you badly outnumbered. There is no hope that you can make it back to Germany. You don't have the food or ammunition, and you're cut off from supply lines. Let's stop this now before all your men are dead."

The major said nothing for a time. He asked another question of Captain Lipp, and then he said, "I have no authority to surrender. I must speak with our *Oberst.*"

Andy felt a chill run through him. An *Oberst* was a colonel. How many troops was he dealing with? He could see men along the main street of the village, probably more than a hundred just in sight, and now the major was talking about a colonel. Booker had ninety or so men up there on the mountain, and the Germans, unless their units had been decimated, might have hundreds, even a thousand.

"Speak with your colonel, if you have to, but your time is running out. We can't wait long."

"I'll bring him here if you can wait a few minutes." The man sounded surprisingly humble—and tired. Andy heard none of the bluster in his voice that he had come to expect from German officers.

"Go ahead. But we won't stay long." He turned to McComb and whispered, "He's going to get a colonel."

"Colonel? What's going on here?"

"I don't know. This must be the remnant of a whole battalion."

"We're in over our heads. Bluff this colonel a little and then let's get out of here."

Andy nodded and they waited. In a few minutes they saw the major tromping down the cobblestone street with *two* colonels, along with a black-uniformed SS major. It was soon obvious that the SS major was going to do the talking. Maybe he had heard that Andy spoke French, and maybe the colonels didn't. In any case, the other officers stayed back a little and the SS major, a powerful-looking man, said, "My name is Major Belz. What is it you are proposing?"

"I've come to represent our commander, Colonel Moore." It was the first name that had come to Andy's mind. "We're giving you a chance to save the lives of your troops. If we're not back in another half an hour, he will begin artillery fire. We have brought in reinforcements overnight, and our airplanes are standing ready to attack. You know that you don't have the weapons or the men to stop us."

"I don't know this. I know only what you claim."

"Colonel Moore isn't fool enough to send me here if I can't back up what I say."

"And what if we simply hold you and this captain here? What would your colonel do then?"

"We volunteered to come. He starts the shelling at the appointed time, whether we return or not. Captain Lipp asked me to give you a chance to surrender before we bring death down upon you, and I told my colonel I would like to end this situation without taking any more lives. You must know, the war is almost over. German troops are falling back from every part of France, racing to stay ahead of more than a million Allied troops that have landed in Normandy and on the south coast. The Allies have taken Paris back. There is no chance that Germany can win the war." Andy was actually not sure that Paris had been taken yet, but he knew it would be true within a few days.

Belz looked resolute, but Andy also saw the weariness in his drooping, red eyes. He saw how tattered his uniform was. The man wore an iron cross at his neck, and no doubt he had been committed to Hitler at one time, but Andy wondered what he was feeling now. Belz turned around and spoke to one of the colonels in German, with deference in his voice. The major Andy had first spoken to stood at attention. So did Captain Lipp, even though he was still standing next to McComb, not with the Germans.

"Where are the Russians now? Do you know?" the SS major asked Andy. It was hardly the question to ask if he were going to remain firm. Andy knew what he was thinking. It was what all German soldiers believed: If they were to surrender, better to the Americans or British than to the brutal Russians.

Andy had no idea where the Russians were now, but he said, "The Russians have taken Austria and they are nearing Berlin."

The major smiled. "You're not a very good liar. If you want to negotiate with me, look me in the eye. The Russians have not come that far."

Andy stared back at him. "I don't know exactly where they are. I haven't heard for a few weeks. But I know that little is left of your German cities. Berlin is being bombed almost daily."

"The Führer is developing new weapons—weapons that can turn the war around. If we can hold out a little while longer, everything will change and you won't speak to me with such arrogance."

"Now who is looking away?" Andy waited for the major to look him straight on, and then he said, "Here is the great question for you. Do you want Berlin to fall to the Russians, or would you rather the Americans and British get there first? The war is over. You need to start thinking about Germany after the war. Don't prolong the dying of your young men."

Again Major Belz turned around and talked to the colonels, this time for much longer. When he turned back to Andy, he said, "We have many troops north of here. The colonel must confer with all our regimental commanders. He won't surrender if his officers feel they must fight on."

This was crazy. He was talking about more than one regiment. The OG was like a fly on a horse's back. The Germans could swipe such a force aside without a second thought.

But Andy held his position. "We may have to talk to our commanding officer," he said. He stepped a few paces away and pulled McComb off to the side where they couldn't be overheard. "They're talking about surrendering," Andy said in a low voice, "but he wants to talk to his 'regimental commanders'—he said it in the plural. We must be dealing with a very large force."

"They're trying to pull something," McComb whispered back. "I don't think they've got that many men. They're just trying to scare us."

"Why? Why should they bother? If they have that many men, they could just march out of here. I think they believe me. They think we have them outnumbered, and they think we can call in our airplanes. These guys want to give up. They're hungry and running out of ammo, and they know they don't have a chance of making it far enough north to cross back into Germany. They just want to get the rest of their officers on board before they agree to anything."

"That's a bluff. Let's tell them we'll go talk to our leaders and just get out of here."

"No. I'm not going to do that, Captain. I'll tell them you have to go back to confer, but I'm staying here. They want to surrender and I want to make it happen."

"How much time do they want?"

"I don't know. They said there are troops to the north. They have to go talk to the officers. Let's do this. You go back now and take Lipp with you. I'll tell them that you have to stop the guns and the airplanes from opening up. We'll say that we can give them a little longer to confer, but we've got to have an answer fast."

"How are we going to take that many prisoners?"

"We'll get them to lay down their arms, and then we'll have to get some troops in here from somewhere. Booker can work on that."

"Andy, I can't leave you here. I don't like any part of this. We can't bluff this clear to the end."

Andy knew that was a danger. He was trying hard to think what he had to do. "Look," he finally said, "I want to do this. I'll stay here by myself, so I'm not putting anyone else in danger. But I've got to give this a try." Andy didn't know how to tell McComb what this meant to him. But it seemed his chance to save his life, not to lose it.

"Okay, okay. Tell them two hours, at most, and we'll send back Wilson to talk to Booker. I'll stay with you."

"You don't have to do that."

"I know. But let's take this all the way—and see if we can make it work."

Andy nodded and took a long look into McComb's eyes. He could see that McComb knew what Andy did—that they might die here together. Andy walked back and told the colonel, through the major, that he could have two hours. He would send a man back to stop the shelling.

"The colonel will surrender only to another colonel," the major said.

"That can be arranged," Andy told him, though he had no idea how.

"We need four hours, at least."

Andy thought for a moment. "I'll give you three," he said.

He stepped back and took a long breath. He felt as though he were coming back to life. He had to make this work.

CHAPTER 28

TWO HOURS PASSED before Andy admitted to Captain McComb that he had actually allowed the Germans three hours, not two. McComb was furious about that. "Andy," he said, "I'll lay you ten-to-one odds they're escaping right now, heading out through the woods, a few at a time. They'll come back and say, 'No, thanks, we're not surrendering, and what are you going to do about it?' Then they can shoot us without a second thought."

Andy had thought about all that, and he knew McComb might be right. At least that was what his mind told him. But he had been praying for the whole two hours, and a calm had come over him that had no basis in anything rational. He just felt that God was with him, supporting him in what he was trying to do.

Andy and McComb had sat in front of a little café to wait. The owner had brought them bread and cheese. The man seemed to know what was going on, and he nodded so often and said "Merci" so politely that he clearly approved of the idea of the Germans surrendering. Sergeant Wilson had returned with the old car, bringing word that Booker was willing to wait but was nervous. He was going to move some men closer, where they could watch from the woods if the Germans tried to grab Andy and McComb. But Wilson seemed calm enough. He was now sleeping in the shade of a tree in the outdoor area of the café.

"This SS officer, do you really think he's going to tell you the truth?" McComb asked Andy. "Those guys are cocky. And they know they're in trouble anyway once the war is over. Right now he's laughing up his sleeve. He's saying, 'I got that fool to wait three hours. I wonder how long they'll sit there before they realize we pulled one on them.'"

"Maybe. But what have we lost? We couldn't have stopped them anyway."

"I'll tell you what we can lose. Our lives. That major might have told some sniper, 'You wait until they try to leave. Then shoot 'em and catch up with the rest of us.'"

"Yeah. That's possible. If they don't come back, we better go through the café and out the back, then—"

"He knows we'd try that. The guy isn't stupid. He's probably got—"

"Look." Andy had spotted Major Belz walking down the street toward them. He was coming down a little hill, walking slowly, as though he weren't eager to say what he had to say.

"All right. Be careful," McComb said. "He's going to try to stall us again, that's for sure. The main thing is for us to get out of here. Tell him we've got a signal we can give that will start the shelling."

But Andy thought he saw sorrow, not defiance, in Belz's face. Andy and McComb stood up from their table. The major came to a halt and then clicked his heels as he came to attention. "The colonel has authorized me to surrender our troops. He won't appear himself until you have someone of his rank or higher he can speak to."

"That's fine. We can do that. But we have to see the weapons. Bring them into the street—here in front of the café—and stack them up. We want everything: small arms, pistols, knives, anything the men have. If we search people and they've held on to anything, it won't go well for them."

"*Oui. Certainement.*" His voice was full of resignation.

"Does your surrender include all the troops in the area, including those north of the village?"

"Yes. Everyone."

McComb was standing shoulder to shoulder with Andy. He took hold of Andy's arm now and asked, "What's going on? What's he saying?"

"They want to surrender to a colonel, but they'll start stacking their weapons here. I told them they have to give us everything they have."

"How many are there?"

Andy turned back to the major. "How many troops, total, are surrendering?"

"I don't know exactly," the major said. "It's close to four thousand."

Andy tried to think whether he had heard right. *Quatre mille*, the German had said. Andy was sure of it. He nodded, trying not to show any reaction. "I want all the soldiers to gather into the village. They should stack their weapons here in the street where our trucks can drive to them."

The major nodded, but then he said, "I would fight you to the death, you must know. But we're out of ammunition and our men are hungry. They have been through enough already. The officers are doing this for them."

"It's as it should be. You're making the right choice. Assemble the soldiers here and set down your weapons. One of us will go back to bring in our troops to take the surrender."

"How many?" McComb was asking again.

Andy tried to speak matter-of-factly, in case the major understood English. "He's not exactly sure. He thinks it's about four thousand."

He didn't look at McComb, but he felt the man stiffen. "We need to get some troops down here," McComb said. "This could be a little complicated."

"The Germans are coming into the village. They'll stack their arms in the street."

"All right. That sounds good."

By then Major Belz had stepped away and was signaling with his arm. Men started to appear out of the buildings and from the side streets. They looked defeated. They didn't march; they walked in little bunches. The major showed them where to lay down their arms, and they followed his order. Andy watched them pull knives from their pockets, even their boots, pistols from holsters. One young officer, also wearing an SS uniform, looked angry, but he put down his machine pistol and then looked at the major defiantly, as if to say, *I'll take orders, but that doesn't mean I like it.*

Others looked relieved. An older man, probably well over forty, dropped his rifle on the stack and stepped back to stand in the lines that were forming on the opposite side of the street. He turned to a young boy and put his hand on his shoulder. He said something Andy couldn't understand, and the boy nodded. Andy thought the man had probably said, "It's over for us, and we're alive," or something of that sort. Andy felt tears come to his eyes. He had saved that man's life. He would go home to his family someday, and so would the young soldier. The boy could get married, have a family, grow old.

"Let's send Wilson back to get word to Booker," Andy told McComb. "Somehow, he's got to work fast to get a whole lot of troops together to take these men."

"No. I'm going to go. I can't believe what's happening here. If they start to figure out we don't have many men in those hills, I don't know what they'll do. I've got to make sure Booker understands the situation. I'll lead our men in here, just to show a little force, but that's not going to be enough for very long."

"I think it is. Look how broken they are. They don't want to fight."

"We'll see. But I'll drive the old car back and see what I can do to get us the help we need."

"All right. Captain, four thousand lives saved. Think of it."

"Yeah, well, it ain't over yet."

McComb began to walk away. But then Andy started after him. "Wait a minute, Captain. Tell Booker that—"

A searing pain tore into Andy's side and back. He hit the ground hard, landed on his chest, tried to fight for consciousness. But something had hit him, taken the breath out of him, torn his flesh. He had seen the blood fly in front of him. Hearing some sort of commotion, he struggled to keep breathing and rolled on his side to see, to understand what had happened. What he saw startled him. McComb had Major Belz on the ground. He was sitting on him with a knife pointed at his neck.

"Anyone move and I'll kill this man," he was shouting in English. But the soldiers weren't moving. The other SS officer, the young one Andy had noticed before, was also down on the ground, and two Germans were holding him.

Belz began to shout, obviously giving instructions. McComb continued to hold him, and more men were coming forward, placing their weapons on the stack. Andy let his eyes go shut. It was still going to happen. He had saved the lives—that was what mattered. But the side of his body was all pain. He reached for the fire, felt the ooze of blood through his fingers. He had saved those lives. At least he had done that first. Andy couldn't hold on any longer. He let himself slip into the dark that was filling his head.

*   *   *   *   *

When Bishop Gledhill walked into the house, Belle came out of the kitchen to meet him. He knew immediately that something was wrong. "Ron, Adele is home," his wife said. "She walked in about an hour ago."

"How did she get here?"

"On the train."

"What about Rex? Is he with her?"

"No. She's broken it off with him. But I know she needs to talk to you. Can you give her some time?"

"Does she *want* to talk to me?" the bishop asked.

"Ron, she's always wanted to talk to you. She just hasn't known it. I think she does know it now. Have you got meetings tonight?"

"Yes. But not until later. And if I need to, I'll call and cancel the one I've got."

"Thank you."

The bishop could tell that Belle was worried, but her voice was also full of resolve. She had a bigger heart than most people he knew, but she was firm as a rock wall when she had to be. "Is Adele in her bedroom?" he asked.

"Yes."

Bishop Gledhill was glad that Adele was home and that she had left Rex, but he wasn't sure that Belle was right. He might be the last person on earth Adele wanted to talk to. He took his suit coat off and walked toward his bedroom.

"Be careful with her," Belle warned.

The bishop knew, of course, what she meant. He pulled his tie off and threw it on the bed with his coat. By then, Belle was next to him again. "Let's say a prayer first," she said.

"Maybe you should be the one to talk to her."

"No. We've already talked for a while. She needs to talk to her bishop now."

"Then you say the prayer. Ask Him to help me."

So the two knelt by the bed holding hands, and Belle prayed that the bishop would be inspired to know how to say the right things, and—as she emphasized—to listen.

Bishop Gledhill thanked his wife and then stepped down the hall and knocked. "Adele, it's Dad," he said. "Do you mind if I come in?"

He heard a soft, "No," and hoped she meant she didn't mind. He opened the door and saw that she was lying on her bed, facedown. When she looked up, he saw how red and swollen her eyes were.

"Hi, honey. I'm glad you're home."

"I doubt that," she said, and rolled onto her back.

He walked over to the bed and sat down, then took hold of her hand. "Why do you say that?"

"Mom told you, didn't she?"

"No. She told me you were here and Rex wasn't. That's all she said."

"He was a big liar, Dad. You knew he was. Everyone knew, except me."

"Well, at least you found out."

"What? Before it was too late? Well, sorry, but it *is* too late."

The bishop continued to hold her hand, and he pulled it to his chest. He remembered when Adele had been three or four. She had been feisty even then, and stubborn, but she had always liked to sit on his lap. When he came home from the bank, she would jabber all about everything that had happened to her that day. It occurred to him now that he hadn't listened very closely to her even back then. She could talk forever if he let her, and he usually had lots of things to do. He had almost always had to end those conversations before she was actually finished talking.

"Adele," he said, "just tell me what you want me to know. Or if you don't feel like talking now, we can do it later."

"I don't *want* to tell you anything. I don't want you to know. But Mom says I'm supposed to tell you. You're my bishop."

"I may be your bishop, but long before that, I was your dad. Maybe you'd rather talk to President Allen."

"No. He scares me too much."

The bishop got up and stepped to the chair at Adele's vanity. He turned it around and sat down, and then he said, "Adele, the last time you were here, I was probably more concerned than I should have been about the impression Rex would make around here. But I was also sick with worry about you. I was pretty sure the man was going to hurt you. And I figured he was going to pull you so far away from us that you would never come back."

Adele sat up. She rubbed her fingers over her eyes. "He did hurt me. And he wanted to pull me away. You were right about all of that."

"But I wish I hadn't given you the feeling that I was mostly concerned about appearances."

"Oh, Dad, I walked him around town on purpose. I knew he would smoke, and I knew the kinds of things he would say. You know how much I love to shock people."

Bishop Gledhill had lots of questions he wanted to ask, but for once, he didn't ask them. He waited.

"Dad, he told me we were going to get married. He said it wasn't wrong for us to . . . you know . . . stay together at his place. I moved into his apartment for a while."

The bishop wasn't surprised, but he felt something like nausea spread over him.

"Then I found out he was fooling around with other girls right while I was living with him. When I told him I knew about that, he said, 'Hey, I can never settle down to one girl. If you can't live with that, move along. There's another girl I'm seeing who wants to move in.'"

The bishop nodded again.

"So that's it. I'm a fallen woman. I'm ruined forever as far as people around here are concerned. I could never marry one of the 'nice boys' from Delta."

"Adele, let's not make the same mistake again. The question isn't what other people think of you; it's what you think of yourself."

"And you think I've shamed myself. You think I'm soiled goods. That's what the Church teaches."

"Who ever taught you that?"

"Sister Passey, at MIA. She says once you've 'gone all the way,' you're like a piece of gum that's been all chewed up. No one else will ever want you."

"Adele, look at me."

Adele raised her head.

"That's false doctrine," Bishop Gledhill said emphatically. "It's not what Christ taught. He said that when you repent, though your sins may be scarlet, they'll be made white as snow. He not only forgives you, he forgets the sin entirely."

"That's Christ, Dad. It's not Sister Passey and everyone else in town. I can just imagine what people will say about me now. They all know I was talking about marrying Rex; they'll guess the rest."

"No doubt there'll be some of that, Adele. But I'll tell you something. These are good people here, and if they see you trying to do the right things with your life, they'll be on your side all the way."

"And what's the right thing—to be like them?"

"To be like Christ."

"I don't see many people around here who remind me of Christ."

"Then you don't know them well enough. You have to get close to them and know their hearts the way I do."

"And give them all my time, the way you do?"

So it came back to that again. Bishop Gledhill looked down at the floor. "I'm sorry, Adele, that I've been gone so much. I know it's true. It was hard enough to be bishop. I shouldn't have agreed to run for mayor. I didn't think it would take me away so much, and then I didn't know how to get out of it when no one else would run."

"You could have quit. Then someone else would have had to run."

"I know." He sat for a long time, and then he told her the rest. "The truth is, I like being the mayor. I have my vanities, and my pride, and it's pretty obvious that I haven't kept my priorities straight."

Adele was crying again. So Bishop Gledhill went to her and put his arm around her shoulders. When he did, Adele leaned in against him and sobbed for a long time. When she could finally talk again, she said, "Dad, when I think of Christ, I think of you. You two are pretty much the same in my mind. I've just always wanted you to pay more attention to *me*. That's how selfish I am."

Bishop Gledhill was crying now too, but he said, "Honey, you're going to be okay. I love you. Christ loves you. Anyone who gets past that front you put up will love you too. I don't know what you want to do with your life, but you're not ruined. You're not chewed gum. You're God's beautiful daughter, and mine. We'll make everything okay together."

Adele was sobbing again, and that was good. The bishop knew that she had needed to do that for a long time.

*　*　*　*　*

Andy woke gradually. He fought his way to consciousness at times, only to slide back into strange dreams, confusing images. He heard voices around him, tried to speak, and then returned to the dream, men dropping their weapons in a long, long line. But finally he could see a man looking at him, speaking in English. "Lieutenant," he said, pronouncing it "Lef-tenant" as the British did. "Can you understand me now?"

Andy concentrated on keeping his eyes open. "Yes," he said. The man was wearing a German uniform.

"I stop blood. This bullet, it has break some bones—ribs—but it have miss your lungs, your organs."

"It hurts. Bad."

"Yes. I have no more morphine. Your doctors, they will have some."

But Andy didn't want to sleep again. He had given up out there in

424

the street, let God take him. He hadn't expected to see this light again. He wanted to grasp it now. "Did your men surrender?" he gasped.

"Yes. It's better this way."

Andy didn't want to sleep, but he realized that he was slipping back into the dark when he heard another voice pulling him out again. "Andy, how're you doing?"

Andy opened his eyes to see McComb, looking grim. "All right, I guess. The German said I'll be okay."

"Yeah. But we're going to get you out of here as soon as we can. We need to have *our* doctors look at you. We've got all our men in here now, and more troops heading this way. They're an hour or two out, coming on trucks. I'm trying to keep the lid on everything that long. Booker's a nervous wreck. I've been running the whole show."

"You're the right guy for the job." Andy finally looked around himself and realized that he was lying on a bed in someone's house. There was a washbasin next to the bed, and some towels. Blood was spattered over everything.

"You say that," said McComb, "but I just might kill some of these men you're so proud of saving. I'm not sure the officers deserve to live."

"Come on, McComb. They're our prisoners now. We have to honor that."

"Yeah, just like they did back in that little town by the bridge. I feel like killing one of these guys for every woman and child they killed back there."

"What are you talking about? These are not the same men."

"They're all the same to me. Maybe some of these kids aren't Nazis—just guys who got pulled into this—but Belz and that little worm who shot you, they believe in Hitler. They're just fine with everything the guy has done."

"But Belz arranged this surrender. I don't think he's a bad man."

"Andy, you'll never grow up. You need to go back to the States and pretend that everything is just okey-dokey—the way your family taught you. It's going to take some guys like me—who recognize evil when we see it—to clear up this mess over here. These SS troops shouldn't be allowed to live, and if we don't kill some of them now, I'm not sure it will happen."

"We can't just kill them. They're our prisoners. That's murder."

"Yeah. Sure. Suddenly it's murder. Don't give me that. I could have killed him yesterday and it's war; today it's murder. Who's going to blame me if I rid the world of some rodents? I should have killed that guy who shot you right on the spot."

"And then the whole thing would have blown up. You did the right thing."

"It's not over yet. He might decide to break out of here, and I might have to shoot him."

"Don't pull something like that, Del. You've got to live with yourself the rest of your life, and you'll never feel right about it if you kill him."

But McComb laughed at that. "I'll feel just fine. I'm going to interrogate all those officers—every one of them. And they better talk."

"Talk about what? Help me sit up."

"Just stay where you are."

Andy struggled to sit up anyway, and McComb helped him. For a moment Andy felt dizzy, but he was feeling more awake all the time. His body ached horribly, but he was starting to think that he would have to stay here for a while yet—and stay awake—if he was going to keep things from going bad. "What is it you want to know from them?" he asked again.

"What their escape plan was. Where they were told to cross the Rhine. That's what Intelligence wants to know."

"Captain Lipp said they had no plan. And he helped us pull off this surrender. Why would he lie about that?"

"Because he's a German officer. He wanted to save his skin, maybe—and some of his soldiers—but he's still one of Hitler's boys."

"He helped us take four thousand men, Captain. He—"

"It's not that many. It's more like thirty-eight hundred."

Andy laughed. "McComb, listen to yourself. We were two guys, and we stood our ground, got thirty-eight hundred Germans to surrender. What more could we have done? Don't mess this up by trying to get revenge on their officers."

"All I'm going to do is question them. That's standard procedure. I'm starting with Belz, right now."

"You can't even speak to him."

"Hey, we have all these French guys here. One of them can translate for me."

"And they want, even more than you, to get at these officers. They'd love to shoot every one of them."

"You got that right."

"I'll translate for you."

"No. I'm going now."

"I'm going with you." Andy stood up next to the bed. He felt the grogginess in his head again, but he wasn't going to let McComb just have his way with these men.

CHAPTER 29

ANDY WALKED FROM the house and saw McComb striding down the street. He leaned against the door frame for a few seconds to catch his breath, but he felt pain every time he inhaled. Still, pushing past the shock he felt with every step, he followed McComb down the sidewalk past the great stacks of rifles. He was gasping for air, feeling faint, but he couldn't let McComb get away from him. He had seen the old building McComb had entered, and he walked through the same door. Inside, he asked one of the OG soldiers where the captain had gone.

"He's got that SS officer in the first room on the right. Are you all right, Lieutenant?"

"Yes. I'll be all right." Andy walked down the hall, losing strength fast. He knocked on the door that the soldier had pointed to, and in a moment McComb opened it. "Let me come in," Andy said.

"Get out of here, Andy. Go back to bed."

But Andy stepped into the gap of the half-open door, and McComb didn't push him back. Andy stepped sideways past McComb and saw that Emil, a *Maquisard,* was also there. Belz, the SS major, was sitting on a chair in the little room. It appeared to be a storage area. Wooden crates had been pushed against the back wall, creating a space maybe eight feet square. Belz was in the middle and Emil was sitting on a chair in front of him, holding a pistol. That seemed unnecessary, since Belz's arms were tied behind his back and secured to the chair.

"All right, you can stay," McComb said. "But Emil is my translator, and I don't want you to interfere in any way." He looked at Emil. "Let the lieutenant take your chair."

Emil got up and brought the chair to Andy, who sat in a corner. He felt close to passing out, but he wasn't going to leave.

"All right, Major," said McComb. "You can make this hard or you can make this easy."

Emil translated, the words in French seeming less harsh, but his tone as intense as McComb's. Andy knew how much the Resistance fighters hated the Germans, and especially the SS. For years now, Emil's children had suffered for food and other basic necessities while the German troops had had all they needed. This was a moment of reversal for him, and Andy knew he was as eager for violence against the Germans as McComb was.

"Simply tell me your planned route of retreat and where you hoped to cross the Rhine."

Emil translated, and then Belz said, in French, "We had talked about trying to reach Strasbourg. We fell in with other battalions, and Colonel Lang took command. But he had no instructions, and we had no contact with higher leaders. Frankly, we didn't know how we could get past Lyon."

This all sounded reasonable to Andy, but Emil had not even translated the whole statement before McComb was yelling, "That's the hard way, Major. You better give me more than that or I'll use some of the techniques your Gestapo boys have used on the French."

Belz listened to the translation and then said, "It's all I can tell you. It's all I know. Perhaps Colonel Lang had something more specific in mind, but if he did, he didn't tell me."

Suddenly McComb's fist flashed out and struck Belz with full force in the side of the head. Belz fell over sideways, still tied to the chair. He hit the floor hard.

"Captain, you can't do that," Andy shouted.

"Shut up. Stay out of this." McComb stepped closer to Belz, stood over the top of him. "Here's the thing," he said. "You don't take me seriously. You don't think I'll do what your people do. But you don't know me. I'll break your bones and then twist them. I heard that's a little trick your Gestapo boys like to pull. If you want that, just keep lying to me."

Emil struggled to translate the exact words, but he was standing over Belz himself, shouting at him, adding a few phrases of his own.

"I'm willing to tell you *anything* I know," Belz said. He took a long breath. "I thought we would try to cross somewhere around Strasbourg, but we didn't know whether your troops would cut us off before we could get there. The truth is, I didn't believe we had much chance of making it back to Germany. That's why I convinced the colonel to surrender."

Emil translated all that as McComb waited and listened.

Andy said from the corner, "That sounds true, Captain. It makes sense. Their troops are confused. Everyone is retreating at the same time. It's not surprising that they didn't know where they could make a crossing."

"Yeah, that does *sound* kind of reasonable. And it also sounds like something a liar would say—just to keep us from knowing what we need to know."

"Why do we need to know? What difference does it make now?"

"Look, Andy, I have my orders. The high command told me to get some intelligence from these men—to find out what they had been told to do. So I'm going to find out."

He suddenly drove his boot into Belz's ribs. A huge grunt came out of the man, followed by something like a whimper.

Andy tried to get up, making it halfway to his feet before his knees gave out and he dropped back to his chair. "McComb, you can't do this!"

"Why? Are you afraid I broke some of his ribs? Well, that's what this guy's friend did to you with that bullet he put into you. I say this is fair enough."

"Belz didn't shoot me."

"Don't worry, that other SS guy is next."

"Come on, Captain. We don't do this. This is what we're fighting against."

"And if this war were left up to guys like you, we wouldn't win it. Someone has to be as tough as they are." He reached down and pulled the knife from his boot. Crouching next to Belz, he said, "Can you see this knife?"

Belz didn't wait for the translation. He said, in English, "Yes, I see it. I know nothing more. You can kill me. It's better for me that way."

"You don't think I will. But I can do it and not feel a moment of regret." He moved the knife closer to Belz's neck.

Andy got to his feet this time. "McComb, stop." He took a step forward, but he knew he couldn't do anything. McComb could push him back with one hand.

"Get out of here, Andy. If you don't want to see this, leave."

"I'll report you. You'll be charged for this."

"Charged for what? Doing what I have to do? This is a war, Andy."

"You can't murder this man."

"I won't kill him if he'll tell me the truth. He knows a lot more than he's saying."

Andy took another step forward. "I don't think you even believe that, Captain. You just want to kill him."

McComb twisted enough to look at Andy. "Get out of here right now or I'll throw you out."

By then Andy knew what he had to do. "All right," he said, and he walked to the door. As he stepped out, he heard McComb yell at Belz again. Andy leaned against the wall in the hallway and said, "Corporal, come here." The soldier at the front door walked back to Andy. "Let me take your rifle."

"I'm supposed to guard this—"

Andy saw that the man had a side arm. "Give me your pistol." The corporal pulled it from his holster, a .45 semiautomatic. "Is it loaded?"

"Sure."

"Chamber a round."

"What's going on in there?"

"Chamber a round."

The corporal pulled back on the slide mechanism, racked a bullet into the chamber, then handed the pistol to Andy. "You don't look good," he said. "Do you need me?"

"No. Go back to your post."

Andy took a deep breath and turned back to the door. He swung it open just as McComb kicked Belz in the ribs again.

"Stop," Andy said softly, but only because he had no strength. McComb had knelt next to Belz by then. He glanced up and saw that Andy was pointing the pistol at him. He looked curious, not frightened. "I want you and Emil to leave this room right now," ordered Andy. "If you don't, I'll shoot you."

McComb stood, looked at Andy, and laughed. "You're going to fall over any minute now."

Andy leaned back against the wall and held the .45 with both hands. "Start moving now." Then in French, "Emil, I want you to leave."

Emil hesitated and McComb told him, "Don't go anywhere. The lieutenant's not going to shoot you. He doesn't have the guts."

"I will, Emil. You're committing a crime. I won't let you do it. Get out."

Andy saw the confusion in Emil's face, perhaps from doubt over what they were doing more than fear of Andy. In any case, he nodded, walked past Andy, and left the room. Andy took a step sideways, staying against the wall. He didn't want Emil to make a quick move back into the room and grab the weapon.

"Now you, Captain."

"You can't shoot me, Andy. You aren't *capable* of it." McComb was still smiling, standing his ground. "You've regretted every life you've taken since we've been over here. You sure aren't going to start killing Americans."

"I can't let you do this. I promised this man we'd take care of him and his men if they gave up their arms."

McComb grinned. "All right, Andy, I guess you mean it. Go ahead and shoot me. That's the only way I'm going to stop."

Andy aimed high and fired. The bullet crashed into a wooden crate very close to McComb's head—closer than Andy had intended. Andy saw the reaction, the sudden terror in McComb's eyes. If nothing else, he had to fear Andy's shakiness.

"Walk out now, Captain. The next one will be in your chest." Andy aimed directly at McComb.

"Now who's going to be court-martialed?"

"I'll take my chances."

"You're a fool, Andy. You don't understand one thing about this war." He stared at Andy for quite some time, didn't really seem afraid, but he gave way to Andy's will. He walked out.

Once McComb was gone, Andy said, "Major, you'll be all right. I won't let anyone else hurt you." But he was sliding down the wall, and black was filling his head again.

* * * * *

Whisper was standing on the Gledhills' porch, feeling nervous. Lamar was next to her. She knocked on the door, and Belle appeared from the kitchen. Whisper saw her look pleased for a moment and then notice Lamar. She obviously knew what this was about; her smile faded quickly. "Oh, Whisper," she said. "I'm glad you came by. I tried to call you just a little while ago."

"Did you? Lamar and I were out running around. We had some things we had to take care of."

"Well, come in. I do want to talk to you." She sounded nice enough, but she didn't acknowledge Lamar. Whisper wondered what she was thinking—and why she would have called.

Whisper and Lamar followed Belle toward the living room, but Whisper glanced into the kitchen and was amazed to find Adele sitting at the table, alone. "Adele, I didn't know you were home," Whisper said.

"I know. I just got here a couple of days ago. I haven't looked anyone up yet. I was going to call you one of these days."

"Is Rex with you?"

"No. That's over. You were right about him. I guess that doesn't surprise you."

"I'm sorry, Adele."

"It doesn't matter."

Whisper could see that it did. She had never heard Adele sound so subdued. But now was not the time to ask any questions. "I think you've met Lamar Jones, haven't you?" Whisper asked, and she turned and took hold of his arm.

"I don't know that I ever have. But I saw him at one of our dances."

"He's from Fillmore."

"I know. You've told me about him." But Whisper could see that Adele was less than pleased to see him there standing in the kitchen door. "I can see the ring on your finger," Adele said.

"Oh . . . yes. He gave it to me last night." Whisper lifted it, but she didn't really hold it out. It was a small set of diamonds, a little arrangement on a thin band.

Belle had stayed in the hall, but now she stepped into the kitchen and took Whisper into her arms. "Congratulations, sweetheart," she said. "I hope you'll be very happy." But the flatness of her voice was more than obvious. Whisper found this terribly awkward. She had known it would be, but she had also known it was something she had to do.

Belle shook Lamar's hand, and Adele finally got up from the table and gave Whisper a halfhearted embrace. "Well, good luck," she said. "When are you getting married?"

"Soon. Lamar got a leave after Basic Training. He's only going to be here a few days. We're not going to have anything fancy. Just a quiet little wedding at home. We'll go to the temple later, when we have a chance. Lamar has to go back for some more training and then I'll join him in San Diego when he's finished with that."

"You mean you're getting married in a day or two?"

"Yes. I wanted to ask the bishop when he could come over to our house and perform the ceremony. We were thinking maybe tomorrow afternoon, but I know he's always busy on Sundays."

Whisper could see tears in Belle's eyes. "I'll get Ron," she said. "He's out in the garden; he's got the kids out there working with him."

Belle walked out. Whisper was left standing in front of Adele, who had returned to the kitchen table. "I guess this is kind of a whirlwind thing," Whisper said, "but he got the leave and came up on a bus. We could wait until he's finished, but we don't know when he might have a chance to come home again. We just thought we'd rather get married here than down in San Diego."

"Sure. I can understand that. And once you make up your mind, I guess there's no reason to wait." Adele stared down at the table. She looked pale and tired. Whisper knew she needed to find some time, somehow, to talk to her alone. "I guess you haven't heard the news we got this morning," Adele said.

"What's that?"

"We got a telegram a couple of hours ago. Andy's been wounded." She looked up and gave Whisper a reassuring nod. "But he's going to be okay. He might even get sent home to recover, at least for a while."

Whisper felt the jolt. Andy would be home. She knew what she had always felt whenever he had come to town. But this time wounded—maybe needing help. Last night Lamar had been so sweet, and Whisper had told herself she had strung the boy along long enough. He'd said to her, "I need to know, Whisper. I love you and I want to marry you, but I've never known whether you really feel that way about me. If you don't want to marry me, say so now, and I'll finally know where I stand."

Whisper had realized that if she turned him down, she was passing up her chance with Lamar, and she didn't know whether others would come along. She had decided that thinking wasn't going to help. She needed to move ahead with her life. "I'll marry you, Lamar," she had said, without saying a word about how she felt about him.

But now this. How was she going to feel about Andy being here—and Lamar gone?

Bishop Gledhill walked into the house first, with Chrissy and Marie close behind. The girls hugged Whisper, but she could see that Chrissy was fighting not to cry. The bishop hugged Whisper too, and then Adele said, "She wants you to perform the wedding tomorrow, Dad. Can you pull that off?"

"Tomorrow?" He stared at Whisper, and she could see how thunderstruck he was. "Do you have a marriage license?"

Finally Lamar said something. "Do we have to have that before, or can we—"

"Yes, you have to have it. And you can't get one today. You'll have to wait for Monday for that."

"Maybe we could have the wedding Monday evening, if that would work out for you. The only thing is, I leave Wednesday, and we wanted a day or two together first."

"Well, of course. I understand. But you're not jumping too fast, are you?"

"It might be the only time I'll be home."

"I was just thinking, it would be so much better if you could wait long enough to go up to Salt Lake and get married in the temple."

"I know. But I didn't know until a couple of days ago that I could get home. We're just trying to figure this all out."

The bishop looked away from Lamar, looked at Whisper. "I guess you heard about Andy coming home?"

It was a terrible moment. Whisper could hardly believe that the bishop would be so obvious. Poor Lamar had to be humiliated. "Yes. I hope he's going to recover all right."

"Sounds like a million-dollar wound, as we used to call it," the bishop said. "It gets him out of the war for now. But he thinks he'll heal completely."

Whisper was nodding. "Do you think Monday would be all right?"

"I guess I could work that out."

"Well . . . that's good." And now the silence again. But Whisper heard the front door open and she heard footsteps in the hall. That had to be Flip. She turned just as he appeared at the kitchen door. He nodded but said only, "Hi." For just a moment he made eye contact, and Whisper couldn't tell whether she was seeing anger or hatred or hurt. She knew only that he was holding back, his face stiff, his eyes unblinking.

"Did Mom tell you?" Adele asked. "Whisper's getting married."

Flip nodded again. "Congratulations," he said, but he didn't walk toward her, and he didn't so much as glance toward Lamar. "I've got to turn the water," he said, and then he disappeared. In a moment Whisper heard the screen door slap shut.

Whisper wanted to chase after him, talk to him. She thought she knew what was going through his mind. But what could she do? So she turned back to Belle, who was trying the hardest to be nice about all this, and she said, "Well, thanks. We've got a lot to plan, so I guess we better be on the run."

"Sure," Belle said.

But no one else spoke, so Whisper took hold of Lamar's hand, and they walked out together.

*   *   *   *

Flip pushed down the headgate on the irrigation ditch and stopped the water from flowing into the garden. And then he took off. He didn't want to see anyone, didn't want to talk. He didn't want to hear his mother or dad or sister tell him that this was "all for the best," or some such thing. He walked hard and kept going, through the streets of Delta and all the way out the road to the farm. It was the only place he knew to go. Life had been fiercely lonely lately, with his friends in town telling everyone he was a Jap lover and Tom still in jail in California. Now Whisper was gone. Before long, Flip would have to look Andy in the eye.

Flip walked to a cottonwood tree down by the irrigation canal and sat in the shade. For a while he threw rocks into the canal, but he soon wearied of that, and he merely sat and stared. He tried to think what he would do with his life now. School would be starting in a couple of weeks, and he dreaded that. He knew what he would be hearing from a lot of the guys. It had crossed his mind, since he was finally growing, that he might go out for sports again, but why embarrass himself? Who would want him on their teams anyway?

Flip's big hero brother would come waltzing into town before long, and everyone would be falling all over him, all the more impressed because he'd been shot. Flip was almost sure that Andy had been a spy, too. All he would have to do would be to hint a little about that and everyone would treat him like the biggest thing that ever happened in Delta. But as far as Flip was concerned, he was just a big phony.

However, Flip saved most of his anger for Whisper. She had about as much backbone as an angle worm. Lamar just had to come home and pop the question and she jumped on board like she didn't have a brain in her head. Couldn't she just look at that guy and know he'd always be a dirt farmer without enough gumption to amount to anything? Whisper would be cooking for ten kids and a bunch of farmhands in a few years, and she'd turn uglier than an old sow. If Andy wasn't coming back to her, she'd just settle for Lamar. That was about as far as the girl could see.

Flip smacked his fist into his thigh. He told himself he was going to be *somebody* someday. He would run the bank if Andy would give him the chance, and he'd maybe run for mayor himself. He'd go up to the U or the Y and find him the prettiest girl on campus, and he'd bring her back to Delta. He'd be a banker and a mayor and anything else he could manage to be. The word would get over to Fillmore, no question, and Whisper would know what he was. It wouldn't matter one bit by then that he was a little younger than she was. She would know what he'd done with his life.

"Flip?"

His muscles locked. He knew the voice, of course, but he didn't want to talk to her.

"I figured this was where you'd come."

"And this is where I'm going to stay. You go smooch with Lamar. He can't stand to be away from you for five minutes."

Whisper actually laughed. "I knew you were mad at me."

"I'm not mad. What do I care? Marry that ugly little rabbit and go off and get yourself a litter of bunnies. What difference does it make to me?"

She didn't laugh this time. She sat next to him on the grass, so close her arm touched his. But he pulled his arm back. She was only trying to use something like that to soften him up.

"Listen to me a minute, Flip. I know you don't like Lamar, but that's mostly because you think you had to hold onto me for Andy. He's really—"

"What do I care about Andy? When they hold the big parade, I'm not going."

"Parade?"

"Sure. They'll bring him into town in a convertible, like he's General Eisenhower."

"Are you really that upset with him?"

"No. I don't care anymore. I made one big mistake in my life. I didn't turn out enough like Andy. But look out for me. I'm going to do more than he ever does. You'll be hearing about me." He picked up a rock by his feet and threw it hard into the water.

"That's good, Flip. I guess. But I don't like to see you so mad."

"Oh, yeah. Sure. You just can't *imagine* why I would get upset. Never mind that everyone I know is a liar, including you. Just take off, okay? Go find Lamar and *neck* with him some more. I don't want to talk to you. I just . . ." But the anger had run out, and he realized his voice was starting to shake. He bent his head forward, held on with all his muscles, but he couldn't stop his tears. When Whisper tried to put her arm around his shoulders, he pulled away and slid across the grass away from her.

"Flip, you know what I'm doing. I want to be married, and this is my chance. I'll—"

Flip spun toward her. "You don't love him. You know you don't. And that's wrong, Whisper. Lamar knows it, too. Or if he doesn't have it figured out yet, he will. And then what? You're going to be miserable your whole life, and you're going to make him the same way."

Whisper drew her knees up, rested her arms on them, then dropped her head onto her arms. She was wearing a thin little dress, and he could see her ribs quiver as she began to cry. He suddenly wanted to take her into his arms and hold her. But he knew she wouldn't want that, so he sat and let her cry, though he could hardly stand to hear it. He finally turned toward her and said quietly, "Whisper, it's not your fault. It's Andy's. He put you in this mess. I shouldn't have said all that stuff."

"Oh, Flip, if he had loved me as much as you do, I would have waited for him forever."

Tears filled Flip's eyes again, but he didn't let himself cry. He shifted back close to Whisper and put his arm around her back. "Don't marry Lamar, Whisper. It's the biggest mistake you could make."

"I know."

"You do know?"

"I didn't sleep all night after I told him yes. I've been sick at my stomach all day. I can't do it, can I?"

"No."

"I've got to go back and tell him. Flip, you're going to have to be my friend after I send him away. I don't have anyone else."

"I'll always be your friend, Whisper. You know that."

CHAPTER 30

ANDY WAS RIDING another train. He had crossed the ocean on a troop ship and then traveled on a train across the country. He was still weak, and the ride had been hard, but the closer he got to Delta, the more he liked looking at the countryside. It was early October now, and the Wasatch Mountains near Salt Lake were showing their color—the aspens yellow, the oak brush rusty red. Even better to Andy were the distant blues of the mountains and the gray-green of the sagebrush. And yet, there was still far too much numbness inside him. He had imagined his return on the day he had left home, and back then he had hoped for a euphoric joy, but feelings of that kind simply weren't part of him any longer.

He had ended up in a hospital in Marseilles, had gone through a surgery there, and had spent some weeks recovering. After his release, he had borrowed a jeep and driven to Tarascon, back where he had spent the summers of his childhood. But that had been troubling to him. What he had felt there was mostly what he had lost. He had come across a little boy playing on the cobblestones in front of his house, seemingly oblivious to all that had occurred in his country the past few years. The boy was tossing a stick, urging his dog to run after it, laughing when the dog responded. Andy remembered the simple way that he had thought as a child. It struck him that in many ways he had remained pretty much the same most of his life. He hadn't really grown up all that much before he had joined the army. He had known what was right and what he had to do about it. But nothing was so clear to him now.

Andy's bluff had worked. The little OG unit had taken more than 3,800 prisoners, and he and McComb had each received the Distinguished Service Cross. Their leaders in London knew nothing about Andy pulling a gun on his commander. McComb had backed off, hadn't harmed any of the other prisoners, and hadn't reported Andy's insubordination. But the bitterness of the confrontation lingered in Andy's mind. McComb had shown so clearly that the evil wasn't only in the Nazis. And Andy wondered whether he was really any better. In the end, he had used a gun to try to set things right.

On that day in Tarascon, Andy had wanted to be himself again, the boy he remembered. He had found a quiet place on the edge of town where he had knelt down and prayed. He had tried to pray in the hospital, but this was his first chance to say out loud the things that were on his mind. He told the Lord that he had done his best to save those lives, that he felt good about that, and then he asked the Lord to heal him, to let him believe in goodness. But certain images wouldn't leave his mind.

All during this train ride he had tried to sleep, but when he did, the dreams would come, and he would see the faces and the blood and hear the explosions. When awake, he tried to clear his mind of those memories, but he kept thinking of his friends who were dead. Raul, whose real name he would probably never know. Evan Roberts. The Bertrands. So many of his comrades in the Resistance. And above all, Elise. Rarely could he get through so much as an hour without her pale face appearing in his mind, her body lying in that dark alley. But he also thought of the others—the ones he had killed.

Andy had another worry, too. The war was far from over, and his wound would heal. He hadn't been released from the service. He doubted he would return to Europe, but the war in the Pacific would probably last for a long time yet. Eventually, Japan would have to be invaded, and that was going to take hundreds of thousands of troops. He could easily be called back to his airborne unit and have to make a drop into Japan during the landing. He could still die in this war, and he may still have to kill.

Still, he liked the look of this land, this desert. There had been a time when he didn't think he could return to his home. Now he hoped that little Delta could bring him back to life. He wanted to believe that he really was the Andy who had come home for Christmas less than two years before. And when he thought of that, he thought of Whisper. He had learned of her engagement, and then he had learned that she had called it off. He almost wished she hadn't. She would know immediately how empty he was, and that would only hurt her.

Andy had contacted his parents. They knew he was coming home, but he hadn't been able to tell them exactly when. Troop trains were too unpredictable. When he had reached Ogden, he had thought of calling, but it was very early in the morning, so he hesitated—and something else had stopped him. He didn't want to create a big scene at the train, with his mother hugging him and people noticing. He just wanted to slip quietly into town. And so, when the train stopped in Delta that afternoon, he hoisted his duffel bag over his shoulder and hiked west into town. He walked along Main Street and then down "Silk Stocking Row," the bag weighing him down, tiring him out.

Andy saw some people he knew along the way, but he didn't look them straight on. They said hello, as everyone always did, but they didn't seem to recognize him. He had lost a great deal of weight. When he had looked at himself in a mirror on the train, he had thought he was looking at a haggard old man. He considered stopping at the bank, but he decided he'd rather see Dad at home, not there, with other people around.

He reached his house, stepped up on the porch, and set his duffel bag down, then waited and caught his breath. It seemed strange to him that so little had changed. The porch needed a coat of paint, he thought, but it usually did, and the old screen door had a new little tear, but this was home, and it reached him as nothing else had. He kept taking deep breaths, recognizing something familiar in the smell of things, the dry air, the sound of crows somewhere not far off.

It was Tuesday. Andy figured Mom would be the only one home. Adele would be at the bank. His parents had written that she was home and working for Dad now. Marie and Chrissy were both at college, and Flip was probably not home from school yet. So Andy opened the door, stepped in, and said, "Mom?"

He heard something in the back of the house, and then his mother poked her head out of a back bedroom. She had a scarf over her hair and an apron over an old blue housedress she had been wearing for years. "Oh, Andy!" she said. Her hands flew to her face, and then she pulled her scarf off before she ran to him. She was reaching for him all the way down the hall. Andy had conjured up a fear this last year that his parents, his family, would see him and instantly know that he wasn't what he was supposed to be. It was what he felt now: that fear. But she kept coming, and then she had him in her arms. "Oh, Andy, Andy, my little boy. I was so afraid I would never see you again."

Andy hadn't expected to cry, even to feel, but he did.

"Am I hurting you? Where is your wound exactly?"

Andy stepped back a little and put his hand on his side. "It's here, but it doesn't hurt much now. I'm afraid I'm healing too fast."

"Will they take you back?"

"They might. I'm not sure."

She didn't say what she thought of that, but he could see it in her face. Still, she looked pretty, not really older, and the tears in her eyes were for her happiness. "At least I've got you now," she said. "I'll keep you as long as I can." She took him back in her arms.

But now Andy was feeling pain in his side, bending the way he had to. She seemed to sense that and let go of him. "I'll call your father."

"That's all right. Let's just sit here for a minute. It feels good to be in the house."

"Flip will be home in a few minutes. But Andy, he needs you. He's having a terrible time right now. He sounds the way Adele did at the same age. He wants to get out of Delta and he's stopped going to church."

Andy knew something about that from letters his parents had sent him, but it was hard to imagine that Flip could be anything but his good, simple self.

"You must be hungry. What can I fix for you?"

"Anything real. I've been wanting your good bottled peaches for a long time now."

"Oh, that's easy. I'll open some."

"And some of your bread."

"I baked yesterday. I do have bread. But we can't get any butter. It's just that oleomargarine with the dye in it."

"That's okay. Just the bread. And some peaches."

So they walked into the kitchen, and Andy sat at the table while his mother sliced bread for him and then, with her strong hands, twisted the lid off a bottle of peaches. Things seemed almost shockingly as they had always been. "I was in Tarascon a few weeks ago," Andy told his mother. "It looked about the same."

"Can you tell us what you did in France, Andy? In your letters, you told us nothing, and for all those months, you didn't write at all."

"I couldn't, Mom. I hope you understand that. And I still can't say much. Not yet."

"But it must have been terrible. I know you were behind enemy lines."

"It wasn't easy." Andy took a long breath. He was glad he couldn't tell her. But when he looked up at her, she seemed to know. She came to him again, knelt by his chair, and wrapped her arms around him. "I'm so sorry," she said. "You don't ever have to tell us, if you don't want to."

Andy didn't say it, but he knew he would never tell her very much.

Belle continued to hold him for a long time. "Are you going to be all right?" she finally asked him.

"I'm tired from everything, Mom. I don't know how to tell you how tired I am."

She stood and kissed him on the top of the head. "I know. I see it in your eyes. But we'll make you better. I promise we will."

Andy had doubted that for such a long time, but it seemed true when his mother said it.

"And what about Whisper? She didn't get married. I think she still holds out hope that you two might feel the same about each other. She tells Flip that she isn't thinking that way—but I'm almost sure she is."

"That's all changed, Mom."

"But how?"

"It just has. Maybe she hasn't changed, but I have. She wouldn't like me now."

"Oh, Andy, don't say that. You'll be all right again. I know it's hard to imagine, after going through so much, but you'll see. You'll be fine. I watched your father go through some of the same things, and look at the man he is now."

Andy wanted to believe that, but he didn't say so. He told her how good the peaches and bread tasted, and then they talked about people in town, his friends who were at war.

Andy had finished eating but was still sitting at the table when he heard the screen door open and then slap shut. Then he heard a deeper voice than he remembered. "Hi, Mom. I'm home."

"Come here a minute," Belle said.

Flip stepped into the kitchen. Andy watched him, waiting for his reaction. He saw some surprise but not much excitement. "Andy," he said, "when did you get here?" But he didn't rush to the table.

Andy got up and walked to him. He was about to take Flip in his arms when the boy stuck his hand out. "You've grown a whole lot," Andy said. "You'll be as tall as me pretty soon."

"I doubt it. But I've grown four inches since my last birthday."

"Why didn't you go out for football?"

"I'm not good at sports. I've quit trying."

Andy could see he had asked the wrong thing. Flip glanced down the hallway, as though he wanted to get away.

"Sit down. Let's talk. Do you want some peaches?"

"No, thanks. I've got some homework I need to do. Maybe we can talk a little later."

Flip turned and walked on down the hallway toward his room. Andy looked at his mother. "I told you," she said. "He's got a lot on his mind right now."

"Was it this thing with his Japanese friend? Is that still bothering him?"

"Sure. His friends have finally let some of that go, but he's not close to anyone at school. And Andy, you have to understand, you put him in a difficult spot with Whisper. He feels like you backed out on your end of the deal."

Andy nodded. He hadn't thought enough about that. He had been in his own world in France and had hardly been able to think of things back here. "I'll talk to him."

"Yes. But don't push him. He's at that age when he wants to think for himself."

"Okay."

Andy walked down the hall to Flip's room. "Hey, Flip," he said, "everyone's going to be home pretty soon. Could you spare a few minutes to talk to me before they get here?"

Flip was lying on his bed. He had set his books on his desk. He glanced at them, as though he wanted to claim again that he had to do homework, but then he said, "Yeah, okay."

"Let's walk out on the porch. I like feeling this good, dry air here."

So Flip got up and walked to the porch with Andy, and they sat down on the old metal chairs that had sat on the porch for as long as Andy could remember. They needed a coat of paint too. "I get the feeling you're mad at me," Andy said.

Flip exhaled, then slumped down in his seat. "Wow! You must be brilliant. But then, that's what everyone always says about you."

Andy was surprised by the anger; he hadn't expected that. "Just tell me what you're upset about."

"Well, let's see. It's hard to figure, isn't it? You make me promise to hang onto your girl, and then you break her heart and ruin her life— while I watch. I thought a promise meant something to you, but it doesn't."

"Flip, I don't know how to explain this to you."

"Hey, I don't care. You don't have to. Just don't expect me to show up at your welcome-home parade."

"That's the last thing in the world I'd ever want."

"Oh, yeah. Right. You'll show up when the band starts playing."

"You don't know me, Flip. I know you're mad, but don't accuse me of things I wouldn't do. I feel bad enough about the things I've done."

"What's that supposed to mean?" Flip was staring out toward the old willow tree out front, not looking at Andy.

"Flip, things happen in a war—things that change who you are. I got to a point where I didn't feel worthy to look Whisper in the eye ever again, let alone marry her." Andy probably needed to tell Flip about Elise—if he really wanted to explain—but he couldn't bring himself to do it.

"Andy, I don't even know what you're trying to say."

"I'm not the same man I was, Flip. That's all I'm telling you."

Flip looked down at the porch. "I don't get that. A lot of guys go to war, and then they come home and get married. You don't know how it was. You didn't have to be here looking at Whisper, seeing how sad she was."

"I never should have asked you to help me out that way, Flip. I should have seen that from the beginning."

Flip's head popped back up. "That's not what you did wrong. What you did wrong was let her down. She's the best girl on this earth, and you don't even know it. And she still loves you, whether she says so or not."

Andy let that sink in a little. He wanted to find Whisper and tell her he was sorry. But he still hadn't told Flip the whole truth. "Flip, there came a time in France when I didn't believe in God. I knew Whisper would never want me back in that state of mind."

"Well, at least we're not so different," Flip said. "I found out everything I learned in church is a bunch of lies. People don't love each other the way Jesus says. That's just all talk. I tried to help a guy because people were stealing from his house. So do my friends tell me that I'm a good guy? No. They call me a 'Jap lover.' It's supposed to be, you love everyone, and you're all brothers and sisters and everything, but it's not like that. And *no one* keeps promises."

Andy felt limp. He had experienced a lot of doubt in the last year, but it was worse to see Flip going through the same thing. Andy had been trying to find his faith again, but suddenly he felt the need to make a better effort—Flip needed him to be stronger than he'd been. "Flip, let me tell you something that happened to me."

Flip was staring straight ahead again. A little breeze was picking up, and narrow, yellow leaves were dropping off the willow tree, twisting and rolling as they fell, just as he had watched them do his whole life.

"I'm not supposed to tell you about this, but I'm going to. A few weeks ago I was fighting with a little army made up mostly of French troops—*Maquis,* they're called. Resistance fighters. We had some German troops caught in a valley. They had us outnumbered, but they didn't know that. Another officer and I went down there with a white flag, and we bluffed the Germans into believing we had them cold and they better give up. It turned out there were a whole lot more Germans than we bargained for. We took almost four thousand prisoners, and there were less than a hundred of us."

"Well, that's great, Andy. I'm sure you'll get a medal. You always do."

"No, Flip. That's not my point. We took a big chance, but we saved all those lives. I've killed people, Flip—killed them face-to-face. But on that day, I kept a whole bunch of men from dying. It's the best thing I did in the war."

Flip nodded, but Andy could tell he didn't understand.

"Flip, when we realized how badly outnumbered we were, I knew that if I made a mistake, I'd be dead. I thought about getting out of there with my life, and letting those Germans keep getting picked off as they retreated up the valley. But I wanted to save their lives. I prayed about it, and I felt like the Lord told me what I had to do."

"I told you, they'll give you a medal."

"Don't do this, Flip. Come on. God helped me make the decision. He guided me to save some lives, even showed me how to do it." Andy stopped. He wanted to bear his testimony to Flip, but he didn't want to lie—or to make himself look better than he was. "What I felt right then was that there really is a God, and he does care, no matter how much bad stuff is going on in the world all the time." Andy was suddenly crying, and he knew why. He was feeling it again—the same surge of confirmation that he had felt that day in France. God really had worked through him, used him. He felt sure of it again. "I wanted to do something that was right, and I got a chance to do it. I felt some life come back into me that day."

"Then go see Whisper. She's so miserable she could die. And I know she still wants you."

Andy had to think about that. But for the moment, he was a lot more concerned about Flip. "What's happening to your Japanese friend now?"

"He's still in jail. He wants to get into the army, but the director out here at Topaz won't let him. All he has to do is say the word and sign some papers. Down in California, they're saying they'll release him back to Topaz, and he's eighteen now so he can join the army, but this guy out here, the director of the camp, is saying he has to stay in jail as an example—so other people won't try to run from the camp. He'll probably end up in a federal prison for the rest of the war—and maybe longer."

"Let's go talk to the guy."

"What guy?"

"The director out at Topaz."

"Dad's talked to him over and over."

"I don't care. Let's do the right thing. Let's not stop trying."

Flip was staring at Andy now. "Yeah. You're the big war hero. You figure you can just walk in there and change his mind."

"Lay off, Flip. I'm not saying anything like that. Let's just go see what we can do."

Flip actually smiled. "You mean right now? Really?"

"Sure."

"Dad's coming home before long, and—"

"That's okay. Let's go."

*   *   *   *   *

Flip was amazed by all of this. He wanted to stay angry with Andy, but the guy was willing to try to do something for Tom.

Andy got the keys to the old car from Mom, and they drove out through the farms east of town and on to Topaz. At the gate, Andy—still wearing his uniform—told the guard that he had army business with Director Schneider. The guard saluted Andy, let him park inside the gate, and then he led Andy and Flip to the administration building.

Flip had ridden his bike out to Topaz with Cal one time, and he had driven by in the car with his dad, but he had never been inside the gate. Up close, the place looked drearier than ever. The black, tar-papered barracks sat in lines, in blocks spread out a mile square. Gray dust covered everything.

Andy seemed to know how to pull everything off. He walked up to a receptionist and said, "I need to see Director Schneider. I've just come here from New York City." That was true, of course, but not in the way Andy was making it sound.

"Yes, Lieutenant. Can I tell the director your name?"

Flip was glad to know the man was in. Sometimes Dad had trouble making contact with him. "Gledhill. Lieutenant André Gledhill."

"Oh. Are you . . ." She looked at Flip and seemed to put two and two together.

"The director will want to see me, Miss. He's well aware of the matter I wish to speak to him about."

She got up and walked into the director's office. Andy looked at Flip. "I know I'm stretching the truth, Flip. But we need to get in there, and then we can be on the level. I've learned you have to show confidence when you're bluffing."

"It's fine with me. But this guy'll tell you to kick a rock down the road, the same as he keeps telling Dad."

"We'll see."

When the receptionist stepped out of the room, she said, "Is this about—"

But Andy was walking toward her by then, and he said, "I can't really

453

discuss it with you." He kept right on walking into the office with Flip behind him.

"Director," Andy said, "I'm Lieutenant Gledhill. You know my father, the mayor in Delta. This is my little brother, Phillip. He's the one who drove with Tom Tanaka to California. We have to talk to you about that."

The director stood up. "Look, Lieutenant, I know your father wants me to let the boy join the army, but I've talked to folks back in Washington, and we all feel the same. The boy runs off, commits a felony, and we reward him for it? We're trying to get people out of this facility in an orderly way—letting them move toward the middle of the country if they can get jobs, and quite a few of our boys have joined the army, but we can't let people go on work leave and then slip back to their homes on the coast."

"You understand that his home was being burglarized and that he only wanted to bring back some of his belongings. He didn't plan to stay in California." On the way to Topaz, Flip had filled Andy in on all the details.

"I've heard all that. He still broke the law."

"What about the people who robbed his house?" Flip asked. "No one did a thing to stop them. That's what's wrong, if you ask me."

"No one's justifying that."

"Sir, could we just sit down for a minute?" Andy said. "It seems like there ought to be a better way to solve this whole thing."

Mr. Schneider was still standing. "I'm sorry. I have a lot to do before I get out of here today, and there's really nothing more to say."

"Sir, I just got off a train. I was wounded in France, and I've come home to recover. I haven't had a good night's sleep in three days, but when my brother told me what was happening, I came straight out here. You could give us ten minutes of your time, and you could at least think about trying to find a solution."

"Go ahead. You can sit down. But I've heard your solution. That boy is not getting into the service."

Andy sat in a chair across the office from the director's desk. Flip took the chair next to him. "Here's my problem," Andy said. "I've been over in Europe fighting the Nazis. I've seen what they do to people, the way they've treated the French. They take away their rights, round up people and make them do forced labor, and if anyone stands up to them, they throw them in jail or shoot them on the spot. That's what I've been fighting *against.* Now I come home and my little brother tells me he's lost his faith in just about everything. He saw something that was wrong, tried to make it right, and who gets punished? The victim. How would you feel if you knew your house was being broken into? Wouldn't you want to see what you could save? By leaving the state, he may have committed a felony—technically—but if you ask me, his real mistake was to be born to a Japanese family. He's an American, but he's being treated as though he has no rights."

"Look, I've heard all the arguments," the director said. "Our government felt threatened by the Japanese on the coast. I've come to have great respect for the people here, and I doubt that many of them were any threat at all. But the decision was made in time of war to protect our citizens, and to protect the Japanese themselves. Whether that decision was right, we'll let history decide, but I was hired to enforce the law."

"What you call enforcing the law is actually stealing a young man's life from him. My brother says Tom is a great young man."

"He was a good boy while he was here. But he's the one who took off. Don't blame me for that."

Flip could see it was no use. It was the same old thing. But Andy wasn't moving.

"Now, if you'll excuse me, I need to get on with what I was doing," Mr. Schneider said.

"Fine. And then I'm going to start calling newspapers."

"What?"

"You know the most decorated unit in the army these days, don't you?"

"Of course. We're very proud of our Japanese soldiers."

"What a story. Here's a boy who wants to join that unit and fight for his country, and a hard-nosed administrator is using the letter of the law to ruin his life. You know what he found in his house, that he wanted to save? Pictures of his family. And his *baseball glove.* Everything else had been stolen, but he at least saved some pictures for his family, and that baseball glove for himself. That's a great American story. It'll play well in the *New York Times.* Some people out there are starting to ask why we chose the most desolate spots in America to place the Japanese. Some want to know why they had to be interned in the first place. And most of all, they want to know why they're being housed in such terrible conditions. I'll bet I can have a reporter on his way out here in the next couple of days. You'll be portrayed as the guy who punished a boy for wanting to save his *baseball glove,* after everything else he owned was stolen—while the police didn't bother to protect his home."

"I don't think a reporter will look at it that way."

"Well, maybe not. I'll just go call and see." Andy stood up.

"That isn't right, Lieutenant. I don't see why you want to make us look bad here. I'm just trying—"

"Sign the papers. Let him join the army. That can't hurt anything."

"It's not that easy. I would have to confer with some other people before I could do something like that."

"Fine. Start making calls. Tell your friends back east that a young lieutenant out in Utah is not going to stop until this story is in every newspaper in America. They'll be interested to hear that."

"Most Americans respect the law. They'll understand my decision."

"Maybe so. But they love their families, too. And they love baseball. The story sure pulls at a person's heart, doesn't it?"

"Maybe I could—"

"Maybe you could sign the papers and let a boy go fight for his country. It's hard to see that as a bad solution."

"I could discuss this with a few people and get back to you, Lieutenant."

"Yes. And I'll discuss it with a few reporters and they'll get back to you."

Mr. Schneider sat for at least thirty seconds, and Flip held his breath the whole time. "All right," he finally said. "I don't want a big fuss, and Tom *is* a good boy. I'll sign the papers."

Flip felt something like an explosion in his chest. He had believed for so long that he had ruined Tom's life. It meant everything to him to be released from that.

He followed Andy back to the car, now considering the possibility that his brother was the guy he had always thought he was. In the car, he said, "You did it, Andy. I can't believe it."

"Schneider knew darn well what was right." Andy laughed. "He just needed to look at the whole matter a little differently."

Flip wondered. The guy had only given in when he was worried about looking bad, and that didn't exactly change Flip's recent view of the world. But *someone* had finally stood up for what was right, and best of all, it was Andy. There was still the whole matter with Whisper, though. "Now you have to go make one more thing right," he said. "You've got to talk to Whisper."

"Are you sure she would want to talk to me?"

"She shouldn't—but I think she would."

"Flip, I don't know. I've had my mind made up for a long time that I need to let her go on with her life. It won't take long for her to find out how much I've changed."

"You haven't changed so much. All you did was learn how to bluff."

"But I can't bluff Whisper."

"You're right about that." But Flip wasn't sure. Whisper would probably take him back. And Andy would have her for himself again, the way he always had before. Flip felt himself slip down in the seat a little, not quite so pleased. Whisper was his only friend.

CHAPTER 31

WHISPER WAS TAKING Sister Winslow's blood pressure. She was a woman who knew everything that happened in town—and never stopped talking. Whisper had been paying little attention to her chatter until she said, "My husband said he thought he saw Andy Gledhill sitting on his porch here about an hour ago—talking to Flip. Is that possible? He's not home, is he? Stan wasn't even sure. He said if it was Andy, he was just a shadow of himself, he was so thin. But then, I know he was wounded and . . ."

On and on she went. But Whisper's breathing had almost stopped. She told herself she wasn't going to do this again; she wasn't going to wait and wonder this time. After all, Andy was out of her life. "It was probably him," Whisper said, interrupting. "I know his family was expecting him any day now."

"I would think *you* would be the first to know."

"It's not like that now, Sister Winslow. We haven't written to each other for a long time."

"Oh, well . . . I guess I don't keep up."

Whisper felt like saying, "You know every rumor that goes around; I'm sure you knew this one, too." But she didn't say it. She was thinking instead that maybe she would see him soon; then he could at least tell her what had happened to change his mind about her. Chances were, though, he wouldn't want to do that. He would probably avoid her until they bumped into one another somewhere. Maybe she'd see him at church. All the same, every time the door to the doctor's office opened, she held her breath again.

But that was so pathetic, and as an hour stretched into two and he didn't appear, she became increasingly disgusted with herself and with the meaninglessness of her life. She wanted to get out of this town and away from here. She didn't want to be walking around wondering when she would finally run into him.

She was sitting at the desk in the front office filing some papers when Dr. Noorda walked up front and was about to ask her for something. "Doctor, I'm not feeling well," she said on a sudden impulse. "Would it be a problem if I left a little early?"

"No, that's fine. Go ahead. You haven't caught something from around here, have you?"

"No, I'm . . . Doctor Noorda, I might be leaving. I have a friend in California who has a good job. She says she could get me on with the same company. I'm thinking I want to see some other places, or . . . I don't know, just . . ." She hardly knew what she was talking about. But suddenly she said, with more emotion than she had intended, "I want to give notice. I want to leave as soon as you can find someone else." She had started to cry, and she was humiliated. She needed to get out of the office before she made a complete fool of herself.

"Whisper, it's hard to find anyone. It might take me a while."

"But I was going to leave before. You knew that."

"Yes, of course. I just wonder . . . should you make such a sudden decision?"

Whisper knew what he was thinking. Dr. Noorda thought California was a big den of iniquity. He didn't like to see so many young people from Delta being drawn there. "I'll talk to you about it later," she said. "I just need to go home now. Is that all right?"

"Yes. Of course. Do you need anything? Are you feeling sick at your stomach, or—"

"No. I'll be all right. I'll be back in the morning." She reached in the desk and got her purse, then hurried out the door. She walked home, but when she got there, she didn't want to go in. Her mother would only start asking questions. So she slipped around the house, hid her purse under the back stairs, and got her bicycle. Her dad's car still wasn't running, but she used the bike sometimes when she wanted to hurry to the grocery store or just ride in the evening and let the wind blow over her. This time she pumped hard, not wanting to see anyone she knew, and hoping to get out of town as quickly as she could. What she realized was that she wanted to talk to Flip—the only person who really understood her—so she headed out to the Gledhill farm, hoping maybe he was there this afternoon.

Flip, as it turned out, wasn't there. She supposed he was probably staying home to be with Andy, no matter how angry he claimed to be with him. She didn't want to ride back home yet, so she sat under the old cottonwood tree, where Flip liked to sit, and tried to think what she was going to do. She thought about Lamar again and wondered whether she shouldn't reconsider. But she couldn't do that, and she knew it. Maybe she really would go to California and work. She had to get away from this town.

* * * * *

Andy liked the change he saw in Flip. On the way back from Topaz, the boy talked about Tom and how happy he was going to be to get out of jail and into the army. He told Andy a little, too, about the hard time he'd had around town, with so many people down on him for helping an internee "run away," as they called it. "Tom wants to get to the war before it's over, but maybe he won't make it now," Flip told Andy.

"I don't know. Some think it'll be over in Europe before much longer, but we might have a long fight in the Pacific."

"So far, they aren't letting any Japanese fight over there. But I could go. And that's what I want to do. Dad said he won't sign for it, though. He says if I go, he wants me to wait until I'm eighteen."

"I hope you don't have to go."

"I know. That's what Dad says. And Whisper keeps hoping that the war will end. She only wants me to think about college. I guess I do want to go to college, and Mom says I have to, but my grades have been pretty bad lately."

"You'll go, Flip. And you'll do well. You're smart. You could end up running the bank."

"What are you going to do?"

"I don't know. Nothing's very clear to me right now. I might be back in the war myself. I've thought about buying some land out by the farm and raising alfalfa seed. People around here have done really well with that. I never thought I wanted to be a farmer, but now I don't know. I think I'd rather do that than sit behind a desk at the bank."

"I've thought about that myself."

"Maybe we could be partners. We could run some businesses here, the way Dad has done, and farm besides."

"So you're saying you want to live here?" Flip asked.

"I'm not sure. But I'm feeling that way today. I really am." Andy glanced at Flip, who nodded. He knew the boy was pleased about Tom, but he seemed to have other things on his mind. Maybe he didn't want to be partners with Andy.

Andy was entering Delta by then, passing over the railroad bridge and heading onto Main Street. He was also admitting to himself what he had wanted to do since the moment he had stepped off the train. He wanted to see Whisper. He liked that he had done something for the Japanese boy, and he liked that he had made Flip a little happier. It was all part of what he had been trying to feel since that day he had saved those lives: that he was a decent person.

"Flip," Andy said as they drove down Main Street, "I'm thinking I might stop at Doc Noorda's office and just say something to Whisper. You know, so she'll know I'm home."

"Yeah, sure. You ought to."

Andy heard something in Flip's voice, maybe some concern, but he drove to the office anyway. He was starting to feel a little excited. "Do you want to come in with me?" Andy asked.

"Naw. That's okay. I'll just wait for you."

Andy could feel his breath coming faster; he was scared. This was really awkward, but he didn't want Whisper to think he'd been in town all afternoon and hadn't bothered to let her know he was home. He knew how she had always felt about that. Maybe things had changed, but they didn't seem so different now that he was here. He opened the door and stepped inside, but Whisper wasn't at the front desk. No one was. Andy just stood there for a time before he called, "Hello."

"Just a moment," Andy heard the doctor call back, and then in a minute or so, he appeared from the hallway where the rooms to his little office and hospital were. He clearly didn't recognize Andy for a moment, but then he said, "Oh, Andy. My, how good it is to see you."

"What's left of me, anyway."

"Well, you have lost weight. But you'll get that back all right."

"Isn't Whisper here?"

"She left a little while ago. She said she wasn't feeling well. Did she know you were in town?"

"No. I just got in this afternoon."

"Well, she left about half an hour earlier than usual. She seemed upset. She was talking about moving to California."

"Oh. I see." Andy had no idea what else to say. "Well, I'll give her a call at home. Nice to see you, Doc." He turned and walked back to the car.

When he told Flip what the doctor had said, Flip said, "I can tell you what's happened. Someone came into the office and told her you're in town. When you didn't come over, she figured she knew what that meant."

"But why would she expect me? It's not like it used to be."

"Andy, I know you're considered really smart and everything, but you're sounding pretty stupid right now. What she wants is for you to come home to her—more than anything in this world—no matter what she told me or you or anyone else."

"She told Doc Noorda she was sick. Do you think I ought to go over to her house?"

"Yeah, you better. But I doubt she's there. She'll want to be alone."

"You sound like you know everything about her."

"Not really. But I know a few things."

Andy drove to Whisper's house and knocked on her door. But he only managed to get Sister Harris upset by doing that. "No, she didn't come home early. In fact, by now I was starting to expect her. I thought she was staying late, the way she does so many times."

"Well, maybe she had to run an errand or something. I might have misunderstood what Doc Noorda told me."

Sister Harris wanted to know all about Andy at that point, but he broke away as quickly as he could. When he came out of the house, Flip was standing outside by the car. "I just checked in back," he said. "She took her bike. My bet is, she rode out to the farm to see if I was out there. We talk when things like this happen."

"Let's drive out there," Andy said, but he was trying to think what all this meant. Flip really had become her best friend. Andy hadn't thought that possible when little old Flip had first said he would try to help out.

"She told Doc Noorda she might be moving to California," Andy went on. "Why do you think she would do that? Do you think she's changed her mind about that fellow she was engaged to?"

"No. She just wants to start over on everything. She's afraid that she'll never find anyone to marry around here, and she's tired of the way her life is—living with her family and just going back and forth to work every day. I can see her heading for California if you don't say the right things to her."

"Flip, I've told you, I'm not sure I should try to change her mind. I feel like I need to talk to her and sort of set things right—but I don't see us getting married after everything that's happened these last two years."

Flip was staring straight ahead, but when he finally spoke, there was anger in his voice again. "All I can say is, if you don't tell her you love her and talk her into staying, you're the stupidest man who ever lived. And I mean that."

Andy thought maybe he was starting to understand some things. "You've grown up, Flip. I can't believe how much you've changed."

But Flip didn't respond to that. He only said, "When you get there, walk out behind the house. If she's at the farm, she'll be sitting under that old cottonwood tree by the irrigation canal."

And that turned out to be true. Andy walked back and saw Whisper's bicycle against the tree. She was sitting on the other side of the tree, facing the canal. He walked closer and said, "Hi, Whisper."

She didn't seem surprised, but then she had certainly heard the car on the gravel driveway. She must have guessed who it was. Without looking around, she said, "How did you know I'd be here?"

"Flip knew."

"That's right. Flip *would* know."

Andy walked around her and looked down. He had thought he remembered how pretty she was, but he was surprised. She was older, beautiful, more a woman—or the sadness in her eyes made her seem so.

"Flip and I just got back from the camp. We talked to Mr. Schneider, and he agreed to let Tom join the army."

She looked up, her face brightening. "Are you serious? How did you do that?"

"It's a long story. But that's where I've been."

"You didn't have to come looking for me."

"I know." Andy wasn't sure where to begin. "I just talked to Doc Noorda, and he said you might be leaving."

"I'm thinking about it."

"Flip said you're tired of Delta and want to get away."

"That's true. But it's not the town so much. I just want to start over and have some new experiences."

"That's also what Flip said." Andy knelt down in front of her, looked at her more closely. "That kid's in love with you. Do you know that?"

She looked down at her hands, which she had gripped together. "Yes, I know. I shouldn't have let that happen. But I've needed him. I feel bad that I've hurt him so much."

"He'll find someone his age one of these days. And he'll be a better man for what he's learned from being around you."

"Maybe. But he's mad at the whole world right now."

"My guess is, half the reason is that he can't have you."

She nodded, as though she had realized that herself. "He's just too good to stay so mad," she said. "What you did for Tom is going to make a big difference to him."

Andy turned and sat down next to Whisper. He was starting to feel his weakness and his weariness from all the travel.

"Are you okay?" Whisper asked. "You look pretty beaten up."

"I lost a lot of blood, and I didn't get the help I needed at first. I came close to dying before I finally made it to a hospital."

"But you're okay now?"

"In some ways, I am. But I'm beat up in lots of ways. I don't know if you can understand that."

"I guess I don't understand it all. But I believe it."

"I've done things I'll never talk about with anyone, Whisper. What I feel right now is that I'm not fit to be around decent people. Especially not you."

"So that's what you came out here to tell me?"

"No. I'm just telling you the truth. I've changed, and I don't know whether I'll ever be the same. I don't know if I can be."

"So if I leave for California or somewhere, that's fine with you?"

"I don't know, Whisper. Maybe that would be the best thing for you."

"You sound like your letters."

Andy heard the resignation in her voice, even a touch of anger, and he didn't know what to do about that. "Whisper, I thought I was going to die. I didn't want to ruin your life. I thought it was better to cut things off before it happened, so it wouldn't be quite so bad for you."

"That's a good one. You thought it might be better to kill *me* before you died."

"I didn't think of it that way. When you're out there, it's hard to remember how things are back home."

"Andy, when Flip and Tom and I drove to Berkeley, we had a blowout, so the boys walked to a town to get the tire fixed. When they came back, a man was trying to break into the truck and drag me out. Flip took in after that guy and fought him. He could have gotten himself killed, but he fought for me. I don't care what your reasons were; you were way too quick to decide you didn't want me. Flip would have fought his way through any war to get back to me."

"I know it seems that way. But no one knows what war is until—"

"Andy, you're home. I just told you I'm about to leave town, and what do you say. 'Go ahead. I've changed. It's probably better.'"

"Whisper, you don't even know what I'm talking about. It's not just that I was in a war."

"Then explain it to me. I feel like I deserve that much."

Andy sat with his arms on his knees. He tried to think what he could say. "I wasn't a regular soldier. I was sneaking around like some snake in the grass. I killed people with my bare hands. After a while, the evil just builds up in you, and it doesn't seem possible that a place like this even exists. I thought you would see it in my face when I got home, that I was all filled up with that stuff."

"Are you?"

"I don't know now. I'm telling myself I was a soldier and I did what I was supposed to do. But I can never tell you how evil I felt." He sat for a time and then, in a softer voice, said, "Whisper, there was a woman in the Resistance—a very pretty young woman. For a while, it seemed as though she knew all the things I knew, and she was better for me than you were. By then, I wasn't sure I believed in God anymore. There was a night when she wanted me, and I turned her down—because I've been taught all my life not to do that. But later she was killed saving *my* life, breaking me out of a jail, and for a time, I thought I had done the wrong thing not to have given into what she wanted. It still seems as though I committed a sin with her, just by thinking that way. I wasn't really true to you."

"Is she the real reason you're willing to let me go?"

"Not her. But what I did."

"But you said you didn't do anything."

"I broke with the Church, Whisper, with everything I believed. It all seemed a bunch of silliness to me. All of you back here were people who just didn't understand what life was all about."

"But what about now? Do you still feel that way?"

"I had something happen there at the end. I saved some lives—a whole lot of German lives. And God seemed to speak to me and help me to do it. Since then, I've been trying to pray. I have some hope now that maybe I'm not entirely lost. Maybe God can forgive me. But I don't know if you can."

"Andy, I gave up on you. I agreed to marry someone else. I didn't really love him, but I let him believe that I did. It's not like I sat at home the whole time you were gone."

"I know. I told you to find someone. But still you seem like the same person I left behind."

"No, Andy. I'm not. I was a little girl when you left, and I thought my only happiness could come from you. But if you don't care about me now, I can live with that. I'll leave town, and I'll start over. I can do that. When you didn't come to see me this afternoon, I started thinking the way I used to, like that girl who always just waited for you to show up. But I'm not going to be like that from now on. I do some things pretty well, and I'm going to see how my life turns out, once I stop thinking it begins and ends with you."

"Whisper, stay for a while. Let's see what happens. I want to be myself. Maybe being around you will help."

"Andy, you haven't said how you feel about *me*. All you want to talk about is how you feel about yourself."

"Whisper, when I look at you, I feel all those old feelings. You're beautiful, and you're good, and you're what I've always wanted. But—"

"Don't say it, Andy. Just say you love me, or say you can't. But don't tell me there's something wrong with you." She had started to cry.

"Do you still love me, Whisper?"

"You know I do. I wish I didn't, but I never stopped, no matter what you wrote to me."

Andy felt a vibration run through him. "I do love you, Whisper. I never stopped either. But I thought it was wrong to feel that way about you, after what I'd done."

She turned toward him finally and kissed his cheek. Andy felt as though he'd been touched by God. He felt his heart start to beat. And then he kissed her lips and held her in his arms.

*　*　*　**

Flip waited in the car for a while, but the air got hot inside, so he stepped out, walked over to the house, and sat in the shade of the porch. Andy was gone a long time, and Flip knew what that meant. At least it wasn't Lamar, he told himself, and at least Andy was acting like the guy he was supposed to be. He had made things right for Tom.

Finally Andy and Whisper appeared from around the house. Flip didn't have to ask what had happened. He could see that they had both been crying, and he saw the way Whisper was leaning against Andy. They stood in front of Flip and Andy said, "You kept your promise, Flip. She's still here—even though I didn't deserve to have her wait."

Flip nodded, but he didn't feel like talking. He stood up, ready to go.

"We're going to spend some time together," Andy said, "and just see how things go. But we're feeling pretty good about each other right now."

"That's good," Flip said, stepping off the porch.

"Andy," Whisper said, "could I talk to Flip for a minute?"

"Sure. I'll get your bike and stick it in the trunk." He walked back around the house.

"Flip," Whisper said, "things are going to work out okay for you. I hope you know that."

"I'll be glad when I can get out of here," was all Flip could think to say.

"When you get to college, you can start over. You're so handsome now, and no one at college will know anything about Tom."

"Yeah, I know. I've thought about all that. I'll be fine." But Flip was fighting against showing any emotion. He didn't want Whisper to know what he was feeling.

"I couldn't have had a better friend, Flip. You got me through these years."

"Yeah. You did the same for me."

"I love you."

Flip nodded, and he fought. He bit the inside of his lip.

"Maybe you'll be my brother-in-law, and we'll be friends for life."

Flip couldn't do this. He stepped past Whisper, heading for the car.

Whisper grabbed his arm and stopped him. "Things will work out great, Flip. You're the best person I know."

Flip nodded. He tried to walk away again, but Whisper turned him and put her arms around him. "I needed to be loved, Flip, and you gave me that gift when it was so important to me. It's the loveliest thing that's happened to me in my life so far. But you always knew, didn't you, that it had to be this way?"

"Sure I did," Flip said, pulling away again. He walked to the car, where Andy was shutting the trunk gently onto the bike, which was sticking out the back. "I'll have to drive really slow," he was saying.

Flip got into the car, in the back. Andy and Whisper got in the front. Flip wiped his eyes, swallowed, took a couple of breaths, and then he said, "I guess I should have told you two congratulations."

Whisper looked back at him and nodded. Tears were in her eyes, too. But she looked happy, and she hadn't looked that way for a long time. Flip still wanted to join the army, still wanted to show people in town what he could do. But he liked what Andy had said about being part-ners. He tried to think of college, of maybe meeting some nice girl there and bringing her back here.

Whisper was sitting close to Andy in the front seat, and Flip liked to see that. It made him feel he'd done what he had set out to do. But he could see the side of Whisper's face—the prettiest face he had ever seen—and he knew what would happen now. She would be with Andy all the time, and Flip wouldn't have much chance to talk to her. He was going to miss her more than anything he'd ever lost in his life.

Whisper turned again and gave Flip a careful look, as if to see whether he was all right. He nodded to her, so she would think he was doing just fine. But he wasn't—not yet. He just hoped that a better time would come.

"Flip," Andy said, "I don't know how I can ever thank you."

Flip didn't know either, but it was what he had needed to hear Andy say. Flip settled back in his seat and watched out the window as Andy drove back into town. Big leaves were falling off the horse chestnut trees in front of Doc Noorda's house, and old Brother Larsen, up the street, was working in his yard, pruning back his roses. Andy didn't take Whisper to her house; he took her home with him. As they pulled into the driveway, it finally occurred to Flip that this was the day he had been waiting for so long. Dad would be there now, and word would be spreading all over town. Andy was home.